Colin Forbes, born in Hampstead, London, writes a novel every year. For the past twenty years he has earned his living solely as a full-time writer.

An international bestseller, each book has been published world-wide, including the United States. He is translated into twenty languages.

He is an enthusiastic traveller and visits all locations appearing in his novels. 'It is essential for an author to see everything for himself to achieve vivid atmosphere and authenticity.'

He has explored most of Western Europe, the East and West coasts of America, and has made excursions to Africa and Asia. He lives with his wife in Surrey.

Surveys have shown that his readership is divided almost equally between men and women.

COLIN FORBES

The Heights of Zervos

AND

Double Jeopardy

PAN BOOKS
in association with Collins

The revised edition of *The Heights of Zervos* was first published
in 1972 by Pan Books Ltd
© Colin Forbes 1970, 1972

Double Jeopardy was first published in 1982 by
William Collins Sons & Co. Ltd
© Colin Forbes 1982

This two-volume edition first published 1993 by Pan Books Ltd
a division of Pan Macmillan Publishers Limited
Cavaye Place London SW10 9PG
and Basingstoke
in association with William Collins Sons & Co. Ltd

Associated companies throughout the world

ISBN 0 330 33429 8

This two-volume edition © Colin Forbes 1993

1 3 5 7 9 8 6 4 2

A CIP catalogue record for this book is available
from the British Library

Printed and bound in Great Britain by
Cox & Wyman Ltd, Reading, Berkshire

The Heights of
Zervos

Author's Note

I wish to record my thanks to Mr Michael Willis of the Imperial War Museum for his invaluable technical assistance.

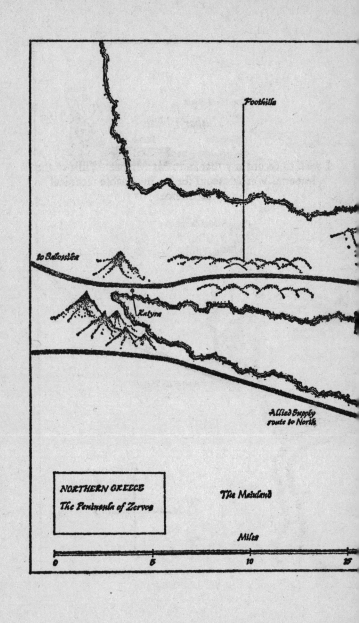

Foothills

to Salonika

Katyna

Allied Supply
route to North

NORTHERN GREECE
The Peninsula of Zervos

The Mainland

Miles

0   5   10   15

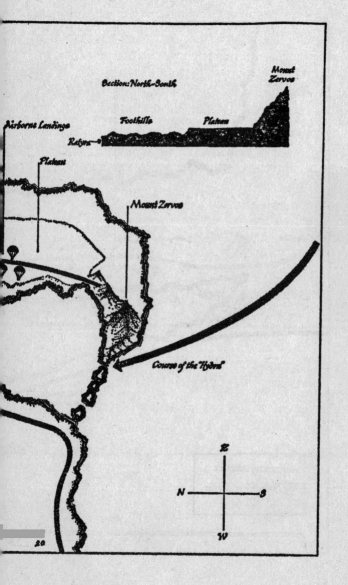

Section: North-South

Mount Zervos

Foothills

Plateau

Airborne Landings

Plateau

Ravyra

Mount Zervos

Course of the 'Hydra'

E

N ——————— S

W

20

CHAPTER ONE

Thursday, April 3, 1941

Less than ten minutes to zero, to detonation point, Macomber, lying on his stomach along the top of the oil tanker wagon, listened to the German patrol closing in round the Bucharest railyard. His escape route was blocked, his body chilled to the bone by the snow which drifted down through the night, and the frightening barks of the Alsatian dogs assaulted his ears, a sound punctuated by orders rapped out in German. 'Watch the wire... At the first sign of movement open fire ... Gunther, take the signal-box – you can see what's happening from up there...'

It was the third night of April and Rumania was still gripped by winter, still showed no inkling of spring on the way, still lay numbed under the icy wind which flowed from the east, from the Russian steppes and Siberia beyond. The insidious cold of 2 AM was penetrating Macomber's leather coat as he remained sprawled over the curve of the tanker, not daring to flex even a gloved finger as a German soldier walked beside the track below, and the crunch of boots breaking the crusted snow came up to the trapped Scot like the sound of twigs snapping.

The sub-zero temperature, the realization that arms, legs, feet were gradually losing all feeling, the trudge of marching troops below the wagon – these were the least of his worries when he remembered what was supporting his precariously poised body. He was lying on top of several thousand gallons of refined aviation spirit, petrol already bound for the Luftwaffe even though the Wehrmacht had occupied Rumania only recently, and a ten-kilogram composite demolition charge was attached under the belly of this huge tanker. The time fuse he had set was ticking down to zero, synchronized with other charges spaced out along the petrol train. And now the patrol had arrived and was checking for an intruder, searching for a saboteur – although perhaps sabotage had not yet entered their minds as they systematically surrounded the petrol train.

The snow, damp and paralysingly cold, was building up over his exposed neck, forming an icy collar where his woollen scarf parted company with his bare skin, but he remained perfectly motionless, thankful that his head at least was protected by the soft hat squashed over his brow. There's too damned much of me for this concealment game, he was thinking. Over six feet tall, over fourteen stone in weight, there was far too much of him, but he dismissed the thought as he stared at the illuminated hands of his watch, a watch strapped to the inside of his wrist as a precaution against the phosphorescent face betraying his position. Eight minutes to zero. Eight minutes before the charges detonated – and the tankers detonated seconds later – turning the railyard into a flaming furnace, a furnace which would cremate Ian Macomber. And there was yet a further hazard which made it impossible for him to protect himself against the elements which were slowly embalming him with a covering of freezing snow – as though to prepare his body for the imminent cremation. Ice had formed over the metal surface of the cylindrical tanker, ice which would send him slithering down into the path of the searching patrol if he altered his position by so much as a centimetre. So he lay still as a dead man while he watched a field-grey figure pass under a lamp close to the wire, mount the steps to the signal-box and enter the stilt-legged structure which overlooked the petrol train.

The lamp was hooded against direct observation from aircraft flying overhead, as were all the lamps inside the yard – hooded to avoid giving guidance to Allied planes which might appear on their way to bomb the vital oil-fields at Ploesti. Not that Macomber was expecting an RAF raid – the chronic shortage of bombers, the lack even of a machine which could fly the distance, guaranteed the Germans the safety of their newly acquired oil reserves – which made the sabotaging of oil for Germany vital. More footsteps crunched in the snow and then stopped immediately below where Macomber lay. His muscles tensed involuntarily and then relaxed. The metal ladder attached to the tanker's side ended a few inches beyond his head where the final rung rested close to the huge cap concealing him. Was someone coming up the ladder to investigate? His brain was still wrestling with this contingency when it received a further shock: something metallic clanged against a wheel. The demolition charge was hidden behind the front wheel. Christ, they'd found it!

'Get under the wagon – cross to the other side and wait there!' The voice spoke in German, a language Macomber understood and spoke fluently. An NCO issuing an order to a soldier – so there were two of them standing not fifteen feet below him. The voice continued, harsh and keyed up by the sub-zero temperature. 'If he runs for it, he'll run for the wire. I'm posting men the whole length of the train...' So they knew someone was inside the railyard. Macomber blinked as a snow flurry percolated under his hat and clouded his eyes; fearful lest the snow should begin to freeze his eyelids, he blinked several times while he waited for the soldier to crawl under the tanker. He would, of course, find the demolition charge. At least there was little sign of activity from the signalbox where he could see two shadowed figures under a blue light behind the windows – Gunther was checking with the signalman presumably. Feet crunched through the snow again, were swallowed up quickly as the NCO continued his march to post more men along the train – men who would inevitably close the door to escape. Not that he had a chance in hell of covering the hundred yards which would take him to the hole in the wire where he had cut his way through, and the wire-cutters in his pocket were now so much dead weight; with the place so well covered he could never hope to cut a fresh hole before they spotted him. He heard a fresh sound from below, the rasp of metal against the tanker as the soldier began clambering under the wagon. A clumsy Jerry, this one. Perhaps a stupid one, too, but not stupid enough to miss seeing the charge...

More scrabbling noises, hurrying noises from under the tanker. The German didn't like passing over the track in case the train started moving. An illogical fear since the wagons would never be moved during the search, but Macomber

11

understood the reaction and had experienced it himself. Wondering whether he would ever be able to stir again, Macomber lay motionless and waited for the noises to stop suddenly, which would warn him that the charge had been found. And then he would wait again, but only briefly before the soldier's shout announced his lethal discovery. The scrabbling sounds ceased and Macomber held his breath, waiting for the shout, but he heard only a wheezing cough and a shuffle of frozen feet. The damned fool had missed seeing it, thank God. He was now standing on the other side of the tanker, the side nearest the signal-box – which put him between Macomber and the wire. The Scot checked his watch. Five minutes to zero.

The uncanny silence of winter's darkness descended on the railyard once more. The dogs had been taken farther up the line, the sound of feet crunching through the snow had ceased, and the wind was dropping. The stage was set, the Wehrmacht were in position, and now it only remained for Macomber's nerve to break, for him to be apprehended when he climbed down the small ladder and ended his career by the tracks of a desolate junction few people had ever heard of. As the snow fell more slowly the silence was so complete he heard in the distance coals going down the iron hopper in the eastern railyard. The silence was broken by the sound of a window opening in the signal-box, opening with a fracturing crack as ice on the ledge shattered. Gunther leaned out of the window and stared directly at the snow-shrouded hump on top of the last petrol wagon.

Macomber stared back at Gunther's silhouette, moving only his eyes to take in this new source of danger. He was boxed in: observed from a distance and trapped by the soldier below. His eyes swivelled back to his watch. Four minutes to zero and still no way out, not even the ghost of a diversion he could take advantage of. It was his swansong as a British saboteur, the end of his dangerous passage down through the Balkans, a trail not only blazed by the series of devastating explosions which had destroyed vast quantities of strategic war materials – but also a trail which the German Abwehr Intelligence service had followed, often only one step behind him. He weighed up his chances.

With a great deal of luck the Luger in his coat pocket would eliminate the soldier below the wagon, but then there was the German in the signal-box who had apparently noticed nothing amiss, who had left the window while he talked to the signal-man again; there was the wire fence he could never hope to climb; and there was the line of Wehrmacht troops posted along the train with instructions to watch that wire, to shoot on sight. His mind raced, estimating possibilities, and his watch raced faster. Three minutes and thirty seconds to go. He had calculated the odds and decided they were loaded impossibly against him. The sound of the car starting up so startled him he almost lost his balance; he hadn't even realized it was there, but now the driver switched on a light inside the vehicle and he saw it parked close to the signal-box on the far side of the wire. A Mercedes. The driver was having trouble firing the motor. A chance in a thousand – but the repeating rattle of the car's engine struggling to fire revived his hopes enormously, stirring the blood inside his half-congealed body as he worked out how to exploit this heaven-sent diversion.

Between the misfires of the numbed engine he heard feet clumping below the wagon as the unseen soldier stamped the ground to bring back the circulation into his frozen system, then the wheezing cough again. The feet began tramping through the snow, moving away from the wagon and over the empty neighbouring track, and Macomber guessed that he was improvising his own sentry-go to neutralize the appalling cold. The open window in the signal-box was still unoccupied as the marching German moved farther away; if only that bloody engine would start, would begin shifting the Mercedes – because stationary the car was useless. His nerves prickled with desperate impatience as the driver tried again and again to wake up the dead motor, and Macomber's prayers were with the driver as he went on struggling to spark life from the sullen engine. The motor caught, ticked over unenthusiastically, died again. God, he'd really thought it was going. He gritted his teeth to prevent them chattering with the cold, stared at the empty window in the signal-box, watched the marching German cross a second track close to the lamp. Another laboured spasm when the car seemed to be going, another false start

13

which faded away – and Macomber suddenly realized that the wheezing German was growing curious about the car because he was marching towards the wire now. Then the engine caught, ticked over, continued ticking as the Scot moved for the first time in ten minutes, breaking the stiffened rigidity of his posture to reach inside his coat pocket and haul out the Luger.

He aimed the Luger, fired once. The car was moving slowly, and he had aimed at the rear window – away from the driver who must remain in control of his vehicle, who must be panicked if the plan was to have any chance of working. The bullet shattered the rear window and its report echoed in the darkness as a voice roared out across the railyard in German. 'He's in that car ... on the other side of the wire ... Don't let him get away!' The darkness, the falling snow, distorted the direction from which the voice came, but Macomber's bellowed command carried a long distance. Someone opened fire, a burst from a machine-pistol which sprayed the rear of the accelerating Mercedes. A fusillade of shots crackled in the darkness and men ran forward, leaving the train. A German, finding the wire barring his way, shouted a warning, retreated behind the signal-box, threw a grenade, then another. The explosions were bright flashes, muffled assaults on the ear-drums, the men were pouring through the hole in the shattered wire, a muddle of field-grey figures rushing past the hooded lamp as men already beyond the wire fired long bursts at the retreating vehicle. The Mercedes was still moving, turning a sharp corner and accelerating afresh when the patrol left behind the wire and vanished into the night.

Macomber wasted no time on the ladder. Levering himself over the side farthest away from the signal-box, he fell heavily in the snow, cushioning his fall by rolling away from the wagon. The shock of the impact was still with him as he forced himself to his feet, glanced quickly in both directions and scrambled under the tanker between its wheels. He emerged from underneath gripping the Luger, and his gaze was fixed on the point of maximum danger – the signal-box. Gunther had taken up position, was leaning out of the window with his rifle, unaffected by the headlong rush away from the railyard.

14

There's always one who uses his head, Macomber thought grimly as the German leaned out farther, raised his rifle and took swift aim at the blurred shadow moving away from the last petrol wagon. Macomber jerked the Luger high, hoped the damned barrel wasn't blocked with ice from his fall, steadied the gun and fired. The sound of his shot was drowned in the rattle of firearms beyond the wire as the German flopped over the window ledge, lost his rifle and hung in mid-air, face downwards. Macomber ran towards the wire, ran awkwardly because his legs were still stiff and unwieldy from the long wait, and as he ran he hoped to God the signalman wasn't the courageous type who raised alarms, but from a brief glance at the window he saw no sign of him – he was crouched on the floor between his levers.

He slowed down to pass through the tangle of wire and then began running in earnest, running to the left – away from the signal-box and away from the road where the Mercedes had driven off. Behind him, some distance up the yard, dogs were barking excitedly; the other section of the patrol had gone to the front of the train to start a systematic search. He ran slowly but steadily, his eyes growing accustomed to the unlit darkness as he threaded his way between man-high piles of wooden sleepers, ran with his Luger held well forward so he could aim it quickly in case of emergency, but this fringe area of the railyard was deserted and he reached the parked Volkswagen safely. Now to start his own engine. At the sixth attempt the car fired and he paused only to haul off the German army blanket he had draped over bonnet and radiator, stuffing it on the passenger seat before driving away across the snow. The blanket had frozen into a natural canopy and it retained its strange shape as he left the field and drove onto a road which would take him the long way back into Bucharest. Remembering what he had deposited under the petrol train, he pressed his foot down as soon as he reached the road, building up speed dangerously as the wheels whipped over the ice-coated surface. His watch registered thirty seconds beyond zero.

He swore in German, the language he had accustomed himself to speak always, to think in, even to dream in as part of his

15

German cover. Surely all the bloody time fuses couldn't be defective? Or had he gone through all this for nothing? He shivered uncontrollably as he accelerated to even greater speed, gripping the wheel tightly to overcome the tremor. Reaction? Probably. Beyond his headlight beams the flat countryside was a mystery, a realm of darkness which might have contained anything, but from frequent reconnaissance in daylight hours he knew there were only bleak, endless fields stretching away to the Danube. A paling fence rushed towards him, disappeared as he lost speed and started to take a bend, then the skid began. He reacted instinctively, guiding rather than forcing the steering, following the spin while the headlights swept a crazy arc over the snowbound landscape. When he pulled up, by some miracle still on the road, the Volkswagen had swung through one hundred and eighty degrees, so he faced the way he had come at the moment of detonation.

The first sound was a dull boom, like the firing of a sixteen-inch naval gun, followed by a series of repeating booms which thundered out across the plain. A tremendous flash illuminated the snow with a searing light, then the flash died and was succeeded by an appalling roar, a deafening, blasting sound as the petrol went up, wagon after wagon in such swift succession that the night seemed to break apart, to open up with volcanic force, to burst and boil with fire. During all his sabotage missions Macomber had never seen anything like it – the moonless night was suddenly lit with a vast orange conflagration which showed the huddled rooftops of Bucharest to his left, rooftops white with snow and then palely coloured by the glow of the seething fire enveloping the railyard from end to end. He was turning the car when the smoke came, a billowing cloud of blackness which temporarily smothered the orange glow and rolled towards the city. Reversing cautiously, he edged the rear of the Volkswagen into the paling fence, which cracked like glass in its frozen state, pitching an intact section into the field beyond. He changed gear, turned a cautious semi-circle, straightened up, accelerated and headed for Bucharest.

The sabotaging of the petrol train was Macomber's last assignment in the Balkans, since the taking over of Rumania by the

Wehrmacht would soon make any further explosive excursions well-nigh impossible, and while he drove into the outer sub-urbs of Bucharest his attention was concentrated on the haz-ards which lay ahead – the hazard of escaping from Rumania, of crossing German-occupied Bulgaria and entering neutral Turkey where he could catch a boat for Greece. The Greek mainland – where Allied troops had recenly landed to meet the threat of German invasion – meant safety, but reaching the haven was quite a different matter. He could only hope to pass through the intervening control points by preserving his impersonation of a German up to the last moment, but it was the Abwehr he feared most. It was the Abwehr who had sent men into the Balkans to end the wave of sabotage and Macom-ber knew the Abwehr were closing in on him, might even be within twenty-four hours of discovering his true identity. So it was back to his flat to pick up the already packed bag, then on the road again, south for Bulgaria and Istanbul beyond.

Lord, he was tired! Macomber rubbed the back of his hand over his eyes as he drove slowly through the deserted streets – driving at speed inside a built-up area might attract attention. The old stone buildings, five storeys tall, were in darkness, except where here and there a high window showed a light – some family woken by the unnerving explosions which had broken over the city – but the lights were going out again as he drove along a devious route which avoided the main highway, feeling the tension rising as he drew closer to the flat. Return-ing late at night it was always like this – because you never knew who might be waiting for you on the darkened staircase. Reversing the Volkswagen into the garage which had once served as a stable, he parked it facing the double doors, ready for a speedy departure in case of emergency; then, lighting one of the foul-tasting German cigars he had come to like, he began the five minute-walk to the apartment block.

As he walked steadily through the crusted snow he found his thoughts wandering back over the years to when he had walked through other cities without fear. Through New York as a boy when they had lived there with his American mother, and later, as a youth, through the streets of Edinburgh when his father, a Scot, had decided he should be educated in his home country. He thrust the memories out of his mind quickly, reminding himself that sentiment blunted the edge of alertness. He was nearly there. It would have been more convenient to rent a garage opposite where he lived, but the stopping of a car in the small hours could signal his arrival to anyone who might be waiting for him.

At the entrance to the narrow street, hardly wider than an alley, he dropped the cigar in the snow where it sputtered and extinguished itself. No point in illuminating your approach. He had deliberately chosen this apartment block because its entrance led off from a side street, which made it more difficult for anyone following to be sure which doorway you vanished inside. As he walked along the twisting, canyon-like street, his head bowed with fatigue, he automatically noted the footprints in the snow which preceded him, but people in this district worked a late shift in the factories and so far the footprints did not disturb him. Providing the doorstep to his own entrance was virgin snow – no one in the apartment block worked at night. The footprints went on past his entrance and the doorstep was hidden beneath unspoilt snow. Now for the worst part, the trip up the staircase. Inside his coat pocket his right hand gripped the Luger he had reloaded in the garage; he used his left hand to insert the key gently, turn it quietly and push the door open until it was backed against the wall. Stepping inside, he shut the door with equal care. Then he listened before switching on his pocket torch and aiming it up the staircase. Dry steps. The oppressive silence of three in the morning which always hinted at menace in the shadows.

He went up slowly, pausing at each landing to swivel his torch up the next flight, looking for the shadow which shouldn't be there. When he arrived on the fifth floor outside his own door he paused again, in no hurry to unlock it. A sixth flight led up to the caretaker's cramped quarters in the roof and a brief swing of his torch showed dry steps to where the staircase turned up the last flight. In any case Josef was away in Constanta. Taking out his key, he was about to insert it when he changed his mind. He should never have come back here; this was pushing his luck a shade too far. It must have been the sapping fatigue, the temptation of a few hours in bed which had made him take this needless risk. The place where you stayed was always the most dangerous – they'd taken Forester in his Budapest flat. I'll damned well hold out a few hours longer, let sleep wait until I'm well clear of the city. He had the torch still in his hand when a hard, pipe-like object was rammed into the small of his back and a voice spoke in German.

'Be very careful, Herr Wolff. This is a gun, so why die so early in life? Put on the landing light, please, but do not turn round.'

Macomber's hand, which should have been gripping the Luger, now gripped the torch – another sign of the dreadful weariness which had made him overlook his normal precautions. He raised the hand still holding the torch, wondered briefly whether he could utilize the weapon, whether he could swing round and wield the torch as a club, and dismissed the idea as soon as it entered his head. The man on the landing knew exactly what he was doing, had the gun muzzle pressed firmly into his back, so firmly he would have plenty of time to squeeze the trigger and blow his victim's spine in half at the first hint of a wrong movement. Macomber fumbled for the switch, pressed it down. Light from the low-powered bulb percolated dismally across the landing.

'We will go inside,' the voice continued, a mature experienced voice. 'Use your key to open the door – and be careful!'

Thirty seconds later the pistol in the German's hand was aimed at a point a fraction above Macomber's stomach as he backed through the doorway into his small bedroom. As requested, he pressed down the switch and only the far bedside light came on. 'What is the matter with the overhead light?' the German demanded.

'It's defective – the same switch operates both lights.'

The German, having flashed his own torch into each room, had chosen this one because it was the smallest. Macomber continued backing inside the room where the space for manoeuvre was precisely nil, which presumably was why the German had preferred it, and the watchful look on his adversary's face produced the same reaction in the Scot as the

19

steadiness of the pistol: this was a man who wouldn't be taken by surprise, who wouldn't make a single mistake, a man who would squeeze the trigger instantly if he considered such drastic action necessary. Thin-faced, a shorter man than Macomber, he was in his early forties and he wore a similar leather coat and a similar soft hat. Behind rimless glasses his eyes were unblinking as he gestured for the Scot to sit at the far side of the bed.

'If we're going to talk in here may I take off my coat,' Macomber began, 'and then you can start telling me what the hell this is all about.'

The thin German nodded and issued no further warning about being careful; he simply held his pistol levelled and watched the slow careful movements of taking off the coat. Macomber had noted the rubber overshoes peeping out of his visitor's own coat pocket, which explained his mode of entry – he must have used a skeleton key to open the street door, must then have taken off his overshoes and stepped over the doorstep without disturbing the snow. A man who thought of everything – or almost everything. The Scot hung his coat on a hook at the end of the huge wardrobe which was the other main item of furniture in the room, taking up so much space with the double bed that he had to squeeze his way round in the morning when dressing. He hung the coat carefully to conceal the instability of the wardrobe, the fact that it wobbled easily on its rotting plinth, and he hung the coat with one pocket outwards, the pocket containing the Luger. When he turned round the German reacted instantly. 'You have a gun inside your jacket – take it out very carefully and drop it on the bed, Herr Wolff.'

Macomber used his fingertips to extract the second Luger by the butt, keeping his index finger well away from the trigger as he eased the weapon out of the shoulder holster and let it fall on the bed. The shock had gone, his brain was working again, and at least this manoeuvre had succeeded – by drawing the German's attention to the second gun he had distracted his attention from the coat. The German used his left hand to pick up the Luger and slip it into his pocket. 'Now sit on your side of the bed, Herr Wolff. Incidentally, your

German is quite flawless. I congratulate you. My name is Dietrich. Of the Abwehr, of course.'

'Then why the devil do you want to see me?'

Dietrich said nothing while he closed and locked the bedroom door to guard against the arrival of an associate of Macomber's. The precaution taken, the Abwehr man leaned against the door as he began his interrogation.

'It has been a long time to this moment, Herr Wolff – I will call you that until you decide to tell me your real name.'

'My real name?' Macomber stared at Dietrich as though he must be mad. 'I am Hermann Wolff . . .'

'It has been a long time since January 1940,' the Abwehr man continued as though he hadn't heard the Scot. 'A long way, too, from Budapest to this apartment. I almost caught up with you once in Györ, but I made the mistake of letting my assistant come for you. What happened to him? We never saw him again.'

'As a citizen of the Reich . . .'

'You demand to be taken to police headquarters?' Dietrich was amused and smiled unpleasantly. 'Do you really think you would enjoy that experience – particularly if I take you to Gestapo headquarters instead?'

'I shall complain direct to Berlin – I know people there,' Macomber growled. 'I am a German businessman sent here by my firm in Munich and I have correspondence with me to prove this . . .'

'I'm sure you have,' Dietrich replied sarcastically. 'I'm also sure that it would stand up to superficial examination – until we checked back with your so-called employers. You nearly had me killed tonight, Herr Wolff – and by my own people. I was inside that Mercedes the Wehrmacht opened fire on and I had to drive like a maniac to stay alive, so I decided it might be interesting to come straight here – in case you escaped. I have been following you for some time but I lost you this evening on your way to the railyard.'

'I still haven't the least idea what the hell you're talking about,' Macomber told him coolly. He re-crossed his legs and put his hands together in his lap where Dietrich could see them, and at the same time he hooked his right foot round the electric cord attached to the table-lamp plug. Dietrich smiled without humour.

'I was at the railyard tonight, Wolff – when the shooting started. Now do you understand?'

'Which railyard? What am I supposed to understand about this rubbish?'

'That there is no way out, that you have come to the end of the line. That railyard was the end of the line for you – literally.'

'I don't understand one damned thing,' Macomber rasped, 'but if you open the drawer in that other bedside table over there you may grasp what a bloody fool you're making of yourself.' Then the Scot waited.

It was a chance, no more, and Macomber knew that within a few minutes he would be dead or free. He scratched at his knee as though it tickled and this covered the slight movement of his leg testing the cord. The cable felt to be looped firmly round his ankle, but he could only test it by feel; if he dropped his eyes for even a second Dietrich would guess that something was wrong. Macomber waited, saying not a word while the Abwehr man wondered about the closed drawer. Everything depended on whether Macomber's offhand tone of voice, his arrogant manner, had half-convinced the German there might be something important in the bedside table. The Scot's expression had changed during the past minute, had become a mixture of boredom and contempt, as though the pistol had no existence, as though he thought the Abwehr man an idiot and had proof of the fact – inside the closed drawer.

The bait was tempting. The little table was close enough for Dietrich to lean forward, to reach out with one hand and open it, to see what was there. And he still had Macomber safely on the far side of the bed, his hands pacifically clasped in his lap, unable to come anywhere near the Abwehr man without standing up and running down the narrow space between wardrobe and bed – with Dietrich holding his pistol.

'What is in this drawer?' the Abwehr man asked waspishly.

Macomber said nothing and the battle of nerves continued as the Scot used the only weapon available – silence. The German watched him a few moments longer and then he

22

nodded again, as much as to say very well, we will have a look at this great revelation. He stood up from the door, took a step towards the table, his pistol aimed point-blank at Macomber's chest, but his prisoner was looking at the door with a bored expression. Dietrich used his left hand to reach down for the handle, the hand closest to Macomber, who had foreseen his dilemma. With his gun in his right hand while the other reached for the drawer it was physically impossible for him to keep the pistol muzzle trained on the Scot. Macomber was sitting with his hands limply at rest when the telephone beyond the locked door began to ring.

'Who will that be at this hour?' Dietrich demanded.

Macomber shrugged his shoulders, made no reply. The Abwehr man was becoming rattled – the Scot's refusal to speak was getting on his nerves and the muffled ringing of the phone irritated him. And he wanted to see what was inside the drawer before he found out who was calling Wolff, so everything became urgent. He grabbed at the handle, jerked open the drawer, saw a leather-bound book which might have been a diary, and while he stared at the book he wasn't watching the Scot. Still sitting on the bed, Macomber gave his right foot a tremendous jerk. The plug came out of the wall socket, the room went dark, the table lamp fell onto the bed. Macomber lay sprawled on the floor, waiting for the first shot. But the German didn't fire, which showed extraordinary self-control and quick thinking – a shot would reveal his position. To avoid his boots making a sound, Macomber swivelled on his knees, felt up to the coat, scooped the Luger out of the pocket, then pressed his shoulder against the wardrobe and waited for endless seconds. Had he heard the quietest of noises, a swift slither? He was certain the Abwehr man had changed position, that he had moved along the wall and was now standing with his back to the locked door, facing the other end of the unstable wardrobe. Still on his knees, Macomber heaved massively. The wardrobe toppled, left him, over a hundredweight of solid wood moving through an angle of ninety degrees. It struck something brutally and Macomber heard a muffled cry which cut off suddenly as the wardrobe completed its turn and landed on its side. He used his left hand to locate the coat still

23

attached to the hook, fumbled inside the other pocket and pulled out the torch. The beam showed Dietrich lying under the great weight, the upper half of his body turned to one side, crumpled and motionless, although he still wore his glasses. The left side of his head was oddly misshapen where the wardrobe had crushed his skull.

The phone bell had stopped ringing in the outer room but from its limited duration and the lateness of the hour Macomber guessed who had called him. He had difficulty easing open the door past Dietrich's sprawled body and then he went across the living-room and opened the front door. No sound from below. Locking the door, he went back into the bedroom, turned off the light switch, rescued the table lamp, fixed in the plug and then switched on again. The identity cards were inside the dead man's wallet which he levered from his breast pocket. Two of them, and Dietrich was who he claimed to be. One card – the card tucked away inside a secret pocket – identified him as a high-ranking officer of the Abwehr, but it was the other card which interested Macomber. *Dr Richard Dietrich, archaeologist.* He had heard of this practice – the carrying of a civilian card for use when the Abwehr wished to conceal its true identity. Amid the shambles of the room, with the body lying under the wardrobe he couldn't move without help, Macomber sat on the edge of the bed and lit a cigar while he studied the card for several minutes. Then he went back to the living-room and called a number, puffing at his cigar while he waited for the operator to put him through. Baxter answered sleepily, became alert within a few seconds. 'Hermann here . . .' Macomber began.

'I tried to call you a few minutes ago.'

'I know. Get over to Marie's – she's had some news from Munich.'

He slammed down the receiver, hoping the line wasn't tapped, but they had spoken in German and 'Marie's' identified no address; only the mention of Munich warned Baxter that a grave emergency had arisen. While he waited, Macomber sat calmly smoking because there was nothing more to do; the flat held not a single piece of incriminating evidence and the only papers concerned the fictitious Wolff, papers prepared

24

by the ingenious Baxter. Ten minutes after their brief call had ended, the Englishman who was posing as a Spanish mineralogist with Fascist sympathies arrived and he listened without speaking while Macomber explained what had happened, then looked at the two cards the Scot gave him. 'Roy, I want to use that card to take me out of Europe – the civilian version. Can you fix it up for me damned fast – you've still got some of my pictures, haven't you?'

'Should be able to.' Baxter, a wiry, sallow-faced individual in his late thirties stared up from his chair in the living-room, 'You really think you can get away with it – using the card of a man you've just killed? I'd say you were carrying it a bit far this time. The risk is colossal.'

Baxter studied the huge Scot who stood smoking his cigar without replying immediately. An impressive figure, Mac, he was thinking, but the last man he would personally have chosen to lead a sabotage team: he was too prominent, stood out too much in a crowd. It was characteristic of Macomber that he should have turned this seeming disadvantage into a major asset, always taking up an aggressive role when he was in the company of Germans, which in itself made his impersonation so much more convincing in Nazi-occupied Europe. The brutal thrust was absent from his personality now as, for a brief period only, he was able to be himself, to let the natural, dry-humoured smile show at the corners of his mouth. But to impersonate a senior officer of the Abwehr! The idea alone made Baxter want to shudder. Macomber smiled easily as he spoke.

'Look, Roy, as a cover Hermann Wolff is blown sky-high – the presence of Dietrich in there proves that. So I need a fresh identity. Audacity always pays – it's paid me all the way down through the Balkans and it will get me safely home to Greece.'

'Sometimes, Mac, I think you like the big bluff. You play it that way because it suits your temperament as much as for any other reason...'

'I play it that way because it works. And I need that card fixed during the next few hours, so you're going to have to break all records. As soon as you've gone I'm clearing out of Bucharest and I'd like you to deliver the card to me in

25

Giurgiu. I'll wait at that inn where we once spent a weekend. Can you manage it by noon? Today.'

'I might manage it.' Which was Baxter's way of saying he would be in Giurgiu by noon. 'There's the description to change as well as the photo, but the new quick-drying inks should help. I might even fix up the other one too,' he grinned quickly, 'just in case you want to go the whole hog.' He gestured towards the bedroom. 'Leaving the late Herr Dietrich in there?'

'No, he's got to disappear for several days, but if you'll help me shift that wardrobe I'll cope with the rest. And this, by the way, is your last job. Get that card to me and then make your own way home.' Macomber paused, a gleam of humour in his brown eyes. 'That is, unless you'd sooner come out with me?'

'Thanks, but no thanks. The sort of tricks you go in for would leave me a nervous wreck before we were halfway to the Turkish border.' Baxter grinned wryly. 'If it's all the same to you I'll creep out all by myself.' He looked towards the bedroom again. 'You really think it's wise trying to move him? The city is stiff with German army trucks swarming out to the railyard. Seems someone left a few bombs lying around the place earlier tonight.'

'Then I'll avoid the trucks. But if I'm using Herr Dietrich's card he has to disappear for a while. So long as they don't find him his local people won't know for sure what's happened – don't forget the Abwehr operate on their own a good deal.'

'Better you than me.' Baxter stood up, hoping he wasn't showing too great an eagerness to get away from the flat. 'What do I do with the store of demolition charges? Smash the time fuses and leave them there?'

'Don't bother.' Macomber checked his watch and moved impatiently. 'The Germans have a few more of them, so it's pointless and takes time. Now, I've got to get that body out of here.'

'I'll help you to shift that evidence if you like ...'

'Just help me to shift the wardrobe and then push off. I'd sooner deal with this on my own.' A typical reaction, Baxter thought, and he marvelled at the Scot's steady nerves. Forester, Dyce, Lemaitre – all the rest of the sabotage team were dead and Mac was the sole survivor, possibly because of his habit of working alone. And he can have it, he told himself as he followed Macomber inside the bedroom.

Macomber felt a little more relaxed as he drove the Volkswagen through the still-dark streets of Bucharest, a reaction which would have astounded the less phlegmatic Baxter. Down side roads which led to the main highway the Scot had already seen several army trucks trundling through the snow and for a short distance he must travel along that highway himself. The army blanket, thawed out by the heat of the car on his journey from the railyard, was thrown over the back seat, but it still assumed an odd shape – it had proved impossible to disguise completely the hump of Dietrich's body underneath. So relaxation was perhaps not a correct description of the Scot's present frame of mind. Even so he was relieved, relieved to have accomplished the mind-numbing trip he had made down the apartment block's fire-escape with the Abwehr man looped over his shoulder. The iron treads of the fire-escape had been coated with ice, he had heard a window open in the darkness during his grim journey down the staircase, and there had been no cover to hide his progress across the walled yard to the back street where he had parked his Volkswagen. But for Macomber the worst phase of this problem was over – providing he could avoid those army trucks.

He drove very slowly as he approached the exit to the main highway, then pulled up with his engine still ticking over. He waited half a minute and when nothing passed the exit he drove out and turned left, north towards the railway, the direction which would take him into open country most quickly. He drove steadily at a medium speed and his headlights showed up sombre buildings, their iron balconies laced with snow; later a desolate square, the trees naked and frosted with a bowed statue in the centre; later still shabby tenements forming a continuous wall of poverty. Lord, he'd be glad to leave this place. He was close to the outskirts when the emergency began. Driving at a sober speed along the empty highway, although the fog of fatigue was settling on his weary mind, he still watched the road keenly as he glanced at his watch. 4.15

AM. A little over two hours ago he had been lying on top of that petrol wagon with the sounds of the dogs in his ears. He turned a bend, saw an army truck emerging from a side street ahead, and then he was driving behind it as the vehicle rattled forward over the uneven road. Headlights glared in his rear mirror, roared up behind him, only slowing when he thought he was going to be run down by the second army truck. He was boxed in by the Wehrmacht.

There was no side turning he could take now except the turning a mile ahead he intended using, so he had to put up with the unwelcome escort as they drove on into the country-side. He glanced back quickly, saw the truck behind within twenty feet of the Volkswagen, and when he looked back again where the road curved he saw a stream of headlights coming up. He had slotted himself inside a whole convoy of German trucks. Clenching the cigar more tightly, he concentrated on holding the same speed as the vehicle ahead, his eyes fixed on the red light, the closed canvas covers, while in his rear mirror the oncoming headlights behind remained a constant glare. Even leaving this damned convoy was going to be tricky. He timed it carefully, drawing nearer to the vehicle in front as the vital side turning approached, and he was on the verge of signalling when he saw the pole barricading the side road, the German military policeman behind it. They had blocked it off to prevent civilian traffic entering this route. He drove past his escape exit without a glance while he searched for a solution, tried to foresee the next move. A mile farther on the road forked; the left fork leading to the railyard, the right one across the plain. But logically they would have blocked this off, too, so he would be forced to continue with the convoy until it reached the railyard he had half-destroyed, an area which must be swarming with troops. Perhaps, after all, Baxter had had a point.

As they drove on through the night the fatigue grew worse, encouraged by the monotonous rumble of the truck engines, increased by the necessity to go on staring at the red light ahead, and when the German vehicle's canvas covers parted briefly his headlights picked up the silhouette of a helmet: the trucks were packed with German troops. Wiping sweat away from his forehead, Macomber began to conduct the only possible manoeuvre which might extricate him from the trap, gradually reducing speed so that the truck in front moved farther away. But there was a limit to the loss of speed the driver behind would tolerate, and Macomber was gambling on the lack of enthusiasm for his job which might be expected in the middle of the night. He drove on until there was a gap of twenty yards between the Volkswagen and the truck ahead and then held it at that distance, expecting at any moment a furious burst of hooting from his rear. He had decided to try and use a very minor road turning off to the right, a road which was a dead end, leading over the fields and across the railway to a large farm, but he wanted to conceal the fact that he had turned off up this dangerous dead end. If the driver behind reported the presence of the lone Volkswagen when he reached the railyard they mustn't know where to look for him. The next bend was the crucial point and it needed split-second timing.

A copse of trees flashed into the lights of the vehicle in front and then vanished as the truck turned the corner. Macomber glanced in the mirror, saw the headlights locked onto him, suddenly speeded up. The car raced forward over the wheel-gutted snow, left well behind the truck in his rear as he accelerated, praying he wouldn't go into another skid. As he reduced speed to go round the curve his lights shone on the trees, then he was momentarily out of sight of the truck behind. The wooden gate was set back from the road and he almost missed it, but he saw it just in time, swung his wheel, crashed through the obstacle, turned behind a stone wall and felt the Volkswagen wobble from side to side as it passed over iron-hard ruts. Leaving the engine running, he switched off the lights and waited.

He was chewing at his cigar-end when a glow of lights appeared beyond the wall, silhouetting the naked tree-trunks like a natural palisade. The truck's engine was losing speed as the driver saw the bend, and too much loss of speed enormously increased the danger of his seeing the smashed gate, the tracks left by the Volkswagen in the snow when it plunged into the field. Macomber sat motionless while the truck lost even more speed and lumbered ponderously round the bend, then it

29

sounded as though it were stopping. He had been spotted – the smashed gate, the tyre tracks had been seen! He grabbed the door handle, ready for a futile flight into the wasteland, knowing that the truck had only to follow him once the headlights picked up the fugitive, doubtful whether his legs had the strength to carry him far, when the engine ticked over more strongly and the truck rumbled past the gateway towards the railyard.

He left the car at once, stumbled his way over the ruts in the darkness, found a buttress which he used to haul himself up to where he could see over the wall and back along the road. Between the pole-shapes of the trees he observed the headlights moving towards him, saw a gap between the fourth and fifth set of lights. There would be orders about maintaining an even distance in convoy but there was always a laggard – if only he would continue to lag behind! Macomber ran back towards the Volkswagen, sprawling headlong in the snow when his foot caught in a rut, clambering swiftly to his feet again and reaching the car as the first set of headlights lit the top of the wall. The second vehicle followed closely, then the third and the fourth. Now! The Volkswagen rocked unsteadily as he drove towards the gateway and when he arrived at the exit the road was clear. Turning out of the field, he pressed his foot down and sped after the retreating rear light of the truck in the distance.

The turning onto the farm track came sooner than he expected and he swung the wheel automatically, glancing back the way he had come. No headlights behind: the fifth truck had not yet arrived at the bend. Within a hundred yards the track dropped into a bowl and his own lights were hidden from the main road. As he drove along the track, his headlight beams showing up clumps of frosted glass on either side, he concentrated on the immediate problem – the disposal of Dietrich. In summer, with the grasses grown tall, he could have dumped him in a dozen places, but with the ground frozen to the consistency of iron, the grasses ankle-high and the fields a white sheet against which the body would show up clearly, any unlucky chance might disclose the evidence in daylight. He would have to do better than that.

Five minutes later he was driving up a slope as he approached the bridge which crossed the railway; even in the daytime it was a lonely spot but at this hour there was an atmosphere of eerie desolation about the place and spiked reeds caught in the headlights reminded him he was driving across marshland. He slowed down to take a dangerous turn beyond the bridge and heard the clanking of goods wagons moving up from the south. On the spur of the moment he pulled up, left the engine running and got out to look over the bridge. A hooded lamp a short distance away shone down on a steam engine which passed under him hauling a train of empty coal trucks bound for the eastern section of the railyard, a section unaffected by the explosions. The trucks were on their way to the coal hopper where they would be filled and sent on their long journey to Germany. Macomber felt a sudden lightening of the dreadful fatigue which was steadily wearing him out, making even thought difficult. There could be a ready-made solution to his problem twenty feet below him.

Long weeks of observation had made the Scot an expert on the workings of that railyard, and he knew the coal would be loaded into the trucks as soon as the train arrived. The first trucks were already passing under him as he gauged their speed and the moment when the centre of a truck was exactly below where he stood. Without further calculation he switched off the car lights, opened the rear door and wrestled out the blanketed bundle. Hoisting the German on his shoulders, a major effort in itself, he staggered to the parapet and waited, gauging the right moment afresh, knowing he couldn't afford to misjudge his timing by so much as a second. He waited until one truck was centred under the bridge and flopped the bundle across the wall; as the rear of the truck rolled out of sight he heaved and held his breath. The body dropped, landed in the centre of the next coal truck, vanished under the bridge. Dr Richard Dietrich, archaeologist, was on his way home to Germany.

CHAPTER TWO

Saturday, April 5

Dietrich.

The name on the identity card immediately caught the attention of the Turkish passport control officer. *Dr Richard Dietrich, German national, born Flensburg. Profession: archaeologist. Age: thirty-two.* Officer Sarajoglu buttoned up his collar against the cold and studied the card thoughtfully as though he found it suspect. Behind him in the harbour of the Golden Horn a tugboat siren shrieked non-stop, a piercing sound which the raw, early morning wind from the Black Sea carried clear across Istanbul. Sarajoglu, a man sensitive to atmospheres, was unable to define the feeling of suspense which hung over the waterfront. At half past six on a morning when winter still gripped the straits, the worst always seemed likely to happen.

'You are travelling on business?' the Turk inquired.

'I am leaving Turkey.' Dietrich took a small cigar out of his mouth and flicked ash which fell on the counter separating them. He was a very large man, dressed in a belted leather coat and a dark, soft hat. His reply had been arrogant in manner and wording, implying that since he was leaving the country his activities were of no concern to this bureaucrat. Sarajoglu concealed his annoyance but proceeded to make a gesture of independence, conveying that although German troops had recently marched into Rumania and Bulgaria, his country was still neutral territory: using a gloved finger, he poked the German's ash off the counter. It fell off the edge and landed on Dietrich's highly polished boot. Sarajoglu, who had watched the fall of the ash, looked up and stared at the German. No reaction. Dietrich had clasped his hands behind his back and was staring through a frost-coated window at the harbour.

He was a man whose sheer physical presence was formidable – a man over six feet tall who must weigh at least fourteen stone, Sarajoglu estimated. Even so, the head seemed a little large for the body, a squarish head with a short nose, the mouth wide and firm-lipped, the jaw-line suggesting great energy and enormous determination. But it was the eyes which the Turk found most arresting, large brown eyes which moved slowly and deliberately as though assessing everything. He might be on the list of known German agents, Sarajoglu was thinking. Without much hope, he held onto the card and asked Dietrich to wait a moment.

'I have to catch that boat, the *Hydra*,' Dietrich informed him roughly, 'so hurry it up,' he rumbled as the Turk moved away into a small room behind the counter. Pretending not to have heard, Sarajoglu closed the door, opened a filing cabinet, took out the confidential list of German agents and ran his eye down it. No, his memory had not deceived him: Dietrich was not on the list. He turned to a youth who was typing at a desk close to the wall.

'The *Hydra* – she hasn't changed her sailing schedule so far as you know?'

'No, she's sailing at 7.30 AM and making the normal ferry run – Istanbul to Zervos. Why, sir?'

'Nothing really. But there are three Germans aboard the vessel already and now I've got a fourth outside. It's just unusual – Germans travelling to Greece at this stage of the war.'

'Greece isn't at war with Germany – only with Italy.'

'Yes, and that's a curious situation.' Sarajoglu bit the edge of the identity card between his teeth and failed to notice that some of the ink had flaked off. 'Curious,' he repeated. 'The Greeks have been fighting Germany's ally, Italy, for over six months but the Germans still remain neutral. I heard yesterday that British forces are landing in Greece – one of our captains saw their transports in the Piraeus. They must anticipate a German attack.'

'They probably hope to prevent one.' The typist peered through the window towards the counter beyond. 'Is that him – the big brute out there?

33

Ah, so you don't like the look of him either, Sarajoglu thought. He stared through the window where he could see the German standing passive and immobile, and this total lack of nervousness impressed him. When a passenger's papers were taken away even the innocent ones displayed a certain perturbation, as though they feared an inadvertent mistake in their documentation. Dietrich, however, stood so still that he might have been carved from wood except for the curl of cigar smoke rising towards the roof of the shed. 'Yes,' Sarajoglu replied, 'that is Dr Richard Dietrich. He is thirty-two years old – so why is he not in the German army, I wonder?'

'Better ask him.' As the typist resumed work Sarajoglu's lips tightened. He flicked the cutting edge of the card sharply across the youth's ear, noted with satisfaction that he had flinched, then went outside to the counter. The German was standing in exactly the same position as when he had left him, hands behind his back, staring out at the harbour, his manner outwardly unruffled by this deliberate delay. Sarajoglu felt even more irked as he laid the card on the counter and spoke with exaggerated courtesy. 'You may go now, Dr Dietrich. A pleasant trip.'

The German picked up the card without haste, put it away inside his wallet, his eyes on Sarajoglu all the time. He stood with that typically German stance, his legs splayed well apart, his body like a human tree-trunk. The Turk began to feel uncomfortable: there had been precise instructions from above as to how to deal with German tourists – don't offend them and treat them with every courtesy so there can be no cause for complaint from Berlin. He felt relieved when Dietrich turned away, nodding curtly to the porter who hastily picked up the single bag and followed him out of the shed and up the ice-sheathed gangway. Inside his cabin Dietrich was feeling in his pocket for the tip when the porter, still nervous of his German passenger, clumsily knocked over the water carafe. Dietrich shook his head brusquely as the porter stooped to pick up the remnants, told him he'd done enough damage already and handed over the modest tip, a sum which normally would have provoked a sarcastic response. But as the German went on staring at him, clearly inviting his immediate departure, the

34

porter thought better of it and left the cabin with a polite mumble.

As soon as the porter had gone, Macomber locked the door, picked up the two largest pieces of broken carafe and deposited them in the wastepaper basket. God, it was a relief to be inside neutral Turkey, to be on board, to be alone in his cabin. And within thirty hours he would be able to revert to his real identity, to be known once more as Ian Macomber, to talk in English all day long if he wished. He went over to the washbasin and looked in the mirror above it, gazing into the glass like a man seeing the result when surgical bandages have been removed.

For the first time since he had left the flat in Bucharest his features relaxed, the crinkles of humour appeared at the corners of his mouth, and even though still wearing the German hat and leather coat the Teutonic image was gone. It was going to be irksome – keeping up his German impersonation until he landed safely on Greek soil – but it was necessary. He was travelling with German papers and the Greek captain might not appreciate his sudden conversion to another nationality. So for one more day and one more night he must go on playing the part of Dr Richard Dietrich, German archaeologist. The knock on the door startled him, reminded him of the extreme fatigue he was labouring under – and also that the danger might not be past yet. He unlocked the door, his hand clutching the Luger inside his coat pocket, opened it cautiously. It was the chief steward and he showed surprise when Macomber addressed him in fluent Greek.

'What do you want?'

'You speak our language – it is most unusual for a German . . .'

'I said what do you want?'

'Is everything to your satisfaction, sir? Good. If you need something you have only to call me . . .' The voluble steward chattered on while Macomber stared at him bleakly, then he said something which again startled the Scot. 'I'm sure you'll be interested to know we have three of your fellow-countrymen also on board . . .'

For a muddled moment Macomber thought he was referring to three Englishmen, then he recovered his tired wits. 'Are they together?' he enquired in a bored tone which concealed his anxiety about the reply.

'No, sir, they are all travelling separately.' The steward paused and there was a malicious gleam in his quick-moving eyes. 'There are also two British passengers.'

'You find that amusing?'

'No, sir.' The steward replied hastily, taken aback by the grimness of this overbearing German. He tried to correct his blunder. 'I shall be in the dining-room where breakfast is being prepared, so if you require anything...'

'Then I shall ask you! And take this – I want a comfortable trip, so do your duty.' Macomber had handed the flabbergasted man a generous tip before turning his back and closing the cabin door, but it had suddenly occurred to him that the steward could be a valuable source of information and he had already decided to question him further about the other passengers. But not now – it would arouse too much interest. Alone again, Macomber stripped off the hat and coat and doused himself in ice-cold water. Three Germans aboard, he was thinking as he dried himself slowly; perhaps it wasn't all over yet. When he had reached Istanbul he had avoided going anywhere near the British Legation – because the Legation was the very place the Abwehr might be watching for his arrival. It was too late to arrest him but it certainly wasn't too late to have him killed. Not that he feared the Abwehr's revenge – they had a far more powerful motive for ensuring that he never reached Allied territory alive, and they were perfectly capable of putting an assassin aboard the *Hydra*, an assassin not necessarily of German nationality. It's what I'm carrying in my head they'd like to destroy, he reminded himself. Information gathered over months of patient observation in the Balkans – data about assembly points, storage depots, the routes along which supplies were being sent to the Reich ...

He finished drying himself, glanced at the inviting bunk and looked away quickly. Lord, it had been a swine of a trip from Bucharest. Four hours' sleep in forty-eight, his reflexes shot to hell, but he'd better check this damned ship – and forget any ideas about sleep until he was actually on Greek soil. He put on the leather coat and the hat, tested the action of his Luger, glanced in the mirror. He was back in business again. The arrogant, uncompromising image of Dr Richard Dietrich stared back at him. Replacing the gun inside his coat, he left the cabin to carry out his inspection of the 5,000-ton Greek ferry.

The bitter wind raked his face as soon as he reached the deck, a wind unpleasant enough, he soon found, to keep the handful of fellow-passengers below decks. Half an hour later, his tour of the vessel completed, he stood near the stern where he could keep an eye on the gangway for late arrivals. It was just possible that the Abwehr might send someone on board at the last moment. Standing by the rail, Macomber seemed impervious to the weather as he quietly smoked his cigar. The lifeboat covers were still crusted with last night's snowfall, the masthead rigging still encased with glassy ice, but the battered yellow funnel was dripping moisture as the ship began to get up steam. To all outward appearances Macomber had wandered round the vessel with the idle curiosity of the newly arrived passenger who is interested in his temporary home, but now as he smoked his cigar he was cataloguing his discoveries in his mind.

From the chief steward he had learned that the *Hydra* carried a crew of six, that the captain's name was Nopagos, and that he had plied this regular passage between Istanbul and Zervos for the past fourteen years. Macomber stirred at the rail as the chief steward reappeared at his elbow, chattering amiably.

'Looks as though we've got our full complement of passengers aboard, sir.'

Macomber nodded, wondering whether he had overdone the tip: the steward was becoming his shadow. He checked his watch. 'There's still time for last-minute arrivals.' Again he was subtly probing for information.

'Doubt that, sir. I was talking to the ticket office manager a few minutes ago on the phone – he sold seven tickets for this trip, so it looks as though that's the lot.'

Macomber nodded again and the steward, sensing that he was no longer in a talkative mood, excused himself. Left alone once more, the Scot continued his mental inventory. Two British civilians he hadn't yet seen, one man in his late twenties while his companion was probably a few years beyond thirty. Which was interesting, since both men were of military age. One Greek civilian who lived on Zervos and apparently had something to do with the monastic order which owned the ferry – again a man of military age, but Macomber presumed that his slight limp had kept him out of the Greek Army. And, finally, the three Germans. He had seen two of them briefly, both civilians in their early forties who had the appearance of businessmen, but the third, a man called Schnell, had apparently come aboard very early in the morning and locked himself away in his cabin. 'With his cabin trunk,' as the voluble steward had explained earlier. On this point the Scot had detected an uncertain note in the steward's voice and he had asked a question.

'You find that odd – that he should keep a trunk in his cabin?'

'Well, sir, it takes up a lot of space and I offered to have it put in the hold when he came aboard. After all, we shall be docking at Zervos in twenty-four hours. He was quite abrupt with me, the way some...' He had paused and Macomber, knowing he had been about to say 'the way some Germans are', had smiled grimly to himself. But the steward had changed his wording in time. '...the way some people are when they arrive early. He insisted it stayed with him in the cabin so he must be carrying something valuable.'

Something valuable? Macomber frowned as he recalled the steward's words – it was this cabin trunk and its unknown contents which occupied his thoughts as he gazed out over the muddle of decrepit-looking tramps and coasters which congested the Golden Horn harbour. He heard a sound behind him and remained staring out across the water, one large boot resting on the lower rail. Was it likely that an attempt would be made to assassinate him at this late hour – a few minutes before putting to sea? Out of the corner of his eye he watched the Greek approaching, heard the faint slur of his limping step.

38

The man's name was Grapos and even with that slight limp Macomber thought he would be an asset to any army: of only medium height there was, nevertheless, a suggestion of tremendous physical strength in those broad shoulders and that powerful chest which swelled the coloured shirt. Not a prosperous individual, Macomber decided: his grey jacket and trousers were of poor quality, the red tie round his neck was faded and his boots were shabby. The steward had told him of an unexpected facility Grapos possessed – the monks had taught him to speak English. The Greek was very close now, stopping almost behind the Scot, and his eyes were shrewd and alert.

'Always it seems so long before the boat sails,' he began. 'You have been to Zervos before?'

'Once.' Macomber replied in Greek and turned his head away to study the harbour. Grapos might have been surprised had he known how much Macomber had registered in that brief glance. The Greek's face was strong-featured, the jaw-line formidable, and the long straggle of dark moustache which curved round the corners of his wide mouth gave him the look of a bandit or guerrilla. He was one of the most villainous-looking characters Macomber had encountered since entering the Balkans. But the point which had alerted the Scot was the fact that Grapos had spoken to him in Greek. Which could only mean that he had eavesdropped while Macomber was conversing in that language with the steward, unless that talkative individual had informed Grapos that they had a Greek-speaking German aboard.

'There is bad weather on the way,' Grapos remarked and looked upwards.

'Why do you say that?' Macomber's tone was brusque and unencouraging, but the Greek seemed not to notice.

'Because of the birds.' Grapos lifted a hand and pointed to where a cloud of seagulls wheeled and floated in erratic circles high above the white-coated domes and minarets onshore.

'Don't you always get birds over a harbour?' Macomber sounded bored with the company which had thrust itself upon him, but now he was observing the large, hairy-backed hands which gripped the rail as though they might pull a section loose bodily.

'Yes, but not so many, and they are uneasy – you can tell by the way they fly. I have seen them fly like that over Zervos before the great storms. This will be a bad voyage,' he went on cheerfully. 'We shall run into a storm before we land at Katyra. Let us hope it does not strike us off Cape Zervos. You see,' he continued with relish, 'the entrance to the gulf is very narrow and the cape has been the graveyard of a hundred ships or more . . .' He broke off, grinning savagely as he displayed a row of perfect white teeth. 'But, of course, you know – you have been there before.'

Macomber said nothing as he hunched his broad shoulders and threw the smoked cigar butt into the water. Two ships away along the wharf another vessel was preparing to leave, her white funnel belching out clouds of murky smoke which the wind dispersed in chaotic trails. Behind him he heard footsteps retreating, one of them out of step. Grapos had taken the hint and was on his way to find someone else who would listen to his chatter. Extracting a Zeiss Monokular glass, a single-lens field-glass, from his pocket, Macomber focused it on the other vessel getting up a head of steam. The Rumanian flag whipped in the wind from her masthead and she was, he knew, the *Rupescu*. Her decks were strangely deserted for a ship on the point of departure and at the head of the gang-plank two seamen stood as though on guard. It was quite clear that shortly she would follow the *Hydra* across the Sea of Marmara and into the Dardanelles, which he found interesting.

From the steward he had learned that the *Rupescu*, a fast motor vessel, was twelve hours out of the Bulgarian port of Varna and the situation could be a little tricky since she was bound for the Aegean. German troops now controlled Bulgaria so technically the Allies might regard the *Rupescu* as an enemy vessel, a prize to be sought out by the Royal Navy. Certainly the British Legation at Istanbul would already have wirelessed Egypt of her presence in the straits, but Macomber doubted whether she would be seized – the British Government had broken off diplomatic relations with Rumania

40

but had not yet declared war on that unhappy country. Satisfied with what he had seen – nothing out of the ordinary – Macomber put away his glass and then stiffened as a shabbily dressed man dashed up the gangway. Under his arm he carried a batch of newspapers and he flourished one in the Scot's face when he came along the desk. Macomber bought a copy, glancing at the banner headline before he went below. *German Army Poised To Attack?*

The engines were throbbing steadily as he made his way along a narrow companionway and walked calmly into the saloon, a small cramped room with panelled walls which was already reeking of acrid cigar smoke. Pulling out his copy of the *Frankfurter Zeitung*, Macomber sank heavily into an ancient arm-chair in a corner which allowed him to see the whole room while he pretended to read. Hahnemann, a thin-faced German in his early forties and dressed like a travelling salesman in a cheap suit, sat in the diagonally opposite corner smoking one of the cigars responsible for the bad air. In another corner, a heavily built German of medium height, his clothes well-cut and dark, sat reading some typed sheets and also smoking a cigar. That would be Volber. The fourth corner was occupied by a small bar where a man in white uniform was polishing a glass. Thank God, Macomber was thinking, those two don't exactly look like sociable types. I could do without useless conversation in German at the moment. The thought had hardly passed through his head when two men opened the doors and stood hesitating as though not sure whether to come in. Their first words warned Macomber. They were British.

'Go on in, for God's sake,' Prentice said impatiently to Ford, who was standing in the doorway. 'Don't just stand gawping. We've paid our fares just like the rest of these johnnies.'

Ford's face was expressionless as he carefully made his way through the smoke to a table close to the bar. As they settled behind a low table the steward took Macomber's order and a minute later placed a glass of beer in front of him. Ford kept his voice low as he made the remark. 'That chap who's just got his beer looks like another bleedin' Jerry.'

'I think they all are,' Prentice murmured nonchalantly.

41

'This is a funny, funny war at times.' Unlike Ford, who sat stiffly and kept an eye on the other three men without appearing to do so, Prentice was outwardly the soul of relaxation. When the steward arrived for their order he deliberately raised his voice so the whole room could hear. 'A beer and a glass of *ouzo*, laddie.'

'Beg, please?' The steward looked at a loss. Prentice leaned round him and stabbed a finger in the direction of Macomber's table, his voice louder still. 'One *ouzo* and a beer – beer – like that chap over there ordered.' The other two Germans glanced in his direction and then looked away, but the Scot, who had lowered his paper, stared hard across the room with an unpleasantly inquiring expression.

'Tough-looking basket, that big one,' Ford remarked, keeping his own voice quiet. 'If I met him in Libya I'd let him have two in the pump. Yes, two – just to be sure.'

The drinks were served and Ford sipped at his palely coloured beer cautiously, then grimaced. 'They've got the washing-up water mixed in with the beer.' He eyed Prentice's glass with even more distaste. 'You're not really drinking that, are you?' But his question was purely rhetorical – Prentice would drink anything, smoke anything, eat anything. Some of the dishes he'd consumed during their brief stay in Turkey had astounded and appalled the conservative Ford. Prentice pushed the glass of yellowish liquid towards him.

'Go on, it tastes just like whisky.' He watched with amusement while his companion took a gulp and then almost dropped the glass, looking round suddenly to make sure his experience hadn't been observed. Macomber was still watching him over his paper.

'Lovely!' Ford choked. 'A delicate mixture of nail varnish and turpentine. If that's the Greek national drink no wonder the Romans licked them. It still seems odd travelling with a bunch of Jerries for company.' He looked round the saloon as he heard a distant rattle. The gangway being hauled up probably. In one corner the thin-faced German was absorbed in a book while the man crouched over some typed sheets made notes with a pencil. They might have been aboard a normal peacetime boat and the war seemed a long way from Istanbul

'It really is damned funny,' Prentice began, his lean, humorous face serious for a change. 'Here we are on a Greek ferry just leaving for Zervos – in the middle of a life-and-death war with Adolf Hitler's Reich – and because the Greeks are fighting the Italians but not the Germans, we can travel with three Jerries we mustn't even bump into if we meet them in the corridor. I must remember this trip when I write me memoirs, Ford.'

'Yes, sir,' said Ford automatically, and received a sharp dig in the ribs for his pains. He understood the hint and swore inwardly. He'd be glad when this ferry trip was over and they could get back to normal service life, to being Lieutenant Prentice and Staff-Sergeant Ford. Before they had boarded the *Hydra* Prentice had given him a stern lecture in their Istanbul hotel bedroom and he had tripped up already.

'Ford,' Prentice had begun, 'for the purposes of this sea trip back to Greece and while we're on board the ferry, I want you to forget I'm a lieutenant and, what's more important still, forget that you're a staff-sergeant. We're sporting civvies, but if you keep on calling me "sir" it's a dead giveaway. There may even be a German tourist on that broken-down old Greek ferry.' Prentice hadn't really believed that this would happen but he was dramatizing the situation to try and make Ford forget his years of professional training for a few hours.

'I'll watch it, sir,' Ford had replied and had then watched Prentice throw his trilby on the bed with a despairing cry.

'Ford!' he had bellowed. 'You've just done it again! Look, I know we're at the fag-end of our trip with the military mission to carry out liaison with the Turks in case Jerry attacks them, but we really have got to watch it . . .'

The trouble really had been the Turks themselves. Anxious to keep out of the war if they could – and who could blame them for that? – they had invited the British to send a military mission to discuss possible defence measures if the worst happened. But to avoid provoking the attack they feared, or rather, to avoid giving Berlin an excuse for launching that attack, they had insisted that the mission should travel in civilian clothes. A Signal Corps man, Prentice had found plenty to discuss with his Turkish opposite numbers in the way of a plan for setting up communications, and Staff-Sergeant Ford, ex-Royal Artillery, was now one of that rare breed, an ammunition examiner, an expert on explosives, both British and foreign. In this role he had also finished his work late when he had been taken to see a Turkish dam it was proposed to blow up in the event of a German invasion. So both of them had returned to Istanbul to find the plane with the military mission aboard had already left for Athens.

'When's the next one?' Prentice had light-heartedly asked the chap at the Legation.

'There isn't one,' the Legation official had informed him coldly. 'You'll have to catch a boat out of here. The very first available boat,' he had added. 'I've already looked it up for you – it's a ship called the *Hydra*. Sailing for Greece to-morrow morning. Just after dawn,' he had concluded with a twinge of waspish humour which Prentice, who hated rising early, had not fully appreciated.

Later, Prentice had discovered that normally there was a regular service operating between Istanbul and Athens, but the Turks had just cancelled this because of rumours of German troop movements along their northern borders. So, that left the ferry to the peninsula of Zervos, which was in northern Greece, much closer to Salonika than Athens, but at least it would land them on Greek soil. The Legation, of course, had been in the devil of a hurry to see the last of them. Prentice had a shrewd idea that the Ambassador was having kittens at the thought of British soldiers disguised as civilians wandering the streets of Istanbul. As he expressed it quietly to Ford in the saloon of the *Hydra* while he swallowed the *ouzo* in two gulps: 'I really think if there'd been a boat leaving for Russia they'd have pushed us on that.'

'Maybe. I still think it's queer there should be three Jerries all on the same trip on this leaky old tub,' Ford persisted. He could hear the rattle of a chain somewhere. They'd be off any minute now.

Prentice grinned. 'They may be embassy staff transferred from Istanbul to their place in Salonika.' He studied Ford, noted again the stocky build, the neatly cut black hair and the

44

alert eyes which watched the room constantly. Always wanting to have a go, was Ford. An aggressive, controlled chap who carried an air of competence and energetic ability. As for Prentice, he never went out of his way to have a go, but if the necessity arose he was more than able to cope with his leisured, laconic manner. The difference was that for Ford, the army was a way of life, whereas for Prentice it was a necessary but time-wasting interval which kept him from his advertising job in the West End of London.

'But if they're embassy staff,' Ford went on obstinately, his hands cupped to hide his mouth, 'why are they travelling separately? They don't know each other, that's obvious enough.'

Prentice felt the ship moving away from the quayside and checked his watch. 7.30 AM. Ford had a point there, he was thinking. And if they were embassy staff going to Salonika why the devil hadn't they taken the train from Istanbul along that line through Macedonia? By all accounts it was a nightmare trip, stopping at every little out-of-the-way village and taking anything up to a couple of days, but at least it would have got them there direct. So why were they in such a rush to reach Greece by the earliest possible hour? Why, Prentice kept asking himself? Why?

Field-Marshal von List stood up from behind the desk at his GHQ in southern Bulgaria and walked to the window, still holding the meteorological report. Beside the desk his staff officer, Colonel Wilhelm Genke, waited patiently. The field-marshal was worried and from long experience Genke knew that this was not the moment to speak. The clock on the desk registered 7.30 AM.

His face seasoned and grim, List gazed out at the view, and this didn't please him either because it was a reminder of the piece of paper he held in his hands. It was an hour after dawn and beyond the stone houses of the village he could make out where the mountains rose to meet the clouds which hung low over Bulgaria, clouds which promised more snow on the way. Which the Met report also promised. He could vaguely see the

45

snow from where he stood – great drifts of it piled up on the lower slopes under the cloud ceiling. His voice was harsh when he spoke.

'It's foul, unspeakably foul weather. They could be wrong, I suppose. They're wrong half the time, these so-called weather experts. Look at what happened in Norway.'

Genke coughed, timing his intervention carefully. 'Spring is late all over Europe, sir. There is still deep snow across the Russian steppes and no sign of a thaw ...'

'Don't let's talk about Russia yet. We have to settle this business first.' List turned round, a tinge of sarcasm in his voice. 'Berlin, of course, is quite confident.'

'Berlin is always confident when other people have to do the work, sir. But you have exceptionally powerful forces under your command.'

On that point, at least, the field-marshal agreed. The Twelfth Army comprised two motorized, three mountain Alpenkorps and light infantry divisions, three regiments of the Liebstandarte Adolf Hitler Division – and five Panzer divisions, the spearhead of the coming onslaught on Greece and Yugoslavia. A force of enormous strength and great mobility – theoretically powerful enough to overwhelm everything which stood in their path. But there was deep snow on the Greek mountains, deep snow on Olympus and Zervos. Could the machines overcome the hazards of this damnably prolonged winter? The question was never far from his mind – and zero hour was almost here.

Gazing out of the window, he thought that Bulgaria was the most Godforsaken spot he had encountered in his life, and even as he watched, white flakes drifted down outside the window, several clinging to the glass and beginning to build up opaque areas. Would spring never come? Yes, zero hour was very close indeed. Beyond the window he heard a familiar sound – the grind and clatter of tank tracks moving over cobbled streets. The supporting Panzers were rolling towards the border and would be in position before nightfall. The time-table had been set in motion and the operation was under way. Now no power on earth except Berlin could stop it. And within hours even Berlin would have forfeited that prerogative.

From outside the house came the sound of a vehicle stopping, its engine still left running. Genke shuffled his feet.

'The car has arrived, sir.'

List buttoned up his coat to the neck, put the peaked cap on his head and started for the door. But on the way he paused to glance at the wall map which an orderly would take down as soon as they had left, a map of the southern Balkans and eastern Mediterranean zones. Then Genke opened the door and Field-Marshal von List strode out with his assistant following. Genke had noted that pause to glance at the map and he knew which area had attracted List's attention. He had looked first at Istanbul, then his eye had followed the sea route through the Dardanelles and across the Aegean where it had finally alighted on a certain peninsula.

Zervos.

'The *Rupescu*?' The Senior Naval Intelligence Officer at Alexandria looked up at his assistant, Lieutenant-Commander Browne. 'Is that the Rumanian ship the Legation people at Istanbul sent the message about?'

'Yes, sir. It left the Bulgarian port of Varna yesterday and arrived at the Golden Horn a few hours ago. There's some mystery as to her ultimate destination.'

'What mystery?'

'It's a bit vague, sir. Apparently she's bound for Beirut – but it's her first trip out of the Black Sea for months and I suppose the Legation's bothered because the Germans control Rumania now.'

'I see. That's rather delicate – we still haven't declared war on Rumania. You're suggesting we keep an eye on her? To make sure she is heading for the Lebanon?'

Browne looked out of the window where a white jetty sparkled in the early morning sunshine, its arm enclosing a basin of brilliant blue water where warships lay at anchor. A transport bound for Greece was just beyond the jetty wall, sailing north-west and leaving behind a clear wake of white on the blue. 'It's the only vessel in the area which has the remotest connexion with the Axis powers – and so far we have no idea what she's carrying.'

'Probably collecting rather than carrying – trying to pick up a cargo before war is eventually declared and we can pounce on her. We're very stretched, you know that, Browne.'

'I was thinking of the *Daring*, sir. She's patrolling off the Turkish coast and could intercept the *Rupescu* soon after dark. I'm not thinking of boarding her – but it might be interesting to get her reaction when a British destroyer comes in close.'

'Send Willoughby a message, then. And radio another one to Istanbul. We've had two requests already from those querulous diplomats.' The senior officer looked at the wall clock. 7.30 AM. Yes, it would be after nightfall before Willoughby arrived.

CHAPTER THREE

Saturday, 10 PM

The tension had slowly risen aboard the *Hydra*, a tension which seemed reproduced by the steady beat of her throbbing engines as she left the Dardanelles and proceeded far out into the open Aegean. By nightfall she was midway between the Turkish and Greek coasts, steaming through seas which were beginning to curdle. The tension rose from small, meaningless incidents. The meeting at a doorway between Prentice and the squat, dark-haired German, Volber, when the latter had started to push his way through first and had then changed his mind, offering prior entry to Prentice. The episode at dinner when a cork came out of a bottle like a pistol shot and for several seconds the company had frozen. The careful way in which passengers of different nationalities turned to go in another direction when they saw someone coming towards them.

'It's not frightfully funny any more,' Prentice had remarked over dinner irritably. 'Look at the way they're sitting – like pallbearers at a funeral.'

'They'd have more fun at a funeral – afterwards, anyway,' Ford had pointed out. 'It's almost as though they're waiting for something to happen.' All the others occupied a table to themselves. Macomber, Hahnemann, Volber and Grapos – all sitting in splendid isolation with empty tables between them while each ate and drank as though he were the only person in the room, taking care to make no sound except for the occasional clink of cutlery. Even the captain, Nopagos, who came in later, was unable to help. He had explained this briefly to Prentice in his careful English while visiting each table in turn before taking a table of his own.

'It is difficult, Mr Prentice – British and Germans on board, you understand.'

49

'Frightened there'll be a rumpus?' Prentice had inquired genially.

'Rum ... pus?'

'A battle, a fight.' Prentice had play-acted with his fists, glad of the chance to pull someone's leg, then had relented when he saw the Greek's doleful expression. 'Don't worry, we'll be good. But I bet you'll be damned glad to drop this lot off at Katyra in the morning.'

'The safe arrival in port is always the happy time,' Nopagos replied ambiguously and went away to his solitary table.

When dinner was over one passenger, Macomber, lingered in the room long after the others had left, smoking his cigar and drinking coffee from the pot the steward had provided after clearing his table. Like the saloon, the dining-room was panelled and small gold curtains were still drawn back from the porthole windows. Occasionally, he glanced out of the nearest window which gave him a view across the moonlit sea to the north-east, a sea which had now ceased to tremble with small waves and was already developing massive undulations which heaved towards the vessel with foam-topped crests. The dining-room was beginning to sway ponderously and the Scot shifted his feet wider apart to counter the movement as the woodwork creaked ominously, the horizon beyond the porthole dipping out of sight and then clambering into view again. The fourth German, Schnell, had still not appeared, and Macomber had mentioned this to the steward when he had brought the extra pot of coffee. 'Perhaps he's dead,' he had said with rough humour, 'he could be for all we've seen of him.'

'He had dinner served in his cabin,' the steward had remarked, 'and he wanted a Thermos of coffee made up for the night. Probably he doesn't sleep well at sea.'

'He won't if he drinks a whole Thermos of this,' Macomber had replied. The coffee was Turkish and the prospect of consuming it in such quantities suggested a steel-plated stomach and an inability to sleep at all.

'We get passengers like that occasionally,' the steward had prattled on. 'They just don't seem to like mixing with strangers. This man is like that – he was in the toilet when the dinner was taken in, as though he didn't even wish to see the

50

steward. He's Austrian, I think,' he had added.

'Indeed? Why do you say that?'

'His big cabin trunk has labels on it from the Hotel Sacher in Vienna. The steward thinks he spends a lot of time sitting by his porthole gazing out to sea – there was a pair of field-glasses opened by the table next to his wrist-watch. Call me if you want anything else, sir.' Left alone by himself Macomber had drunk two cups of the strong-tasting liquid while he thought about the invisible Herr Schnell. It was ten o'clock when he walked out of the deserted dining-room to take a final tour of the vessel, and at this hour the *Hydra* had the feel of a ghost ship, one of those phantom vessels which drift round the seaways of the world and are only seen as a mirage in the night. There was no one about as he descended a creaking staircase and began to walk along the empty companionway on the deck containing the passenger cabins. He had chosen this staircase deliberately and his rubber-soled boots made no sound as he paused by the first cabin which the Austrian occupied. Cabin One was silent but there were narrow streaks of light in the louvred upper half of the closed door. He made no attempt to see through the louvres – he had tested that possibility with his own cabin door earlier in the evening – but clearly the mysterious Schnell was still secreted inside his own quarters. He might not be awake, Macomber was thinking as he stood quite still, since a man who spends hours inside one small room is likely to get drowsy and fall asleep with the lights still on.

The next cabin was the wireless-room. Here, instead of pausing, Macomber walked past slowly, seeing through the half-open door the Greek wireless operator reading a newspaper as one hand reached out for a sandwich. So far everything seemed normal, perfectly normal, but the Scot could not rid himself of a feeling of growing unease. The next cabin was in darkness. Volber's. The German who looked like the owner of a small business – or a member of the Gestapo. Often the two types could easily be confused. Cabin Three still had the lights on and from behind the closed door came the faint sounds of dance music. Herr Hahnemann was tuned in to Radio Deutschland, perhaps feeling a little homesick aboard

51

this swaying ferry in the middle of the Aegean. There were lights in the next cabin, too, the temporary home of the two Britishers. Macomber paused outside and then walked steadily on as the mumble of voices died suddenly. When a cabin door opened behind him he was careful not to turn round. An interesting thought had struck him: was Volber really asleep inside that darkened cabin or was he somewhere else, having deliberately given the impression that he had gone down for the night? Silently he passed his own darkened cabin and began to mount the staircase at the other end of the companionway. The vessel was steaming steadily westward and as he opened the door at the top he faced the stern, consciously bracing himself and squaring his shoulders as the moan of the wind took on a higher note, rasping his face with its icy blast. Macomber had experienced the wind from the plains of Hungary, a wind which swept straight in from the depths of faraway Siberia, but as he slammed the door shut he thought he had never felt a more penetrating chill.

The deck was deserted. No sign of Volber. But the boat was still there, the vessel he had seen through the porthole from his dining-room table. She was moving along a course parallel to the *Hydra*'s, ploughing through the rising seas perhaps three kilometres to starboard. The deck was lifting sufficiently for him to hold onto the rail as he made his way to the stern, his face muscles drawn tight and not from the bitter wind which froze his skin. Taking out his Monokular glass, which was small enough to conceal inside the palm of one hand, he looked back along the deck. Lifeboats, the snow melted and gone during the day, swung slowly on their davits, reproducing the movement of the sea. A thin trail of smoke floated from the *Hydra*'s funnel, was caught up by the wind and thrown into a spiral. There was no sign of life anywhere. He aimed his glass, saw the other ship as a blur which merged in one long glow-worm of light, focused, brought the lights forward as separate portholes, noted the white funnel and the unidentifiable flag which whipped from the masthead. For perhaps a minute he stood motionless, one part of his mind on the lens, the other part alert for the slightest sound which might warn him that he was no longer alone on that empty deck, a sound which might

52

warn him of the attempt on his life he had feared ever since coming aboard. Then he closed the glass, pocketed it and checked his watch once more. 10.10 PM. Yes, it was the *Rupescu*, the vessel which had got up steam as soon as the *Hydra* had made preparations to leave the Golden Horn. Shoulders hunched against the wind, he made his way back along the unstable deck and went down into the warmth which met him as soon as he opened the door. Inside his own cabin he took off his hat and coat, lit a fresh cigar, put the Luger within easy reach and settled down to wait. Assassins often preferred to operate at night.

'It was the big German,' Ford said as he closed the cabin door and re-locked it. 'I caught him on the staircase at the far end – he still had his coat and hat on and he was going up on deck. I don't like it.'

'Don't like what?' Prentice withdrew his hand from where it had rested near the pillow which concealed his Webley .455 revolver and began studying the patience cards spread out over his bunk.

'The feel of this old tub – those Jerries being aboard and not talking to each other. They come from the same country and they haven't said a blasted word to each other from what I've seen.'

'Perhaps they're English in disguise – that would explain the non-fraternization.' He picked up a card, placed it over another. 'Not been formally introduced, you see.'

Ford lit the last of his army issue cigarettes, the ones he could only smoke when they were alone, and started thudding a heel against the woodwork as he sat down on his bunk. Prentice looked up and stared pointedly at the thudding heel until Ford stopped the noise, then went back to his game. 'You could always get some kip,' he suggested hopefully.

'Couldn't sleep a wink,' the staff-sergeant told him emphatically. 'Not with those Jerries aboard creeping all over the shop when it's long past their bedtime.' He got up and went over to the porthole, pulling the curtain aside with a jerk. 'That ship's still there, too. Wonder why it's keeping so close to us?'

Prentice slammed down a card and lit a Turkish cigarette quickly while he watched the sergeant who continued staring out of the porthole in his shirt-sleeves. 'Ford, there are things called sea-lanes. Ships are liable to follow them. If you've ever crossed the Channel you'll see quite a few ships not far from each other the whole way across. I really think that Turkish food must have done you a power of harm – you're not normally as jittery as this.'

Ford turned away from the porthole, closing the curtain again. 'And I'm not normally travelling on a boat with a load of Jerries for company. There's something strange going on – I can feel it.'

'Three Jerries . . .' Prentice started to point out.

'Four! There's that other one the captain mentioned to us earlier in the day – the one that never comes out of his cabin at the end of the companionway.'

'All right, four! But hardly a load of Jerries – you make it sound as though there's a division of them aboard. What can four of them do aboard a Greek ferry in the middle of the Aegean which – when I last heard of it – is controlled by the Royal Navy? If you go on like this, Ford,' he continued with a mischievous grin, 'you'll end up in sick bay with some MO asking you what scared you in your cradle! Now, how do you expect me to get this game out if you persist in banging your foot and peering through portholes as though you anticipated a whole German army arriving at any moment?'

'Sorry. It's probably that last meal we had in Istanbul. What was that dish again?'

'Fried octrangel,' said Prentice absent-mindedly as he turned his attention to the cards. 'It's a baby octopus. A great delicacy.' He didn't look up to see Ford's face, but a few minutes later he became aware again of the restless sergeant's movements and glanced up to see him putting on his coat over his jacket.

'Feel like a breath of fresh air,' Ford explained. 'Don't mind, do you?'

'Yes, I think I do.' The lieutenant spoke sharply. 'Going out on your own isn't really a very good idea.'

Ford's eyes gleamed as he dropped the coat onto his

bunk. 'You don't much like it either, then?'

'I just don't think it's too clever for us to separate at this time of night. There!' He dropped a card on a small pile. 'You see, it's coming out.' Prentice smiled grimly to himself as he went on playing: Ford had smoked him out there. No, he wasn't entirely happy about the situation aboard this ferry, but he saw no point in alarming the staff-sergeant at this stage. Prentice was a man who, despite his outwardly extrovert air, preferred to keep his fears to himself. Those Germans who were worrying Ford could, of course, be spies, and if they were they had chosen the right place to come – the strategically important peninsula of Zervos. As he played out his game Prentice was thinking of a military conference he had attended in Athens just before departing for Turkey, a conference he had attended because a question of communications had been involved. He could hear Colonel Wilson's clipped voice speaking now as he automatically placed a fresh card.

'It's the very devil,' Wilson had said, 'getting permission to send some of our chaps to Mount Zervos. The official in the Greek War Ministry who's responsible says Zervos is seventy miles from the Bulgarian frontier and in any case the peninsula comes under the command of the Greek army in Macedonia. He just won't have us there.'

'Not even to send a small unit to set up an observation post?' Prentice had ventured. 'From what I gather the monastery under the summit looks clear across the gulf to the coast road taking our supplies up to the Alkiamon Line.'

'You gather correctly,' Wilson had told him crisply. 'But the monastery seems to be the stumbling-block. Apparently for many years the whole peninsula has been a monastic sanctuary and you need a government permit even to land there. They won't grant one of those to a woman – the only women allowed in the area are the wives and relatives of fishermen who live there ...' He had paused, his expression icy until the ripple of laughter had died. Perhaps he had sounded unnecessarily indignant on that score. 'The guts of the thing is that this Greek official practically suggests we'd be violating something sacred by sending in a few troops ...'

'You believe him?' Prentice had interjected quietly, never

backward in speaking up when his interest was aroused. There had been an awkward pause before Wilson had answered that one. Only a tiny fraction of the Greek population was believed to hold secret Nazi sympathies, but it was feared that one or two of these undesirable gentry might occupy key positions inside the Greek government.

'We can only take his word,' Wilson had replied eventually. 'But the thing that sends shivers up the spines of our planning staff is the idea of German troops capturing that monastery. It's perched nearly three thousand feet up at the southern tip of the peninsula and has a clear view across to that vital coast road. And that's not all. There's some freak in the weather up there which means the summit of Mount Zervos is nearly always cloud-free – so you get an uninterrupted view of that road even when visibility's nil a few miles away. A Jerry observation post stuck up there would put us in a proper pickle.'

Afterwards, a Royal Artillery major had further enlightened Prentice : beyond the head of the gulf a range of hills formed a natural defence line, but if the Wehrmacht attacked and were able to emplace heavy guns on the lower slopes they could bring down an annihilating fire on the coast road from behind these hill crests – *providing they had an observation post on Mount Zervos which could guide the fall of the bombardment.* The major ended up by saying that if the Germans ever did get the Allies in such a position it would be little short of a massacre.*

Prentice dropped another card in place and sighed as the *Hydra* tilted again, a slow, deliberate roll as though revolving on an axis. While in Turkey he'd almost forgotten that conference, never believing for one instant that he would ever set eyes on Zervos, and here he was less than eight hours' sailing time from that benighted peninsula. And why the hell did ships always have to leave almost at dawn and arrive somewhere else at that Godforsaken hour? Finishing the game, he started shuffling the cards, uncertain whether to play again.

* Later in the war the same threat materialized at Monte Cassino where a German observation post reported to the gunners every movement of Allied troops.

Then he stopped shuffling. Ford was again standing by the porthole, the curtain drawn back, and there was something in his manner which caught Prentice's attention. 'What's up?' he asked.

'It's this ship – she's coming in damned close, whatever you say about sea-lanes.'

Prentice stood up quickly and went over to the porthole. The unknown vessel was now sailing on a parallel course less than a quarter of a mile from the *Hydra*'s hull and even as he watched the gap seemed to be narrowing. 'She is damned close,' he agreed, and felt a faint prickling of the short hairs at the back of his neck. He watched for a little while longer to be sure the ship wasn't simply passing them, then took a decision. 'I think we'd better pay our friend, Captain Nopagos, a little visit . . .' He broke off in mid-sentence. 'What was that?'

'Sounded like someone falling over in the passage – I think he hit our door . . .'

'Better see – and watch it!' Prentice dropped the pack of cards on his bunk, sat down and idly let his hand rest on the bunk close to the pillow which hid the Webley. He looked half-asleep as he watched Ford, who had now reached the locked door. Ford hesitated, listened for a moment, then heard a groan and a shuffling sound. He unlocked the door, opening it cautiously.

The Greek steward who looked after the cabins was lying face down in the companionway, his body wriggling as a slight moan escaped him. Ford looked both ways along the passage and saw that it was deserted. The *Hydra* was moving in a heavy swell, rocking slowly as the sea lifted and lowered it. He bent down quickly and noted that the man's hands were underneath him as though clasped to his stomach. There was no sign of injury so far as he could see – the poor devil must have been taken sick while walking down the companionway. He looked back inside the cabin and called out to Prentice.

'It's the steward. I think he's had an attack or something. I'd better go along and find someone . . .'

'Hold it a minute!' Prentice's nerves were on edge and his mind raced as he took in the implications of this unexpected incident. Ford going off to seek help would mean they were separated, a situation which could be dangerous. There was something queer going on, very queer indeed. 'No, don't do that,' he told Ford quickly. 'Can we get him in here? Let's have a look at him first.' He stepped into the companionway to give Ford a hand, stooping down to hoist the steward by the shoulders while the sergeant took the legs. They were standing in this position, still in the companionway with their hands encumbered, when the cabin door next to them was thrown open and Hahnemann came out. At waist-height he held a German machine-pistol, the weapon aimed at Ford's chest as he spoke in English.

'Put the Greek down and lift your hands. Be careful! If I shoot, the Greek dies, too.'

They put the steward down gently and as he reached the floor his hands and feet began to scrabble about in a more life-like fashion. His face turned and Prentice saw that he was scared stiff, his complexion whiter than the jacket he wore. With Ford, he raised his hands, turning slowly as he stood up so that he could look down the passage where he caught a glimpse through the half-closed door of the wireless-room. The radio operator still sat in front of his seat but now his hands were tied behind the back of his neck and then the view closed off as Volber came out holding a Luger pistol.

'Look at the wall!' snapped Hahnemann. 'And keep still.'

They faced the wall and Prentice felt Volber's quick hands pat his clothes and explore his body for hidden weapons. The shock of the hold-up was going now and Prentice's mind coldly searched for a way of upsetting the enemy who had decided to continue the war on neutral territory. The Greek steward was standing up and faced the wall when Hahnemann gave the order. The German issued his instructions in a crisp, controlled manner which warned Prentice that any counter-action would have to be swift, unexpected and totally effective.

'And now you go inside the cabin. Quickly!'

Prentice obeyed the order without hesitation. In fact, he went inside so quickly that Hahnemann was caught off-balance as the lieutenant tore through the open doorway, hooked his right heel behind the panel and slammed it in the German's face. His instinct was to dive for the revolver under the pillow, but knowing he hadn't the time, he jumped close to the wall as the door was thrown open again. Hahnemann jumped into the room, literally leapt through the doorway, turning as he saw Prentice a fraction of a second too late. The lieutenant grasped the machine-pistol by the barrel and swung the muzzle viciously to one side, still holding on, then jerked it backwards beyond the German who had expected him to pull it away from him. The muzzle was still aimed futilely at the outer wall. Continuing the rearward jerk, Prentice felt the weapon come free and in the same second felt his feet slip under him. He went over on the back of his head, still gripping the weapon as clouds of dizziness addled his brain and he saw only shadows through a mist. He was still struggling through the mists, seeing them clear gradually, when something hard and heavy hit him in the side. Hahnemann had just kicked him. When he recovered a grip on himself the German was standing over him with the machine-pistol aimed at the centre of his chest. In the doorway Ford stood grimly silent with Volber's Luger pointed at his stomach.

'Get up!' said Hahnemann savagely, backing away as Prentice, wondering why the hell he was still alive, clambered painfully to his feet. That hadn't been too clever. The back of his head felt to be split in two and an iron hammer was banging down the split. He gulped in several breaths of air, trying to hear what Hahnemann was saying. 'Over by the wall. Quick!' Tottering a little, Prentice went over to the outer wall and leant against it where Ford joined him a moment later. Volber went out of the cabin, closing the door behind him. It had all happened so swiftly that he was still wondering what the hell they hoped to achieve, was still suffering from a partial sense of shock. Alongside him Ford stared at the German with an intent look, waiting for him to make just one small mistake. The trouble was he didn't look like a man who repeated his mistakes – letting Prentice break loose had put him in a state of total alertness, and although he was guarding two men on his own he stood back far enough to give his gun a good field of fire. One brief burst would kill both of them: Ford, as a weapons and explosives expert, was under no illusions on this point.

'Why are you aboard this ship, Lieutenant Prentice?' demanded Hahnemann.

Prentice glanced at the table where Volber had left the papers and paybook he had extracted from their pockets while searching them for weapons. Hahnemann must have looked at these while he was coming up out of the mists. He wasn't in any hurry to reply – time was a factor the German clearly valued, as though he were following a carefully worked out timetable, and Prentice had detected a note of anxiety behind the question, so his reply was deliberately non-informative. 'To travel from Istanbul to Zervos,' he said. For a horrible second he thought he had made a fatal mistake. Hahnemann's finger tightened on the trigger and Prentice braced himself for the lacerating burst of bullets, but the German regained control and smiled unpleasantly.

'That I understood! Now, Lieutenant Prentice, before I shoot Sergeant Ford in the stomach I will ask the question again. Why are you travelling on this particular ship on this particular night? You understand? Good.'

Prentice found he was sweating badly on the palms of his hands and under his armpits. He hadn't the least idea of what Hahnemann was talking about but he doubted whether he could convince the German of this. His brain reeled as he sought desperately for words which might half-satisfy their interrogator, and with a tremendous effort he managed a ghastly smile in an endeavour to lower the temperature before it was too late. 'I take it you're in the German army?' For the first time Hahnemann showed a trace of uncertainty and Prentice followed up his tiny advantage quickly. 'Then you'll know that according to the Geneva Convention all we have to give you is name, rank and number. You've got those there on that table already.'

It was a hair-line gamble, switching the conversation to this topic, but Prentice was counting on the German's training to make him pause, to cool his anger, to gain control again. To his great relief he saw the machine-pistol muzzle swing to a point between himself and Ford where it could fire in either direction. The German had, at least temporarily, recovered his balance. Prentice had now assessed Hahnemann as a highly trained individual who normally kept an ice-cold grip on his emotions, but who also, occasionally, in a state of fury, lost that grip and went berserk. They had just witnessed such an occasion when their lives had trembled on the brink.

'What were you doing in Turkey?' Hahnemann asked suddenly.

'Trying to get a berth home to Athens.' Prentice's quick tongue rattled on. 'And the civilian clothes were loaned to us by the Turks. Our ship struck a mine off the Turkish coast two days ago and we were dragged out of the sea more dead than alive. We were the only survivors – and don't ask me the name of the ship or how many she was carrying because you wouldn't answer that either if I were holding the gun. And don't ask me why the Turks didn't intern us because I don't know – except that they seemed damned glad to get rid of us at the earliest possible moment. They'd have put us on the normal Istanbul–Athens service, but that was cancelled at the last minute so we were hustled aboard this ferry. The first available ship out, they said – and this was it.'

It had been a long speech and he hoped to God that it had satisfied Hahnemann on the one question which seemed to bother him – why were they aboard the *Hydra*? There was a hint of respect in the German's eyes now and Prentice decided to press a point home, forgetting that it's always a mistake to overdo a good thing.

'So we're your prisoners-of-war at the moment,' Prentice continued, 'but don't forget that the Royal Navy controls the Aegean. If there's a British destroyer in the area you may find me holding that gun within a few hours, so let's drop the threats.'

'There is a British destroyer near here?' The gun muzzle was aimed straight at Prentice's chest and the note of cold fury had come back into the German's voice. 'You know this?' The words were an accusation and Hahnemann's jaw muscles were rigid with tension, a tension which instantly communicated itself to the two men with their backs to the wall. The tip of the gun muzzle quivered, the outward sign of the nervous vibration bottled up inside the man holding the weapon. Christ! Prentice was thinking, we're a nervous twitch away from a fusillade. Where the devil did I go wrong? He spoke carefully but quickly, his eyes fixed on Hahnemann's as he struggled to gauge the effect of his words while he was talking. 'I'm not thinking of any particular destroyer – I'm in the army, not the navy – you know that. But these seas are constantly patrolled so it's just a matter of luck – yours or ours.' He shut up, hoping for the best, determined not to overdo it a second time. His shirt was clinging to his wet back and he daren't look at Ford in case Hahnemann thought he was passing a signal. It was becoming a nightmare and he had a grisly feeling they might not live through it.

'Turn round and lie on the floor – stretch out your hands to the fullest extent.'

The unexpected order threw Prentice off balance; it was impossible to keep up with this German through his swift changes of mood, but at least there weren't going to be any more of those trigger-loaded questions. He was on his knees when he grasped the meaning of the order, saw out of the corner of his eye the vicious arc of the machine-pistol butt descending on poor Ford's head, and as the sergeant slumped unconscious over the floor he swung round to swear at the German. The muzzle was aimed point-blank at his chest. Prentice was obeying the fresh order to look at the wall when a ton-weight landed on his tender scalp. A brilliant burst of light flashed before his eyes and then vanished in the flood of darkness which overwhelmed him.

The rifle muzzle was pressed into Macomber's face when he opened the cabin door in response to the urgent knocking, and the threat was accompanied by an apology in German. 'You must remain in your cabin until further orders, Herr Dietrich. I am sorry . . .'

'Whose orders?' Macomber stood with his hand behind his back, his manner harsh and unimpressed by the sight of the weapon. For a moment it seemed as though he would push Volber out of the way by walking straight into him. The German had paused, uncertain how to handle this aggressive reaction, but Hahnemann, who stood close behind with a machine-pistol in his hands, was not taken aback.

'By order of the Wehrmacht!'

Macomber stared past Volber, ignoring the squat man as he gazed bleakly at Hahnemann. Again it seemed as though he would push the rifle barrel aside and Hahnemann instinctively raised his own weapon. 'That is not enough,' Macomber rumbled Teutonically. 'The officer's name, if you please.' He might have been a colonel addressing a subordinate.

'Lieutenant Hahnemann, Alpenkorps.' The German had replied automatically and had felt the reflex of snapping his heels to attention, but he desisted just in time. Now he was furious with his own reply, but there was something about the passenger which he found intimidating, an air of authority which was disturbing. 'You will stay in your cabin,' he barked. 'Do you understand? Anyone found outside their cabin without permission will be shot!' Immediately he had spoken he had doubts, and the steely look in Macomber's eye was anything but reassuring. Who the hell could he be? 'Lieutenant Hahnemann?' Macomber repeated slowly, and there was an uncomfortable, mocking note in his voice. 'I think I can remember that for later!'

Hahnemann persisted, but more quietly. 'Please give my sergeant the key of your cabin so it can be locked from the outside.'

Macomber gazed thoughtfully at Hahnemann a moment longer, then turning on his heel so that the cabin door hid part of his body, he slipped the Luger back inside his coat pocket and re-entered the cabin, ignoring the request for the key. Volber he could have dealt with, but the lieutenant's machine-pistol was quite another matter. With a muttered expression of annoyance Hahnemann walked forward, extracted the key himself and locked the door on the outside. The Scot straightened up from the newspaper spread over the table, his expression grim. This was even worse than he had imagined: they were taking over the whole ship.

His initial reaction on opening the door was that the assassins had come for him. This fleeting impression had been succeeded by the revelation that they were not interested in

63

him at all, that a major Wehrmacht operation was under way, a stroke as audacious as the Norwegian campaign*. He stood listening, his head cocked to one side. Yes, he was right – the *Hydra*'s engines were slowing. For the mid-sea rendezvous, of course. They must have taken control of the engine-room at an earlier stage and by now they would command the bridge. An efficient operation planned with the usual meticulous care and attention to detail – including the bringing aboard of Herr Schnell and his outsize cabin trunk containing the weapons. Retrieving his smoking cigar from the ash-tray, he switched off the light and used his torch to find his way across the cabin to the porthole.

The *Hydra*'s engines had almost stopped and the *Rupescu* was so close that a collision seemed likely. Standing by the porthole without any attempt at concealment, his cigar glowing for anyone who cared to see it, he watched the transfer of the German troops from the Rumanian vessel to the Greek ferry. The soldiers, wearing life-jackets, were coping with a heavy swell – had they arrived later or had the weather worsened earlier the operation might have proved impossible. German luck again, Macomber thought bitterly – like the luck of the marvellous weather over France in 1940. You can't get far without luck, he was thinking as he watched a boatload of troops being lowered to the sea. There must have been almost twenty men aboard and he was praying for an accident as the craft almost capsized when the waves heaved up to meet it, but at the last moment someone released the ropes and the boat followed the natural curvature of the sea. The uniformed troops wore soft, large-peaked caps and were heavily laden with equipment. Alpenkorps. A unit of the élite mountain troops who had conquered Norway, men trained to fight in appalling terrain such as the peninsula of Zervos.

He remained standing there for some time, his body now fully accustomed to the sway of the ship under his widespread feet, and during that time he counted the transfer of over two hundred men to the Greek ferry. More than enough to take

* Norway was seized by apparently innocent merchant ships full of German troops which sailed up the Norwegian coast within gun range of the unsuspecting Royal Navy.

64

Zervos, providing they received heavy reinforcements in the near future. After all, unless the Allies had put their own troops ashore on the peninsula the only people who stood in their way were a handful of monks at the monastery and a few fishermen at Katyra. Even when the transfer had been completed, when a boat containing, so far as Macomber could make out, the crew of the *Rupescu*, had accomplished the narrow crossing, he still waited at the porthole as the *Hydra*'s engines began to throb with power.

The ferry had resumed its interrupted voyage, was moving away and leaving the Rumanian vessel behind like an empty carcass, when Macomber opened the porthole and thrust his head out into the elements. The rising force of the knife-edged wind chilled his face as he watched the *Rupescu* slowly settling in the growing turbulence of the sea. They had switched off all the lights before they left her but by the light of the moon he saw her bows awash, the curling waves submerging her decks, the water-logged wallow of the doomed vessel. The sea-cocks had been opened, of course. He was still leaning out of the porthole when her superstructure disappeared under the billowing waves, leaving for a brief moment only the white funnel thrust up like some strange lighthouse in mid-Aegean. Then that, too, sank and there was no trace left that the *Rupescu* had ever existed.

Macomber withdrew his head, rammed the porthole shut, switched on the cabin light and began slapping his hands across his body to warm up. Sitting down on the bunk, he resisted the fatal temptation to sprawl his legs along it, and lit a fresh cigar. Still no chance to sleep, and it looked as though it might be a long while yet before he dared close his eyes. The period of standing by the porthole had tired his limbs horribly but his growing fury and the night sea air had made him steadily more alert, and now as he smoked the anger helped him to think. All his eager anticipations of returning to a haven of peace had temporarily left him, had left him at the first sight of those uniforms he knew so well. He had to do something to upset the timetable, the careful plan they would be working to, because they were bad improvisers and when things went wrong they reacted badly. His main hope was to persist in his impersonation, to throw them off-balance at the outset, to gain the freedom to move around the ship freely. He stood up to fight down the sleepiness he felt again, shoved the hat on his head, the hat which made him look even more Germanic, and glanced in the washbasin mirror. No need to assume an expression of grimness: that was already only too evident. You're *Dietrich*, he said softly, so from now on forget a chap called Macomber ever existed. And they'll have to maintain radio silence so they can't check anything. It's the first encounter that matters. You're Dietrich, Dr Richard Dietrich. He sat down again in the chair, impatient for the first confrontation, and when they came for him it was close to midnight.

CHAPTER FOUR

Saturday, Midnight

With his machine-pistol cradled under his arm, Lieutenant Hahnemann, now dressed in Alpenkorps uniform, unlocked the door, turned the handle and kicked it open with his foot. Dietrich was sitting at the little table, still wearing his coat and hat with his legs stretched out before him and crossed at the ankles. He was smoking a fresh cigar and the rude entry had no effect on him, caused no change in his relaxed stance; rather it seemed as though he went out of his way to demonstrate his bored unconcern. Dietrich folded his arms. He was regarding Hahnemann as he might have regarded a piece of badly cooked meat, then he transferred his attention to the tall, beak-nosed man who walked briskly in behind the lieutenant. A striking-looking German in his early forties, he held himself very erect as his cold blue eyes studied the seated passenger, and under his civilian coat, which he wore open at the front, Dietrich saw the boots and uniform of the Alpenkorps.

'This is Colonel Burckhardt,' Hahnemann informed him harshly. He paused as though expecting some reaction. 'People normally stand in the colonel's presence,' he went on bleakly.

'Tell this man to go away so we can talk.' Dietrich addressed the suggestion to Burckhardt who was looking down at him with interest. The passenger hadn't moved since he had entered the cabin.

'You can talk with both of us,' Burckhardt began tersely. 'Unless you have a very good reason for wishing to speak to me alone.' Like Hahnemann earlier, Burckhardt was wondering why he had reacted in a way he had hardly intended. And yet...

'What I have to say is not for junior officers.' Dietrich's brief mood of amiability was vanishing rapidly and he looked at the colonel grimly. 'I should have thought you hadn't a great deal of time to waste, so shall we get on with it?'

Burckhardt's expression showed no reaction, but inwardly he felt a trifle off-balance – he had been going to say almost precisely the same thing and now this aggressive-looking brute had forestalled him. He had the odd feeling that he was losing ground so he spoke decisively to the lieutenant. 'Hahnemann, you have duties to attend to. Leave me with this man until I call you.'

'He may be armed,' Hahnemann protested.

'Of course I am armed,' Dietrich replied swiftly, anticipating Burckhardt's next question. A lesser man than Colonel Heinz Burckhardt might have felt annoyance, but the colonel had risen to command an élite arm of the Wehrmacht and he had a grudging appreciation of an independent attitude. 'I am going to take out a Luger pistol,' Dietrich explained, staring at Hahnemann as though he doubted his ability to grasp plain German, 'so kindly keep a hold on yourself – and your weapon.' Producing the pistol from his coat pocket, he laid it on the table. 'It is fully loaded, incidentally – I never bluff when I have to use a weapon, which, fortunately, is a rare occasion.' The sight of the regulation pistol, a minor point, subtly reinforced Burckhardt's growing interest in the huge German passenger. For a moment Hahnemann hesitated whether to pick up the gun, but Dietrich's attention was so clearly concentrated on the colonel, was so obviously no longer aware of his presence, that he felt at a loss and glanced at Burckhardt for instructions.

'Leave us,' the colonel told him brusquely. 'I shall be on the bridge in a few minutes.'

Dietrich waited until the cabin door had closed and then stood up slowly. The action startled Burckhardt, who was six feet tall; he had realized that Dietrich also was a tall man but now he was able to see that the German civilian stood two to three inches above him. Rarely impressed by another man's physique, Burckhardt found himself a little overawed by the formidable figure who stood before him with his shoulders hunched and his hands clasped behind his broad back. Dietrich waited a moment, then put a hand inside his coat, extracted something and dropped it on the table. 'My papers, Colonel Burckhardt.'

With a mounting sense of irritation Burckhardt looked at the card carefully, glancing up to find Dietrich watching him without any particular expression. 'You're an archaeologist, I see, Dr Dietrich?' He couldn't keep the flatness out of his voice: he had suspected that this passenger was someone important from Berlin; it was the only explanation for his arrogant manner.

'Look at them carefully,' Dietrich urged him gruffly. 'See anything unusual about them?'

'No!' Burckhardt replied after a second perusal and there was a snap in his voice now.

'Good!' Dietrich lifted his shoulders and towered over the colonel as he went on with withering sarcasm. 'I was travelling aboard a Greek ferry which might at any time have been stopped and searched by a British destroyer. Under those conditions would you really expect me to present them with papers showing I am a senior officer of the Abwehr?'

Burckhardt stood quite still and his heart sank. Here was the explanation for Dietrich's overbearing attitude since he had entered the cabin. God, the Abwehr! That damned Intelligence organization of the incredibly influential Admiral Canaris. They never told anyone what they were going to do – not until they had done it. And they never told anyone where they were going until they had been there and arrived back in Berlin. They were responsible to no one except the wily old admiral who had started his career with naval Intelligence, and who was now answerable only to the Führer himself. The Abwehr was disliked – feared might be a better word – by all the regular Intelligence services because it lived a life of its own, but even more because of its legendary record of coups. In some uncanny way the admiral managed to be right every time in his forecast of enemy intentions. Oh yes, Burckhardt had heard of the Abwehr, but this was the first time he had met one of them. That is, assuming Dietrich was who he claimed to be . . . He looked up suspiciously as something else landed on the table.

'Now you can see what I would have dropped through the

nearest porthole if we had been stopped – along with the Luger, of course.'

Dietrich's tone was ironic, close to sneering, and Burckhardt caught the tone and felt the blood rush to his head, so for a short time while he examined the second card Baxter had doctored and handed over in Giurgiu, his normally ice-cold judgement deserted him. Dietrich walked across the cabin to look out through the porthole, still talking over his shoulder.

'You will require absolute proof of my identity, so you had better send a wireless message to Berlin. I can give you the signal code.'

'Not while we are at sea,' Burckhardt rapped out. 'We must preserve radio silence at all costs.'

'I had assumed that,' Dietrich retorted brusquely. 'I meant after you had gone ashore. You have dealt with the two Englanders, I hope?'

'Yes, Hahnemann dealt with the whole operation most efficiently. They are only a lieutenant and a sergeant travelling home from Turkey.'

'You knew then beforehand that these two men were being put on board?'

Burckhardt paused, staring at the back of the Abwehr man who continued gazing out to sea. There was something in the way the question had been phrased which disturbed him, which made him delay his departure for the bridge. Had there been some awful slip-up somewhere? 'Knew?' he repeated warily.

'Yes, "knew", I said. Did you know?' Dietrich had swung round and was talking with his cigar in his mouth, his legs splayed as he continued to dominate the conversation.

'No,' the colonel admitted reluctantly. 'I was worried when I first heard about them but they are of very junior rank...'

'Are you certain of that? Papers can be easily forged or doctored – including army pay-books. These two men could be far more important for all we know.' He paused to give his insidious suggestion maximum impact. 'They could be on board because some hint of your operation has reached the Allies. You may be lucky they never reached the wireless-room.' He leaned forward grimly. 'I take it they did not reach the wireless-room?'

70

'Of course not! That was part of Hahnemann's job ...'

'Any idea which arm of the service they're attached to?'

Burckhardt felt himself go very cold. Until this unnerving interview he had assumed that the two Englanders were only on board by chance, but now the Abwehr man was raising diabolical possibilities. 'Ford, the staff-sergeant, is an ammunition examiner,' he said slowly.

Had Dietrich detected the note of reluctance in his voice? He pressed the colonel for further information instantly. 'And the other man, the so-called lieutenant – Prentice?'

'He is with the Signals Corps.'

'Ah! So undoubtedly an expert wireless operator ...' Dietrich shrugged his shoulders, his devastating point made. He puffed at his cigar for several seconds and then said something equally disturbing. 'Since we know they have been in Turkey for several weeks it seems an even stranger coincidence that they should choose this particular trip for returning to Greece. Don't you agree?'

'Several weeks? You know this? Is this why you are on board?' Burckhardt took a step towards Dietrich who regarded him without replying. 'They were supposed to have been saved from a ship which sank off the Turkish coast a few days ago ...'

'What ship?' Dietrich pounced on the statement. 'Is this the story they have told you?'

'Yes, when Lieutenant Hahnemann was questioning them ...'

'He has Intelligence training, this Hahnemann?' The ironic note was back in Dietrich's voice.

'No, but he is clever and he said their story rang true. The lieutenant – Prentice – told him this ...'

'I have seen this British lieutenant,' the Abwehr man replied slowly and deliberately, 'and I would say he not only has his wits about him – he is also capable of making up a convincing story on the spur of the moment. I don't like the way the situation is developing, Colonel Burckhardt. You should have the two Englanders questioned again.'

Burckhardt's expression was remote. Under other circumstances, without the enormous responsibility of the expedition

71

resting on his shoulders, he might have thought differently, and he had no way of knowing that he was confronted by a master of the art of psychological aggression. Without realizing it, he had been subjected to a kaleidoscope of changing impressions and anxieties from the moment he had entered the cabin, and during this ordeal he had subconsciously accepted the Abwehr man's credentials at face value. In fact, the subject of the identity of Dietrich had subtly been turned into questioning the identity of the British prisoners. He was also becoming a little worried about his own position. Had this devil been put aboard the *Hydra* to check up on the operation because it involved a naval phase – the seizure of the *Hydra* and its subsequent voyage to their objective! 'I'll get Hahnemann to have another word with the prisoners,' he said crisply.

'This Prentice, he speaks German, then?' Dietrich was staring through the porthole again as he asked the question.

'Not so far as I know – but Hahnemann speaks excellent English. I must leave for the bridge now.' He was talking again to Dietrich's back as the Abwehr man used his hand to smear a hole in the steamed-up glass. The temperature was probably at least thirty degrees higher inside the cabin than on the high seas.

'Did Hahnemann find out anything else when he was interrogating the prisoners?' Dietrich went on peering intently through the porthole and something in his attitude made the colonel wait a few seconds longer.

'I believe there was some mention of a British destroyer being in the area, but I'm convinced he was bluffing.'

'Bluffing!' Dietrich straightened up, swung round abruptly. 'First you talk about it being a coincidence that those men are aboard and now you hope he was bluffing! I'm afraid a very serious situation has arisen – a strange vessel is coming in fast from the north-east and unless I'm very much mistaken it is a British destroyer.'

Burckhardt turned to go quickly, and when Dietrich was left to his own devices he had, by default, been granted the privilege to roam round the vessel as freely as he wished.

Burckhardt was leaving the cabin when he very nearly collided

72

with Hahnemann who was rushing down the companionway. Halting abruptly, the soldier saluted and spoke breathlessly. 'There's an emergency, sir. Lieutenant Schnell would like to see you on the bridge – it's very urgent . . .'

'I know!' Burckhardt was already pushing past him, heading for the staircase. Hard-faced young men of the Alpenkorps, fully uniformed, pressed themselves against the companionway wall with their rifles at their sides to let him pass. One man hastily extinguished a cigarette under his boot. The doorways to the three cabins recently occupied by the German passengers were open and inside more men of the Alpenkorps sat on the floors and leaned against the walls, their faces tense as they watched their colonel pass. The grapevine had worked already, reporting the rumour that a British destroyer was approaching fast. The whole atmosphere of the Greek ferry had changed, had become more akin to that of a troopship. Dodging round kit piled in the passage, Burckhardt made a mental note to get that shifted and then leapt up the staircase. Pushing open the door at the top he received a blast of cold wind and a douche of icy spray full in the face. Without even bothering to wipe himself he glanced quickly along the deserted, wave-washed deck. All the troops were under strict instructions to remain below decks and he was satisfied with the outward appearance of normality. Strange how the sea seemed far worse up here than down below. The thought flashed through his mind as he went into the wheelhouse.

Inside the enclosed area everything was quiet and there was a feeling of disciplined control, but under the silence Burckhardt sensed an atmosphere of nerves tautly strained as the *Hydra* ploughed on through mounting seas. Lieutenant Schnell of the German Navy, wearing inconspicuous dark trousers and a dark woollen sweater, was holding the wheel while the ferry's captain, Nopagos, stood a few feet away with a signalling lamp in his hands. Behind him, crouched on his knees out of sight, an Alpenkorps soldier held a machine-pistol trained on the captain's back.

'Over there. To starboard.' It was the helmsman who had spoken, nodding his head towards the north-east. Schnell was a typical German naval officer, round-faced, his dark hair neatly trimmed, a man of thirty with watchful eyes and a steady manner. Taking in the situation at a glance, Burckhardt accepted a pair of field-glasses from another soldier whose uniform was covered with a civilian raincoat. To starboard a slim grey silhouette was bearing down on the *Hydra*, a silhouette with lights at her masthead. Burckhardt focused the glasses on the ship and his lips tightened. Yes, it was a British destroyer sailing on an oblique course which would take her across the bows of the ferry within a mile or two. He handed back the glasses and moved into the shadows in case other glasses were aimed in his direction from that distant bridge. They wouldn't be able to pick out individuals yet, but within a few minutes they'd pick up all the detail they wanted if the destroyer maintained its present course. He spoke quickly to Schnell. 'What is Nopagos doing with that signalling lamp in his hands?'

'He will have to use it in a minute . . .'

'I don't like that.'

'We have no alternative.' Schnell had half-turned round to stare at the oncoming warship. 'She is bound to signal us, so tell the Greek I understand the use of signals at sea.'

Burckhardt thought quickly. It was a damnable situation: the very existence of the expedition now depended on the signal-lamp in the hands of a Greek whose ship had just been shanghaied from under him. He saw the knuckles of Schnell's hands whitened under the overhead light as he gripped the wheel and steadily kept to his course. Still crouched on the floor, the Alpenkorps soldier with the machine-pistol moved gently with the sway of the ship, his face drawn with tension as he watched Burckhardt and then transferred his gaze to Nopagos' back. Burckhardt maintained his outward appearance of calm confidence, his hands thrust into his coat pockets, although inwardly his nerves were screwed up to fever pitch. He began speaking to Nopagos in his careful, Teutonic-sounding Greek.

'The British destroyer may start signalling. If that happens you only use your lamp when I give the order. I want you to understand this clearly – the man at the wheel is a German naval officer thoroughly conversant with signalling procedures. He will be watching. If you make any attempt to send a distress signal, we shall know. If there is an emergency we shall engage the British destroyer and we shall undoubtedly be sunk. I hope you realize that it is unlikely anyone will be saved in seas like this...' Without putting it in so many words he managed to convey that Nopagos' crew were hostages. He had just finished speaking when the moonlit wake of the oncoming destroyer became clearly visible. A few seconds later the door to the bridge opened and Dietrich came inside. Burckhardt swung round and turned away again when he saw who it was. Completely unruffled by his reception, the Abwehr man walked across to join the colonel after glancing at the approaching destroyer.

'It's probably just a routine check,' he remarked, 'but let's hope they are not expecting a signal from their friends locked up below.'

A nerve jumped by the side of Burckhardt's neck underneath his collar. Dietrich had hardly arrived before voicing the most alarming suggestion at this critical moment. He had just quietened his mind after the Abwehr man's remark when the door burst open again and Hahnemann strode onto the bridge with a furious expression. He had hesitated to stop Dietrich following Burckhardt up to the bridge but now felt he should keep an eye on him. Burckhardt turned on him instantly. 'Hide that gun you bloody fool – they may be watching the bridge. And while you're here – had either of those British soldiers any means of signalling in their possession?'

'No signalling lamp,' Hahnemann reassured him quickly. 'They definitely had no signalling equipment of any kind. The lieutenant, Prentice, had a revolver under his pillow. But nothing to send a message with.'

Burckhardt glanced at Dietrich with an expressionless face, but the Abwehr man was still studying Hahnemann, who glared back at him defiantly. 'And no torch?' Dietrich queried in a deceptively mild tone. 'Not even a pocket torch?'

Hahnemann looked confused. He started to answer Dietrich, then his face stiffened and he addressed Burckhardt. 'One of them had a torch, yes, sir. It was inside the pocket of his coat hanging up behind the door.'

Dietrich caught Burckhardt's glance and he lifted his eyebrows in an expression of foreboding, then frowned at Schnell who had turned to say something. 'Here it comes, sir. They've started.' Across the swelling Aegean where the waves were growing higher a light began to wink on and off from the destroyer. Schnell had half-turned to starboard, his eyes fixed on the flashing lamp which went on with its brief explosions. On the bridge no one moved or spoke as all eyes were fixed hypnotically on the signalling light and Burckhardt could feel the stillness of men suspended in a state of horrible anticipation. So much depended on the next few minutes but Burckhardt had no intention of surrendering, whatever happened. He had had some experience of the devastating fire a British destroyer could lay down; in Norway he had seen a German troop transport reduced to a burning hulk by only a few salvoes. What those four-inch guns might do to the hull of the *Hydra* was something he preferred not to contemplate. The lamp stopped flashing and Schnell spoke.

'We are asked to identify ourselves.'

Burckhardt stood up a little straighter and gave Nopagos his instructions in Greek. 'Signal that we are the Greek ship *Hydra*. Nothing more. And remember that Lieutenant Schnell is a naval officer.'

The tension on the bridge was becoming almost unbearable, like a physical affliction. Nopagos wiped his lips and glanced behind to where the Alpenkorps man gazed straight at him, the muzzle of the machine-pistol aimed at the small of his back. Burckhardt nodded confidently without speaking, as much as to say get on with it. The captain adjusted his cap and started to flash the lamp while Schnell watched him coldly, his hands still on the wheel. To the colonel it seemed to take an age to send the short message. Was marine signalling really so complicated? Was Nopagos managing to trick Schnell while he inserted a desperate SOS among the jumble of flashes? A dozen appalling possibilities ran through his mind but he could do nothing but wait, hoping that his threat had struck home to the Greek. The lamp stopped flashing. Nopagos mopped the back of his neck with a coloured handkerchief as Schnell addressed Burckhardt over his shoulder.

'He has identified us simply as the *Hydra*, ownership Greek. Nothing more.'

With a supreme effort Burckhardt resisted the impulse to let his shoulders relax; both the Alpenkorps soldiers kept glancing towards him for reassurance. German soldiers, Burckhardt had noticed before, were never entirely happy at sea – the existence of the British Navy probably had something to do with their lack of enthusiasm for water-borne expeditions. He watched the destroyer still moving on her oblique course. Would her captain be satisfied with that signal? Just a routine check, Dietrich had suggested. But a moment later he had raised the unnerving suggestion that the two British soldiers might have been put on board deliberately – that the destroyer out there was expecting another flashing signal from a porthole confirming that all was well aboard the *Hydra*. Blast the Abwehr!

'They're signalling again!' Schnell spoke quietly, his eyes on the distant flashing light which was now less than a quarter of a mile away. Burckhardt stood quite still, resisting the impulse to pace up and down the bridge: it was vital at this moment to preserve an absolute outward calm. He felt that his feet had been glued to the deck for hours and God knew there were enough signs of tension on the bridge already. The signal lamp in Nopagos' hands wobbled slightly – if he had to carry on answering these bloody questions much longer he was going to crack. The soldier crouched behind the Greek captain was sweating profusely, his forehead gleaming from the light over the bridge. Hahnemann was lightly tapping a nervous fingernail on the butt of his machine-pistol and Burckhardt wanted to roar at him for God's sake stop it! Schnell, a highly experienced naval officer, was still holding the wheel tightly. All these little details Burckhardt took in automatically while the lamp on the British destroyer blandly went on flashing its message. Only Dietrich seemed undisturbed, almost at ease as he stared at the ceiling with the unlit cigar motionless in the centre of his mouth. He dropped his eyes and caught the colonel watching him.

'There is a Greek called Grapos aboard,' Dietrich commented. 'I think he could be dangerous if he isn't watched carefully.'

'I dealt with him myself,' said Hahnemann in a flat tone. 'He was sleeping in the saloon -- he had no cabin – and I was able to knock him out before he knew I was there. He's tied up in one of the holds.' The endless strain of waiting had neutralized his natural dislike of the Abwehr man and he looked at Dietrich without resentment.

'I do have this ship under control,' Burckhardt added icily.

'Perhaps it might be better if I went below,' Dietrich said almost amiably. He glanced to his left and saw that Hahnemann was leaving the bridge as a cloud of spray broke over the bows of the *Hydra*. When the lieutenant had gone there was a loaded silence as the light from the destroyer continued flashing, the ferry's engines went on throbbing heavily, and the sea heaved endlessly under them. After the winking light had stopped, Schnell cleared his throat twice before speaking. 'They wish us to report where we're from, our ultimate destination and the time of arrival.'

Without hesitation Burckhardt rapped out more instructions in Greek. 'Tell them we're bound from Istanbul, that our destination is Katyra, Zervos, and our estimated time of arrival 05·30 hours.' Nopagos blinked, glanced again at the sweating soldier behind him, took a firmer grip on the lamp and began signalling. The gun muzzles of the destroyer could be clearly seen in the moonlight as the vessel remorselessly continued on course without altering direction by as much as a single degree. Burckhardt found it unnerving – why was all this interest being shown in an ancient Greek ferry which spent its life plying between Istanbul and the remote peninsula of Zervos? He kept a tight grip on himself as Dietrich's rumbling voice spoke again behind his back. 'I'm wondering now whether this signalling isn't a smoke-screen put out until they get close to us. If they were expecting their own private signal from the prisoners below the course they are maintaining would make sense – they would keep on that course until they fired the first shot across our bows. Ten minutes should tell us the worst.' And having fired this last shot across the colonel's bows he quietly left the bridge and went out on deck.

Tight-lipped, Burckhardt heard him go, relieved that at long last the Abwehr man was leaving the bridge. But secretly Burckhardt agreed that Dietrich's estimate was just about right. In the next ten minutes they should know the worst.

CHAPTER FIVE

Sunday, April 6

As he struggled in the darkness with the ropes which bound his wrists, Prentice was bathed in sweat from his exertions. He lay in his bunk sprawled on his side, his ankles also tightly bound together while a further length of rope joined his wrists to his ankles, a rope drawn up so tautly that his knees were permanently bent. The fact that they had thought of turning out the cabin lights didn't help him either; it meant he had to work blindly by feel and this made ten times more difficult a task which already seemed insuperable. And because his hands were tied behind his back he had soon given up the attempt to fiddle with the knots he couldn't see, and a little later, when it struck him that they had probably used Alpenkorps climbing rope, he gave up his efforts to break the cords by stretching his wrists against them – a rope which could support a man dangling from a cliff face was hardly likely to weaken under the mere pressure of two straining wrists. So it seemed hopeless: a rope which couldn't be broken and which couldn't be untied. There was, however, one other alternative. Prentice was thin-boned and he had unusually slim wrists, so now he was concentrating all his strength on compressing his hands into the smallest possible area and then trying to pull them upwards through the loops which imprisoned him. His success to date had fallen rather short of the milder achievements of Houdini and for a few minutes he stopped struggling while he rested.

He was turned on his left side, facing inwards to the cabin, and while he rested he contented himself with straining to see the time by the light of the phosphorescent numerals of his watch on the table. Almost 12.10 AM so far as he could make out. In that case the guard would be looking in on them shortly – he checked the cabin every quarter-hour. With typical

Teutonic punctuality he had, so far, arrived at precisely the quarter-hour. He lay listening for the sound of footsteps and heard only the distant murmur of voices. Twisting his head round, he called out in a loud whisper. 'All right, Ford?'

The sergeant, similarly bound in the next bunk, was just recovering from the pounding headache which had assailed him when he regained consciousness after the blow from Hahnemann's machine-pistol. From the sound of Prentice's voice he guessed that the lieutenant had enjoyed a less painful return to the land of the living, something which didn't entirely surprise him when he recalled Prentice's speedy recovery from a hangover after a night of Turkish hospitality. He wet his lips before replying. 'Fine and dandy, sir. We'll have to sue the *Hydra*'s owners for damages when we arrive back.'

Prentice grinned in the darkness. 'We might just do that, laddie. Now, the guard'll be looking in any minute, so pretend you're still out cold.'

'Got it, sir.' The faint hammering inside his brain was sending waves of dizziness through Ford, a sensation which wasn't improved by the Aegean waves outside which regularly lifted the ship and tilted the cabin with an unpleasant rolling motion. Combined with his dizziness, Ford had the feeling that he was turning over and over and over. It cost him a certain effort to make his enquiry. 'Making any progress, sir?'

'A bit,' Prentice lied cheerfully, 'but not enough yet. I think they used steel hawser cable to truss us up.' He checked his watch again. Nearly a quarter past twelve. Was the guard going to be late this time? The curtains were closed over the porthole so the cabin was in almost total darkness except for the light seeping in from the door which was not quite closed. He found that slightly ajar door tantalizing – for all the use that unlocked door was to Prentice at the moment it might have been locked and bolted on the outside. But it did give him warning of the guard's approach as he proceeded with his unvarying patrol. After he had entered the cabin to make his quick check on the prisoners he continued his slow tread along the companionway and Prentice, who had exceptional hearing, found previously that he was able to follow the tramp of the retreating boots and their progress up the distant staircase

81

which ended with the thud of a door closing. So his sentry-go also took in the open deck aloft, God help him. But for Prentice this made sense – the German commander, knowing there was little risk of an emergency while they were on board, was conserving his manpower, letting his troops rest as best they could before morning. Prentice lifted his head, then called out quickly. 'Here he comes!'

The Alpenkorps guard reached the door and reacted with his normal caution, switching on the light and entering the cabin with his rifle levelled. He stood there for a moment, watching the two inert bodies, then peered round the cabin to make sure that it was empty. As he left he switched off the light and closed the door firmly. Lying on his bunk, Prentice used a little army language wordlessly – now he couldn't hear the basket marching away and, more to the point, he wouldn't be able to hear him coming back again. Gritting his teeth, he renewed the struggle to free himself, pushing down his left hand to hold the rope taut while he compressed his right hand and pulled upwards, wriggling a wrist which was now moist with sweat. The moisture might help, might eventually make it a little easier to slip his wrist upwards out of that biting rope. To give himself extra leverage he pressed his bound feet against the side of the bunk, breathing heavily as he strained desperately at the rope. Five minutes later he lay limp and exhausted by his exertions, taking in great breaths of muggy air as he summoned up his strength for a renewed onslaught. The cabin seemed to be tilting more steeply now and the woodwork was groaning as though the timbers might give under the enormous pressure of the sea. The effort to free himself had been so great that his head was beginning to ache badly and he felt that he had a steel band drawn round his temples. A light flashed briefly and he bit his lips. God, this was no time to black-out. A second later he lay still as a dead man, his heart pounding with excitement. That flash of light hadn't been his eyes playing him tricks. The light had flashed from the companionway as someone opened and closed the door soundlessly. *Someone had come inside the cabin!*

Fear. Uncertainty. Growing alarm. The emotions darted across his fatigued brain as he continued to lie quite still, straining his ears, trying to accustom his eyes to the darkness quickly. The trouble was that damned sentry lighting up the cabin had taken away his night sight for a few minutes and he wished he hadn't watched him through half-closed eyes. Had Ford also realized what had happened – that some unknown person had crept inside their cabin with uncanny silence? He had no idea. His ears had still provided no evidence that there was someone else present but instinctively Prentice knew that they were no longer alone. He found the stillness unnerving, the creaking of the ship ominous, and the thought that someone who moved like a ghost was approaching him terrifying. His mind was strained, his nerves strung up to fever pitch with their recent experiences, and now a nightmare idea flooded over him – someone had been sent in to kill them quietly. A knife in the chest, then a swift despatch overboard into the Aegean. Feverishly his imagination worked it out: the German commander might not want his unit to know about an episode like this, or perhaps there was an SS section aboard. Lying helpless in the darkness, his nerves close to breaking-point, he foresaw the next step – the hand coming out of the darkness to feel over his chest, finding the right place, the upheld hand striking downwards with one savage thrust. Keep a grip on yourself, for Christ's sake, Prentice ... His heart jumped, his throat went dry, he felt he was choking – now he could see something, a shadow which had interposed itself between the bunk and the phosphorescent hands of his watch on the table. The intruder was feet away, standing beside his bunk, looking down at him. He tried to call out, but croaked instead, a sound like a bullfrog. A hand touched his cheek and he jerked involuntarily.

'Keep quiet! Listen!'

Prentice was stunned, lay absolutely still with sheer shock. The voice had spoken in English with a distinct Scots burr. He swallowed quickly and kept his voice down to little more than a whisper.

'Who is it?'

The voice ignored the question, speaking in an urgent Morse-code fashion. 'Keep still! I have a knife ... I'll cut the ropes on your hands ... a British destroyer is close ...' Prentice felt cold steel between his wrists, stiffening the rope as the knife began to saw the fibres apart. '... at the back of the ship is a raft ... use the knife to cut it free ... when the raft is on the sea and you are away from the ship...' The knife sawed steadily, one of the ropes snapped. '... you send up a distress light ... they're on the raft...' Another rope snapped as Prentice pulled his hands away from each other to increase the tension on the remaining rope. He spoke quickly.

'I ought to know who you are – I may be able to help you later...'

'Shut up!' The knife was sawing more slowly now and Prentice realized that the man who was freeing him was taking care the knife didn't jab into him as the last rope snapped. The voice went on speaking. 'The distress light will be seen ... by the destroyer ... but Burckhardt won't dare shoot at you since that will warn the destroyer something's wrong...' Prentice felt the last rope part, freeing his hands, then heard the measured tramp of an Alpenkorps guard approaching along the companionway, the boots clumping dully on the wood.

He froze, his feet still tied. It wasn't time, not nearly time, for the guard to check on them. The intruder had entered the cabin soon after the guard had left – deliberately so. Prentice had already grasped that. So had the guard changed his routine? He was going to enter the cabin and catch him with his hands free – and catch this unknown helper in the act. The guard's tread was closer now, was slowing down prior to switching on the light and coming inside. Another thought struck Prentice and he felt a shiver run through his body – since he could hear the guard coming the door must be slightly open. Yes, it was! A thin line of light showed round the door frame. The intruder hadn't closed the door properly and the swaying of the ship had opened it wider. Lying quite still in the darkness, Prentice realized that they were finished. The guard had closed the door last time, so when he noticed that it was open, and even if he hadn't intended coming in this time... He wondered what the feelings of the unknown Scot were who was waiting with them in the unlit cabin without making a sound. He still had the knife – would he use it on one of his own men? Would he even get the chance? That partly opened door would alert the guard and he'd come inside prepared for anything. Lying back on the bunk, he turned himself sideways and hid his hands, hoping they would still look to be roped up. Another huge wave caught the vessel, thudding against the hull with such force that he felt it was coming through. A second later he heard a further thud outside in the companionway and a muttered oath in German. The wave had caught the guard off-balance. Bathed in sweat, his heart pounding solidly, he waited and listened. For a moment there was a drawn-out silence, followed by a metallic click. The guard cocking his weapon? Prentice had a fierce impulse to call out a warning, but he kept his mouth closed, then heard the tread of the guard's footsteps again just beyond the cabin door. He had turned his head sideways now, his eyes almost closed as he watched the entrance for the first shaft of light which would tell him the door was being opened. Then he heard more footsteps coming along the companionway, brisk footsteps which hurried. He could imagine the scene clearly – the guard noticing the door which should have been closed, his beckoning to a comrade who was hurrying along the passage to join him. Then the two of them would burst inside the cabin and it would be all over. The hurrying footsteps stopped outside the door and voices were raised in German. Prentice knew a little German, but not enough to speak it, and they were talking too rapidly for him to grasp what they were saying. Perhaps the new arrival was the sentry who normally checked their cabin? His mind was still grappling with possibilities when he heard feet hurrying away along the passage, followed by the deliberate tread of the sentry's footsteps as he also proceeded into the distance and up the staircase. A door thudded shut. Both men had gone.

'You must cut the ropes on your feet yourself...' The voice of the unknown man spoke quickly again. 'There's a coat and cap on the floor ... you turn left when you leave the cabin ... hurry!'

The knife had already been placed on Prentice's leg and he was working on the ropes round his ankles when light flooded briefly into the cabin and then the door closed again. Prentice looked up quickly but he was too late – he saw no more than the departure of a shadow as the intruder disappeared. While he was sawing at the ropes the ship began to roll more violently, the angle of the cabin's tilt increasing steadily. They were moving into dirty weather. Behind him he heard a creak inside Ford's bunk and the sergeant's voice was a careful whisper. 'Who the devil was that?'

'God knows, but the Scots accent was unmistakable. He must be a stowaway.' Prentice was free now and he nearly stumbled full length as the vessel rose abruptly while he was feeling his way across the darkened cabin. He'd have to risk a light — there had been a fierce urgency in the intruder's final words and in less than fifteen minutes the sentry would be back. And this time he would come inside their cabin. Switching on the light, he noted that the door was firmly closed, then ran across to Ford's bunk. He used his knife to cut the ropes as he talked. 'We've got to get on that raft and away from this ship pdq. Then we can loose off a signal to that destroyer...' Ford was rubbing the circulation back into his wrists when Prentice tried on the coat which had been dropped on the floor. An Alpenkorps greatcoat, it was a little too long and fitted loosely across the shoulders, but he thought it might serve. The soft, large-peaked cap was also ill-fitting but he settled it on his head as the sergeant looked at him.

'You're the spitting image of a Jerry,' Ford informed him. 'And your face fits, too.'

'Thanks very much...' Prentice was moving towards the door, the knife concealed inside his pocket. 'I'll walk on the left — you keep to my right. That way I'll try and cover you if any cabin doors are open.' Switching off the light, he paused while he listened with his ear pressed to the inner side of the door. He thought he understood now the restless wakefulness of those murmuring voices he had heard earlier — if the Alpenkorps men below decks knew of the destroyer's presence that would be more than enough to spoil their beauty sleep. It also meant that they were likely to be alert, which would make their walk along that companionway a hundred times more dangerous. He whispered to Ford quickly. 'Here we go. If anyone calls out to us we just keep moving as though we haven't heard. Now!' Opening the door quietly, he peered out.

The passage was deserted in both directions. He walked straight out, closed the door behind them, and began walking down the companionway with Ford at his side.

The first cabin door was half-open and before he had reached it he heard voices speaking in German. He walked at a steady pace, not too quickly, not too slowly, staring ahead as they drew level with the doorway. Out of the corner of his eye he had a glimpse of a smoke-filled cabin, a blur of uniformed bodies, and then they had passed it. Maintaining the same pace, Prentice kept his eyes fixed on the distant staircase where a pile of army packs lay huddled near the lowest tread. The next cabin door was also open, wide open. Smoke drifted into the companionway as the vessel heeled violently and Ford had to grab at the rail to save his balance. Prentice briefly slowed his pace while the sergeant caught up. That had been lucky – if it had happened opposite the open cabin door, Ford, dressed in British civilian clothes, would have been completely exposed to view. Prentice's mind was coldly alert as they came close to the doorway. From inside he could hear more animation, the sound of raucous laughter as a voice ended in a shout. Someone telling a story, he guessed. One Alpenkorps soldier, his fair hair cut to a stubble, lounged inside with his shoulder resting on the door frame and his back turned towards the companionway. Prentice kept walking forward and as he began to walk past the doorway another burst of laughter echoed inside the cabin. An NCO stood in the middle of the room, half-turned away from the doorway, waving his hands as he pantomimed something. An energetic attempt to keep up morale, Prentice was thinking, something to take the minds of the men off that destroyer outside in the night. But he thought the laughter was a little forced and short-lived. The main thing was it concentrated attention inside the cabin as they walked past it. Only one more cabin to pass, and the door was closed.

Then they were walking past the door and within a few paces of the staircase. At the foot of the steps Ford glanced down, saw inside a German army pack which had its flap drawn back. With his interest in explosives he paused involuntarily as he saw the demolition charge and the timing mechanisms. By his side Prentice sensed the pause and grasped his arm, urging him upwards without a word. The lieutenant was mounting the steps when the bows of the *Hydra* plunged downwards, elevating the staircase in his face so suddenly that he nearly fell over backwards, tightening his grip on the rail just in time. Half-way up, he looked quickly back along the companionway as he continued climbing. It was still deserted.

When he pushed open the door at the top it was almost torn from his grasp by the force of the wind. He waited until Ford was safely on deck, then used both hands to close it without a slamming noise. With the howl of the wind and the heavy slap of heaving water it seemed a needless precaution, but the thud of a door closing is a special sound and that guard might be somewhere on deck. The water-washed deck gleamed in the moonlight and beyond the funnel to port a burst of spray exploded near the rail. With Ford motionless at his side Prentice scanned the deck which seemed to be deserted. A moment later a gust of wind whipped the ill-fitting Alpenkorps cap from his head and blew it into the sea. He had lost the most distinctive part of his disguise. He looked to starboard and was staggered to see how close the destroyer was steaming, frowning when he saw the signal lamp flashing. Was she calling on the *Hydra* to heave-to? With a very slight turn of his head he looked towards the stern and saw the raft waiting for them, its canvas cover drawn back, and by the light of the moon he could see the rescue loops hanging from its sides and bobbing with the *Hydra*'s motion.

The raft had been covered with the canvas when he had last seen it and he hadn't recognized what the cover concealed. If it really carried distress lights they might just make it, might attract the destroyer's attention and be picked up. Not that he was too enthusiastic about the prospect of being aboard that tiny craft in seas like these. The whole surface of the Aegean was heaving up in a series of mountainous crests which raced towards the ferry with an insidious gliding movement as though intent on overwhelming it. He was about to make his way towards the raft, waiting for a moment when the ferry was pulling itself out of one of the great rolling dips, when he caught a brief twitch of a shadow to starboard beyond the

88

funnel. The shadow of a huge man wearing a soft hat and standing close to a swaying lifeboat. Putting a warning hand on Ford's sleeve, Prentice kept perfectly still. It was the big German who had come aboard as a passenger at Istanbul. From the way he was standing he appeared to be talking to someone who was out of sight under the wall of the bridge. Go away, Prentice prayed. Get lost! The German began to move, to turn in his direction.

'Italian mines have been sown in the Gulf of Zervos.' This latest signal from the destroyer should have reassured Burckhardt but it sent a chill through him.

It should have reassured him because the destroyer's commander had sent the captain of the *Hydra* a friendly warning, but instead he was appalled. The passage from the narrow entrance to Katyra, at the head of the gulf, was a distance of twenty miles, and the prospect of sailing twenty miles at night through mine-strewn waters was not an experience he contemplated with great enthusiasm. Mechanically, he ordered Nopagos to signal a message of thanks to the destroyer while inwardly he cursed his allies. In the interests of security the Italian High Command had been given no warning of the Zervos operation, but it was the most fiendish luck that on this night of all nights they should suddenly decide to sow mines from the air in the vital gulf. This, he told himself grimly, is going to be a voyage to remember.

'Go down and have the British prisoners escorted to my cabin.'

He gave the instruction to the soldier not preoccupied with guarding Nopagos, his eyes still on the warship as the soldier left the bridge. There might be something in what that damnably arrogant Abwehr man had hinted at . . . His thought broke off as Nopagos completed signalling and stood waiting with a resigned look on his face as the destroyer sent a short series of flashes in reply. Yes, Burckhardt decided, it was a good idea to have the British prisoners questioned again, but this time he would let his second-in-command, Major Eberhay, undertake the interrogation. Like Lieutenant Hahnemann, Eberhay also spoke English.

'They wish us *bon voyage*!' Schnell was unable to keep the relief and exultation out of his voice.

Burckhardt could hardly believe it, but the feeling of salvation which flooded over him did not affect his judgement. He issued the warning swiftly to Schnell. 'Be sure to maintain exactly the same course and speed – it may be a trick to test our reaction.' He switched to speaking in Greek. 'Captain Nopagos, kindly stay exactly where you are until I give you further orders.' From the destroyer they would easily be able to see the *Hydra*'s bridge, Burckhardt was thinking as he remained in the shadows, and if the British commander were shrewd his glasses would at this moment be focused on the ferry's bridge. He watched the destroyer's course without too much hope and inside his coat pocket his hands were clenched tight. Had they really got away with it?

'She's still on course.' It was Schnell who had spoken and the note of anxiety had crept back into his voice. With an expressionless face Burckhardt continued to stare at the warship as more steam emerged from her funnel and she began to change course for the north-west. Incredibly, they had got away with it. Speaking a word of congratulation to Schnell, he left the bridge and went down the staircase in time to meet Major Eberhay who was at the foot of the steps. Behind him strolled Dietrich and behind the Abwehr man Hahnemann was running along the companionway towards them. Several Alpenkorps soldiers were moving away in the opposite direction. 'What's the matter?' he asked Eberhay.

'The British prisoners have escaped...'

'They were tied up!'

'We are searching now,' Eberhay explained crisply, his manner quite unruffled. 'Put two more men on the bridge,' he told Hahnemann, who issued an order, summoning two soldiers from the nearby cabin and then going up the staircase as they followed him. 'And I have met Herr Dietrich,' he went on as Burckhardt appeared to be on the verge of saying something, 'we have been discussing the British destroyer...'

'It's turning away...' Burckhardt began.

'You are sure?' Dietrich interjected.

Eberhay stared up curiously at the Abwehr man as Burckhardt stood on the bottom stair and glared at Dietrich with a look of thunder. More troops were filing out of the cabins under the orders of Sergeant Volber who was instructing several to search the engine-room, to mount a double guard on the wireless operator's quarters, but not to go out on the open deck yet. Volber would take a small section to the deck himself.

Dietrich was facing the colonel bleakly, not at all disconcerted by Burckhardt's attitude. 'I heard of a similar case,' he told them. 'One of our merchant ships off Norway raised the Argentinian flag as a British destroyer approached. The warship turned away as you say this one is doing now. But it made a complete circle and came up unexpectedly on the stern of the ship and boarded her before the sea-cocks could be opened. So the danger may only be starting.' Burckhardt stood quite still on the step, his feeling of relief ebbing away; he remembered the incident this damned Abwehr man had just recalled. Dietrich turned to Eberhay without waiting for a reply. 'So, if you don't mind, I'll come on deck with you and see what that ship is doing.'

Burckhardt said nothing as he walked past them, heading for his cabin while Dietrich followed the major up the staircase, turning up his coat collar when they reached the deck. A guard stationed permanently outside the door stood to attention as Eberhay went briskly to the bridge. Inside he noted that Hahnemann had stationed two more soldiers in the rear away from the light and stared with keen interest at the destroyer as Dietrich joined him.

'It will be an hour before we know whether they've really gone,' Dietrich commented as he looked at Eberhay. The contrast between the two men was startling. Whereas Dietrich was easily the largest man aboard the *Hydra*, Eberhay was small and lightly built, his face lean and alert as a fox's and his manner almost dandified. In his early thirties, he wore over his uniform a civilian raincoat belted close to his slim waist. The name sounded Hungarian in origin, Dietrich reflected, and there was certainly Balkan blood in his veins. Which probably accounted for the air of intelligence and sophistication which radiated from him.

'The escape of the prisoners is unfortunate,' Eberhay remarked, offering his cigarette case, 'but we shall soon find them.' Dietrich shook his head, noting that the contents were Turkish as he extracted his own case and took out a cigar. Eberhay lit the cigar for him as he stooped low to reach the match. 'I'm going on deck now to supervise the search.'

'It is the manner of their escape which is more than unfortunate – it could be catastrophic,' the Abwehr man observed.

Eberhay glanced sharply up at him and then, without replying, made his way onto the open deck followed by Dietrich. As they arrived in the open the *Hydra* plunged its bows into a massive wave and a torrent of spray drenched them. Dodging close to the starboard side of the funnel, Eberhay mopped his face with a silk handkerchief. Dietrich had also moved and now he was standing by a swaying lifeboat where he caught the full blast of the icy wind. He had to pull his hat down tight over his large head and on another man the compressed hat might have looked absurd, but on this man, Eberhay reflected, it only emphasized an air of physical menace which seemed to emanate from him.

'Your name suggests a Balkan heritage,' Dietrich rumbled, switching unexpectedly to an entirely different topic.

'My grandfather moved from Budapest to Munich last century,' Eberhay replied stiffly and a little uncomfortably. 'The family has been entirely German since then.' Something about Dietrich suggested to the sensitive Eberhay a whiff of the Gestapo, and he was reminding himself to mention this to Burckhardt when he saw two Alpenkorps soldiers slip past on the port side, their bodies crouched low as they made their way towards the stern. Dietrich had turned and was also looking towards the stern as though something had caught his attention, then he turned away again, and a moment later they heard one of the Alpenkorps call out.

Eberhay ran forward, saw two men standing near the raft as the Alpenkorps soldiers charged along the deck and within seconds a furious struggle had begun. Prentice found himself thrown back against the rail, temporarily winded. A clenched fist scraped his jaw as he jerked his head aside and lifted one

92

knee. The soldier twisted to avoid the thrust, lost his balance and Prentice crashed down on top of him, his right hand reaching for the man's throat. But the German foresaw the attack again and buried his head in his chest to ward off the hand, trying to grab blindly for the lieutenant's hair. They fought ineffectually for a short time and then Prentice tore himself loose from the soldier's grasp and jumped up as though fleeing. The German came to his feet confidently, ran forward and received Prentice's aimed shoe on the point of his kneecap. He was doubling up as his opponent crashed into him and rammed him against the rail. Prentice had used the natural tilt of the vessel to port to give him added momentum and now the German was half-spreadeagled over the side as the vessel went on dropping to port, lifting the German over the rail. Scooping his arm under the German's crooked legs he hoisted and the soldier went over the side head first into the heaving sea. Eberhay had seen the danger and had run forward with his pistol held by the barrel to club Prentice. He himself had earlier given the order that under no circumstances must there be shots fired which might alert the destroyer which now presented its stern to the *Hydra*. Eberhay was close to the lieutenant when he slipped on a wet patch and sprawled headlong on the deck. In front of the funnel he saw running men as he lifted his head. 'Volber!' he shouted and then dropped his head just in time to escape Prentice's aimed shoe. Volber and two other men were struggling with Prentice while Ford still fought on the deck with the other Alpenkorps soldier as Eberhay looked quickly over the side. The seething waves had swallowed up the man who had gone overboard and there was no sign of him amid the churning crests.

In less than a minute both Prentice and Ford had been overpowered and were being taken along the deck with their arms pinioned behind them. Eberhay had warned Volber that they were wanted for questioning and that they must be looked after carefully, a necessary precaution after one of their comrades had been thrown overboard. Accidents could happen so easily and he didn't want Prentice tripped and thrown down the full length of the staircase. When he turned round, Dietrich was supporting his balance with a hand against a ventilator while he stared at the raft as though it might be alive.

'They almost got away,' were his first words.

'But they didn't . . .' Eberhay was unsure how to reply. The remark infuriated him since Dietrich seemed completely unconcerned that one of their men had just drowned.

'Three more minutes and they'd have been over the side,' the Abwehr man growled. He glared at Eberhay as though it were all his fault. 'And you wouldn't have dared open fire for fear you warned that destroyer.'

Eberhay rubbed his bruised hands with his silk handkerchief, almost lost balance again as the deck started to rise, then leant against the ventilator. The trend of Dietrich's remarks greatly disturbed him: he had heard that the Abwehr's chief, Canaris, had such a contempt for soldiers that he refused to allow any man who wore a military decoration to enter his office. It looked very much as though his aide shared his chief's views of the Wehrmacht. It had been a most unfortunate incident and the only officer present had been Eberhay himself. He tried flattery. 'You took a risk yourself coming out into the open like that.'

'So far as I could see they had no guns. I am not interested in displays of courage, Major Eberhay,' he went on bitingly. 'My usefulness to the Reich lies in staying alive as long as I can. Considering what has happened I must have a word with Colonel Burckhardt immediately.' He looked across the Aegean in a westerly direction. 'There are certain things which must be cleared up before we reach the entrance to the Gulf of Zervos. Have you ever made this trip before? No? It will be an experience for you – going into the gulf through that narrow entrance on such a night will be like entering the gates of hell.'

CHAPTER SIX

Sunday, 3 AM

At 2.50 AM the *Hydra* was steaming into the eye of the storm as seas of unimaginable violence began to take hold of her. The hull shuddered under the impact of the seventy-mile-an-hour wind, the bows of the vessel climbed a rolling wall of water, a Niagara of spray burst in the air and was flung against the window of the bridge with hammering force, blinding their view for several seconds. To stay upright, Burckhardt gripped the rail tightly as he watched the mighty waves swarming in endless succession towards the ship from Cape Zervos, waves which seethed and heaved with a dizzying motion, advancing relentlessly as though bent on the ship's destruction. Close to the colonel stood his shadow, Dietrich, his hat jammed low over his head and an unlit cigar between his lips. A few feet in front of Burckhardt the wheel was held by Schnell, standing with his legs apart and braced, the strain showing in his stooped shoulders, while to his right Nopagos, his face lined and drawn, held onto the rail as he gazed fixedly ahead. Turning, he spoke quickly to Burckhardt, his manner so harsh that for a moment it seemed the Greek had once more resumed command of his own ship.

'We must wait till morning – if you continue you will wreck us on the rocks.'

'For the sake of your crew you must see that does not happen.'

Burckhardt answered decisively but his outwardly determined attitude did not reflect his thoughts. The view from the bridge was quite terrifying; although the moon was fading there was still sufficient light to see what lay before them as a series of menacing shadows, and to the north-east the cliffs of the peninsula soared up into the night towards the three-thousand-foot summit of Mount Zervos. As the *Hydra* straddled the crest of another giant roller Burckhardt was able briefly to see the entrance to the gulf, a gap between the shadows so frighteningly narrow that from a distance it seemed as though the hull of the ship might well scrape both sides of the bottleneck. The bows plunged downwards into a fresh trough, the view was lost, and Burckhardt comforted himself with the thought that distance across water at night was doubly deceptive. So when they came closer the entrance must widen, even comfortably so, if that was a word which could be used under such turbulent conditions. Schnell, who didn't understand a word of Greek, asked the colonel what Nopagos had said.

'He wants us to wait until morning. I have said no.'

Dietrich noted that Schnell made no reply to this and he suspected that the German naval officer secretly agreed with Nopagos, who was acting as pilot. But Burckhardt would continue on course, he was sure of this, and his assumption was correct. The colonel was in an impossible dilemma: he was compelled to maintain the pre-arranged timetable, to land the expedition at Katyra by dawn. Under no circumstances could there be any possibility of turning back or waiting – his key force had a vital role to play in a far more gigantic operation and play it they must, whatever happened. Or perish in the attempt. And as Burckhardt stared from the bridge it seemed highly likely that they might indeed perish – his staff and the two hundred Alpenkorps troops huddled below decks.

The men on the bridge wore life-jackets – a precaution which Nopagos had insisted on – and the troops below were also similarly protected. But to Dietrich, as he surveyed the way ahead, the precaution seemed futile. If they struck the cliffs the *Hydra* would be pounded to pieces and no one could hope to survive in the boiling waters which surrounded them. As the vessel climbed again, breasting a further crest, he saw with appalling clarity – even through the foam-flecked window of the bridge – the mouth of the gulf, a rock-bound narrows which would require skilful seamanship in the calmest of seas in broad daylight, but at three in the morning, at the height of an Aegean storm, Schnell was going to have to take the ship on a course which most Greek sailors would have pronounced suicidal. And the weather was definitely deteriorating.

Eberhay stood a few feet away to the Abwehr man's left, and he stood so quietly and inconspicuously, almost like a wraith, that once Dietrich had looked to see if he were still there. He was watching the grim spectacle with interest and it might have been assumed he was nerveless, but in that earlier glance Dietrich had noticed a gleam of sweat across the small man's forehead. He made his remark to the major, knowing that Burckhardt was bound to hear him. 'If the vessel founders we mustn't forget that Greek tied up in the hold.'

'The guard has his instructions,' Eberhay replied. 'In the event of an emergency he will bring Grapos on deck. I gave the order myself.'

Burckhardt pretended not to have heard the exchange but the muscles across his stomach tightened a shade and he cursed the Abwehr man silently. 'If the vessel founders . . .' '. . . in the event of an emergency.' The phrases pointed up dramatically the desperate course of action he was committed to and he found the reminders unpleasant. Despite the hardening experiences of war Burckhardt was now frightened as he realized that the storm was growing worse. The deck rocked under his feet, the engines throbbed with the agonized vibration of machinery strained to the limit, and the howl of the gale was rising to a shriek. If they weren't careful the ferry was going to slip out of control. He could feel the tension reacting across his shoulder-blades from standing erect in one position, but he remained standing like a statue, determined to give an example of fortitude, compelling himself to watch the rise and fall of the sea which was going up and down like a lift. Yes, conditions were much worse, dangerously so. Beyond the bridge the world was a series of shifting shadows, shallow mountain peaks of sea which were now soaring and surging high above the *Hydra*'s masthead as the ship sank into another trough. It was weird and nerve-shattering – to see the waves jostling all around and high above them, dark, sliding slopes of water which might overwhelm them at any moment. He had a horrible feeling that exactly this could happen – the sea closing over them as the ferry capsized and plunged down to the floor of the Aegean. Then, once more, the ship seemed to gather itself to mount wearily and falteringly yet another glassy slope as it dragged itself up out of the depths. At the very moment when he least wanted it, he heard Dietrich speaking again.

'Nopagos could be right – we may end up as a wreck on the rocks.'

'That is a chance we must take. Personally, I am confident that Schnell will take us through.' Burckhardt paused, struggling to control his sudden rage. He had purposely left out that remark of Nopagos' when relaying what the Greek had said to Schnell, and it infuriated him that Dietrich should have repeated it for all to hear. But in spite of the immense pressure, the almost unbearable responsibility resting on his shoulders, Burckhardt's brain was still working and he had registered something he hadn't previously known.

'You understand Greek, then?' he asked abruptly.

'Perfectly. I speak it fluently – rather more fluently than yourself, incidentally.' Dietrich's tone of voice became scathing, a tone of voice which prickled the colonel's raw nerves. 'Why the devil do you think they chose me for this trip – one of the first qualifications, surely, is a mastery of Greek?'

'Any other languages?' It was just something to say and Burckhardt wasn't in the least interested in the reply.

'Yes, French. I don't anticipate being able to employ that particular talent on this voyage.' He spoke banteringly and his brief outburst seemed forgotten. This was another aspect of the Abwehr man's character which Burckhardt found so disconcerting: his moods changed with astonishing swiftness and kept you off-balance. He stiffened as Nopagos turned and spoke urgently, his eyes pleading.

'There is still time to change your mind – but you must decide now.'

'We are entering the gulf at the earliest possible moment. It is your duty to see that we make safe passage. For the sake of your crew, if for no other reason.'

Nopagos' manner altered. He stood up very straight and stared directly at the German with an authoritative expression. 'In that case we must change course. There is a dangerous cross-current from the east we must allow for if we are not to pile up on the rocks to the west. Tell your wheelsman . . .'

Burckhardt relayed the instructions automatically in German, instructions which he didn't understand completely and which he mistrusted. Nopagos had given the incredible order that they must steer straight for the cliffs of Zervos and the strangeness of the order raised an entirely fresh spectre in Burckhardt's already anxiety-laden mind. Quickly, he tried to resolve the fear before it was too late. Nopagos was undoubtedly a Greek patriot – his whole attitude had confirmed this to Burckhardt hours earlier – so to what lengths might he go to prevent the *Hydra* and its cargo of Alpenkorps troops ever reaching Katyra? Would he deliberately wreck his own vessel on those fearsome cliffs? He had a crew of his own countrymen aboard but would this prevent him from taking action which could only end in the death of every man aboard? Like Dietrich, Burckhardt was secretly under no illusion as to the chances of survival if the ship went down. If anything, they were less than they might have been ten minutes ago. It all depended on the inscrutable mind of one middle-aged Greek.

'There *is* a cross-current.' It was Dietrich who had spoken and now Burckhardt could feel the first signs of the ship heeling from starboard to port. The *Hydra*, its overstrained engines thumping heavily, began to move chaotically in the churning seas, like a gyroscope out of control. Sick with dread, Burckhardt watched Schnell struggling with the wheel to keep the vessel on the nightmarish course Nopagos had dictated, a course which seemed to have no direction at all as the ferry wallowed amid the inferno of near-tidal high waves rolling in all directions as the cross-current grew stronger. Soon the ship was being driven two ways – forward by the labouring engines and sideways by the powerful current from the east. Then for several minutes they suffered the illusion that they were making no progress – until the illusion was shattered in a particularly terrifying manner. Burckhardt had been under the impression that great bursts of spray in the near-distance were the product of huge waves colliding with each other and disintegrating, but as the spray settled briefly he saw an immense shadow rising in the night and knew that he was staring at the almost vertical rock face of the towering cliffs which barred their way. The surf was exploding at the base of the cliffs as the waves destroyed themselves against the barrier. Horror-struck, he heard Dietrich's voice close to his ear, a low rumble like a knell of doom. 'I estimate we are six hundred metres from them...' The *Hydra* reached the crest of a wave and now they were near enough to see huge billows shattering against the awful monolith of rock, sending up blurred spray which rose a good hundred feet above the gyrating crests of the Aegean far below. Burckhardt felt a constriction of the throat as he gazed with fascination at the spectacle – the rock face rearing upwards, the spurs at its base momentarily exposed as the sea receded, the lift of the *Hydra*'s bows, so close now that with their next fall it seemed they must ram down on that immovable rock base. And from the heaving bridge they could hear a new, sinister sound – the boom of the sea as it drove against the massive bastion of the headland. For the first time Burckhardt felt compelled to speak, to voice a navigational question. He had to lift his voice so that Schnell, still crouched over the wheel, could hear him above the shrieking wind and the steady roar of sea breaking against the cliff face.

'What's gone wrong? We're nearly on top of Cape Zervos!'

Schnell made no reply, didn't even turn round as Burckhardt took a step forward, grabbing Nopagos tightly by the arm as he spoke harshly in Greek, trying to trap the man into an admission by the suddenness of his approach. 'We're too close, aren't we? You've done it deliberately...'

Nopagos stood perfectly still, his body frozen rigid under the German's grip. As he turned to gaze directly at the colonel, Hahnemann arrived on the bridge, slamming the door shut behind him and then waiting. Nopagos spoke with dignity. 'You think I would destroy my own men? Because you are a soldier you think you are the only one with responsibilities?' He looked down at the gloved hand which held his forearm. 'You are hurting me, Colonel. This is no moment to panic. You must leave it to Schnell – or hand over the wheel to me.' Burckhardt relaxed his grip, let go, his eyes still on the Greek's face. No hint of triumph, no suggestion of treachery in those steady eyes; only a touch of resignation. Burckhardt was unmoved by the suggestion that his nerve was going – it was immaterial to him at this moment what Nopagos thought so long as he got the truth out of the man. And he believed him. The tilt of the deck almost threw him clear across the bridge as the *Hydra* heeled over again, but the soldier who was guarding Nogagos saved him. Holding firmly onto the rail Burckhardt listened while Hahnemann reported that all was well below but more than half the unit was sea-sick. As Hahnemann spoke Burckhardt was waiting for the first grind and shudder as the ferry struck. The lieutenant completed his report, saluted, and left the bridge. He closed the door as water surged over the port side, enveloping him when the wave broke against the bridge, and for a moment Burckhardt thought he had gone, but when the flood subsided Hahnemann was still clinging to the rail and he took advantage of the respite to dash below.

The not unexpected news he had brought depressed Burckhardt: within three hours the unit had to go ashore and the landing might be opposed. For such an operation the troops should be in the peak of condition and already half their energy must have drained away under the impact of their experiences so far – and the voyage was not yet accomplished. In fact, the worst probably lay ahead. Suppressing a sigh, he turned to face the cliffs and saw only spray. A second later every man on the bridge was petrified and their expressions of hypnotized fear were etched on Burckhardt's mind – a long drawn-out grinding noise was heard and the ship shuddered. *She had struck!* The message flashed through his brain and then the engines, which had missed a beat, started up reluctantly, and he knew that it was this which had caused the diabolical sound and tremor. He caught Dietrich's eye and the Abwehr man nodded, as much as to say, yes, this is gruelling. Burckhardt turned to look ahead as the vessel climbed, the spray faded and the entrance to the gulf appeared again. Within minutes their position had changed radically and they were now lying close to the narrows and well clear of the Zervos cliffs. But within a matter of only a few more minutes an even graver crisis faced them.

The enormously powerful cross-current which had carried them clear of the cliffs now threatened to carry the *Hydra* to a new and equally total destruction. From the bridge Burckhardt could now see why Nopagos had advised the apparently suicidal course of steaming directly for the notorious cape – it was an attempt to take them close enough to the narrows to pass through the bottleneck before the cross-current swept them sideways beyond it. The Greek mainland to the west lay several miles away, but from its distant coast a chain of rocks stretched out across the gulf entrance, a chain which ended close enough to the cliffs of the Zervos peninsula to compress the entrance dangerously narrow. And the only navigable channel, Schnell had explained earlier, lay through the bottleneck, guarded by the last rock in the chain. Burckhardt was staring grimly at that rock as the ferry ploughed its way forward towards the entrance, half its engine-power neutralized by the insidious sideslip motion of the cross-current which, only a few minutes before their saviour, was fast becoming their most deadly enemy.

In size the rock was more like a small island, a pointed island which rose straight out of the sea to its peak, a saw-toothed giant against which a warship might well destroy itself at the first impact, whereas the ferry they were aboard was a little more fragile than a steel-plated cruiser. Mountainous waves were surging half-way up the rock's face and the bursting spray smothered its peak. It had the appearance of waiting for them.

'It is fortunate that we did not plan to scale the so-called cliff path,' Eberhay commented. He had said the first thing which came into his head to break the tension permeating the bridge like a disease. 'I hardly imagine it would have been a great success,' he went on lightly. 'There might have been some difficulty in disembarking the troops at the base of the cliff.'

'I don't believe there is a path,' Burckhardt replied. When the operation had been planned one of the experts had mentioned this path which he said climbed the apparently sheer face in a series of zigzag walks leading eventually to the summit close to the monastery. Superficially, it had seemed an attractive idea – Burckhardt could have taken his main objective soon after landing instead of going to the head of the gulf

102

and then marching twenty miles back down the peninsula. From the monastery he could have sent out patrols to the north to occupy the peninsula from the heights – the operation would, in fact, have taken place in precisely the reverse direction from the one now contemplated. The operation had been revised to its present form when the planners had realized that the Greek ferry reached the cape in the early hours of the morning; the prospect of scaling the cliffs at night had been considered impracticable and the ferry had to complete its run to preserve the appearance of normality up to the last moment.

'Yes, there is a track,' Dietrich informed the colonel. 'It links up the anchorite dwellings built into the cliff face. The anchorites are hermit monks who spend all their lives in isolation from their fellows – hence the extraordinary places they live in.' He chuckled throatily. 'I have always thought it must be similar to solitary confinement during a lifetime in prison.'

'How do you know this?' Burckhardt was twisted round one hand still gripping the rail as the bridge swayed alarmingly.

'Because I paid a visit to Zervos five years ago.' Dietrich regarded the colonel ironically. 'Which is simply another of my qualifications for being here. I travelled all over the peninsula.'

'You went to the monastery?' Burckhardt put the question casually but the information interested him intensely. He had only one man among the two hundred aboard who knew Zervos personally – Lieutenant Hahnemann – and he had worried over this ever since the expedition had been planned. Perhaps, after all, the Abwehr officer was going to prove extremely useful during the dangerous hours ahead.

'Yes, I visited the monastery. Why?'

'I simply wondered how widespread your travels had been. I understand there is no landing place along the peninsula coast between the cape and Katyra at the head of the gulf.'

'There is Molos – twenty kilometres south of Katyra.'

'Yes, I know. It is a small fishing village – but has it access to the interior?'

'It depends what you call access.' Dietrich was still holding the cigar unlit in his mouth and he didn't bother to remove it to reply to the colonel. 'There is a footpath which goes up into

103

the mountains but often it is washed away during the winter.'

'I see.' Burckhardt replied as though this were news, but he had heard this at the planning stage and it confirmed that Dietrich did know the geography of the peninsula. 'There is a road south from Katyra, of course?'

'You know perfectly well there is, or I presume you would not be on board this ship. It is little more than a track and winds its way among the hills. You should have brought mules with you,' he told Burckhardt bluntly.

'We considered them – but it was hardly practicable to transfer animals from the *Rupescu* to this ferry.' Satisfied with Dietrich's replies he turned away, but the Abwehr man had the last word.

'All this is assuming that we ever penetrate that gulf. You see what is happening, don't you?'

Burckhardt, who had let his attention slip for the shortest period of time, looked ahead and stiffened. During the very brief interval while he had conversed with Dietrich, the *Hydra*, caught up in the main force of the cross-current, had been swept three-quarters of the way across the entrance and now he heard a fresh sound, a sound more muted than the breaking of the sea against the cape but no less sinister – the dull boom of the swaying Aegean against the base of the saw-tooth. They were very close to the narrows – close enough to see that there the water was quieter, although still it heaved and bubbled like a tidal race, but they were equally close to the saw-tooth. He looked away to starboard where the big rollers were rounding Cape Zervos and hurtling towards the ferry, a piling-up of the sea which had more than once shaken the vessel as though she were a toy ship. It was these mountainous rollers which posed Burckhardt's second nightmare. If a big one came just at the wrong moment as they were passing the saw-tooth... He noticed Schnell again turning his head to look to port, and Schnell's frequent glances in that direction worried him. The naval officer was clearly aware that they were engaged in a lethal race – to pass through the narrows before they piled-up against the rock. There was no longer anything they could do except to hope. Everything seemed to conspire to screw up their tense nerves to an unbearable pitch –

104

the engines were beating foggily as though on the verge of breaking down altogether; the vessel's movements were becoming laboured and had a discouraging, waterlogged feel; the cross-current seemed to be carrying them sideways faster than the bows of the ship moved forward. He heard Eberhay clear his throat and the sound alerted him, made him look again to port. They were about to enter the narrows but the saw-tooth was less than thirty metres from the hull. A wave broke on the rock's side and spray reached the apexed summit. Out of the corner of his eye Burckhardt caught a slight movement – Nopagos was staring in the opposite direction towards the cape as though transfixed.

Following his gaze, the colonel clenched his teeth and felt coldness like an affliction chill his spine. Another roller was coming, a roller more mountainous than any Burckhardt had seen. There must have been some accumulation of the waters, even an overtaking and merging of three giant waves to form the foam-crested colossus bearing down on them like an upheaval from the deep. All heads were turned in that direction now, even Schnell's before he dragged his gaze to for'ard by some supreme effort of will. The crest of the monster was well above funnel height. Hands gripped the rails tightly, bodies stood rigid with fright. Even Burckhardt took several steps back as Dietrich moved aside for him to brace his back against the rear wall. With the wood pressed against his shoulderblades he stared incredulously at the appalling spectacle. The wave seemed to be climbing higher and higher, swallowing up more of the sea to swell itself to mammoth proportions. We'll be overwhelmed, Burckhardt thought, we'll never emerge from this: we'll plunge down to the floor of the gulf like a submarine out of control. God, had there been some frightful underwater upheaval, some shift in the earth's surface on the Aegean floor? The wave was within ten metres now. Half the wave's height would be clear over them ... His hands locked on the rail, felt the greasy sweat inside his gloves, and then the *Hydra* tried to climb, to carry itself up the side of the monstrous wave – and instead was swept sideways. Lifted like a paper boat, it seemed no longer to move forward at all as the screw churned frantically inside the pounding sea. Eberhay lost his grip and was hurled bodily across the bridge where he collided with the Alpenkorps soldier. Bracing himself afresh, determined not to follow Eberhay, the colonel looked to port again. For a moment he saw nothing except the wave travelling westward, a shifting wobble of sea which shimmered his vision, then a window appeared in the water and his jaw muscles tautened. Just beyond the ship, it appeared, the sawtooth was rushing towards them like the wall of a building toppling over on the port deck. He waited for the shuddering crash of hull disintegrating against immovable rock, the sinking sensation as the *Hydra* foundered.

Spray blinded the view. Unexpectedly he realized that the ferry was listing to starboard, was over the crest. Ahead lay the smoother water where the gulf was protected from the fury of the storm by the wall of the cape. He looked back through the window at the rear of the bridge in time to see the saw-tooth submerging under the surge of the sea, the spray bursting high above the summit as the whole rock was temporarily drowned under the immense fall of water. Then the rock began to reappear as water drained down its sides and Burckhardt's mind functioned again. *The rock was behind them.* They had moved inside the Gulf of Zervos.

Three minutes later he was about to leave the bridge, his mind concentrated on the peril of the Italian sea-mines, when Hahnemann reported that the unit's wireless set had been sabotaged.

'The Gestapo? Dietrich a member of the Gestapo? What the devil put that crazy idea into your head, Eberhay?'

Burckhardt stared grimly across the table at his second-in-command. It was a suggestion he could have done without at this stage of the operation as the *Hydra* proceeded steadily up the gulf through the darkness. All its lights were ablaze to preserve the appearance of normality and from the bridge a powerful searchlight was beamed ahead as Schnell and Nopagos strained their eyes for the first sight of the dreaded mines. Inside the colonel's cabin Eberhay crossed his slim legs and smiled faintly. The two men were alone and it had seemed an ideal moment to voice his doubts. 'It is just a feeling I had,' he explained, 'when I was talking to him on deck some time ago.'

'Just a feeling!' Burckhardt was more annoyed than ever. 'No evidence – just a feeling. And why should Berlin secretly put a Gestapo official on board this ship?' His voice became more biting. 'You have a theory on that, I'm sure.'

'Yes, I have.' The little major, accustomed to the colonel's moods, was unruffled. 'Since there appears to be a traitor on board it could be someone the Gestapo has previously suspected. We know someone helped the Englanders to escape, and if the unit has been infiltrated this would account for Dietrich's presence – he is trying to locate the spy. Naturally, if he is Gestapo, he doesn't take us into his complete confidence. They never do. And the sabotage of the wireless set proves that someone is trying to hinder the expedition...'

'I agree,' Dietrich spoke the words from the door he had opened silently and Burckhardt's manner became icier as the Abwehr man came inside and joined them at the table after carefully closing the door. The sentry outside the cabin should have stopped him, of course, and the colonel reminded himself to deal with that later. But it was an interesting example of how the Abwehr man's powerful personality was dominating almost everyone on board. A short while earlier Burckhardt had overheard an Alpenkorps soldier explaining to his cabin mates that the Abwehr officer had been sent personally by the Führer to watch over the operation, a suggestion which had not endeared him to the huge German who now sat at one end of the table holding his cigar while he spoke.

'Major Eberhay is, of course, correct. Someone aboard this Greek ferry is trying to prevent you from ever reaching your objective. And he has the freedom of action to sabotage your wireless set. That I personally find most inconvenient – I wished to send a message to Berlin via your GHQ in Bulgaria at the earliest possible moment. When would you have been able to break radio silence?'

'Not while we are on board,' Burckhardt replied evasively. 'But you may still be able to send your message later.'

Dietrich looked relieved, nodding as he lit his cigar. 'That is certain?'

'I cannot be sure yet when that will be.' He paused, conscious of a feeling that he was being too close-mouthed with this Abwehr officer. For all he knew he could be Admiral Canaris' right-hand man. 'We have a second wireless set in perfect condition,' he said briskly. 'Military signals will, of course, have priority, but you will be able to communicate with Bulgaria at a certain time after we have gone ashore.'

'The other set is permanently out of action?'

'Possibly not. Someone smashed the tuning coil but the wireless op may be able to repair it in time.'

'It had been left unguarded?'

'No, not originally. But the man who was guarding it became sick and went to the lavatory. He was there for some time and because of his condition he didn't check the set immediately when he returned.'

'How can you smash up a tuning coil?'

Eberhay, who had seen the damaged set, explained this. 'Anything heavy would do the job – a pistol butt, or a rifle's – anything. It could be done in less than a minute.'

'Why did Schnell keep to his cabin during the early part of the voyage?' asked Dietrich. The sudden switch in topic surprised both German officers and again it was Eberhay who replied. 'He made the same trip aboard the *Hydra* a fortnight ago to study the vessel and its route. Although he was disguised on that earlier trip we wanted to eliminate any risk that one of the crew might recognize him this time.'

'And he carried the weapons for use in taking over the vessel inside that cabin trunk which caused so much comment?'

'Yes!' It was Burckhardt who answered now, disliking the final qualification in Dietrich's question. 'Both wireless sets, incidentally, are now under heavy guard. And the seizure of this vessel went exactly according to plan.'

'I agree that that part of the operation was well organized,' Dietrich said blandly with the underlying implication that the later stages had been little better than a dog's breakfast. Withdrawing suddenly from the conversation, he sat back in his chair and regarded both men through his cigar smoke. The German officers had taken off their outer civilian coats and wore field-grey Alpenkorps uniform: a tunic buttoned up to the neck, trousers ankle-wrapped with puttees, and heavily nailed boots. The footgear, Dietrich thought, was an improvement on the normal Wehrmacht jackboot he so disliked. Round his waist each man wore a wide leather belt with a hip holster slung on the left side and the Luger pistol set butt forward. He remained motionless while someone hammered urgently on the outside of the door and a moment later the knocking was repeated. Burckhardt called out for them to come in and Lieutenant Hahnemann appeared.

'What is it?' Burckhardt asked quietly.

'One of the ten-kilogram demolition charges is missing and a time fuse.'

Dietrich came to life suddenly, was standing up as he fired the question, his great body overshadowing Hahnemann. 'That sounds like a large bomb?'

In his agitation Hahnemann replied immediately before the colonel could say a word, addressing Dietrich directly. 'If it is placed in the right position it could destroy the entire ship.'

'Something's upset their apple cart, all right.' Ford spoke quietly as he stood alongside Prentice by the porthole. Their cabin was being methodically searched by Alpenkorps soldiers who prodded the bedding gingerly with short-bladed bayonets, opened cupboard doors as though expecting something to fall out, and peered cautiously under chair seats without moving them.

'They're nervy, too.' Prentice watched the searching process curiously and he thought he sensed a desperate urgency in their efforts, like men working against a clock. Near the door Sergeant Volber stood directing operations, although his main task, under orders from Eberhay, was to protect the prisoners. During the search more than one man glanced murderously at Prentice who was responsible for the death of one of their comrades, and Volber was present to exercise strict discipline. A moment later the sergeant spoke in German, and when Prentice failed to understand, he waved his Luger to indicate they must move to one side. A soldier who pointedly did not look at them opened the porthole, peered outside, then rubbed a hand round the outer rim as though seeking something which might be suspended there. Satisfied with his search, he closed the porthole and Volber motioned them to take up their former position.

'What the hell's going on?' Ford whispered.

'Don't know – but they're as jumpy as hens with a fox in the yard.' Prentice was glad of Volber's presence: all the Germans carried carbines,* as the technically minded Ford insisted on calling them, and it had been known for a weapon to go off accidentally when aimed at a lethal spot. From the look on the faces of some of these hard-bitten youngsters a carbine could have discharged quite easily in his direction if Volber had omitted to attend the ceremony. Ford continued gazing out of the porthole where he could see on the mainland side of the gulf a chain of pinpoint lights crawling up the coast road to the north. He pressed his hand lightly on the lieutenant's arm.

'Look – must be our chaps across there.'

'I know, I've seen 'em.' Prentice hadn't relaxed his own gaze from the interior of the cabin. He could feel the deep animosity radiating from the dozen men who went on turning the cabin inside out. One soldier walking past him chanced to let go of his carbine and Prentice had to move quickly. The metal-sheathed butt of the weapon thudded heavily on the cabin floor where a moment before his right foot had stood. If that butt had contacted, it could have crippled him. Volber called out sharply in German and was still barking vehemently when the soldier left the cabin.

'Sounds as though he's going on a charge. With any luck,' Ford added. 'You know, sir, I don't think they really like us.'

'Just be ready to do a quick tap-dance if the occasion arises,' Prentice told him and continued to stare at any man who caught his eye. Yes, Ford had been right: it was a damned queer situation. On board the *Hydra* there must be at least a company of well-trained German troops and some of them expected to operate at high altitudes – he had seen several pairs of skis inside one cabin when they had been taken along earlier for interrogation by that slip of a German officer who spoke English. And behind them, a few miles across the gulf through that porthole, they could see the hooded lights of traffic moving through the night along that vital mainland road

* Ford was referring to the Gewehr 98 K bolt-action carbine.

to the north. Prentice had no doubt that those were the lights of Allied convoys driving up to the Alkiamon Line, completely ignorant of the fact that the ship whose lights they could see across the water was carrying a German spearhead aimed at Zervos. For by now Prentice had little doubt of the Alpenkorps objective – the Germans on board were on their way to seize that vital monastery observation post overlooking the road Ford was watching through the porthole.

'A whole load of them on the way,' Ford went on, 'I can see lights right up the coast.'

'What the blazes can this lot be looking for?' Prentice wondered out loud. 'And it bothers them. They're sweating.'

'They can melt away for all I care. What I can't make out is why they're still wearing their Mae Wests. It's as calm as the Serpentine outside now.' Ford's description of the gulf had an element of exaggeration because the *Hydra* was still steaming through a moderate swell, but contrasted with the seas off Cape Zervos it could indeed have been the Serpentine. The Aegean, one of the most unpredictable seas in the world, had subsided again.

'I told you, they were nervy,' Prentice replied. Inwardly, he assumed the wearing of Mae Wests was just another example of Teutonic discipline, but it was the object of the search which was nagging at his tired brain. Come to think of it, these boys didn't look as though they'd just got up in the morning. Which was a thought that gave him a certain amount of satisfaction: if they went on prowling round the ship like this they'd be exhausted before they ever got ashore. The soldiers were trooping out of the cabin when he went up to Volber. 'Speak with German who speaks Englische ...' he began. It took him a pantomime of gestures to convey that he wished to talk to the little officer who had interviewed them earlier, and when Volber returned he came back with Lieutenant Hahnemann instead.

'What is it?' Hahnemann rapped out. There was tension here, too – tension and irritability in the manner and expression with which he regarded the two prisoners.

'What are you looking for? We might be able to help,' Prentice told him blithely.

The reaction was unexpectedly violent. Hahnemann took a step forward and his right hand rested close to his hip holster. It had been a mistake, Prentice realized at once. The Jerries were more at their nerve-ends than he had realized. He spoke quickly and tersely, letting a little indignation creep into his tone. 'I meant what I said. Why wouldn't I? If I could tell you where it was – whatever you are looking for – it would have saved us having the bedding bayoneted to bits.'

'You will stay here and not send for me again.' He turned away and then looked back. 'Why are you not wearing the life-jackets?'

'Because there isn't a storm any more.'

'You put them on now and they stay on. That is an order. For your safety,' he ended abruptly. They were left alone with the guard while they tied on their Mae Wests again. Prentice was relieved to see that it was the same guard, a thirty-year-old who sat some distance from them with his machine-pistol always aimed in their general direction. A sturdy-faced character, he had shown no exceptional signs of hostility although he was careful never to let them come within ten feet of where he sat.

'I'd still like to know what they were after,' said Ford as he sat down on a pile of massacred bedding. He looked up at Prentice. 'How much longer?'

'About an hour, if they're keeping to the ferry's schedule.' Prentice's watch registered 4.30 AM and the *Hydra* had been due to dock at Katyra at 5.30 AM, a little before dawn. To keep awake he went over to the porthole again for another look at those tantalizing hooded lights of the convoy moving along the coast road. Another hour. Nothing much could happen in that time.

The ten-kilogram composite demolition charge stood on the table. It was enclosed inside a black-painted zinc container about the size and shape of a deep attaché case and there was a web carrying-handle at the top. Inset into the top face were two standard igniter sockets.

'Like that?' queried Dietrich innocently. He gave the impression that this was the first time in his life he had seen a ten-kilogram demolition charge.

'Its twin is hidden somewhere aboard this ship – with the difference that the clockwork time fuse has undoubtedly been attached and set in motion. Show him the fuse, Hahnemann.'

While Burckhardt waited, the engines of the ferry ticked over steadily, unpleasantly suggestive of the ticking of a time bomb. They were alone in the colonel's cabin with the exception of the temporary presence of Hahnemann who had brought in the demolition charge at the Abwehr man's request. As Dietrich had so unfortunately put it, he wanted to see what was going to blow him to kingdom come.

'The fuse,' said Hahnemann.

It was roughly shaped like an outsized egg-cup. Measuring a little over two inches across the top in diameter and six inches in overall depth, the casing was chocolate-brown bakelite, and when Dietrich picked up the device Hahnemann showed him how it worked. The top was a hinged glass lid which had to be lifted to set the clock. Still holding the time fuse, he looked up at the lieutenant.

'And one of these is definitely missing with the charge?'

'Yes. They were in a rucksack at the bottom of the companionway stairs.'

'Not guarded?' Dietrich was looking down at the mechanism.

Hahnemann glanced at the colonel, who nodded. 'There was a mix-up of rucksacks. I'm sure it would never have happened if half the men hadn't been sea-sick. Corporal Schultz thought he had the rucksack with the charges inside with him in a cabin. It was only discovered later that he had someone else's while his own rucksack had been left outside.'

Dietrich ignored the explanation. 'Corporal Schultz is waiting in the passage? Good, I'd like to see him.'

Hahnemann went to the door and let inside a slim man in his late twenties who was clearly not at ease, and his embarrassment increased when he slipped on the polished floor. He glanced at the colonel as he saluted and Burckhardt merely told him to answer questions. He had already had a word with the negligent NCO.

'These fuses are totally reliable?' enquired Dietrich. The pink-faced corporal glanced at Hahnemann who told him briskly to answer the question. Schultz was uncertain how much to say and the colonel barked at him to get on with it.

'No, sir, not always,' Schultz began. And having begun he gained confidence and spoke rapidly. 'They have a habit when set of stopping for no reason at all. Then they can start up again of their own accord – again for no particular reason. We do know that they can be affected by jolting or vibrations. They're weird – I heard of one case where a fuse was set to detonate the charge in two days. It was put under a bridge during training and then the man who had put it there died in a motor crash. Everyone forgot about it.' He paused, his eyes on Dietrich who was staring at him fixedly. 'Two years later the bridge blew up. Yes, sir – two *years* later.'

'Thank you.' Dietrich returned the time fuse to Hahnemann who picked up the charge by the handle and left the cabin with Corporal Schultz.

'And where does that get us?' asked Burckhardt.

'It gets us into a worse state of nerves than we were before, I should have thought. You heard what he said?'

'Of course! Which point were you referring to?'

Dietrich clubbed one large fist and began drumming it slowly on the table. It took Burckhardt a moment to grasp that he was drumming in time with the beat of the *Hydra*'s engines. He pursed his lips uncomfortably as Dietrich rammed the point home verbally. 'Affected by jolting or vibrations,' he said.

'We shall not be on board much longer.' He hesitated. It must by now be patently obvious when they were going ashore to anyone who knew the *Hydra*'s timetable. 'Barely an hour. In the meantime the search continues and they may find it.'

'Colonel Burckhardt.' Dietrich was standing up now, his hat in his hand. 'This is likely to be the longest hour of your life. I think I'll go and help them try to find it. You never know – they say heaven protects the innocent.'

As he went along the companionway, hands thrust deep inside his coat pockets, he heard the frenzied clump of nailed boots everywhere. The boots rarely stayed still for more than a short time, as though their occupants were finding it impos-

114

sible to keep in one place while they continued their frantic search for the missing demolition charge. Inside one cabin he found men with moist faces pushing aside a pile of dark brown hickory skis which could not possibly have concealed the charge. A soldier who didn't look a day over nineteen was peering behind a fire-extinguisher, another impossible hiding-place. There had been tension aboard the *Hydra* ever since the Alpenkorps had arrived, tension initially through the know-ledge that at any minute they might be stopped by a British warship, tension because they were aboard the vessel of a country which Germany still officially treated as a neutral in the war. But the earlier tension brought on by the secrecy, by the storm, by the sabotage of a wireless set and the death of one of their men overboard – this tension had been serenity compared with the stark, livid tension which now gripped the *Hydra*'s illegal passengers.

It manifested itself in little ways. The lift of a rifle as Dietrich came round a corner. The kicking over of a bucket of sand by an Alpenkorps soldier hurrying past. The disorganized clump of those nailed boots on the ceiling when he was walk-ing along the companionway of the lower deck. The sentry who guarded Grapos was still at his post, his back to the port-holed steel door leading down to the hold where the Greek was imprisoned. Farther along the companionway Dietrich looked inside the half-open door which led down to the engine-room. He had one foot on the iron platform when a rifle muzzle was thrust in his face, reminding him of the muzzle which Volber had thrust at him as he opened his cabin door when they had taken over the ship. But this time he withdrew swiftly – the muzzle had wobbled slightly. In that brief glimpse he had seen below at least half-a-dozen field grey figures searching among the machinery while another man mounted guard over the chief engineer. The fear was a living mounting thing which he saw in men's faces as he climbed back to the top deck, faces damp, baggy-eyed and drawn with strain as they went on searching amid the ferry's complexities for something no larger than an attaché case. This is a formula for driving men mad, he was thinking as he went on climbing, for slowly shredding their nerves to pieces.

On the open deck it was quieter because there were fewer searchers: Burckhardt had given strict instructions that despite the gravity of the emergency only those men who could cover their uniforms with civilian coats were to be sent up here. Even now he was not prepared to risk a British motor-torpedo boat suddenly appearing and flashing its searchlight over the deck to illuminate men in German uniform. So far as Dietrich could see there were no more than a dozen, hatless men flitting in the shadows. But here again he heard the disjointed hurrying clump of those heavily nailed boots pounding the wooden deck. It was quite dark now, the impenetrable pitchblackness of the night before dawn, and a cold wind was blowing along the gulf. He leant against the ventilator amidships to light his cigar and a soldier came round the side and cannoned into him. When he saw the silhouette of the hat against the match-flare he apologized and hurried away. Dietrich sighed. Again he had seen the lift of the rifle prior to recognition. He went to the stern and looked over the rail where the screw churned the sea a dirty white colour, stumbled over a piled loop of rope, and went back along the deck to the illuminated safety of the bridge. It was 4.45 AM.

The ten-kilogram composite demolition charge swayed at the end of the rope. The vibrations of the ship's engines shuddered it in mid-sway and the rock of the ship's movements reproduced themselves in the sway itself. The charge thudded regularly against the metalwork as it continued its endless pendulum motion, but the sound of the thuds was camouflaged by the same engine beats which shook it. A man standing close by might not have heard those warning thuds as the charge dangled and swayed and shuddered. The clock was set and the mechanism was ticking, but the most vital sound – the ticking – was muffled by the larger noises. Occasionally the vessel plunged its bows a little deeper into the waters of the gulf and then the charge would strike the metal heavily, its rhythmic sway temporarily upset by the unexpected jolt. For a minute or more it would sway erratically, its pendulum balance disturbed, then it would recover its poise and resume the same even swing backwards and forwards with the regularity of a

116

metronome. It was suspended a long way down the shaft, suspended from an Alpenkorps scabbard which still held its bayonet, a scabbard which had been jammed inside the shaft at an angle which might hold it there indefinitely. And as it went on swaying none of the hatless men who thumped along the open deck in growing desperation had, as yet, carefully examined the ventilator shaft amidships.

CHAPTER SEVEN

Sunday, Dawn

'The Greek has escaped – I have instituted an immediate and intensive search of the ship.' Hahnemann reported the news to Burckhardt whom he had found on the bridge standing next to Dietrich. He waited nervously for the colonel's reaction, but Burckhardt, holding a pair of field-glasses, simply looked at him as he asked the question.

'How did it happen, Hahnemann? He was tied up in the hold and Private Kutzel was standing guard over him.'

'He must have freed himself in some way.' Hahnemann hesitated: the next item of news was bound to provoke an explosion. 'Kutzel is dead – I found him on the floor of the hold with his neck broken.'

'And his rifle?'

Dietrich smiled grimly to himself as he heard the question and he gave the colonel top marks for competence under stress. The weapon, of course, was vital, could make all the difference to the degree of menace posed by the escaped Greek.

'I found that on the floor close to his body . . .'

'Good. He shouldn't be difficult to round up. You said an "intensive" search, Hahnemann. How intensive? How many men?'

'Fifty, sir.' Hahnemann at least felt confident that he had organized the hunt for Grapos on a sufficiently massive scale, even though there was something else which he dreaded mentioning. He wished to heaven that the Abwehr man wasn't standing there with his hands behind his back, his great shoulders hunched forward as he took in every word the lieutenant was saying. The colonel's reaction gave him an unpleasant shock.

'Fifty? You mean you have taken fifty men off the search for the missing demolition charge?' Burckhardt was facing the

118

unfortunate Hahnemann now, his hands on his hips as he went on bitingly. 'When will you get your priorities right? An explosive with a time fuse has been planted somewhere aboard this vessel, an explosive powerful enough to sink us in the middle of the gulf before we ever go ashore. That, since it appears you don't realize it, is a far greater risk than one unarmed Greek civilian who is probably gibbering with fright in some cupboard. You will tell off no more than twenty men to look for him – the other thirty must immediately resume the search for that demolition charge.'

'He is armed, sir – with a rifle . . .'

'You said you had found Kutzel's rifle.'

'That is correct, sir.' Hahnemann's rigid stance reflected the extent of his unhappiness as he went on stolidly. 'I think the Greek must have surprised Private Wasserman also when he was asleep in a cabin on the lower deck . . .'

'Asleep!' Burckhardt changed the direction of his attack: what a soldier had been doing asleep during these vital hours was something he could inquire into later. Doubtless Wasserman had sneaked off into the cabin hoping no one would find him there. 'What has happened to Wasserman?'

'He's dead – strangled as far as we can tell. And his rifle and ammunition belt are missing so the Greek must have them.'

Burckhardt paused only briefly while he wished to God that the Abwehr man wasn't listening to all this, but he was still perfectly clear as to what must be done. 'You will still use only twenty men to hunt for the Greek. Issue a general warning that he's armed.'

'I have done that already, sir.'

'Then issue a special warning to those on the open deck – we don't want them starting to loose off at each other.' As Hahnemann hurried away he thought no, that would be the final disaster – to incur further casualties with the men shooting one another. Taking up a firmer stance, he stared ahead to where the searchlight beam shone down the gulf. It was 5.15 AM. A quarter of an hour to disembarkation. Coldly, he catalogued in his mind the risks and setbacks which had bedevilled the expedition since he had come aboard the *Hydra*.

A boatload of troops which had been very nearly capsized during the transfer from the *Rupescu*; one soldier sent into the sea by the Englishman, Prentice; one wireless set sabotaged by smashing the tuning-coil; the encounter with the destroyer which had almost proved fatal; a demolition charge of great explosive power planted somewhere in the bowels of the vessel; the escape of the armed Greek; and the death of two more Alpenkorps men during that escape. So three men out of two hundred were dead even before they set foot in Greece. Surely nothing more could happen during the remaining quarter of an hour? Actually, it was likely to be twenty-five or thirty minutes – they were behind schedule with this infernal ferry having to move more slowly because of the danger of mines – and Italian mines of all things. Schnell had insisted on the further reduction in speed to ensure that they sighted them in time. The irony of it was they hadn't seen a single mine since entering the gulf.

'I think I'll go and have a word with Major Eberhay – if I can find him.' Dietrich was already moving away and leaving the bridge to Burckhardt's relief – the large German seemed to dominate wherever he went, to hang over the ship like a prophet of disasters to come. Barely a minute later Sergeant Volber came onto the bridge and the colonel only had to take one look at his face to know it was not good news.

'What is it, Volber?' he rapped out sharply.

'We think Private Diehl may be missing, sir'.

Burckhardt instantly thought of the Greek who was prowling about somewhere with a loaded rifle. 'You *think*? Either Diehl is missing or he isn't?' Which is it?'

'We don't know, sir.' Volber lacked Lieutenant Hahnemann's capacity for telling a complete account quickly, forestalling his commanding officer's questions so far as he could, and the sergeant's habit of replying without explaining was a foible Burckhardt found intensely irritating. He felt the blood going to his head as he forced himself to reply coldly.

'What the devil does that mean?'

'He hasn't been seen for a long time – I've asked several of the men and they all thought he was somewhere else. They're very scattered . . .'

'You've allowed your section to become scattered?'

'We're on the open deck and it takes time to check everyone in the dark...'

'Report to me as soon as you can whether he's definitely missing. Definitely, I said, Volber.'

The strain was telling everywhere, Burckhardt thought as the sergeant hurried away. Schnell was being over-cautious, the NCOs were getting rattled, and the men were being steadily drained of their aggressive energies as they plodded round the ship searching for time-bombs and armed Greeks. And soon they would have to fight a campaign. Armed Greeks? The thought reminded him of a few vital questions he had to put to the captain. He took a step forward which placed him at Nopagos' elbow.

'The man called Grapos has escaped,' he said harshly. 'He has taken a rifle and ammunition – can he use them? Before you reply, remember that he is a civilian with no rights in war and I shall hold you responsible for the death of any of my men if you withhold information.'

Nopagos turned and stared at the German. His skin was lined and pouched with fatigue but he still held himself erect; what little responsibility he still held for his own vessel as its pilot would only cease when they docked at Katyra. He was tempted to tell Burckhardt to go to hell but he sensed something of the tremendous pressure the colonel was undergoing and it seemed senseless to take a risk when they had almost landed. 'He has been able to use a rifle since he was a boy,' he replied.

'But he has something to do with the monastery.' Burckhardt did not understand this at all and his mouth tightened as he held the Greek's eyes.

'He was a novice monk who had no vocation. When he left the monastery it was agreed that he should do odd jobs for them – like going to Istanbul on this ferry to bring back supplies of books and things like that. He has shot birds on the peninsula from an early age. Yes, he can use a rifle.'

'Well?'

'A marksman.' Nopagos gave this reply with a certain relish.

121

'His limp kept him out of the army?'

'It was his greatest regret. He would be an asset to any army in the world. Has he caused any trouble yet?'

'He has killed two of my men.'

'You see what I mean, then?' For a moment Nopagos thought he had gone too far. Burckhardt stiffened and a hint of fury came into his eyes and then faded as he regained control. He was careful to keep strict control as he put his next question.

'He knows this ship well?'

'Well enough to hide until we have reached Katyra as you have not found him now.' And with this last thrust Nopagos turned away and attended to his duties once more. But he was not able to resist asking a question which he carefully put in a polite tone. 'Have they found the time-bomb yet?'

'No.'

'So, there is still time.'

This simple comment stung Burckhardt more than anything Nopagos had said previously. He had given Eberhay orders to leave assembly for disembarkation until the last possible moment so they could keep on looking for that missing demolition charge – Burckhardt's greatest fear was that it would detonate just before they landed. He was thinking about this when Schnell, almost exhausted from his long hours over the wheel, straightened up as a soldier ran along outside the bridge and came in breathless. Burckhardt recognized him as one of the two men posted as lookouts as soon as they had passed through the narrows. In his anxiety to speak the man had trouble in getting out his message.

'Mines sighted, sir ... on the port bow.'

The explosion came at 5.45 AM as the *Hydra*, listing to port, her engines beating uncertainly, began the ninety-degree turn which would take her inshore to the distant light of the Katyra landing-stage. They were almost there, Burckhardt reflected as he stood on the bridge behind Nopagos, but the last mile was likely to be the longest of the voyage. The dangers surrounding the expedition were now so overwhelming that his mind had reached the point where it could hardly take in any

122

more – those damnable Italian mines were growing more numerous with every quarter-mile they glided forward; an armed Greek was loose somewhere on board, and a marksman at that; and they had still failed to locate the demolition charge which might detonate at any moment. Lifting his field-glasses to focus on the circle of mines ringing the vessel, he ignored the newcomers arriving on the already overcrowded bridge. Because of the risk of imminent disaster he had ordered the British prisoners to be brought up from their cabin.

'Are we abandoning ship?' Prentice asked quietly.

'No!' Hahnemann's reply was savagely emphatic as his hand guided the lieutenant by the elbow to the rear of the bridge. 'We shall be landing shortly.'

'Through that lot!' Ford sounded incredulous as he gazed over the colonel's shoulder along the searchlight beam which cut across the darkness. To port and starboard of the illuminated avenue at least four mines floated, metallic spheres which gleamed palely, their surfaces speckled with small shadows – the dreaded nozzles which caused instant detonation on contact. Burckhardt spoke briefly over his shoulder, instructing Hahnemann to tell them about the missing demolition charge; after all, they were soldiers, so they might as well know the position. With waning enthusiasm, Prentice and Ford listened to Hahnemann and were then pushed to the rear of the bridge, squeezed in between a press of uniformed Alpenkorps troops. Looking to his right, Prentice found he was huddled next to the large German civilian who had come aboard at Istanbul. On their way up from the cabin they had seen him in the distance climbing a staircase and Prentice had enquired who he was.

'Herr Dietrich is with the Abwehr,' Hahnemann had replied with a hint of respect in his voice. Prentice looked up curiously at the huge figure who stared back at him as he lit a fresh cigar with one elbow rested on the shoulder of the corporal next to him. A rum cove, this Dietrich, was Prentice's reaction as he turned to listen to Ford who was keeping his voice down.

'How big did he say that demolition charge was? I couldn't catch all he said in this crush.'

'Ten kilograms. Is that bad?'

'It's not good, I can tell you that straight off. And if it's been dumped near the boilers and they go, too . . .'

He broke off as Burckhardt issued a stream of orders to Eberhay who had appeared at the door to the bridge and then hurried away when the colonel had finished speaking. They were close to the moment of disembarkation, which required disciplined control, and the little major was facing something like near-panic as the troops filed up the staircases. It was then that Prentice saw the Alpenkorps equipment which confirmed his worst fears: he had a glimpse of men with skis of hickory wood passing beyond the bridge. The skis were carried on their backs which also supported rucksacks – which could only mean they expected to be operating in the deep snows on Mount Zervos at the far end of the peninsula. The Alpenkorps' main objective was the natural observation post of the monastery which overlooked the mainland road carrying Allied supplies northward.

'Funny that bomb hasn't gone off already,' he remarked lightly to Ford. He would have liked to feel that he was praying for the charge to detonate, but the truth was that he was sick with apprehension. 'Perhaps the chap who fixed it didn't know what he was doing,' he suggested.

'That's possible, sir. But their time fuses aren't all that reliable – a Jerry we had in the bag told me that. The damned things have a habit of conking out at the wrong moment.'

'You mean they become harmless?' Prentice tried to keep the hope out of his voice.

'Now I didn't say that, did I? Apparently they sometimes stop and then start up again. Vibrations can get them going again as easy as winking. The ship's engines are ideal for the purpose.'

'That's right, cheer us all up.' Prentice did not feel particularly reassured. Ford was an ammunition examiner who spent too much of his life fiddling with things which might go bang in his face at any second – including enemy explosives and equipment on which he was also something of an expert. But here on this German-held vessel he was displaying distinct signs of nervousness as he pulled at the lobe of one ear and kept looking round the bridge as though he expected it to disappear without warning.

'Fasten those straps at once!' Hahnemann had returned briefly to the bridge and had noticed that Ford's life-jacket was loose. Every man on the bridge wore his life-jacket and these cumbersome objects took up more space and further impeded movement. Prentice had the feeling that he would soon be lifted clear off the floor if anyone else crowded in on the bridge. He jerked his head round again to look through the rear window which gave a view along the deck towards the stern, a deck which was almost deserted since the order for uniformed troops to keep out of sight was still in force. Almost deserted, but not quite. Prentice's eyes narrowed as he watched sea mist drift past a lamp near the starboard rail: by its light he saw a short, heavily built man on the wrong side of the rail, a man who carried a rifle over his back. Something about the shape and the movement reminded him of the Greek civilian who had also come aboard at Istanbul. Grapos, the captain had called him. Mist blurred the view and when it cleared the poised figure was gone. He had dived over the side.

'Seen a ghost, sir?' Ford inquired.

'I've got a crick in my neck if you're referring to my expression of almost unendurable agony.' Prentice felt sure that at the last minute Dietrich had also glanced through that window, but by then the mist would have blotted out the lonely figure. He was greatly relieved when the German said nothing and continued quietly smoking the cigar which was now adding to the growing foetid atmosphere inside the packed bridge. So Grapos had made a dive for it and was heading for the shore fast. Some people are lucky, he thought, and then he remembered the mine-strewn waters the Greek was swimming through at that very moment and he suppressed a shudder. Despite the number of men compressed inside the confined space it was very silent on the bridge in the intervals between Burckhardt giving sharp orders as officers and NCOs appeared at the door, a silence of suppressed dread which hung over their still heads like a pall as the engines slowly beat out their mechanical rhythm and the *Hydra* continued to turn eastwards.

The bows of the vessel were now moving through drifts of white mist which were fogging visibility, yet a further source of anxiety to Burckhardt, who had now left off his civilian raincoat and was dressed in full uniform with the Alpenkorps broad-brimmed cap set firmly on his head. Nopagos stood like a man of wax, his eyes trying to bore through the mist-curtain at the earliest possible moment. Schnell was crouched in a permanent stoop over the wheel, glancing frequently to starboard where the nearest mine bobbed gently less than fifty metres from the hull. At least, he hoped that was the nearest mine. From his all-round view at the rear, Prentice was looking from face to face, noting the gleam of sweat on tightly drawn skin, the nervous twitch of an eyelid, the hands which gripped rifles and machine-pistols so tensely that the knuckles were whitened. These men, all over the ship, were under the maximum possible pressure. They were going into action by dawn. They knew that the sea ahead was alive with mines, and that somewhere, perhaps under their feet, the time fuse was ticking down to zero. If someone had determined to bring well-night unbearable pressure on their morale they could scarcely have planned it better than this. He looked to his right again. Dietrich, outwardly the most composed man on the bridge, was still calmly smoking his cigar and looking down at Prentice as though assessing his character and qualities in an emergency.

'Not more than half an hour at the most.' Ford's voice was little more than a whisper, a whisper motivated more by a dislike of breaking the doom-like silence than by a wish not to be overheard.

'Less than that, I imagine. If we ever get there.' Prentice looked again at the landing-stage light which was visible and closer now the mist had temporarily cleared. And there seemed to be light in the east on the far side of the peninsula. Hoisting his wrist upwards, he looked at his watch. Exactly 5.45 AM. Schnell was turning the wheel to straighten course as Burckhardt transmitted an instruction he had received from Nopagos; Dietrich was studying the end of his cigar rather dubiously; a soldier was wiping moisture from his forehead; and

Ford was looking round the bridge with quick darting glances when the explosion came.

The silence on the bridge was ruptured by a shattering roar. The *Hydra* shuddered from bows to stern as though struck by a mammoth blow and then wobbled. A wave was carried away from the ferry and swept towards the shore as it gathered up more water in its headlong flight from the vessel. For a few brief seconds it had been as light as day to starboard where a brilliant flash temporarily blinded those who had been looking in that direction. From beyond the open door of the bridge came a babble of panic-stricken voices and the sound of nailed boots scattering across the decks. Stark gibbering panic had seized the ship and on the packed bridge the hysterical murmuring was only silenced by Burckhardt thundering for quiet. He pushed aside Nopagos who had been leaning out of the window to starboard and leaned out himself. The sea appeared to have gone mad as it heaved and bubbled frothily. For a second Burckhardt thought that they had been struck by a torpedo and that a submarine was surfacing. Then the water began to settle. Schnell still held the ship on course, heading for the landing-stage which was coming closer and closer in the darkness, and he spoke without looking at the colonel. 'The mine was very close when it detonated.'

'It was a mine, just a mine, we have not been hit...' Hahnemann shouted out the news in German and then in English to stem the signs of panic.

'Well, if that doesn't start it ticking, nothing will,' Ford remarked grimly.

'It?' Prentice was still a little dazed with relief as well as shock.

'The demolition charge,' said Ford, whose mind was never far from explosives. 'If the time fuse mechanism had stopped only temporarily that thump was quite enough to get it moving again, believe you me.'

'I was under the impression that we had hit a mine,' Prentice told him icily. 'That's enough to be going on with, I should have thought.'

'Well, obviously we didn't – we're still steaming on course

at the same speed. The mine just went off on its own accord rather too close for comfort.' He was having to lift his voice for Prentice to hear him above the shouts on deck as Burckhardt thrust his way roughly off the bridge and went out on deck himself.

'You mean they can be defective, too?'

'Frequently. They can go off without rhyme or reason. On the other hand something else may have bumped into it – although I can't imagine what.'

Prentice began to feel slightly ill. He could imagine what else might have bumped into that mine in its frantic efforts to reach the shore. He had a picture in his mind of Grapos diving overboard with that protruding rifle attached to his back, of him swimming among the mines and so easily forgetting the barrel projecting beyond his body. There would be nothing left of the poor devil now. Prentice didn't like to think of what explosive which could take out a ship's bottom might do to a single human being as it detonated within a few feet of the swimming body.

'I think that little bang has rattled them,' Ford remarked.

'It rattled me,' Prentice replied with feeling. He looked back through the rear window where there was a state of confusion on the deck below. Alpenkorps men in full uniform who had been huddled close to the rail were being sent under cover by Volber who was waving his arms like a man shepherding sheep back to the fold. Within a minute the deck was clear and the babble of voices beyond the open door had ceased when Burckhardt came back to take up his post behind Nopagos. But the damage had been done. Another heavy blow had been dealt at the morale of troops who, on land would have taken the explosion in their stride, but cooped up on the unfamiliar sea the experience was having an entirely different effect. Prentice thought he could see in the faces in front of him a little extra strain, a trace more tension as the cold light from the east died in the false dawn and the landing-stage light at Katyra drew steadily closer.

Schnell was showing great skill as he steered the *Hydra* on the last stage of her perilous course, threading his way between a scatter of mines which floated in the path of the searchlight beam. An oppressive silence had fallen on the limping vessel as she moved through the dark water which was impenetrable beyond the beam, water supporting perhaps a hundred more mines for all Burckhardt could tell. The men on the decks below were waiting – waiting for the final collision with a mine, waiting for the still-hidden demolition charge to detonate under them, waiting for the tension-fraught moment of the landing – although which of these hazards was uppermost in their strained minds it was impossible to guess. The engines ticked over monotonously as the ferry slipped towards a blurred shadow which was the coast.

Plagued by a dozen anxieties, Burckhardt maintained his outward appearance of calm confidence while inwardly he fretted at the damnably crawling progress of the vessel. He was already nearly thirty minutes behind his timetable and he was praying that the news of the general offensive launched at 5.45 AM was not yet on the air. It was unlikely – an hour or two should pass before the world read the reports of the German onslaught on Greece and Yugoslavia spearheaded by the Panzers and reinforced with airborne troops – and the peninsula was still devoid of Allied troops and wide open to his attack. The whole key to the operation was a swift dash back along the peninsula and the capture of the monastery before the Allies had time to recover their balance. Just so long as there really was nothing standing in his way – and that they were able to land safely. He felt the chill of the early morning air filtering through his uniform and braced himself to control a shiver as Dietrich appeared at his elbow.

'The inhabitants of Katyra are bound to have heard the mine explode,' the Abwehr man remarked.

'I realize that,' Burckhardt replied non-committally.

'So there is a serious risk that someone may have phoned through to Salonika.'

'We have attended to that, so once again you can put your mind at rest,' Burckhardt began ironically. Then he paused: they were so close to going ashore that really he was free to speak more openly. 'There is only a single telephone line out of the peninsula, Herr Dietrich, and that was cut several hours ago.'

'Good. But Salonika may wonder why the line has gone dead.'

'Last night's storm will account for that. In a way it was lucky – it has provided an explanation.'

'And you have transport waiting for you as well?' Dietrich inquired genially.

'There are mules on the peninsula. It was impossible to bring them with us but we shall find mules available. The planning has taken into account every possible contingency. As to transport, other arrangements have also been made...' Burckhardt trailed off vaguely and lifted his glasses, focusing on a mine which floated, so it seemed, only a few metres off the port bow. The vessel was already changing course to avoid the menace.

'And you expect no opposition?' Despite the atmosphere of suspense on the bridge Dietrich's manner was almost pleasant as he bowed his head to listen to the colonel's reply.

'None at all. There is no one to oppose us – except a handful of fishermen.'

'There are two policemen on the peninsula – or there were when I was last here.' Dietrich was very close to becoming jocular and good-humoured, a mood he shared with no one else on the silent bridge.

Burckhardt made a great effort to respond. 'I think we can manage if they appear. You come ashore with me, of course.'

'I had assumed that!' Dietrich stared round slowly as though he found it instructive to see the reactions of a company of soldiers about to go ashore into the unknown as dawn broke. He met stolid eyes, tightly shut mouths, and once he caught Prentice's gaze as the lieutenant stared back at him curiously. 'I have my Luger,' he told Burckhardt amiably, 'just in case of trouble.'

'There is to be no shooting!' Burckhardt spoke sharply and for the first time he turned and looked directly at Dietrich. 'My men have strict orders to go ashore quietly. It will increase the element of surprise and their first task is to set up a road-block at the northern end of the village. The first troops ashore will see to that.'

'And when do you expect to take the monastery?'

'Who said we were interested in monasteries, Herr Dietrich? This is a war we are fighting, not a religious campaign.' And having delivered this rebuke the colonel turned away and devoted his whole attention to the lamp which was now so close that they could see it perched at the end of a stone jetty. Under the lamp stood two men, woken up doubtless by the explosion of the mine and anxious to hear what had happened. They're in for a surprise, Burckhardt was thinking as he saw the Abwehr man easing his way towards the door. I suppose he's checking up on our arrangements for the landing so he can put that in his report to Canaris. Still, with his knowledge of the peninsula he might come in useful yet. Burckhardt looked up as Hahnemann appeared in the doorway when Dietrich went outside.

'Start withdrawing men from the search for the Greek and assemble them for disembarkation,' Burckhardt told him. 'What about the demolition charge?'

'No sign of it, sir. We are still searching . . .'

'Withdraw all men from the search except for those in the engine-room. Any news of the Greek?'

'He hasn't been seen, sir.'

Burckhardt removed the glove he had been wearing from his pistol hand and nodded. 'The Greek doesn't matter any more. Later the search can be continued by the men left to guard the ship.' It was only a minor element in the meticulous plan – guarding the ship to make sure no one tried to take her across the gulf to warn the British. Burckhardt checked his watch. 5.55 AM. Yes, they were thirty minutes late. It would be dawn just about the time they landed; already he could see faintly a low ridge silhouetted against a streak of cold grey light. The countryside in this part of the peninsula was hilly, with a single road to the south which wound its way between the hills until it reached the plateau. From there on the terrain became steadily worse, culminating in the grim wilderness of precipices and sheer ascents of the heights of Zervos.

'You will be responsible for the security of the British prisoners,' he told Sergeant Volber who had just entered the bridge to report that his section was ready for disembarkation. He had already decided that they would be taken half-way along the peninsula and then left there under guard. This obviated any possibility of their being captured and released by a Greek unit which might be sent to the peninsula from Salonika. The information they possessed as to the unit's strength was a little too valuable to share with the enemy. He glanced back at the two men who stared at him with expressionless faces.

'Looks as though they're going to make it,' Ford whispered, 'although I wouldn't bet a brass farthing on the outcome yet.'

'Looks as though *we* might make it,' Prentice corrected him drily. 'And frankly, I wish you hadn't said that – it's asking for that demolition thing to trip its whatnot.'

'There's time yet, sir,' Ford assured him.

Schnell was now having to conduct an awkward manoeuvre to evade a single mine floating dead ahead. He had to steer the vessel round the mine and then alter course afresh to bring the ship up against the side of the jetty. Burckhardt could see that the glowing lamp was a lantern fixed to the top of a low mast and underneath it a small group of figures was huddled. He sent several men off the bridge, ordered the rest to keep in the shadows and joined them. This last mine was causing further delay and he felt the impatience surging up: he wanted to be off this damned Greek ferry, to get ashore and get on with it. And it was not only the timetable which made him curse that so inconveniently placed mine – that object so thoughtfully dropped by his allies was providing more time for the hidden demolition charge to detonate. He prayed to God that it wouldn't happen at the last moment, but a streak of pessimism in his nature made him fear the worst. In war, the chance happenings, the coincidences, were always bad ones. He had learned that in Finland where he had experienced the Winter War as assistant to the German military attaché in Helsinki when the Finns had fought the Russians to a ferocious standstill, in Norway where he had commanded ... He spoke quickly in Greek as Nopagos moved to the starboard window. 'Stay by the wheel!'

'If they see me they will be reassured.' Nopagos still stood by the window as he looked over his shoulder. His face was despondent and he looked as though he could hardly stand up:

132

this was probably the last voyage of the *Hydra* and he was bringing home the most terrible cargo he had ever carried. 'I don't want any harm to come to them – if they start to run away...'

'My men have orders not to shoot.' Burckhardt hesitated. The fight had gone out of the captain and it gave a greater appearance of normality if he could be seen clearly on the bridge. 'You can stay there,' he said, 'but you are not to call out to them.'

Dawn was beginning to spread over the peninsula as Schnell edged his way round the solitary mine, and the bleak light showed a landscape still in the grip of winter. The olive trees on the scrub-covered hills were naked silhouettes and along the jetty a coating of frost glittered with the colour of *crème de menthe* over stones green with age. The little group under the lamp which glowed eerily in the half-light stood hunched up with their hands in their pockets and one man was stamping his feet on the stones. An appearance of absolute normality. Another ferry trip ending its voyage quietly as a matter of seagoing routine. Which was very satisfactory, Burckhardt was thinking. Near the end of the jetty, a simple mole which projected straight out into the gulf, the beach was visible, a beach of rocks and stones. And behind the beach a high sea-wall stretched away into the distance. The intelligence people had warned him about that unscalable sea-wall – had emphasized that the only entrance to the village was a gap in the wall at the end of the jetty where a causeway linked the mole with the road into Katyra. Burckhardt was looking beyond the wall now to the short line of two-storeyed houses which were shuttered and still like abandoned villas. The whole place had the look of a resort which is only open during the summer months. It was all going according to plan. They would land without any fuss, occupy the village, set up the road-block to the north, and within an hour the main body of the troops would be moving south into the heart of the peninsula. An officer Prentice had not seen before came on to the bridge to report and the colonel motioned him back into the shadows.

'Major Eberhay reports everything ready for disembarkation, sir.'

'Good. The wireless set is being guarded by two men, I take it, Brandt?'

'Yes, sir. The major saw to it himself.'

'Tell him those civilians on the jetty are not to be brought on board because of the demolition charge. He can keep them on the beach and they can be escorted back into the village later.'

As Brandt left the bridge Burckhardt thought about the wireless set. Until the sabotaged set was repaired it was their only means of communication with GHQ to confirm that the reinforcements could be flown in. It was, in fact, one of the most vital pieces of equipment in the expedition. Without that he would be on his own and there could be the most appalling muddle when they arrived at the plateau. The vessel had almost circumnavigated the pestilential mine and was creeping in towards the jetty where the little group had shifted position. Prentice had moved closer to the window and Burckhardt warned a guard that he mustn't get any closer. When he looked to starboard again the jetty was almost under the ship's hull.

The lower slopes of the hills were still in darkness as the gangway clattered onto the jetty. Major Eberhay was the first man ashore and a moment later Nopagos joined him, followed by a dozen Alpenkorps soldiers. These troops were unarmed, their collars nearly buttoned to the neck, and one man carried a plaque struck to commemorate the commencement of collaboration between Greek and German peoples. Only the space for the date was left blank. Drawn up in files of threes, they marched steadily along the jetty top in the direction of the causeway which led to Katyra. The plaque was for presentation to the mayor of Katyra. Outwardly, for the first few minutes, the disembarkation had the appearance of an arranged visit as the Alpenkorps paraded away into the distance. Only a band was absent to mark the occasion.*

'No resistance, please! We are overwhelmed!' It was

* The same technique was practised in Norway where the first unit of invading Germans ashore at Oslo was a brass band which played and marched through the capital to simulate a peaceful visit.

134

Nopagos who delivered the urgent message to the group of four men who stood stunned under the lamp as the troops passed them. It was not quite the message which Burckhardt had instructed him to deliver but it served the same effect. One man, larger and burlier than the others, took a step backwards as though to move away, but he was restrained by the leading soldier in the next section of troops leaving the ship. The German put a firm hand on the civilian's arm and ushered him back to the group which stared at the ferry as though hardly able to believe their eyes. The third file of men pouring off the vessel were heavily armed, their rucksacks on their backs, their rifles looped over their shoulders, and short bayonets sheathed in leather scabbards by their sides.

From the bridge Burckhardt watched the landing operation with approval and relief. It was all going according to plan. The leading section had already disappeared through the gap in the sea-wall and within minutes would reach their first objective – the mayor's house. It was light enough now to see the Greek flag fluttering in a breeze from a tower behind the wall. He checked his watch again as the file of armed troops began to cross the causeway. Half-way along the jetty the group of four Greeks was being hustled towards the beach while more troops marched past them. Yes, everything was going according to plan. A moment later the firing started.

The firing, which commenced immediately the Greek civilians were clear of the jetty, came at the worst possible moment for Burckhardt. The entire mole from gangway to causeway was dense with disembarking troops and the ski sections were just filing off the ship. It was one of these men, encumbered with the skis over his back, who fell as the first shot rang out. Instantly, what had been an orderly disembarkation became a scene of chaos as the falling soldier crashed into his comrades and caused several to stumble. A second shot rang out and a second man on the jetty fell close to the first casualty. There was a danger of an imminent pile-up of men as the mole seethed with field-grey figures. Burckhardt swore and leaned over the bridge to look down at the open deck below where Hahnemann was issuing quick instructions, shouting to the men to clear the jetty and move inland. A third shot was fired and four men close together half-way along the jetty paused, then began to run towards the causeway, but as they ran one of their number sprawled lifelessly on the jetty floor. Burckhardt left the bridge and made for the open deck. At the top of the staircase Dietrich was staring across the peninsula and as Burckhardt ran past him he noted a trivial detail: for the first time, so far as he could remember, the Abwehr man was no longer smoking a cigar. He was running down the staircase when he heard a fusillade of shots – the Alpenkorps were returning the fire, although what the God they thought they were shooting at Burckhardt had no idea. From his commanding position on the bridge he had been quite unable to locate the source of the attack.

At the bottom of the steps he noted a less trivial detail – the battalion wireless, the last set still in serviceable condition, was stowed against the wall with the flap opened back. An Alpenkorps soldier stood close by guarding the precious equipment. As soon as they had taken Katyra Burckhardt had to send the vital signal, *Phase One completed*. Despite the air of total confusion which now pervaded the vessel where men crouched low behind the rails or ran down the gangway urged on by Hahnemann, the colonel was still thinking clearly and a disturbing idea had entered his mind. Three shots, three casualties. That was the work of a marksman. It was quickly apparent that Hahnemann was disembarking the troops with all speed so Burckhardt, still concerned with his simple calculation, went swiftly back to the bridge where he could see what was happening. He arrived there in time to see more men hurrying along the jetty too close together as the firing continued. A man near the edge stopped as though struck by an invisible blow, tried to stagger forward a few steps, then plunged over the edge. He hit the water with a splash and when the body surfaced it floated motionlessly.

The fusillade continued for several minutes while the Alpenkorps constantly disembarked and ran the gauntlet of the exposed jetty. During the firing Burckhardt ordered the two remaining guards on the bridge to take Prentice and Ford below ready for going ashore. Schnell had left earlier so now he was alone on the bridge as the fusillade ceased suddenly.

He waited, turning his eyes now to the lower hill slopes still in the fading shadow of night. Hahnemann had carried out his order to cease fire abruptly and then hold fire for five minutes. Earlier, the colonel had assumed that those shots were coming from behind one of the shuttered windows, but so far he had seen nothing to confirm this. Half-a-dozen men were risking the jetty run again, their bodies crouched low as they ran past the huddled shapes lying on the stones. A single shot split the silence only broken by the thud of nailed boots on paved stone. One man fell. The others ran on, disappearing through the gap in the wall. On the bridge Burckhardt twisted his mouth grimly. He had seen it this time – the muzzle-flash in the hills to the south of the village. The marksman was indeed firing long-distance, and now he felt sure it was the work of one man. He left the bridge and Hahnemann met him at the foot of the staircase with news of the disaster.

'The second set is out of commission . . .'

'What!' Burckhardt was thunderstruck. He felt the blood rush to his head and paused before going on. 'How did it happen?'

'A bullet hit it – all the valves are smashed.'

A soldier was crouched over the set and he kept his head lowered as though afraid to face the colonel. Bending close to him, Burckhardt spoke very quietly. 'You were supposed to be guarding it, Dorff.'

'He could hardly have done anything,' Hahnemann interjected. 'He was by the rail firing off a few shots himself when it happened. He was never very far away from the set. It is just the most appalling bad luck, sir.'

'Bad luck, Hahnemann?' The colonel straightened up and stared at him. 'We have had one set sabotaged earlier in the voyage. Someone planted a demolition charge inside the vessel. And someone, at the beginning, set free the British prisoners. Haven't you grasped it yet that some unknown person is making sure that bad luck does come our way?' He turned as Dietrich walked round a corner and stopped to look down at the wrecked set.

'More?' he asked bluntly.

'A bullet has smashed all the valves. The set is quite use-

137

less.' Burckhardt studied the Abwehr man for a moment. 'Herr Dietrich, I believe you possess a Luger. Would you mind showing it to me?'

Without a word Dietrich extracted the pistol from his pocket and handed it to the colonel. While Burckhardt was examining the weapon he stood with his hands deep inside his pockets as he gazed along the jetty where the last troops were hurrying towards the village. It was almost daylight now and the buildings beyond the sea-wall showed up clearly in the pale sunshine. They had a decrepit, unpainted look and several tiles were missing from the shallow roofs which were a dull red colour. Once their walls had been brightly colour-washed but that had been a long time ago; now that the place could be seen properly in the dawn light it had shrunk from a shadowed village of some size to a tiny fishing hamlet of a few hundred people. Burckhardt had checked the gun, had found it fully loaded with seven rounds. He sniffed briefly at the barrel and then returned it. 'Thank you.' He looked at Hahnemann. 'We will go ashore. Tell Volber to bring the prisoners.'

Straightening his tunic, Burckhardt led the way onto Greek soil. Because of the *Hydra*'s list to port, the gangway was inclined at a steep angle, a detail he had overlooked, and he had to run down it onto the almost deserted jetty. Here again, he led the way, walking briskly but without undue haste, pausing to exchange a few words with two medical orderlies who were attending the casualties. One of them looked up and shook his head. Burckhardt resumed his even pace, knowing that men still aboard were watching him from the rails. Behind him came the Abwehr man, hands still inside his pockets, looking towards the south as he trailed the colonel, and behind him followed Prentice and Ford escorted by Volber and a private. At the end of the mole the colonel stopped and called down to Nopagos who was waiting with the other civilians on the beach. 'That Greek, Grapos, what other qualifications had he that you didn't tell me about?'

'He speaks English.'

Nopagos hadn't understood what the colonel was driving at and he saw the German stiffen. Burckhardt's reactions piled on top of one another. Was he being insolent? The question going through the colonel's head had been whether at some time Grapos might have undergone military service, perhaps before he contracted his limp. Grapos spoke English? As he walked on to the causeway Burckhardt tried to recall the sequence of events aboard the *Hydra*. Could Grapos have freed Prentice and Ford? He had been imprisoned in the hold at the time. Had he sabotaged both wireless sets? Was he still on board? Then who was that marksman in the hills ... Firmly, he pushed the riddle out of his thoughts as he went through the gap in the wall where a sentry had been posted. He saluted as the man jumped to attention.

Behind him Dietrich was taking his time about walking towards Katyra, dragging his feet until Volber and the prisoners caught up with him. He even stood quite still for a moment while he looked down at Nopagos, and when he continued along the causeway the prisoners and their escorts had passed and were a few paces in front of him. He appeared to be taking a great interest in the view to the south next, staring fixedly at the hills, and then he switched his attention to the sentry by the wall, noting the hand-grenade which hung from the soldier's belt. Finally, he looked back along the jetty to see if anyone else was close at hand. The gangplank was empty and there was no sign of more troops coming ashore. He turned round and called out.

'Volber! I think you're wanted back at the ship.'

The sergeant gestured to the prisoners to halt. They had just passed through the gap and beyond a dusty track wound out of sight past a stone building into the main part of Katyra. Burckhardt had almost reached the bend and Dietrich's words had not been spoken loudly enough to reach him. The sentry looked puzzled and stared at the *Hydra* where a tall figure could be seen at the head of the gangway with its back turned.

'What is it, sir?' Volber took a few paces towards the Abwehr man and his expression was uncertain. In the distance, over his shoulder, the colonel disappeared round the curve in the road which was now empty. Prentice was standing with his hands on his hips while Ford stared pointedly at the soldier who stood a few paces away with his rifle at the ready.

139

'I think you're wanted back at the ship,' Dietrich repeated. 'I saw Hahnemann beckoning.'

Volber was in a quandary. He had received explicit orders from the colonel to escort the prisoners personally into the village and he had no inclination to vary from Burckhardt's command by so much as a centimetre. But Lieutenant Hahnemann was the officer who could, and did, make life arduous for him. So he compromised briefly, waiting to see whether the beckoning was repeated from the gangway. Dietrich remained where he was, apparently absorbed in the panorama across the gulf. If one ignored the huddled group on the jetty and overlooked the signs of military invasion, it was an extraordinarily peaceful scene. By early daylight the Aegean was an intense, deep cobalt with a backdrop of misty mountains on the mainland which seemed almost unreal. At the head of the lonely gulf, where the sun caught the water at a certain angle, the sea glittered like mercury, and on the nearby beach small waves, rippled by the breeze, slid gently forward and collapsed.

Volber stirred restlessly. 'I can't wait any longer, sir,' he ventured, and Dietrich nodded as though he understood. He followed the sergeant through the gap and stopped suddenly when he saw, to his right, that two Alpenkorps soldiers stationed behind the wall had been concealed from his view. As he appeared they were looking at the hills to the south, but now they lowered their field-glasses, hoisted their machine-pistols more firmly over their shoulders, and walked back to the gap to take one last look at the vessel which had brought them all the way from Istanbul. Volber paused to have a word with them, making some joking reference to pleasure cruises, but Dietrich noticed that he was staring along the jetty in case Hahnemann appeared and started gesturing. Sighing out aloud, Prentice crossed onto the grass verge and sat down with his back to the wall where Ford joined him. Volber, standing in the middle of the gap with the other three soldiers, was about to reprimand him, when hell opened up on the gulf.

The reverberations of the detonation crashed round the hillsides, roared out across the gulf like a cannonade, and sent a shock wave like a bombardment through the gap in the wall. The demolition charge had reached zero. Dietrich, half-protected by the wall, was thrown sprawling onto the grass, and he thought he heard two explosions close together – the charge first, then the boilers going up. The full force of the wave had struck the four Alpenkorps soldiers like a giant hammer and they lay in the road like trampled rag dolls. Only two men were moving feebly and one of them fell limp almost immediately as he lost consciousness. The sentry was bunched up against the outside of the wall in a strangely twisted position. As Dietrich lay on the grass, temporarily deafened by the road, there was a stench of burning oil in his nostrils and Prentice and Ford, whose ears had not been affected, heard debris clattering on the village rooftops like spent shrapnel from ack-ack guns.

For both of them the immensely strong sea-wall had muffled the blast. But Dietrich was recovering quickly. As he staggered to his feet Prentice began to move up behind him with a rock in his fist. The Abwehr man, unaware of what was happening behind him, fished the Luger out of his pocket, looked quickly up the road and along the jetty, and moved towards the soldier who was climbing to his feet in the centre of the road. Prentice, moving soundlessly on the grass, followed Dietrich as he lurched towards the soldier who had now brought himself to his knees and was shaking his head like a dog emerging from a river. He looked up as Dietrich brought the Luger barrel crashing down on his head. He was slumping to the ground when Dietrich tugged the loop of the machine-pistol free. Prentice stared in astonishment, the rock still poised in his hand, but when he saw the machine-pistol he moved forward again. The Abwehr man turned, knocked the unsteady fist aside and thrust the weapon into Prentice's hands. 'This will be more useful – if you can handle the damned thing.'

He had spoken in English and without waiting for Prentice's reaction he hauled another machine-pistol loose from an inert German, tossed it across to Ford, and then extracted spare magazines from the pockets of the two men on the ground. When he stood up he noticed that it was Ford who was familiar with the machine-pistol and shoved the magazines at him. 'Here – it looks as though they'd be more use to you.

141

Now, we've got to get moving pdq. We go that way – along the wall to the south.'

'Who the devil are you?' Prentice demanded.

'Dietrich of the Abwehr.'

The reply was given ironically as the large man stared briefly along the jetty wall. The *Hydra* looked like a refugee from an Atlantic convoy. The funnel was bent at a surrealist angle and her bows were already settling in the shallow water. Around the hull men swam in the sea distractedly as a huge column of black smoke ascended into the clear sky like a gigantic signal which would be seen clear across the bay to the mainland. As he gazed at the wreckage a tongue of red flame flared up at the base of the distorted funnel. Soon the whole superstructure would be ablaze and would go on burning until the hulk was reduced to its waterline and the *Hydra* was a blackened shell. All Burckhardt's efforts at preserving an appearance of normality had gone up with the demolition charge. 'I thought she'd never blow,' he said half to himself, and then he saw Nopagos clambering up onto the jetty. The shock wave must have blown straight over the heads of the group on the beach. He looked back towards the town and the road was still empty. 'They'll be coming soon,' he warned, 'so let's get to hell out of here.'

'Which way? The village is crawling with them ...'

'Along this wall – five years ago I walked all over this place. We've got to head up the peninsula ...'

'But who the devil are you?' Prentice repeated, and when the reply came the Scots burr was even more pronounced.

'I'm Ian Macomber.' He grabbed at the lieutenant's arm. 'Now, if you don't want to get shot, follow me and run like hell!'

CHAPTER EIGHT

Sunday, 10 AM

By ten o'clock in the morning they had marched almost non-stop through punishing hill country which had caused them either to climb or descend most of the way, and they had still seen no trace of Grapos. It was Macomber who had urged them on mercilessly, insisting that they put as much ground as possible between themselves and the oncoming Germans before they rested. Several times Prentice had tried to talk and ask questions, but on each occasion the Scot had brusquely told him to save his breath for the march. They followed a footpath which twisted and turned as its surface changed, sometimes sand, sometimes rock and often merely beaten earth. A path which led them past olive groves, over hilltops ringed with boulders, and down into scrub-infested valleys where the streams raced with swelling waters. But now they had reached a hilltop where Macomber consented to pause briefly because it gave a clear view back to the north where the road from Katyra came towards them in a series of bends and drops down the near sides of hills dense with undergrowth.

'We can see them coming from here,' Macomber announced as he perched on a rounded boulder. 'And water is going to be our problem. There isn't much of it on the plateau.'

'This might help,' Ford suggested as he undid his coat and showed a pear-shaped water-bottle attached to his belt. 'I filched that off one of those dead Jerries while you two pulled yourselves together.'

'Ford gets his priorities right,' Prentice remarked, and then stared hard at Macomber. 'Mind if I hear a little more about you now?'

Macomber took a swig from the water-bottle, handed it on to Prentice and grinned faintly. 'I've spent the last fifteen

143

months in the Balkans. Do you think that sounds cushy?'

'Depends what you were doing,' Prentice replied cautiously. 'What were you doing?'

'I'll tell you, then. I'm like Winston Churchill as far as ancestry goes – half-British and half-American. My mother was a New Yorker and my father came from Aberdeen. I spent a third of my early years in the States, another third in Scotland, and the rest of the time travelling round Europe with my parents. My father was a linguistics expert and I inherited his gift for languages.' There was no modesty in Macomber's tone but neither was he boasting; he was simply stating a fact. 'And that's where the trouble started,' he went on. 'Principally my languages are German, Greek and French – which comes in useful when you're in Rumania. I had lung trouble before the war ...'

'Lung trouble!' Prentice looked sceptical, remembering the tremendous pace the Scot had set up while they were making their dash up and down those endless hills.

'It's cured now – at least so a quack in Budapest assured me. He said it was the pure clean air from Siberia which blows across Hungary in winter that had done the trick. But that lung kept me out of the Forces in 1939, so the Ministry of Economic Warfare asked me to do a job for them. Get your head out of the way, Ford, I can't see that road.'

'What sort of a job?' Prentice asked casually. Without appearing to do so he was trying to check the Scot's story.

'Buying up strategic war materials the Jerries wanted. You'd never believe the funds I had at my disposal. I bought up everything I could lay my hands on and had it shipped out of the Balkans. I had an idea the bright boys foresaw the German *Drach nach Osten* and wanted to denude the place before Hitler arrived.'

'Sounds interesting,' was Prentice's only comment.

'You think so? Just sitting behind a desk and making out orders in quadruplicate for a few thousand gallons of oil or the odd few tons of copper – is that how you see it?'

'I didn't say so.'

'No, but you looked so!' He took out one of his remaining cigars. 'What I don't think you've quite grasped is that I had

144

competitors, Jerry competitors, and they can play very rough, very rough indeed. When I'd survived two attempts to kill me – one in Györ and one in Budapest – I decided my luck was running out and the time had come to go underground, so I acquired some false papers and set up as a German.' He looked quizzically at Prentice over his cigar, put it back in his mouth and went on talking. 'Don't look so damned unbelieving – false papers can be obtained almost anywhere if you have the money, and I had a small fortune to play with.'

'You set up as Dietrich, then?'

'No, he came later. I called myself Hermann Wolff, and, you know, necessity really did turn out to be the mother of invention. I found myself mixing openly with the German community in Budapest, which in the beginning was simply excellent camouflage, but later when I ran out of stuff to buy up it gave our Ministry brains another idea, a diabolical idea.' He turned again to look over his shoulder at the hill behind, in the opposite direction from where the Germans must come, and this was a gesture he had repeated several times.

'Isn't that the wrong direction to fret over?' Prentice inquired. 'Or could they have got ahead of us on the road while we were doing our cross-country route march?'

'Old habits...' Dietrich spread a large hand. 'I've spent so many months looking over my shoulder – because the danger always comes from where you least expect it.' He shrugged and stared at Ford for a moment. 'When it comes, it comes.'

'A diabolical job, you were saying,' Prentice reminded him. As he listened he scanned the deserted countryside to the north where a dark smoke column from the burning *Hydra* was still climbing into the brilliant morning sky. They'd see that smoke as far away as Salonika, almost, if the weather visibility was as good across Macedonia. It seemed incredible that a whole German expedition was mustering itself somewhere beyond those hills for a forced march south to Mount Zervos.

'Yes, truly diabolical,' Macomber repeated. 'There were hardly any more strategic supplies I could lay my hands on, but there was a mass of stuff the Germans had bought up which still hadn't been shipped back to the Reich. It was lying around in warehouses and railway sidings, so the Ministry brainboxes said would I have a go at it? Very obliging they were, too – sent out an explosives man to teach me a trick or two about things that go bang in the night...' He paused again, detecting a sudden freshening of interest from Ford, but when the ammunition examiner said nothing he continued. 'The trouble again was I was made to order for these sabotage jobs. I picked up information from the German community I was mixing with about what was where – and by then I was accepted in Budapest. We even used German explosives – like ten-kilogram demolition charges.'

'Why not British equipment?' queried Ford.

'Because I was operating in neutral territory and the Hungarian government might not have taken too kindly to British time-bombs being planted inside their goods wagons. Those bombs don't always function according to the book and sometimes they don't function at all. Even when they do, the experts can often piece together a few vital bits and tell the type of bomb that was used and where it was made.' He glanced over his shoulder and grinned again. 'And don't ask me how we got hold of German explosives because that's a state secret.'

'You were pretty successful in passing yourself off as a German even in Hungary then?' Prentice suggested idly. He felt close to exhaustion but his mind was still sufficiently alert to go on checking Macomber's identity so far as he could.

'I knew the Reich well by the time war broke out. In peacetime I'd been a shipping broker – some of my business was with the Reich and I spent a lot of time in Germany before 1939 and sometimes, even then, it was convenient to pass for one of the *Herrenvolk*. The trick is to learn to think like them, to feel you are one of them – and that's something I had to work overtime at while we were on the *Hydra*. I may tell you that was the longest voyage of my life, and it took just twenty-four hours.'

'How did you fool the colonel? That must have taken some doing.'

'The ability to bluff big – nothing else. I took a leaf out of the dear Führer's book there: if you want to believe a lie, be sure it's a whopper. If I'd tried to pass myself off simply as a

German civilian, I think they'd have restricted my movements, but the dreaded Abwehr was something quite different. I knew quite a lot about the Abwehr when I went aboard the *Hydra* at Istanbul – in fact, I thought they had somebody on my tail ready to do an assassination act before I could get home . . .'

'You weren't put on that ship deliberately then?' Prentice found it difficult to keep the surprise out of his voice. Ford was emptying the machine-pistol while he tested the mechanism and then re-loaded.

'No, I'd finished with the Balkans and I was on my way to Athens to get a berth to Egypt. The Germans had occupied the whole area and it wasn't possible to operate any more with the key points swarming with their security chaps. I was coming on the direct Istanbul–Athens ferry, but that was cancelled at the last moment. When Burckhardt's lot took over the ship I wasn't completely surprised – the presence of several Germans on the passenger list was something I'd been thinking about ever since I got on board.'

'But why pretend you were the Abwehr?'

'Because I knew how they operated – months ago they'd sent men to Budapest to investigate the sabotage. But mainly because it's the only organization inside Germany today which the armed forces get nervous about. Burckhardt was convinced I'd been put on the ship to check up on how he handled things – which gave me a psychological stranglehold over him from the outset.'

'You make it sound so damned easy.' There was a hint of admiration in Prentice's manner as he sat with his back propped against a boulder and waited.

'Oh, very easy – as easy as moving round inside Hungary and Rumania with top Abwehr agents on your tail. As easy as making frequent trips to wayside railway stations to collect suitcases left by someone you never see – suitcases containing demolition charges. As easy as lugging them across railway lines at two in the morning with engines shunting all over the place and guards with dogs looking for you.' Macomber's voice had risen to a low growl as he glared at Prentice with an intensity of rage which was alarming. 'As easy as going back to

147

your flat late in the evening and noticing that the lock has been tampered with – so you know that inside that darkened flat someone is waiting for you with a knife or a gun or whatever particular weapon they've decided will do the job quickly and quietly. Yes, Prentice, and it was easy on that ship we've just left, too – easy putting those wireless sets out of action with two hundred troops all around you, easy coming into your cabin to cut your ropes to give you a chance to get clear and warn that destroyer...'

'I'm sorry,' Prentice said quietly, realizing for the first time the tremendous pressure this man must have lived under for months, catching a glimpse of what it must have been like to go on living alone in the alien Balkans surrounded by enemies while he went on with his deadly work. He supposed that the outburst was the climax of God knew how much pent-up anxiety and living on the nerves endlessly, until it had seemed it must go on for ever. Macomber made no attempt to apologize for the outburst but he smiled wintrily as he smoked his cigar and started talking again.

'Planting the demolition charge was simpler than you might imagine. I just saw it lying with the fuses in a half-open rucksack and grabbed it. There was a little trouble in the dark on deck when I ran into a soldier, but a knowledge of unarmed combat can come in useful. Afterwards, I pitched him over the side like you did your chap. The vital moment was when we'd just come ashore – I'd always foreseen that.'

'Why then?' asked Prentice.

'Several reasons. Burckhardt's whole attention was taken up with the landing and capturing Katyra quickly. Later, he'd have more time to think, which is just what I didn't want him to have. Then there was the problem of the other wireless set – I'd messed up the tuning coil with the butt of my Luger but I gathered they might be able to repair the thing. The moment they could wireless for confirmation of my identity I was finished. And you can thank whatever lucky star you were born under that the bomb didn't go off earlier – it must have stopped and then started again.'

'What time had you set it for?' Prentice was taking a great interest in the answer to this question and now he saw Ford looking over his shoulder towards the hill behind them. Macomber's fears were contagious.

'I set it to detonate at 3.30 AM while we were still well down the gulf.'

'Good God!'

A trace of the nervous reaction still smouldered inside Macomber and he didn't bother to put it too tactfully. 'I'm sure, Prentice, that by now you know there's a war on. There were two hundred German troops aboard who may yet do untold damage to the Allied cause – if I could sink them I was going to do it. And I still will, although how I haven't the slightest idea. You know they're heading for the monastery on Mount Zervos to set up an observation post, I take it?'

'I had an idea that was the objective. I agree we've got to get there first, if we can, but I can't quite see us forming the monks into a defensive battalion to hold off the Jerries. Is there any means of communication there we could use to get in touch with the mainland?'

'Not so far as I know apart from the telephone line to Salonika and that's been cut.' Macomber dropped the half-smoked cigar into the sand and carefully heeled it out of sight. 'But there's always something that can be done as long as you're there – that's something I've learned.' His expression became ferocious as he growled out the words. 'Whatever happens the Germans have got to be stopped from taking Zervos. Hell! If there's nothing else we'll have to set fire to the place to attract attention. There are British troops driving up that coast only a few miles across the gulf. Setting fire to the monastery may be the only solution!'

Prentice stared at the huge figure stooped forward over the boulder and realized that he meant what he said. Previously he had regarded Macomber as an enterprising civilian, with the accent on 'civilian', but now he began to wonder whether the war he had fought in the Western Desert compared with the shadowy, no-quarter struggle the Scot had waged inside the peace-time Balkans. He blinked to keep his eyes open as Macomber clasped both hands tightly and stared again at the road from Katyra with a dubious expression. It was over twenty-four hours since any of them had slept and the strain

149

showed in their whiskered haggard faces; the brain was beginning to slow down, the reflexes to react sluggishly, and these were danger signals. He was about to speak when Macomber made the suggestion himself. 'I think three-quarters of an hour's sleep would work wonders. We may need every ounce of strength we can muster before the day is out but someone must keep watch.' He grinned. 'So, if you two are sufficiently convinced of my bona-fides, I'll act as lookout while you get some kip.'

'No, I'll stand watch while you and Ford sleep,' Prentice said promptly. 'You've been through more than us, anyway.'

'Suit yourself,' was Macomber's terse reply. Dropping down off the boulder, he lay on the sand after casting one final look back at the hill behind. The hill looked dangerous was his last thought before he fell asleep.

Macomber was a man who, when he woke up, became instantly alert, all his faculties keyed up for immediate action. The trait had been sharpened during his experience in the Balkans and on waking he had developed another facility – the habit of never opening his eyes until he had listened for a few seconds. Lying on the sand with his back against the rock, he listened carefully to the sounds with his eyes still closed. The scrape of a boot over stone, which told him someone was moving nearby. The quick dull click of metal on metal, which was the movement of a rifle bolt. A coldness down his back was the physical reaction of his brain warning him of danger. Then a voice spoke. Prentice's.

'Don't move, Ford, for God's sake!'

Macomber's prone body was still relaxed and lifeless as he half-opened his eyes. Ford was sitting up on the sand, his suit crumpled, his right hand withdrawing from the machine-pistol which lay close by his side. He had a drugged look and had obviously just woken up. Macomber couldn't see Prentice but the thought flashed through his mind that the lieutenant must have dozed off and during those unguarded minutes a German patrol had arrived. Lying on his side, Macomber's hand was tucked inside his coat pocket where it had rested when he had fallen asleep, and now his fingers curled round the butt of the

150

Luger. The problem was going to be to get in an upright position quickly enough. From the direction of Ford's startled gaze he calculated that the newcomers were stationed behind the boulder he was leant against. But how many of them? The boot scraped again and the shadow of a man fell across the sand in front of where he lay, the shadow of a man and a gun.

'Wait! For God's sake wait!' A note of desperation in Prentice's voice chilled Macomber. 'We can explain – don't shoot!'

The silhouette of the rifle barrel angled lower and Macomber guessed that it was now tilted downwards and aimed at him point-blank. He sensed that the slightest movement of his body would activate the shadow's trigger finger, and while he compelled himself to stay relaxed he felt the stickiness of his palm clutching the pistol butt. A strange tingling sensation sang along his nerves and his brain hung in a horrible state of prolonged suspension as every tiny detail seemed weirdly clear. The appalled expression on Ford's face, the mouth half-open, held as though in a condition of rictus. The wobble of the unknown man's silhouette as he shifted balance to the other foot to take the shock of the rifle's recoil. The flitting motion of some tiny insect hopping over the sand in the shade of the silhouette. Macomber's throat had gone so dry that he felt the most terrible compulsion to cough as a tickle crawled in his throat.

'Do you understand any English at all?' Prentice again, his voice throaty with tension. 'We're on your . . .'

'Yes, I speak English.' A deep-chested voice with a rumbling timbre which sounded familiar. 'Why are you with the German?'

'Look, Grapos;' Prentice pleaded quickly, 'he's not a German. He's British. If you let him wake up and speak he'll talk to you in English as much as you want . . .'

'There are Germans who speak English.' Grapos' tone was unimpressed and savagely obstinate. 'I speak English but I am Greek. He has made you think he is English? We have very little time. He must be killed, now!' The gun silhouette moved again as though the Greek was taking fresh aim and

151

Macomber waited for the thud of the bullet, the last thing he would ever feel. And there was an urgency in Grapos' voice as well as in his words which filled the Scot with foreboding. There was some other danger coming very close, he felt sure of it, a danger the Greek was only too well aware of. Prentice was talking again and this time he was adopting an entirely different tactic, abandoning pleading as he spoke crisply as though he were giving a command.

'Look, I'm telling you, mate. His name is Macomber. Ian Macomber. He's a Scot – that's from the topside of my country – and he's the one who planted that bomb which nearly blew up all those Germans, only it didn't go off in time. He speaks fluent German – a damned sight more fluent German than you speak English. To help us get away he half-killed a Jerry – a German – in front of me. He grabbed a couple of German machine-pistols and gave them to us. Since then he's led the way to where we are now because he knows the country and we don't. And if that isn't enough for you, you can go and dive in the sea again. So stop aiming that gun at him and let him wake up and speak for himself.'

'You are sure of these things?' Grapos sounded anything but sure of what he had been listening to and the rifle was still pointed down at the inert figure below.

'I'm perfectly sure! Don't you think I can tell when I'm talking to one of my own countrymen? Wouldn't you know when you were talking to a Greek even if you'd heard that same man speaking good German earlier?' Prentice deliberately lost his temper a little, and seeing the look of doubt on Grapos' face he followed up quickly while he had the Greek off-balance. 'And now, for Pete's sake, can he get up and speak for himself? He must be awake now.'

'Yes ... I ... am ... awake.' Macomber spoke slowly and very clearly, resuming his normal manner of speech only when he saw the shadow of the gun move away. 'So can I get up and let you have another good look at me?'

'Yes, you may get up.' Grapos' boots scraped again as he spoke and when Macomber climbed to his feet the villainous-looking civilian was standing several paces beyond him with his weapon still held so that it could cover Macomber with only a fraction of movement. A German carbine, the Scot noted. The one he had gone overboard with. The one he had used to shoot down the Alpenkorps men on the jetty. Macomber's hands hung loosely by his sides and he gazed at Grapos without friendship as he asked the question with a single word.

'Well?'

'You look like a German.'

'And you look like a bandit.'

The Greek's eyes flashed. The gun muzzle lifted and was then lowered. He stared back grimly but with a certain respect as he slapped his rifle butt once and then turned to Prentice, ignoring Macomber as he spoke rapidly. 'There is trouble. German soldiers are coming up that hill on the other side ...' He indicated the hill which had worried Macomber, the hill he had glanced back at so many times. 'When they come to the top they will see you here. We must go quickly.'

'Which way?' asked Prentice.

'That way.' He pointed towards the hill crest over which he had just warned them the Germans were advancing. Prentice took a step forward, stooped to pick up his machine-pistol, which he looped over his shoulder, and then shook his head uncomprehendingly.

'Grapos, you've just said the Germans are coming over that hill, so we'd better push off in some other direction.'

'No. They come this way – so we go this way. You will see. Come! We must hurry.'

'Half a minute!' Prentice was not convinced and his naturally sceptical mind was now wondering whether he could trust Grapos. 'We haven't seen any Germans come along the road down there and they'd have to do that to get over there ...'

Macomber broke in quickly, relieved to see that Ford's common sense had automatically made him turn round and watch the empty hill crest while the others argued it out. 'Prentice, the Germans were confident they could get hold of mules in Katyra – not enough for all their men, I'm sure, but probably enough to send ahead an advance party. If Burckhardt acted quickly and sent out a patrol on mules in time, they could have passed along that road while we were moving across country. In which case some of them would be ahead of us – that was why I kept looking over my shoulder earlier.'

'Theophilous would supply them with mules,' said Grapos. He spat on the ground. 'Theophilous is at Katyra. He has German mother and Greek father, but he loves Germans. It is known for a long time. And Theophilous has mules . . .'

'And undoubtedly would know where to lay his hands on others,' Macomber interjected. 'All right, assuming they're coming up that hill from the far side, where do we go?'

'We go down here and wait.'

'Wait . . . ?' Prentice still couldn't understand the Greek's plan but Grapos, without attempting to explain further, led the way down the flank of the hill which was fully exposed to anyone coming over the distant hill crest. From the summit of the hill where they had rested the view into the valley below had been obscured by an outcrop of rock, but as they descended through thick scrub which almost closed over the path they were able to see more clearly. A broad stream on its way to the sea ran along the narrow valley floor and at one point it was crossed by a series of stepping-stones which were barely above the water's surface. On the far bank, perhaps a hundred yards to the right of the primitive crossing point, Prentice caught a glimpse of the dusty track winding its way round the base of the hill towards Zervos. The hill crest, which reared above them now as a hard outline against the cloudless sky, was still deserted. What the devil was the Greek up to? He ran down the path and began talking as soon as he was within a few paces of Grapos who hurried downhill without looking back. 'Where are we going? I want to know.'

'To the pipe.' Grapos spoke over his shoulder without pausing, although he had begun to take a keen interest in the hill crest, staring frequently in that direction as he trotted downwards unevenly because of his limp.

'What pipe? What are you talking about?'

'The pipe takes the floods from the hill to the stream. It was built many years since to stop the waters rushing over the road. We go down the pipe. The Germans will not find us there.'

'How big is it, for heaven's sake?'

'It is big. I went down it when I was a boy.'

154

'You were smaller, then,' Prentice pointed out urgently. 'And they'll see us as soon as they come over that ridge.'

'That is why we hide. We are there.'

They were less than half-way down the hill when Grapos plunged into a deep gulley. The sides were lined with protruding rocks and it was deep enough to hide them from view completely. Prentice looked back as Ford and Macomber dropped into the ravine and then turned ahead to see Grapos on his hands and knees while he pulled at a clump of scrub with his bare hands. When Prentice reached him he had exposed the entrance to a large drain-pipe of crumbling concrete. The hole was at least three feet in diameter, a dark decrepit opening but large enough to crawl inside on hands and knees. Crouching beside Grapos, Prentice saw that it sloped down at an angle of about twenty degrees, so it should be navigable. Macomber and Ford were also bunched round the forbidding hole which was damp and smelled of decaying fungus, and the fact that there was no light at the end of the tunnel, no visible end at all, did nothing to increase their enthusiasm for the Greek's proposed escape route.

'Where does it come out?' demanded Macomber.

'By the stream. We cross by the stones.'

'And how long is it?'

'Not long.'

'How long is a piece of string?' Prentice muttered under his breath. 'Look, Grapos, we can't even be sure the Germans are coming in this direction. They could easily have changed their minds and be waiting for us farther along that road.'

'They were coming up the hill. You will see. We can see from here.' Grapos climbed out of the end of the gulley and stood behind a dense grove of undergrowth which was taller than a man's height. In places there were gaps in the vegetation which formed natural windows and when the others joined him they found they had a clear view of the hill beyond. Without much expectation of seeing anything, Prentice stared through a tracery of bare twigs, and it came as a shock when he saw figures against the skyline. There were six of them, well spread out, and they started to descend the slope in a semi-circle with the two in the middle maintaining a higher altitude than those on the flanks. Which was correct procedure, Prentice was thinking – the two men in the centre had better observation and could give covering fire to the men below if necessary. He recognized at once the field-grey uniforms and the distinctive caps of the Alpenkorps.

'Why should they choose this area for their patrol?' Macomber wondered out loud.

'Because Theophilous will have told them about the path,' Grapos informed him promptly. 'There are two main ways from Katyra to Zervos – the road and the path. They have come over the road by mule and when they do not find you they turn back – to trap you on the path.' He stared blankly at the Scot while he pulled at a tip of his straggled moustache and his continuing distrust of Macomber was only too obvious.

'They could seal us off inside that pipe with only one man at each end,' Macomber persisted.

'When they reach the stream and cross it, we go into the pipe. They come up this hill and we pass under them.'

'Sounds feasible,' the Scot commented. 'If it works.' Turning round, he renewed his observation of the patrol which was descending the hill slope rapidly; already they had covered more ground than he would have expected and he reminded himself that these six oncoming Germans were highly-trained Alpenkorps troops, men whose natural habitat was wild, untracked countryside, and who were now operating under ideal conditions. A disturbing thought struck him and he asked Grapos a question quickly. 'I suppose there's no risk that this chap, Theophilous, might have told them about the pipe, too?'

The Greek snorted contemptuously. 'He is not a man who ever walks or hunts – he would be frightened that he gets lost. We wait. When they cross the stream we go into the pipe.'

Macomber moved close to Prentice as he gazed through the dense thicket and he was frowning as though there were something he didn't understand. For a few minutes he watched the patrol, clambering over rocks, sometimes disappearing up to waist-height in undergrowth, but always maintaining their careful formation as they came closer to the stream, then he voiced his doubt. 'I don't like it – Burckhardt is using his men too wastefully.'

'What are you getting at?' snapped Prentice. Still without sleep, he could feel the strain telling and he knew he was trigger-tempered.

'Burckhardt has two hundred men at his disposal to take and hold Zervos. At least he had two hundred when he left the *Rupescu,* he told me. He lost four while on board the *Hydra...*'

'Four?'

'Yes, four. There was the man you threw overboard. Grapos killed two more while escaping, and I put one over the side when I was carrying that demolition charge up on deck. His bayonet and scabbard came in useful, by the way – I used them to support the charge inside the ventilator shaft. That's two per cent of his force without adding in those who died on the jetty and when the ship blew up. Yet he feels he can spare another six men to look for us. Does it suggest something to you, Prentice? Something alarming?'

'It suggests he feels he still has enough left to take care of a few monks.' Prentice was having trouble thinking straight. What on earth was the persistent Scot driving at now?

'It suggests to me that he expects heavy reinforcements in the very near future, which isn't a happy thought.'

'You mean by sea? Another boatload in broad daylight?'

'I doubt that. They may use some entirely different method this time.' Macomber found himself looking upwards. The sky was clear blue as far as the eye could see, its only occupants a flock of seagulls sailing high up in the sunlight as they flew away in the direction of Katyra. 'He wouldn't expend a patrol of six men just looking for us unless he was confident more help was on the way.'

'Just what we need at the moment, a Job's comforter,' Prentice muttered irritably. The Alpenkorps were half-way down the hill and they had begun to converge inwards towards the stepping-stones, although as a target they were still spread out over a considerable distance. Keeping his voice down, Macomber had now turned to question Grapos.

'You know the monastery well?'

'I lived there for two years.'

'Is there any other means of communication whatsoever

157

apart from the telephone which has been cut?'

'When they want things, they phone to Katyra. Sometimes they phone Salonika.'

'There is, of course, no wireless transmitter for emergencies?'

'No, nothing like that.'

Grapos was staring through the thicket as he replied without looking in Macomber's direction, and his replies were grudging, but the Scot appeared not to notice his reticence as he pressed on interrogating the Greek. 'You mean there is no other way ... are you listening to me? Good.' Grapos looked at Macomber directly and the brown eyes which looked back were compelling him to concentrate, to remember. 'Is there no other way at all whereby the Abbot can send a message if the phone breaks down?'

'Only the pigeons.'

'Pigeons?' Macomber's voice was sharp. 'You mean he keeps carrier pigeons? Where do they go to when released?'

'To Livai on the other side of the gulf.'

'On the mainland, you mean?'

'Yes. Livai is near Olympus and there are more monks there.'

Macomber nodded and said nothing more while the German patrol continued its descent to the edge of the stream. Even when they crossed they displayed good military caution, only one man moving over the stones at a time until they had all reached the bank below where Grapos and his group waited. As the last man landed on the near-side bank the Greek grunted and moved towards the mouth of the hole. Macomber had earlier noticed that they were standing in a natural water catchment area; above where they stood three small ravines converged into the gulley and he guessed that during bad weather a minor flood must pour into the pipe. A drift of heavy cloud had appeared in the sky and it was coming their way as he followed Grapos. Once again the unpredictable Aegean weather was changing and he prayed there wouldn't be a cloudburst while they were inside that unsavoury-looking pipe. The Greek was on all fours, about to enter the mouth, when he fumbled under his coat, extracted a knife from his jacket pocket, flicked it to eject the blade, then held it upright. The five-inch blade retracted of its own accord. He was putting it into his coat pocket for easier access when Ford rapped out his question. 'Where did you get that?'

Grapos looked over his shoulder and glared at the sergeant. For a moment it seemed as though he wasn't going to reply and then he answered resentfully. 'It is just a knife. My knife.' Ford glanced at Macomber who had immediately detected the note of suspicion in the sergeant's voice and told Grapos to wait a minute. 'It's a German knife,' Ford explained. 'A parachutist's gravity knife. What the hell is he doing with a thing like that?'

'We have to go into the tunnel,' Grapos reminded them sullenly.

'We have to know about that knife, first,' Macomber replied briskly. 'Where did you get it? Come on – I want to know.'

The German patrol must already have started advancing up the hill towards them but the possession of this strange weapon bothered Macomber and he was determined to get an explanation before they followed the Greek inside the pipe. For precious seconds it seemed like deadlock as the three men stared down at the Greek who gazed back at them with a hostile expression. Then he shrugged his broad shoulders, adjusted the rifle he had previously looped diagonally across his back and addressed Macomber. 'I took it from the German I shot.'

'You were miles away in the hills when you fired on the jetty,' Macomber pointed out. 'Just a minute, do you mean one of those Jerries on the boat?'

'No. The man I shot over there.' He made a gesture forwards to the hill the Alpenkorps patrol had just descended. 'There were seven men when I saw them. I shot the man who was to the right and he fell from a rock into the bushes. They did not find him and when they had gone I took the knife.'

'You mean you've alerted this lot! They know someone is close because you've already shot one of the patrol?' Macomber was appalled. He had accepted the Greek's stratagem for evading the Alpenkorps because he had been confident they were only searching hopefully. Now those six highly trained men below *knew* they were stalking someone who couldn't be far away, which meant they would be in a state of total alert.

'Yes,' Grapos confirmed, 'one is shot. When we go through the pipe they will not know we are on the other side ...'

'So that's it!' Macomber stepped forward and gripped the Greek by the shoulder. 'You want us to go through the pipe and then open fire on them from the other side?'

'We have to kill Germans,' Grapos replied simply. 'When I go to join the army they say I am no good because of my limp. When I have killed many Germans I go to Athens and tell them – then I join the army.'

'Grapos!' Macomber spoke with low intensity. 'We have to get to the monastery before the Germans – in the hope that we can send a message to the mainland in time, or do something to upset them. If the Germans do take the monastery half a division won't shift them – maybe not even a division. Our job is to reach the monastery – to keep out of the way of any Germans we meet on the way, not to fight them.'

'Not fight!' Grapos was outraged. He looked up at Prentice. 'You are a British officer. I was told that when they wanted to know if I knew you. You agree with what this man is saying – this man who pretended he was a German?'

'Macomber's right,' Prentice said quietly. 'We want to get there and the only way we can do that is to dodge them – there are too many to fight. We may achieve a lot more by keeping out of their way.'

'Because it is you who say this.' Grapos glared in Macomber's direction and started crawling down the pipe which left less than a foot's clearance above his arched back. Dropping to his knees, the Scot followed the Greek into the insalubrious hole and the clearance above his back was barely six inches. Prentice, who had decided to bring up the rear, sent Ford down next, took one last look at the gulley to make sure the surface hadn't retained traces of footprints, then went inside himself with his machine-pistol over his back and a fervent hope that the Greek wouldn't start quarrelling with the Scot in this situation. Farther along the pipe Macomber was already finding his great bulk a distinct handicap as he crawled behind Grapos. He had only to lift himself a few inches and he found his back scraping the curved concrete; his contracted elbows

160

grazed the sides of the pipe and his knees were slithering on a film of slime at the base of the pipe as he accelerated his awkward movements to keep up with the Greek's phenomenal rate of progress. The downward slope of the pipe helped him to keep up a certain speed, but he was beginning to dislike the feeling of being shut in as he went on shuffling forward through the total darkness beyond the mouth of the pipe.

Within two minutes he found himself taking great heaving breaths and this was no place for deep breathing – as he penetrated deeper inside the buried pipe the damp smell changed to an oppressive airlessness and the place seemed bereft of oxygen. How the broad-bodied Grapos managed to keep up such a killing pace he couldn't imagine and gradually the sensation of being entombed grew. He had expected his eyes to become accustomed to the darkness but it was still pitch-black and the only sound was the noise of scuffling feet and knees some distance behind him, a sound which reminded him of rats he had once heard scuttering inside a derelict warehouse. He plodded on, hands stretching out into the unknown, followed by the haul of his knees over the scum-like surface of the pipe which he now realized had been embedded in the ground for God knew how long; his hands told him this because frequently the surface of the pipe wall flaked off at his touch and more than once a large piece came away and clattered grittily on the floor. It was badly in need of running repairs but he imagined that when something was built on Zervos it was hopefully expected to last for ever. Nightmare possibilities began to invade his mind – supposing the far end was blocked? The only similar culvert pipe he could remember had been barred at the exit end by an iron grille to prevent small boys swimming in the river from investigating its interior. Grapos had been this way before years ago, but there was no reason why such a grille should not have been fixed more recently. At a rough guess the pipe must be a quarter of a mile long – so what would be the position if the exit were closed? He could never hope to turn round in this confined space and their only hope would be a slow, endless crawl backwards and uphill, a prospect he contemplated with no great relish.

As they went on and the angle of the pipe dipped more steeply, Macomber remembered that the hill slope dropped sharply when it approached the stream. He began to have a horrible feeling that they had taken the wrong decision – that they should never have entered this Stygian cylinder which might be their grave. For a brief second he paused to wipe the gathering sweat off his forehead and then ploughed on, his wrists aching under the weight they had to bear, the palms of his hands sore and tender with groping over the gritty concrete, the pain increasing across his back and down his thighs. When the hell were they going to get out of this blasted tunnel Grapos had led them into so confidently? There had to be a bend soon because only a bend would explain why there was still no light ahead. Unless the tunnel exit was completely blocked: that certainly would account for the continuing state of darkness they were crawling down through. It might also account for the worsening difficulty in breathing.

Macomber was having great trouble in regulating the intake of air now as he shuffled downwards blindly and automatically. But if the exit were stopped up they would be descending into a region of foul and foetid air where breathing might become well-nigh impossible. His great fear now was that they would discover the grim truth too late – that by the time they knew there was no way out they would have degenerated into such a weakened state that they would never be able to summon up the strength needed for the return trip. Years later when they excavated the pipe they would find... He suppressed the macabre thought and concentrated on keeping going, hands first, then that dreadful, wearying haul forward of the knees which it was becoming an agony to move. His head was vibrating gently and frequently he blinked as brief lights flashed in front of his eyes. He was aware of feeling warmer and he couldn't be sure whether this was an illusion or a symptom warning that something was going wrong with his system. He had moved forward mechanically for so long that his heart jumped with the shock when his outstretched hand touched something hard. The sole of Grapos' stationary boot. Was there a crisis? Had the Greek collapsed on the floor of the tunnel under the murderous physical strain? He called out. 'Grapos . . .' Because of the silence which had lasted so long he found he was unconsciously whispering as he called again. 'Something wrong, Grapos?'

The voice which came back out of the darkness was hoarse and breathless. 'We are at the bend. I can see the light at the bottom. When we arrive, you wait inside the pipe. You do not come out until I tell you.'

'All right. You're doing fine.'

Grapos grunted and began heaving himself forward again, on his stomach now because he found this an easier way to progress as the pipe angled downhill more precipitately. Macomber was about to follow when he felt a hand touch his own foot and he called back over his shoulder. 'Nearly there, Ford. We can see the end of the tunnel. Pass it on.' There was a considerable element of exaggeration in his statement but it seemed a reasonable moment to send back a cheerful message. As he rounded the bend, Macomber was able to appreciate the extent of his exaggerated optimism: the pipe was angled downwards at an increasingly nerve-wracking pitch and the blur of light in the distance was little larger than a sixpence. They were probably barely half-way down the hill slope. He was easing himself round the bend when his right knee contacted a particularly slippery patch and before he knew what was happening he lost balance and crashed heavily against the tunnel wall. He felt it crumble under his impact and a large piece of concrete slithered into his thigh followed by a shower of loosened earth. In places the damned thing was little thicker than paper. Calling back to warn the others, he crawled forward again with a sensation of moving down a chute. The brief pause had hindered rather than helped – his knees were wobbling badly and he expected at any moment to keel into the wall for a second time. When the accident happened it was so unexpected, so unforeseeable and bizarre, that it took away Macomber's breath. He had just caught up with Grapos and was within inches of his rearmost boot when the uncanny silence inside the tunnel was shattered by a ripping, cracking sound. Little more than a foot beyond Grapos' head the tunnel roof splintered, caved in and exposed a small hole – and thrust down through the hole was an Alpenkorps boot with a leg showing to the knee.

Macomber froze as Grapos lay rigid, his face inches away from the point where one of the Alpenkorps patrol had trodden through the rotting roof of the ancient pipe. Sufficient light percolated through the small aperture for him to see the pattern of large nails on the sole of the boot. Scarcely daring to breathe, he watched the leg withdrawing. For a few seconds it was held fast by the smallness of the hole when the boot tried to free itself, then it disappeared upwards, leaving the small aperture with ragged concrete edges. Still on all fours, Macomber prayed that the others behind him would lie still, that they had realized something had happened, that they would understand the desperate need for preserving total silence.

Grapos was still lying motionless on the tunnel floor, unable to reach the rifle looped over his back and having the sense not to attempt that dangerous manoeuvre. With agonizing slowness the Scot eased his tender knees forward a few more inches, wondering whether the hole was large enough for the invisible German to peer down and see Grapos, but he doubted whether that was possible. The Greek should be just far enough from the hole to go undetected. But how bright would that Alpenkorps man be? Would it occur to him to investigate the pipe, to kick in a little more of the crumbling roof? Originally, the pipe must have been laid just under the earth's surface, but over the years the rain had probably washed away some of the protecting soil until only a thin layer had remained. He found it an uncanny feeling to be lying there cooped up inside the narrow space, buried just underneath the hill slope and knowing that not three feet above them there was probably a German standing, undecided what to do about this phenomenon. Or had he gone away and climbed farther up the hill over their heads, cursing the pipe and not giving it another thought? He would have his orders to maintain the line of the sweep and German discipline gave little scope for personal initiative. But these were Alpine troops, men very different in training and background from the average breed of

Wehrmacht footslogger. Their training taught them to use their heads, to think for themselves.

All these rattling thoughts passed through Macomber's brain as four men lay absolutely still inside the pipe while two of them – Prentice and Ford – had even less idea of what was happening because they had been farther back. All they knew was that the wriggling, advancing worm of feet and heads had unaccountably stopped after that weird breaking sound had travelled back up the tunnel. Instinct alone, or perhaps a telepathic sense of emergency, prevented them from calling out to ask what had gone wrong. Macomber felt the boots resting against his knuckles begin to wriggle and he understood the signal – Grapos wished to move back a little farther away from the hole. To avoid the risk of two men's movements, Macomber simply perched both hands a little higher up the tunnel wall and the legs wriggled back underneath his own hoisted body, then stopped moving. He had made no sound during his short passage backwards but Macomber wished to heaven that he knew what had caused the Greek to retract that short distance. Was it in anticipation of something? The next moment he had confirmation that he had guessed correctly – a heavy instrument was hammered against the ragged rim of the aperture. Fragments clattered on the floor of the pipe and then the steel-plated butt of a rifle came half-way inside the pipe as a piece collapsed unexpectedly. The German was enlarging the hole to get a better view.

Macomber felt Grapos' body tense and then relax almost immediately – he had been about to seize the rifle butt and jerk it downwards out of the unseen hand holding it. Had the Alpenkorps man been alone it would have been a worthwhile action, but Grapos had remembered in time that the German was not alone on the hill slope. Grimly, Macomber waited for the hammering to be resumed, for the hole to be enlarged to a point where they must be seen, but as the seconds passed the hammering was not resumed and there was an unnerving stillness beyond the aperture. Apparently the soldier was now satisfied that it was simply a deserted culvert and he had continued uphill with the sweep. Or was this too comforting an explanation of the lack of activity above that tell-tale hole?

Had he, in fact, seen Grapos? Probably not – Grapos had moved farther up the tunnel just in time. The complacent thought had hardly passed through Macomber's head when he realized how fatally he had been wrong, realized that the German was still standing there just above them and that this was a man who was going to make sure of the business with very little expenditure of effort. The expenditure of a single hand-grenade, in fact.

The stick-like object fell through the hole and landed on the floor of the pipe. Macomber knew at once that they were going to die, that the grenade would detonate under perfect conditions. Inside that confined space the blast would be enormous with only a fraction escaping through the aperture; the main part of the explosion would be concentrated and funnelled along the pipe in a searing wave of bursting gases which would tear them to pieces. Prentice at the rear might just survive – survive with ruptured ear-drums as the hellish noise roared over him. Macomber felt Grapos stir under him and knew what he was trying to do, but the Greek was sprawled along the floor in a near-helpless position and he would never manage it in time. The Scot's hand closed over the grenade as he pivoted, taking his whole weight on his left hand to give him hoisting room. Gripping the throwing-handle and knowing that he held death in his fist, he looked upwards, calculated in a split-second and then jerked his hand, praying that the missile wouldn't catch the rim of the hole and come bouncing down again. The grenade sailed up through the aperture's centre and vanished as Macomber instinctively huddled over Grapos who now lay perfectly still. The detonation echoed back to the prone men as a hard thump like the thud of a rubber hammer against an oak door. Macomber let out his breath and then nearly fell over as Grapos scrambled out from underneath him, half-stood up, pushed his head through the hole and heaved with his shoulders to force his way through the fractured rim.

What the devil was he up to now? The manoeuvre took Macomber completely by surprise. Was the Greek on the German side, was he taking this last chance to get out of the tunnel and reach his friends? Still standing in a half-crouched

166

position with his head and shoulders only above the rim, Grapos was doing something frantically with his hands and arms. Below him Macomber held the Luger aimed at the lower part of his body while he tried to work out what Grapos was trying to do. He waited a whole minute and then the Greek lowered himself back inside the tunnel, pausing on his knees to reach up outside the hole while he hauled clumps of vegetation over the aperture. His hands were streaked with blood and when Macomber caught a glimpse of the prickly undergrowth he understood – he had been clawing and arranging a screen of vegetation to conceal the hole from the rest of the Alpenkorps patrol. Grapos sagged into an awkward sitting position and wiped his streaked hands carefully underneath his coat while he took in great gasping breaths of air. When he could speak he looked at Macomber and his former mistrust had gone as he dragged out the words. 'The German is dead – the bomb must have landed at his feet. He is alone ... the others will come and will think the bomb went off by accident ... with luck. If they do not see the hole ...'

'You covered it completely?'

'I think so. If they search they will find it – but why should they do that if they think the bomb exploded by mistake? They will see it is not in his belt.'

'Thanks,' Macomber said simply. 'Think you can make it to the end of the tunnel? Good. And now you'd better be extra damned careful how you emerge.'

'I will manage.' Grapos wiped hair away from his face and stared at the Scot. 'And thank you – that bomb came within centimetres of my nose – if it exploded here I would have no head now ...'

'Get moving – those Germans will be here any minute.'

In spite of their cramped state the four men made speedier progress down the last stretch of the tunnel and then waited at the bottom until Grapos signalled that all was clear. Like the Alpenkorps, they crossed the stepping-stones singly, and in less than five minutes they came out from the undergrowth on to the deserted road to Zervos. Grapos grinned as he hoisted his rifle over his shoulder prior to leading the way. 'It will be good from now,' he informed them. 'We are in front of the Germans.'

'I wouldn't count on that,' Macomber replied sharply. 'I've got a nasty idea something very peculiar is going to happen between here and Zervos.'

CHAPTER NINE

Sunday, Noon

The advance guard of the Alpenkorps was in sight and since they were mounted on mules it could only be a matter of time before they overtook anyone moving on foot. Perched on the crag which hung over the road a hundred feet below, Macomber closed the Monokular glass which Prentice had returned to him and looked down at the roadside where Grapos waited for the oxen-carts coming from Zervos. It had been agreed that it would be better if he questioned the peasants riding on the carts alone and the three of them – Macomber, Prentice and Ford – had climbed up from the road to keep out of sight. For the Scot this had been a welcome opportunity to see a long distance back over the way they had come, although the view could have been more encouraging.

'I hope Grapos isn't going to take all day arguing the toss with those peasants,' Prentice said irritably. Lack of sleep was making it increasingly difficult to keep his eyes open and now it was only will-power which sustained his movements. The trouble was that he had missed even the short rest the others had enjoyed before Grapos had appeared on the hilltop.

'He may get some news from them – or at least find out where we can get some food,' Macomber pointed out.

'I couldn't eat a thing. And that lot following us hasn't put any edge on my appetite either.'

'It shouldn't take them too long to get here,' observed Ford. 'They'll drive those mules till they drop – and mules don't drop all that quickly.'

Macomber forced his sagging shoulders upright and began speaking rapidly. It was clear that Prentice was in such a low state that a few minutes of pessimistic conversation might be more than enough to sap his remaining resistance, so he deliberately instilled a rough vigour into his voice. 'We're standing on a good lookout point to check the geography of the area so you know what lies ahead of us. It's about ten miles from Katyra to the plateau, and the plateau itself is about six miles long. Then there's about another four miles from the far end of the plateau up to Zervos. That last four miles is pretty appalling – you climb up a winding road from the plateau which zigzags all over the place – so if we can conscript some mules for ourselves, we'd better do it. Grapos may manage to fix that up – I gather he knows just about everyone on the peninsula.'

'You mean we have another ten miles to do before we get to the monastery?' Prentice started to sit down on a rock and then remained standing; he had the feeling that if he relaxed he might never get up again. 'I don't see us getting there today,' he said firmly.

'Burckhardt will get there today – I'm sure that's the key to his whole timetable. And if you look over there I rather think you'll see Mount Zervos in a minute.'

From their elevated position at the top of the crag they had a panoramic view over the peninsula and to east and west the Aegean was in view, still a brilliant blue across the gulf where they could see the mountains on the mainland above the vital road the Allies were using. The surface of the water glittered in the sunlight and when Macomber scanned it with his glass he thought he could make out small dark specks amid the calm cobalt, the specks of Italian mines floating in the gulf. The mainland was still half-shrouded in mist but here and there the sunlight caught the tiny square of whiteness which must be the wall of a building. To the north a dark column of smoke still hung in the sky from the burning *Hydra*, but the plume was less well-defined now and less smoke drifted upwards to maintain its density. And it was in that same direction where a distant file of men on mules advanced towards the crag at a seemingly snail's pace, a file which was telescoping as the head of the file went down inside a dip in the white streak of road.

To the south a fleet of heavy clouds drifted low over the peninsula, but the clouds were thinning rapidly as they drifted out across the gulf beyond Cape Zervos and, as Macomber had predicted, the mountain slowly emerged from the clouds like a

170

massive volcanic cone, a cone whose slopes were white with snow to the triangular-shaped summit. Prentice stood watching the mountain appear with a sense of awe – had they really a dog's chance in hell of scaling that giant and reaching the strategically vital monastery before the Germans took it? Borrowing Macomber's glass again, he focused and saw that the clouds had never really covered the peak; they had smothered the plateau and intervened between the mountain and the view from the north. So the met men had been right – Zervos was hardly ever obscured by the weather and once Burckhardt was established up there he would have a continuous view of the supply road. Prentice felt temporarily overwhelmed – overwhelmed by what was at stake and by the apparently insuperable problem of arriving on Zervos in time.

'It's not so good to the east, though,' Macomber warned them soberly. 'At this time of year the weather comes from that direction and I don't like the look of what's on the way.'

To the east the sea was still visible, a grey ruffled sea rapidly disappearing under a fresh formation of dense cloud banks which had a heavy swollen look. There was very little doubt that extremely dirty weather was coming, heading for the section of the peninsula they would have to cross. Prentice stared again southwards where the mountain was now fully exposed to its base, and when Macomber told him to focus on a certain spot he thought he saw a tiny rectangle of rock perched close to the sea. 'If you're looking at the right place,' the Scot told him, 'that's the monastery. It's pretty high up, as you'll see.'

'Pretty high. Well above the snow-line, in fact.'

Perhaps a mile farther on from the crag the last remnants of cloud were now clearing from the edge of the plateau which rose abruptly from the foothills like a wall. Again Macomber pointed out a certain spot and Prentice found the road which climbed up to the tableland. On the eastern side of the plateau a wisp of smoke eddied into the sky as it was caught by a strong wind and there appeared to be a huddle of buildings under the smoke. 'That's the village of Elatia,' Macomber explained in reply to Prentice's question. 'We shan't go near that – a spur track runs off the main road to reach it.'

'Main road? Some main road!' Prentice handed back the

171

glass and looked down to where the oxen-carts had stopped below while Grapos talked to several peasants who had gathered round him. At one moment Grapos gestured vigorously towards Katyra and Prentice guessed that he was warning them about the approaching Germans. Shortly afterwards something like panic gripped the gathering. Three of the four oxen-carts filled up with the peasants and began to leave the road to drive straight across the fields which stretched away from the base of the hill. One wagon got stuck as its wheels caught in the ditch and the shouts of the passengers urging the beasts to make greater efforts echoed up to the crag. The fourth cart, empty, remained standing in the road as Grapos stared up at the crag and waved both arms furiously to summon them down. As they started their descent Macomber took one last look northwards and saw the tail of the Alpenkorps column sliding out of view. When it emerged in sight again it would be that much closer to the crag and to Mount Zervos.

'The news is bad – very bad,' Grapos greeted them. 'The Germans attacked my country and Yugoslavia at 5.45 this morning. They say the forts at Rupel have held the first attack.'

'They said the Maginot Line would hold all attacks,' Prentice muttered under his breath. 'Why have they left this wagon?' he asked out aloud. Grapos had turned the cart round so that now it faced away from the Alpenkorps.

'For us! They are going into the fields to escape the Germans so that it did not matter that they knew you were here. With this we can save our strength and some of us can sleep. I know where we can get food and clothes.' He looked at Ford and Prentice. 'With those clothes you would freeze to death on Zervos.'

'Any other news, Grapos?' Macomber inquired quietly. 'And how do your friends know about the German offensive? The telephone line was going to be cut.'

'It has been cut since last night. They heard the news on the wireless.' Grapos' manner had become openly hostile as though he resented the question, and Prentice thought Oh,

172

Lord, those two are at it again! 'I tell you the truth,' the Greek added vehemently.

'Of course you do,' Macomber replied, completely unruffled. 'But I deal in fact and I like to know the details. Where can we get the food and the clothes?'

'At a house where the road climbs. We must go . . .'

'Just a minute! You know this family well?'

'There is no family. There is one man and I have known him many years. He would be in the army fighting but he is old. And he has no German mother – if that would really worry you, Mr Macomber.'

'Then let's get moving. This will be a chance for you to get some rest, Prentice. Make the most of it. I have an idea it may be the last chance you'll get!'

The inside of the ox-cart was carpeted with straw and Prentice, who sprawled full-length after bunching up the straw into a makeshift palliasse, had fallen asleep almost as soon as the cumbersome vehicle started moving. Grapos held the long whip which signalled the animals that it was time to work again and they began lurching forward over the dusty road at a laboured pace across a small plain. The foothills continued on their right, hiding the gulf from them, but they became lower as the wall of the plateau crawled towards them with infinite slowness. It would have been at least as quick to march on foot but Macomber felt that Prentice must recuperate even though the Alpenkorps on mules must inevitably close the gap between them, and the cart provided a means of rest for all four men. Although convinced that it was crucial to conserve their energies for what might lie in front of them, the slow-motion pace of the cart irritated him almost beyond endurance. The wagon was drawn by two long-horned oxen which plodded along sedately as the ancient wagon creaked and groaned as though it might fall apart at any moment. They were coming close to the wall of the plateau when Ford asked Macomber his wry question. 'Anything worrying you – anything in particular, I mean?'

'Well, this ox-cart for one thing. It's not exactly the Orient Express.' He stared ahead as Grapos, who stood between them, glared in his direction. 'For another thing, I can't work out how we're going to communicate with the mainland forces in time to warn them of what is happening here. In time,' he repeated. 'Once Burckhardt has established himself on the heights no one will ever shift him – the place, the position, everything, makes it a natural fortress. But the thing which bothers me most of all is the size of his force – I'm absolutely certain that he's expecting massive reinforcements.'

'Hard to see how – unless they sneaked in by sea again. Could they land somewhere over there?' Ford pointed towards the eastern coastline which was still clear, although out over the Aegean the clouds were continuing to mass.

'There's no way inland. The cliffs go on until they reach the delta area in the north. But I can't see them risking a sea-going expedition twice – and this one in broad daylight. They can't be expecting to break through from Salonika in time or else they wouldn't have sent Burckhardt in the first place...' Macomber trailed off and stared ahead as he put himself in the colonel's position and tried to imagine his next move. Ford was standing with his back to the way they were going so he could watch the road behind but so far it stretched away emptily as far as he could see.

When they reached the base of the plateau wall Grapos took them inside a single-storey stone house concealed by a grove of cypresses and there the owner, a man in his seventies, divided among them the meal he had just prepared for himself. The food was strange and strong-tasting and consisted of balls of meat rolled inside the leaves of some unidentifiable vegetable. He offered to cook more but Macomber said they had no time and they ate with relish food they would normally have rejected as inedible.

Macomber was keeping watch by himself just beyond the cypresses while he drank *ouzo* from a large glass when he saw them coming. His Monokular brought them closer – Alpenkorps on mules, a file which extended back into the distance and which was a far more formidable force than he had imagined from his earlier sight of them. He ran back into the house to find Prentice and Ford trying on two ancient sheepskin coats the owner was providing and then exploded when the lieutenant started to write the man's name in a notebook so they could send him payment later. 'Prentice, you may have just signed that man's death warrant! If the Germans catch us and find that...'

'Of course! I must be half-asleep,' the lieutenant replied apologetically. He went to a stone sink and began setting fire to the page prior to washing away the embers. The room was stone-paved and stone-walled. A hideous place to spend seventy years of one's life.

'And we have about half a minute to clear out of here,' Macomber rapped out.

'I'm just burning a death warrant, as you so aptly pointed out.' Prentice had recovered his normal composure after the sleep in the cart and there was a faint smile on his face when he stared back at the large Scot. 'How close would you say?'

'Two miles. Maybe less.'

'Close enough, I agree. We'll have to hike it up to the top of that plateau. I hope you can walk faster than a mule, Ford.' He dropped the blackened paper into the sink and poured a stone jugful of water over the mess, pushing it down the drain with his finger. 'There's no way up except the road, I suppose?'

'No other way,' Grapos told him.

'Right! The road it is!' He turned to the old man. 'Tell him he has our grateful thanks for his hospitality. I rather fancy it would be a mistake to offer money for the food?'

'A mistake,' Grapos agreed abruptly. He was looking through the open doorway towards the road and hoisted his rifle higher as he moved towards it.

'Tell him also,' Macomber intervened, 'that when the Germans arrive and ask about us, he's to say he saw us get off the wagon we'd obviously stolen and run up the hill. If he tells them something they're more likely to leave him alone. Tell him also to wash up three of those plates and glasses and just leave his own dirty. They'll be looking for things like that. And don't forget the thanks.' He waited while Grapos poured out a stream of Greek and the old man kept shaking his head as though it were nothing, and he was relieved to see as they left that the old man was already starting to wash the dirty plates.

When Macomber looked back as they started to climb the

175

hill, the line of mounted troops was already appreciably closer and he knew that they must hide soon or be captured. With the Scot in the lead they ascended the winding road at a slow trot, but long before they reached the top they were slowing down badly. The gradient was steep and wound its way between huge boulders which seemed on the verge of toppling down the rugged incline. Groves of bare olive trees studded the hill slope and the frequent twists in the road soon hid them from the plain below, which had the advantage of hiding them from the Alpenkorps mule train, but had the disadvantage of preventing them seeing how close their pursuers were drawing. Cover was what they needed, Macomber was telling himself, and he was tempted to leave the road altogether and hide on the hill slope, but this would mean throwing in the sponge: the Alpenkorps would ride past and continue on to Zervos. I'm damned if I'm giving up as easily as that, he thought, after surviving that voyage from Istanbul.

'I'd say we have another thirty minutes left – at the outside,' Prentice called up to him.

'At the outside,' Macomber agreed. Thirty minutes before the leading Alpenkorps troops overhauled them. It was beginning to get a bit desperate and he was pinning all his hopes on seeing a chance to escape when they reached that plateau which stretched six miles to the base of the mountain. This was one area where he had very little idea of the topography because when he had travelled this way five years before it had been drenched in mist while they drove over the tableland. The stitch in his side was getting worse as he forced his legs to keep up the route-march pace and now each thud of his boots on the road pounded up his side like a sledgehammer. To counter the pain he stooped forward a little, cursing inwardly as Prentice caught up with him.

'Take it easy, Mac, you'll kill yourself. You're streaming with sweat.'

'Time is running out – we had a head start on them and we've lost it. We'll have to make a quick decision when we reach the top.' The effort of speaking was a major strain now but he was damned if he was going to give up. Keep moving, you'll work it off! Prentice was walking alongside him now and this gave him a pacemaker to keep up with. He forced himself to resist the impulse to look at the ground because this brought on greater fatigue. Straightening up, he stared at the ridge they were approaching. Was this the rim of the plateau at long last? He had thought so hopefully with three lower ridges and had been disappointed each time. In his state of extreme pained exertion the plateau above was now taking on the character of a promised land, a haven where there must be some salvation from the relentless Alpenkorps coming up behind.

He was hardly aware of the landscape they were passing as the pain grew worse and pulled at him like a steel wire contracting inside his body. Boulders, olive groves, clumps of shrubbery moved past in a blur as he fixed his eyes on the wobbling ridge moving down towards them as they turned another bend and then another. Despite his robot-like condition he was conscious that the air was cooler, that a breeze was growing stronger, and this gave him fresh hope that they were close to the head of the tortuous road which went on and on forever – another bend, another stretch of white dust, another bend...

'Must be nearly there – with this wind,' Prentice commented.

Macomber only grunted and stared upwards. Was he breaking the grip of the stitch? It seemed a little less agonizing, a little less inclined to screw up his muscles into complex knots. It left him quite suddenly and with the realization that he had conquered it he began to take long loping strides which Prentice could hardly keep up with. He wiped his face dry as he walked and then accelerated his pace, feeling a sense of triumph as he saw only sky beyond the lowering ridge. They were almost there! Revived by the small quantity of food and the wine he began moving faster still as the gradient of the road lessened, leaving Prentice behind in his anxiety to catch his first glimpse of the plateau. There must be no hesitation here – they must decide swiftly what they were going to do and do it. There might even be a convenient farm at the top. With a lot of luck there might even be bicycles – he had seen men cycling when he had visited Katyra before the war. A cycle should be a match for a mule. They needed some form of transport which would take them the six miles across the plateau, something which would put them well ahead of that blasted mule train of Burckhardt's. He put on a spurt, came over the top and the plateau lay before him.

The disappointment was so crushing that he stood quite still until Prentice reached him. A classic tableland spread out into the distance, an area of flatness devoid of any form of cover for several miles. In fact, he could hardly have imagined a region less suited for them to escape the Alpenkorps. The road was a surprise, too: a highway of recently laid tar which ran straight across to the mountain, the land greenish on one side and brownish on the other. They must have started the highway from the peninsula tip, a highway which in due course would be extended to Katyra.

'Not quite what we're in the market for,' Prentice remarked.

'It might as well be the sea for all the good it is to us.' Macomber glanced over his shoulder. 'How's the Greek?'

'Had a bit of trouble with his limp coming up. Ford stayed back to keep him company. What's exciting them now, I wonder?'

Ford and Grapos had appeared but they were standing together on an outcrop of rock a short distance from the road as they waved their hands with a beckoning motion. Prentice left Macomber gazing bleakly at the plateau and went back to the outcrop. The ground he scrambled up was dry and gritty, which confirmed that the storm of the night before must have blown itself out somewhere near Cape Zervos. And there was a trace of excitement in Ford's voice as he called down. 'Hurry up or you'll miss it.'

'Miss what?'

The sun which shone on the back of Prentice's neck as he hauled himself up on the rock had no warmth in it and the coldness of the light breeze was a reminder that they were approaching a zone of low temperature. Standing beside Grapos, he adjusted his sheepskin coat. It was too big and flopped off the shoulders; Ford, who was wearing another coat belonging to the same man, fitted far more comfortably inside his sheepskin. Had the Greek possessed a third coat? The thought had never struck Prentice during the flurry to get away from the house. Following the line of Ford's pointed arm he could see the top of the house now, its faded red tiles so levelled by the height that it looked flat-roofed. And only a few yards beyond the cypresses the head of the Alpenkorps column was approaching the foot of the hill road. 'There they come,' said Ford, 'the first of the many.'

'You're sure they are the first? There may be more of them already coming up the hill.'

'No, sir. You and Macomber were in such a perishing hurry to get up here I don't imagine you ever looked back – but we caught sight of them more than once and that's the head of the column.'

Prentice was surprised. Earlier he had been startled to find German troops in front of them when they came over the hill-top near the pipe, and now he was surprised at how long it had taken them to reach this point since he had glanced back when they rushed out of the house below. He waited for two or three men to turn aside and enter the house, but the column went straight past and vanished as it began to mount the hill road. The wagon had been left behind the cypresses, which also concealed the house, and the Alpenkorps were going to ride up the hill without ever realizing its existence. With a feeling of relief he jumped down from the platform and hurried back to where Macomber still stood, stood like a man of stone as he gazed upwards, his hands inside his coat pockets, the expression on his face so grim that it recalled his impersonation of Dietrich.

'What's the matter?' asked Prentice. He tilted his head. 'What's that – I can hear something?'

'The reinforcements – Burckhardt's reinforcements. By God, I expected something but I hadn't expected this. They must have half the Wehrmacht up there coming in.'

The sky to the north-east was still clear, more than clear enough for them to see the huge aerial armada which was descending on Zervos. The steady purr of their engines grew louder as they flew over the peninsula at a height of less than a thousand feet and they were close enough already for Macomber to see that they were three-engined machines with an iron cross on the fuselage and the swastika on the tail. 'Transport planes,' Ford said in his ear. 'They'll very likely have parachutists aboard.' In the distance, flying even lower, came more planes and these were towing other machines with different silhouettes. Macomber was focusing his glass on them as Prentice spoke.

'The Alpenkorps have just started to come up the hill behind us.'

'They'll take Zervos before nightfall. There's nothing to stop them,' said Macomber.

'Unless this airborne crowd is heading for the mainland,' Ford suggested without much conviction.

Macomber stared through the glass, holding his head tilted back as the planes flew in closer. The aircraft towing other machines were losing height rapidly while the transport planes circled above the plateau, their engines a muted roar. There were no Allied fighters to intercept them, of course, although a flight of Messerschmitts had now appeared: the bulk of the over-strained RAF was supporting the Greek war in Albania and even these formations were few and far between. With a feeling of appalled helplessness they watched the aerial fleet droning casually over the plateau like a flying circus putting on a show before an invited audience, although the only audience to watch this display of Luftwaffe air power was the group of four men on the plateau rim. There were probably between twenty and thirty planes, but it was the thought of what they might contain which frightened Prentice. 'Those machines they're towing are gliders,' said Ford. He saw Macomber nod in confirmation and now the shadows of the planes were flitting over the level surface of the plateau, a perfect landing ground for putting down an airborne force. A moment later a cluster of black dots sprayed from one of the transport machines and the dots became cones as the parachutists floated downwards. A machine detached itself from its powered carrier and the gliders started to come in to land.

The four men were retreating from the plateau towards the hillside above the road when Macomber called out. 'Wait a minute, Prentice! Something's going wrong with this one.' A glider detached from its powered transport was wobbling unstably as it headed for the earth and had the appearance of being out of control as it descended towards the rim of the plateau close to where Macomber waited. An ugly, ungainly beast, it was twin-tailed and the fuselage was squat, suggesting great carrying capacity.

Half a mile along the road more parachutists were floating down over the brownish ground which seemed to be the main landing area and the sunlight caught their tilting cones – white for parachutists and various colours for the 'chutes supporting supply containers. Only one transport plane had attempted a landing to the left of the road and his machine was propped at a dangerous angle with the nose well down and its tail angled in the air. On the other side of the road two transports had already touched down safely and a third was just coming in.

'That plane on the left will be in trouble,' Prentice said tersely. 'It's marshland on that side.'

'How do you know that?' Macomber asked quickly.

'Because I persuaded the pilot to make a detour and fly over here on our way to Istanbul. We'd been discussing Zervos before I left Athens and I wanted to see what the place looked like. He told me that the green area was marshy...'

'Those transport machines are JU 52/3s,' Ford interjected professionally. 'I've heard they can carry mountain guns...'

'This is hardly a good time to start cataloguing German equipment,' Prentice snapped. 'I say we'd better get out of here – and fast.'

'And this brute of a glider coming towards us is a Gotha unless I'm very much mistaken,' Ford continued, and then found he was alone as the others ran back towards the boulders and scrub at the top of the hill. As he followed them he could hear the whine of the wind rising and the steady beat-beat of more transports coming in. Ford, who had a fatalistic streak in his make-up had little doubt that this was the end of the line; they would spend the rest of the war in some German prison camp, unless they were shot in the process of being captured. He was close to the first boulders when the machine-pistol slipped off his shoulder and he had to turn back to pick it up.

The huge Gotha assault cargo glider was flying down at an

181

unpleasantly acute angle less than a hundred yards away. If it wasn't very lucky it was going to miss the rim of the plateau and go crashing down onto the plain below. Fascinated by the spectacle of the imminent disaster he stayed out in the open. Macomber seemed similarly affected, because now he came out from behind the rocks and stood close to Ford as the massive glider swooped down, tried to level out at the last moment, and then thudded into the soft earth a bare hundred feet away.

'For God's sake get under cover, you idiots!' Prentice shouted from behind them. Ford, the spell broken, turned to go, but Macomber still waited as he gazed at the machine. The shock of landing had righted the fuselage and now the whole of the nose of the aircraft was lifting back like an immense hood. A soldier stood near the entrance as the aperture yawned larger, exposing a vehicle like a large car which waited to emerge. The German was moving unsteadily as he climbed behind the driver's seat and he paused to wipe something which might have been blood from his forehead. The engine started up and the vehicle began to move slowly out of the nose with a rattling sound as the driver slumped over the wheel as though he could hardly hold himself up. There was little doubt that he had been badly knocked about by the crash-landing. Prentice, who had come out from cover with Grapos, spoke over the Scot's shoulder. 'If we could just grab that . . .'

'Exactly what I was thinking, but there are bound to be more men inside.'

Ford grabbed his arm and his voice reflected a rare excitement for the phlegmatic sergeant. 'It's a bloody half-track! Look!'

The clanking sound grew louder as the vehicle came out with painful slowness and the dazed driver remained still unaware of their proximity. Capless, he was wearing the uniform of the Alpenkorps, but it was the vehicle itself which Macomber was staring at as he put his hand inside his coat pocket and began to move forward purposefully over the grass. A long vehicle without any roof, its body was painted a drab olive-grey and at the front it was supported by two normal wheels, but there were no wheels at the rear; instead it was held up by two large caterpillar tracks. As Ford had said, a half-track – half-tank, half-car. The grinding of the tracks was muffled as they moved down onto the grass and now the driver lifted his head to see where he was going and saw Macomber standing a few feet away. The Scot spoke swiftly, rapping out the words in German.

'Brake! Colonel Burckhardt is here. He needs this vehicle at once!'

The driver reacted automatically to the command in German, braked, then stared hard at the man who had given the order. His eyes travelled over the Scot's shoulder to where Prentice and Ford were moving forward while Grapos watched the road behind. As he made a sudden movement to reach something Macomber pulled out the Luger and struck him across the temples. He had the door open and was hauling the soldier out before he had sagged to the floor while Prentice and Ford ran to either side of the open mouth of the glider. Heaving the driver out onto the grass with one hand while the other still retained the Luger, he looked up as another German soldier appeared at the open nose, his rifle at the ready. Two shots were fired within the fraction of a second. The first, fired by the soldier, struck Ford. The second, fired by Macomber, entered the German's body as Prentice ran round the back of the vehicle, arriving at the moment when the Alpenkorps man slumped down in the space between the rear of the tracks.

'Heads down!' it was Prentice who shouted as he snatched a grenade dangling from the fallen German's belt. The grenade sailed into the interior of the glider and detonated near the back. A moment earlier Macomber had caught a glimpse of movement from inside the plane, but when he raised his head after the thumping explosion there was no further sign of activity aboard the Gotha. Ford was holding onto the side of the tracks as he stooped forward on his knees, but he was trying to clamber up as Prentice and Macomber reached him. The passage of the bullet was marked by a neat tear on the right shoulder of his sheepskin coat. Prentice had an arm round his chest and was helping him to his feet as Macomber spoke.

'Get him aboard quick! I'll have to try and drive this

blasted thing – they'll be on to us in a minute.'

Ford was upright now, one arm clutching Prentice round the waist for support as he clambered inside a cut-out aperture which was the rear-door of the half-track. He spoke through his teeth to Macomber. 'Drives like a car ... any car ... the tracks move with the wheels.' Macomber was turning to go to the front when he saw the distinctive Alpenkorps cap on the head of the soldier slumped between the tracks. He scooped it off and rammed it down over his own head as Grapos arrived, running at a shuffling jog-trot with his rifle between his hands.

'The mules are here,' he gasped out. 'Coming over the hill quickly. I think the first man ...'

'Get in, for God's sake.'

Prentice had successfully manoeuvred Ford into one of the benches behind the two front seats and Macomber was behind the wheel as Grapos climbed aboard. Brake, clutch-pedal, gear-lever – it *looked* like an ordinary car. Ford told Prentice to shut up a minute and leaned forward. 'An ordinary car, Macomber, that's all it is – for driving, anyway.' He sagged back against the bench seat as Prentice grabbed at a first-aid kit attached to the rear of the driving-seat and then the vehicle began moving forward over the grass towards the road. The tracks clanked gently as they revolved over the field and the vehicle had a feeling of great stability.

Macomber was concentrating on three things at once – on getting to know how this queer monster worked, on keeping an eye on the hilltop over which the Alpenkorps might stream at any moment, and with what little attention he had left he cast quick glances to the south where the road ran past the landing zone. The sky was littered with a fresh wave of falling para-chutists and another transport plane had just come to a halt after a bumpy landing. Dammit, he said to himself and speeded up. The half-track reached the road at the moment when the leading Alpenkorps soldier crested the rise on his mule.

Hahnemann! Macomber felt certain it was the German lieutenant on that animal. He must have been hurled over-board into the sea when the *Hydra* blew up, must have been one of those men swimming in the water. The thought darted

184

through his brain as it all became a kaleidoscope and he re-acted with pure instinct. Two more men on mules appeared behind Hahnemann. Parachutists hitting the earth, their 'chutes landing and pulling sideways. A giant glider cruising in to land on the brownish area. The steady throb of planes' engines overhead mingling with the urgent shouts of the men on the mules. Still feeling like a man towing a caravan, he turned the wheel and the half-track climbed onto the road. As its great metal tracks ground their teeth into the hard tar they set up a jarring vibration sound and the unexpected barrage of noise panicked the mules. There was more shouting, fran-tic now, as the animals headed across the hilltop, threading their way nimbly among the boulders and away from the strange machine. Macomber completed his turn, hunched his shoulders, pressed his foot down, and the half-track began to build up speed as the wheels spun and the tracks churned round faster and faster, half-deafening its passengers with the pounding beat of metal on tar.

'How fast can it go?' shouted the Scot.

'Twenty ... thirty ... forty. Fifty would be pushing it.' Ford had his arm out of the sleeve now and was taking off the right side of his jacket as he replied. There were three rows of bench seats across the vehicle behind the front seats and Grapos occupied the rear position. He had aimed his rifle at Hahnemann but the half-track had lurched at the wrong moment, almost throwing him off, and he hadn't fired a shot. Now there was no target – the mules and their riders were lost somewhere inside the tangle of boulders. He swore colourfully in Greek when Macomber shouted over his shoulder for him to get down on the floor out of sight – Grapos was rather too distinctive a figure for his liking at the moment.

Ahead more transport planes were droning in the sky as they waited their moment to come down, and already the plateau to the right of the road had the look of a disorganized military tattoo. So far there were no troops close to the road but a few hundred yards away parachutists were grappling with the supply containers and a number of men were already armed with machine-pistols. Several looked up as the half-track roared past and their uniform was very different from that of the Alpenkorps, so different that they might have belonged to another army. They wore pot-shaped helmets not dissimilar to diving helmets, smocks camouflaged with mottled dark green and brown, and overall trousers which gave them a deceptively clumsy appearance, but there was nothing clumsy about their movements as they began to form up in sections. Macomber, having got the feel of the vehicle, was now sitting very erect so his Alpenkorps cap was prominently on view and frequently he drove with one hand while he waved with the other to the men assembling in the field, a performance which Prentice witnessed with some trepidation. It was typical of Macomber, he was thinking, to carry the bluff to its utmost limit.

'Look out!'

Prentice shrieked out the warning. Like Macomber, all his attention had been fixed on the airborne force's landing area and it was only by chance that he glanced to the left. A Gotha assault glider released from its tow-rope was coming in to land from the east. It was already flying very low, perhaps twenty feet above the ground, flying on a course which would take it directly across the road just ahead of the speeding half-track. Prentice guessed that the pilot was desperately trying to maintain flight long enough to take his machine beyond the marshland area and it was horribly clear that the two very different forms of transport were headed on a collision course. Macomber had time to slow down but nearby a drawn-up section of parachutists was marching steadily towards the road. If he slowed, stopped, they'd get a damn good look at who was inside the vehicle and they had machine-pistols looped over their shoulders. Without hesitation he accelerated and it became a race towards destruction.

His shoulders hunched again, he watched road and oncoming glider. It was an uncomfortably fine calculation – known speed of half-track against estimated speed of glider, with the added element of the plane's angle of descent. The half-track was now thundering down the road, which had begun to slope, at a pace which alarmed Prentice, the tracks rotating madly under increasing tension as the moving metal smashed its way forward with a rattling cannonade of sound.

Across the green field the glider grew larger as it maintained its course unerringly and lost more height. He must be mad, Prentice was thinking. Macomber's going to try and beat the bloody thing, to sneak past ahead of it! The glider was so close now that he wanted to close his eyes, to look away, but he felt a terrible compulsion to stare at the oncoming machine which now seemed enormous.

'We won't make it,' said Ford who had now become aware of what was happening, and Ford was good at this sort of hair's breadth calculation. Prentice would have felt even less happy had he known that exactly the same thought was pressing down on Macomber, and now it was too late to think of reducing speed. The converging projectiles were so close that he would probably smash into the tail of the glider as it passed. The only answer was a little more speed.

The downward gradient of the road was increasing as he pressed his foot harder and prayed – prayed against two catastrophes. He had heard somewhere that if you drive a tracked vehicle too fast a caterpillar could break loose, freeing itself from the small wheels over which it revolved and leave the vehicle altogether. If that happened at the speed they were moving at now there would be very little hope of survival. Grimly, he kept his foot down, his mind totally concentrated on the straight road ahead, the tortured gyrations of the over-strained tracks, and that huge drifting shape about to move across his bows. Prentice had one arm steadying Ford while the other hand gripped the side of the vehicle as the glider lost more height and cruised forward barely six feet above the plateau and less than fifty yards from the road. Grapos, lying resentfully on the floor with his feet under a bench and his back against the rear of the vehicle, had the shock of his life when he looked up and saw the bulk of the Gotha loom up. The half-track raced forward, Grapos involuntarily ducked, and the wing of the Gotha passed over the rear of the vehicle, landing a short distance beyond the road.

Prentice sagged against the back of the bench and stared at the back of the huge Scot, his lips moving soundlessly. Macomber was already slowing down to a safer speed, expecting some uncomplimentary comment from his passengers, but the occupants of the bench were stunned, so he was saved an argument. In the distance a transport plane was stationary close to the road and Macomber whistled under his breath when he saw something which looked like a part of a field-gun coming down a ramp through a large opening in the fuselage. 'How is Ford?' he called out over his shoulder.

'Ford is surviving,' Ford replied.

'The bullet grazed him,' amplified Prentice who was now fixing a bandage to his final satisfaction. 'He's lost a bit of blood and he looks like Banquo's ghost but the fresh air will probably tone him up a treat.'

'There's a plane ahead with something coming out – better try and identify it so we know what we're up against.'

'We can see what we're up against,' Prentice told him bluntly. 'The cream of the Wehrmacht. And I suppose you've seen there are more half-tracks over to the right? One's just nosed its way out of that Gotha which just missed us.'

'Do you think we're nearly clear of them?' asked Ford and there was a note of anxiety in his voice.

'Not much ahead as far as I can see. Why?' Macomber had detected the anxious note and was wondering what had struck the technically minded Ford.

'Because we've been lucky so far – it's wireless communication that worries me. If the Alpenkorps who came over the hill can send a message ahead we may have a reception committee waiting for us.'

It was a point which had worried Prentice but he hadn't seen any point in raising new problems at this particular juncture. So far they had got away with their audacious dash along the fringe of the assembly area, and this didn't entirely surprise him: the Germans had just landed on enemy territory and were taken up with carrying out a certain vital routine – collection of weapons from the supply containers, the unloading of heavy equipment from the gliders and transport planes, and the assembling of the men into their units. They had no reason, when their attention was so divided, to see anything strange in one of their own recently landed half-tracks speeding along the road to Zervos. But wireless communication was a different matter.

'We may be lucky,' said Macomber. 'I made a mess of both of Burckhardt's wireless sets and if he hasn't got that tuning coil fixed he'll have to wait until he finds one with this airborne mob. Now, watch it, Ford.'

He had been travelling at little more than twenty miles an hour to give the tracks a rest but now he began to build up speed again as they approached the transport plane which had landed little more than a hundred yards from the road. Men were scurrying round the machine and he saw beyond it another plane which had been hidden from view. Close to the aircraft stood a complete field-piece. Ford twisted sideways on the bench as they roared past and this time, to Prentice's relief, the Scot did not attempt his cheerful waving act. The planes were receding behind them when Ford spoke.

'They're 75-mm mountain guns – just what they need where they're going. And I saw several 8-cm mortars. This lot is really going places.'

'Some of the half-tracks will haul the mountain guns?' Prentice inquired.

'Yes, that's it. And they'll carry troops aboard as well. They've landed a beautiful heavy-nosed spearhead for the job.'

'Why send Burckhardt's expedition at all?' Macomber asked.

'That's very necessary,' Prentice explained, 'for a variety of reasons. First, if they hadn't had this patch of clear weather the airborne force could never have landed at all and then Burckhardt would have had to do the whole job himself. Second, I can see now that it was vital for them to land men at Katyra to seal off the peninsula . . .'

'And third,' interjected Ford, 'there's a limit to how much a glider or transport can carry. You can have heavy stuff – the mountain guns, the half-tracks – or you can have men, but you can't have both. So it's my bet Burckhardt's expedition is bringing in a sizable portion of the manpower while the airborne fleet brings in the heavy stuff. Together, it makes up a beautifully balanced force.'

'That's the second time you've used the word "beautiful",' Prentice complained. 'Frankly, I can't see one damned thing that's beautiful in what's coming to us.'

'Just a professional observation, sir,' Ford explained blandly.

'I think we've left them behind,' Macomber called out. 'It looks as though those two planes landed closest to Zervos.'

The road stretched away across the plateau and still ran straight as a Roman road, a perfect highway for the advance of the German invaders. They were much closer to the mountain now but it no longer rose from its base with majestic symmetry; a heavy cloud bank from the east was drifting across the lower slopes and the peak had a lop-sided look. The disturbed Aegean was no longer visible from the plateau and another formation of low cloud was gradually obliterating the tableland itself. The road was sloping upwards as it climbed towards the mountain wall and Macomber could feel a distinct drop in temperature as the wind grew stronger. The worsening of the weather was a development he viewed with some disenchantment; his photographic memory for places vividly recalled that murderous stretch of road farther on which zigzagged up the flank of the mountain, a road twisting and turning over precipitous drops as it ascended into the wilderness.

At least Burckhardt's tracked spearhead wouldn't be able to do a Le Mans over that course, but the trouble was he had to take the half-track up the same road. The gradient was increasing more steeply as Prentice called out to him.

'How are we off for petrol?'

'We had a hundred litres – a full tank – when we started, so that's the least of our problems.'

'The pilot of the glider would insist on a full tank before he took off,' Ford pointed out helpfully. 'That minimizes the risk of something going wrong during the flight – an explosion, even.'

Prentice groaned half-audibly. 'And talking about trouble, I don't much like the look of that dirty weather blowing up from the east.'

'Is the Greek still on the floor?' Macomber asked. 'He can get up now if he is and give us his opinion – a Met forecast, in fact.'

Prentice glanced round and lifted his eyes to heaven. Grapos was sprawled on his side with the rifle cuddled in his arms and he was fast asleep. The coil of Alpenkorps climbing rope, which earlier he had pulled from under a bench and examined with interest, lay with a German army satchel at his feet. How anyone could kip down on top of those vibrating tracks passed Prentice's comprehension. 'The Greek,' he announced in a loud voice, 'is in dreamland.'

'Well, wake him up,' Macomber commanded brutally.

Disturbed from his slumber, Grapos sat on the bench behind Prentice who put the question about the coming weather to him. He stared across the plateau, pulling absently at one corner of his moustache and then feeling the stubble on his chin. Then he stared ahead to where the mountain was fast losing itself behind the vaporous pall which was drifting across the plateau in front of them. As he watched, the mountain disappeared. 'It is bad,' he said. 'It is very bad. The worst. There will be much snow within the hour.'

'Exactly what makes you predict that?' Macomber called back to him sharply.

'It is from the east. The clouds are low. They are like a cow with calf – swollen with snow ...'

'First time I've heard of cows with snow inside them,' Prentice commented in an effort to lighten the pall Grapos himself was spreading over them. But the Greek was not to be put off by unseemly levity.

'The sea has gone from the plateau – that is another sign. The top of the mountain has gone – another sign. As we climb it will get worse and worse. It will be very cold and there will be a big fall of snow.'

'Thank you,' said Prentice, 'you're fired! We'll get another met forecaster from the BBC.'

'You ask me – I tell you. There may be landslides on the mountain. There will be ice on the road ...'

'And the sea shall rise up and encompass us, so we'd better find a Noah's Ark,' said Prentice in a kind of frenzy. 'For Pete's sake, man, we asked you for a weather forecast – not a gipsy's warning of doom. Now can it!' And he looks a bit like a gipsy, the old brigand, he thought as Grapos glared at him resentfully and then gazed stolidly ahead as though drawing their attention to the appalling prospect which lay before

191

them. 'That answer your question, Mac?' he called out.

'I think so. Further outlook unsettled.'

It was the reference to ice on the road which most disturbed the Scot. He would have to take this cumbersome half-track up a route which, five years before, a car had found difficulty in negotiating in good weather, because during that trip only the plateau had been blotted out by low cloud. It would make it equally hazardous for Burckhardt, of course, so it really depended on which way you looked at the problem, but Macomber was going to be in front with the Germans coming up behind. He changed gear as the gradient increased again and they were moving at little more than twenty miles an hour when Prentice asked if he could borrow the Monokular glass. He kept it for only a short time and then handed it back as he spoke.

'You were right, the outlook is unsettled – behind us. A half-track is coming after us like a bat out of hell. It could be Hahnemann aboard, but I'm only guessing, of course.'

'How many men?' Macomber was already trying to coax a fraction more speed out of the vehicle.

'Three or four. I couldn't be sure. He's on the flat at the moment so he'll have to slow down when he starts coming up.' Ford and Grapos twisted round on their benches and saw in the distance the half-track coming towards them at speed. Macomber was watching what appeared to be the crest of the hill they were climbing and beyond it the cloud hid the base of the mountain which must be very close. He would have to out-drive Hahnemann up that devilish road : the snag was he would soon be slowed down by the mist while the German could drive full-tilt up to this point, thus narrowing the gap between them to almost zero. The weather was certainly not their friend at the moment. He drove up steadily, reached the crest, and immediately the road turned and dropped into a dip between dry-stone walls where it turned again. The oxen were massed at the bend.

There were three Greek peasants with the animals which had accumulated at this point, and they were shouting their heads off and flailing the beasts with birches made of slim stems. So far as Macomber could see as he drove down towards

192

them their efforts were only adding to the confusion and the road was well and truly blocked. With the thought of that other half-track tearing towards them, he pulled up his own vehicle inches from the chaos of animals and drovers. 'Sort them out, Grapos! Get them moving and damned quickly! They can shove them on to that bit of grass by the next bend till we get past. Then tell them to block the road again.' He waited while Grapos got out of the vehicle and began shouting at the drovers, who, at first, simply shouted back. An ox rested its horned head on the side of the half-track and stared at Ford with interest. Grapos continued his shouting and gesticulating match with the drovers and Prentice felt his temper going. A minute later the animals were still milling round the vehicle and Grapos was still conducting his verbal war with his countrymen. Something snapped inside Macomber. He stood up, pulled out his Luger and fired it over the heads of men and beasts. The animals panicked and began to trot off down the road, followed by the drovers who penned them into the grassy area while the half-track grumbled past them.

'You told them to block the road again?' Macomber shouted back to Grapos who had resumed his seat on the bench.

'I told them the Germans were coming and they must make them wait.'

Macomber swore violently to himself: mention of the Germans coming would undoubtedly frighten the drovers so much they'd keep their animals penned up off the road until the second half-track had passed. They had closed the road to him but he felt sure they would open it to the Germans. Something pretty drastic had to be done to widen the gap between the two vehicles. The road was straightening out once more as it went down a hill between high earthen banks, so he accelerated. The half-track built up speed rapidly under the pressure of his foot and he felt a coldness on his face as the road flew away under him. The mist was floating aimlessly and as it drifted to and fro he caught glimpses of the mountain wall rising up like an immense fortress bastion. Here and there pinnacles of rock spurred upwards and then vanished as the mist closed in again. Glancing at the speedometer, he saw that they were moving at the equivalent of fifty miles an hour and he was well

193

aware that only the weight and stability of the racing tracks were holding them on the road. When the mist parted again momentarily he saw a stone bridge at the bottom and the old route came back to him: beyond the bridge the road veered to the right and then started its fierce climb up the mountain. Within a minute or two he would be reduced to crawling pace as he attempted the first acute bend and the realization of this fact made him exert a trifle more foot pressure.

Behind him Ford was white-faced with the aftermath of his wound, but Prentice was white-faced at the speed they were travelling as he clung tightly to the arm of the bench seat which was shuddering so violently that he was scared the screws attaching it to the floor might soon shake loose. Grapos had wedged himself in against the side of the vehicle, and when Prentice glanced back he thought he saw for the first time a flicker of uncertainty in the Greek's narrowed eyes. Ford's reaction was brief but significant: he leaned forward, stared at the speedometer, then braced his back against the bench. In his determination to out-distance the following half-track Macomber seemed to be going far beyond the bounds of a calculated risk as he drove steadily downwards, the high earthen banks sliding past them in a blur, the sound of the pounding tracks confined inside the sunken road like the noise from a stamping mill, and now the revolving metal was developing a disconnected rhythm which brought Prentice's raw nerves to screaming point. Was the Scot intent on killing every man aboard?

The mist had rolled like a grey fog over the gulley below, temporarily blotting out the narrowing distance between the rushing half-track and the bridge, and it was only when the greyness dispersed briefly that Macomber grasped his mistake, understood that he had overestimated his margin of safety badly, saw the bridge – with the right-angled turn beyond – soaring up towards him, alarmingly close. He began to lose speed knowing that he was too late, that the half-track must still be moving too fast when the moment came to swing the wheel, to turn to the left sharply over the bridge and then turn to the right even more sharply once he was across it. He lost more speed, lost it dangerously quickly, and behind him his three passengers – Grapos now on his feet, grasping the rear of the bench which seated Prentice and Ford – were like frozen men, men who had lost all ability to move even as they stared petrified at what lay ahead of them, knowing that they were going straight through the bridge wall into the river below.

CHAPTER TEN

Sunday, 2 PM

Too late to brake, too late to reduce speed – by orthodox methods. Macomber veered to the left suddenly, immediately veered back to the right, straightened up again. At the speed they were moving the huge tracks at the rear responded a fraction later, as he had intended, and the left-hand caterpillar cracked into the earthen bank with shattering impact, jerking Prentice's bones almost out of their sockets as the caterpillar partially acted as a brake. The vehicle bounced smartly off the bank and a flurry of earth minced up by the revolving track showered over them as the other bank rushed towards them. Macomber had veered to the right now, then to the left, straightened up again, but this time the collision was far more violent and the wheel nearly leapt out of his hands, which would have brought on final disaster, but somehow he maintained his grip as the vehicle shuddered wildly, wobbled uncertainly, still holding its equilibrium as more earth burst in the air and rained down over them. The trouble was he had overdone it this time.

The right-hand caterpillar was acting superbly as an improvised braking system, had lost him a great deal of lethal speed, but the track rammed against the bank had become trapped and now it was rotating furiously inside the earth as it desperately tried to break free. Macomber was holding the wheel with a ferocious grip which signified more than an attempt to regain control – it also signified his fear that the track would come loose, break away altogether from the vehicle. Above the roar of the engine a new sound screamed out, a sound of churning metal rasping over rocks embedded inside the bank, a hellish sound which went on and on as the track revolved frantically and clouds of earth and loose stones soared above them. Then it freed itself and the half-track leapt forward down the natural gradient while Macomber wrestled to keep control, to lose more speed without tipping them over as the right-angled bridge rushed up to meet them. He hit the ice patch at the moment when he felt he might just make it.

The ice patch, starting at a point where part of the earth bank had collapsed into a ditch, was several inches thick, so instead of breaking under the enormous weight of the vehicle it propelled the half-track forward like a sledge sweeping over a skating-rink. Macomber turned the wheels, felt them take on a life of their own, as they hurtled down on the leftward turn over the bridge. He swung the wheels farther to the left, praying for the massive tracks to act as a sheet-anchor, then they were half-way round the bend with the tracks continuing the sweep behind them and Macomber had the feeling some irresistible power had taken hold of their tail as the momentum of track weight carried them farther and farther sideways. The wheels were half-way up the bridge when the right-hand track smashed into the stone wall, a dry-stone edifice of boulders unsealed with mortar. The impact of steel against stone was mind-shattering: Prentice was hurled along the bench, stopped by the side of the vehicle as Ford cannoned into him, and only Grapos, still upright, held his position by the tightness of his grip on the rear of the bench. A few feet beyond them, Macomber took less of the shock, but the impact sound was deafening as the track battered the wall open, tumbled huge boulders into the river below, and then they were suspended over the brink, half the right-hand track in the air over the drop. Prentice shook his head to fight down the stunned sensation, peered over the side and saw he was looking down into the river thirty feet below, a foaming torrent which carried along half-submerged floats of greenish ice. He felt the half-track tremble, begin to tip backwards gently. They were going over . . .

At the last moment Macomber had braked. A swift glance over his shoulder showed him the appalling danger – the jagged gap between the boulders, the greenish swirl, a third of the vehicle in mid-air, so probably at least half the equilibrium, then he, too, felt the tremble, the insidious lifting motion beginning. He released the brake, depressed his foot.

The engine throbbed, built up power; something bumped gently in front. Christ, the wheels had left the ground, had just returned to the road surface! Something had locked on-to the vehicle, holding it fast. He felt the floor rising under him again as they started to tip backwards again, the wheels clear of the ground. They were going to somersault over, the track weight no longer a sheet-anchor as it performed the function of a fulcrum to see-saw the half-track down into the roaring torrent. Mist like smoke drifted over the bridge, obscuring the view like a London fog, the clammy moisture settling on Macomber's sweat-stained forehead. His instinct – of self-preservation – urged him to leave the wheel, to jump for it onto the road still beside him – but for once he ignored the instinct, knowing that the others would go over the edge with the vehicle. He remained rigid behind the wheel, pressing his foot down still farther as the caterpillars revolved furiously among the scattered boulders, metal clashing so savagely with stone that Prentice saw flint-sparks fly in the mist. It lasted perhaps twenty seconds – the final skid, the smash into the wall, the first lift of the vehicle, the brief return to firm ground, the second more nerve-rasping tilt. It was the left-hand cater-pillar Macomber was counting on, the track less thrust out over the drop, the track whose treads still clawed at firm ground, and now the gamble began to work as the caterpillar shifted the mess of boulders and grated its way forward inch by inch – dragging the other track with it until that also gained a firmer grip and did its part in heaving the vehicle farther on to the bridge, farther away from the yawning gap. Macomber felt it coming, felt the wheels hit the road again, released some foot pressure just in time as the vehicle surged free, and in freeing itself the right-hand track let go of a section of wall which had leaned outwards under the shock of the initial impact. Above the growl of the engine they heard a muffled splash as a whole fresh section of wall dived into the river and Macomber steered the half-track over the bridge and started to take the right-hand turn, then braked. He looked back, his engine still running.

'Jesus . . . I thought that was it . . .' Prentice wiped his damp face while Ford licked his lips and held his wounded shoulder where it had cannoned into the lieutenant. Grapos, recovering more quickly than the others, had his rifle gripped in his hands as he stared backwards the way they had come, the way the pursuing half-track would come. 'Not much point in hanging about here, is there? Let's get moving,' Prentice demanded irritably.

'There might be – a point in waiting here for them.' Macomber stared back at the wrecked wall. The vanished section was perhaps twenty feet wide and he was seeing it as the Germans would see it when they reached the bridge, his mind racing while he tried to estimate their likely reaction when they reached the bottom of the hill. The mist, which had thinned but still swirled over the bridge, made the devastation look even worse, like the aftermath of a battlefield. He looked forward again to where the road turned to go up the mountain: the road turned right sharply, but to the left, where the bridge ended, a rock slope continued up from the road and disappeared behind a clump of trees only half-seen in the greyness. A gentle slope which looked firm enough, firm enough to take up the half-track. 'I want you all to get out and take up position for when they arrive. We'll fight it out here,' he said abruptly.'

'What the hell for?' Prentice was vehement. 'If we go on we should keep ahead of them with a bit of luck...'

'Up that mountain road?' Macomber was twisted round in his seat again where he could face Prentice and his expression was grim. 'Look, I've been up that road once before – it's just about wide enough to take this thing, it zigzags backwards and forwards up the mountain with a sheer wall on one side, a sheer drop on the other, and higher up it may be covered with shot ice. There's even ice in the river behind us. We'll be crawling up that mountain like a man going up on his belly...'

'We'll still be in front,' Prentice persisted obstinately, 'and if we have to, we may discover a better spot to ambush them...'

'Not as good as this.' The Scot was eyeing the left-hand slope speculatively. 'And we're more likely to get the element of surprise here – they'll think we went over with that wall.'

'Not when they look over and see nothing there, they won't...'

'So, we'll have to make sure that by the time they discover their mistake it's too late.'

'You'll have to hide the half-track,' Ford pointed out soberly. 'It would give the whole game away if they can see...'

'That's the guts of the thing.' Macomber extracted one of his three remaining cigars, lit it quickly. 'They won't spot it until it's too late if I can work this the way I see it.' He took several puffs and then pointed up the slope. 'I'll be up there inside those trees and I don't want anyone opening fire too soon. They'll come down that road, maybe a bit more slowly than we came down it, and they'll see the ice patch, which will slow them down even more, give them time to spot that smashed-up wall. But they won't stop on the ice – they'll keep on coming and pull up on the bridge to have a look. That's when I come down out of those trees. Then you can shoot as long as your ammunition lasts out.'

'You're going up that slope?' There was an incredulous note in Prentice's voice. 'You'll never make it – you must be bonkers even to attempt it...'

'What are you beefing about?' Macomber growled. 'You're not coming with me – and I'm just beginning to get the feel of this gadget. I could even get to like it. Now, for God's sake get moving – they'll be here any minute.'

Partly because he felt they had lost too much time to continue up the mountain, partly because he sensed the agreement of Ford and of Grapos, who had dropped into the road and was already looking for a good vantage point, Prentice reluctantly helped Ford out of the vehicle, and as soon as they were in the roadway Macomber let off the brake and began driving forward. The slope was a little steeper than he had anticipated but once the tracks gripped its surface he felt them steadily pushing the vehicle up the ascent. The mist was thickening again when he had climbed sixty feet above the bridge and he switched on his lights to see where he was going. The beams were blurred cones and the lights reflected off tiny particles of moisture as they penetrated the trees, showed up a massive slab of rock beyond. Tilted at an angle of perhaps thirty degrees, sagged back heavily against his seat, he steered the half-track cautiously between two tree-trunks, pulled it up with its nose inches from the slab, looked back and swore. The one essential of the ambush was a clear view of the bridge and the mist had closed over it, blotting it out completely. If it didn't shift before the German half-track arrived he was impotent, powerless to help, and the other three would have to fight it out alone. He took out the cigar, moistened his lips and waited with the engine ticking over. Another calculated risk – that the motor of the German vehicle combined with the mist would muffle the sound of his own engine. What the devil was keeping Jerry?

Waiting was an activity – if doing nothing can be termed activity – Macomber had some experience of. Waiting in the shadows of a warehouse on the Danube while he checked the supplies going aboard a barge; waiting beneath a manhole cover while a German soldier patrolled the street above; some of his most gruelling hours during the past fifteen months had been spent waiting. But at the moment waiting didn't suit him; it gave a chance for the fatigue to make itself felt, to settle in his weary limbs and his over-strained mind, and he wondered how much more he could take before his final reserves were drained. Even the slow-motion coils of mist which drifted below as he remained twisted round in his seat seemed to add to the appalling tiredness which was becoming his permanent condition. He blinked, thinking he saw a man creeping up through the mist, but it was only the vapour assuming strange shapes, and then, above the murmuring throb of his own motor, he heard the sound he had been waiting for.

The half-track proceeding cautiously down the hill echoed weirdly through the fogged silence, a distant engine sound combining with a more distinctive noise – the rattle and grind of the descending tracks. And still the bridge was lost, might be a dozen miles away for all he could see of it through the dense pall which smothered the slope so that now it might have been late evening or early morning. Had he known this was going to happen he could have stopped lower down, relying on the mist alone to conceal his presence, but it was far too

201

late to alter position, so all he could do was to wait and hope – hope that damned mist would thin in time. The clanking sound was closer now, the half-track still moving slowly, as he had foreseen it would. His hand went towards the brake, clutched it, and he had forgotten he was smoking as he stared fixedly downwards, trying to make up his mind whether the mist had thinned just a little. His eyes were feeling the strain of staring in one direction and a dull ache was building up behind his temples as the clanking noise grew louder, still a muffled ratchetty sound, but definitely louder. They'd be at the bottom any moment now, turning onto the bridge. It wasn't going to work, there was going to be a tragedy down there, Macomber felt it in his chilled bones, a chill brought on by a feeling of almost unbearable frustration which twitched at his nerves. I may be responsible for the death of three men, he thought.

A breath of wind touched his face as he heard the engine sound slow – they had reached the bottom, they were turning the corner. He suddenly realized his lights were still on and switched them off quickly. A blunder like that would have lost him his life long ago. Pull yourself together, for Christ's sake, this is going to be tricky enough as it is without going to sleep on the job. A noise like gently falling water came from above as the wind rustled the trees, then the mist began to retreat rapidly, to dissolve back down the slope as the wind parted it in melting eddies. He stiffened, his side rigid against the seat, straining to see what was happening down there. Had a voice drifted up from below? He was frowning ferociously, still trying to decide, when the mist cleared from the bridge and he saw the German half-track turning the first corner as it lumbered up to the bridge and stopped, broadside on to the destroyed wall, stopped in the position Macomber had prayed it would stop. Four men inside, and the man standing up by the driver was Hahnemann. Too far away to see clearly, but Macomber knew it was Hahnemann, knew it for a certainty from the way he moved. Now!

He released the brake, accelerated, reversed down the slope at gathering speed as the tracks churned and slithered their way down, the revolutions increasing with every yard of the

202

descent. Had they reacted instantly, remained cool, taking deliberate aim before they fired, they might have killed the Scot, freed the half-track's steering so it would have careered in a different direction. But Macomber had counted on the element of surprise, on the element of terror which can freeze men's minds for vital seconds, on the view as seen from the bridge which a moment earlier had seemed so deserted, on the view seconds later as they heard the harsh grind and thunder of the descending tracks and saw the tank-like projectile coming out of the mist and roaring down on them. Still twisted round in his seat, both hands locked to the wheel, steering by feel alone, Macomber turned the direction of the onslaught a fraction, aiming the half-track square at the vehicle below. He saw Hahnemann react at last, saw him haul out his pistol from his holster, raise it, take deliberate aim, then collapse as Grapos, secreted behind a rock above the bridge, fired at the same moment as Prentice pressed the trigger of his machine-pistol. Hahnemann's three companions ducked, or fell, Macomber had no idea which, as the tracks bounded over a flat boulder and changed direction round the end of the bridge, smashing with enormous force into the side of the German vehicle parked by the gap. The collision was tremendous, a jarring shock which knocked Macomber backward into the wheel, and only his anticipation of what was coming prevented his being impaled on the steering column as he braked at the last moment, a split-second problem of timing since he needed all the force of the rushing descent to strike the half-track before he tried to escape following it to destruction. The battering-ram blow slammed the German vehicle half-way over the edge as one of the Alpenkorps men scrambled dazedly to his feet, acted intuitively and threw himself over the brink, only to be followed seconds later by the half-track which dropped sideways and buried him when it plunged into the river. A burst of water jumped up to bridge height, subsided, and Macomber, turning painfully round saw that his own vehicle was perched on the brink, but perched safely. He was lying forward over the wheel, taking in great gulps of mist-laden air when Prentice reached him. 'Are you all right, Mac?'

'I think so. Stand clear a minute.'

Afterwards he could never remember his automatic action of driving forward slowly and turning the half-track so it faced towards the mountain road before he braked, switched off the engine and staggered out onto the road where Prentice held him as his legs almost gave way. 'I'm not too bad ... I'll survive. I want to see...' He stumbled over to a piece of the remaining wall and leant heavily against it while he looked over. The half-track, upside down, had been caught by two huge boulders thrust above the water, but as he looked down it lost its balance, tipped over sideways, wallowed briefly three-parts submerged and then sank. Bubbles coming up from it reached the surface and were then whipped away in the fast-flowing current, so he couldn't be sure whether his eyes had played him a trick. The sunken vehicle gave up one last memory, the uniformed body of an Alpenkorps man who came to the surface and then was swept away downriver, towards Molos, towards the Gulf of Zervos. 'Poor devil,' Macomber muttered, then he straightened up, still using the wall for support. 'There'll be others on the way, so we'd better get on – up the mountain.'

CHAPTER ELEVEN

Sunday, 2·30 PM

The ledge which supported the road was dangerously narrow – as Macomber had predicted they were hemmed in between a vertical wall of rock to their right, a wall which climbed high above them, while to their left the abyss fell away to unknown depths, unknown because the mist below prevented them from seeing how far down the drop continued. They were fifteen minutes' driving time from the wrecked bridge – no great distance considering he had been compelled to move up at a rate of only a few miles per hour – but in that time they had climbed steadily and Macomber calculated that soon they would have ascended a thousand feet, one thousand nerve-crushing feet. Before they had left the bridge Prentice had offered to take over the wheel, but the Scot refused the suggestion. 'I think I've a little experience of handling her now,' he had remarked drily, conferring a feminine status on the most unfeminine-looking object imaginable, 'you might even say I've had a crash course in coping with a half-track.'

'Crash is the word,' Prentice agreed humorously, 'and that's why I'm wondering whether you're in fit state to drive it up the mountain.'

'If I'm not, you should have time to nip off the back.'

Prentice was recalling this last optimistic remark as he stared over the side to where the world dropped away into nothingness. The tracks were grinding irritably over the shale-strewn road as he leaned forward to speak directly into Macomber's ear. 'You'll watch it, won't you, Mac? This isn't too good a place for nipping off anywhere.'

'You could slip over, too, even if you made it – you've seen what's coming up?'

Prentice stared ahead and was joined in his stare by Ford and Grapos who shared the same bench seat. Up to this moment the road had a dull, powdery look, but ahead it gleamed with a sinister sheen – a sheen of ice which coated the surface from wall to brink. 'That doesn't look too funny,' Ford remarked thoughtfully as he recalled vividly what had happened to the half-track when it hit the ice patch on their way down to the bridge. 'Think we can make it?' Prentice asked softly, subconsciously seeking reassurance.

'It may be all right,' Macomber replied non-committally as he edged the vehicle forward. 'Nothing's ever as bad as you think it's going to be – once you try it.' But his confident reply, deliberately delivered in that form to keep up the morale of his passengers, hardly corresponded with his misgivings. Further evidence that they were climbing steadily was provided by the equally steady drop in temperature and already the mist drifting over his windscreen was lingering, settling to form streaks of blobbed ice. There was no wind worth speaking of at this height yet; just a relentless fall in temperature which caused the Scot to pull the scarf a little tighter round his neck, a purity of cold which inhibited speech and made a man want to sink into the stillness of the mountain. The tracks rumbled forward under them as the ice came closer and Macomber cursed their bad luck – this hazard had presented itself at the very moment when the ledge was narrowing so there was barely a foot of free space on either side of the lumbering vehicle.

He was finding it more difficult to handle in the confined space – no leeway for even the fraction of an error and the concentration required every second was beginning to sap his last reserves of energy, to dull the keenness of his nerves just when he needed every ounce of alertness he could summon up. The vehicle moved on, passing into the ice zone as Macomber sat up straighter, every fibre of his consciousness keyed up for the first sign of slipping, the first hint that the tracks were in trouble – because it was the tracks which would get them through if they survived this ordeal, their weight which would hold the vehicle on the ledge – and conversely it was their malfunction which could bring about the final disaster, the slither backwards which he might not be able to control, ending in their dropping over the precipice, hauled down by the weight which had earlier saved them. Above the slow clatter he heard a new sound, the chilling prickle as the tracks moved onto the ice, followed immediately by a crackle like breaking glass. He let out his breath: it was all right, the ice was breaking. He had to keep up this gradual pace and the tracks would anchor the vehicle while the wheels crossed the treacherous surface, then the tracks would fracture it to allow their own safe passage. Within a minute he was frowning, knowing he had miscalculated dangerously, that his remark that nothing was as bad as you expected was incorrect – things could be worse, infinitely worse. It was the *feel* of the half-track which warned him, something he was becoming familiar with, because now they felt to be moving over a permanent smoothness. The grip of the caterpillars into the road he had noted farther down was missing. They weren't gripping any more – they were moving upwards over a second more solid layer of ice beneath; only the surface had cracked. And he was coming to a bend. And he could see the first of the snow, white streaks garnishing the gleaming surface. Prentice leaned close to his shoulder, careful not to distract him, to keep his tone moderate and calm.

'Look, Mac, I think we have a problem. We're still moving over ice. The stuff must be inches thick.'

'I know. You'd better all move onto the rear bench – just in case.'

'I appreciate the suggestion...' Prentice was speaking with studious calm, a calm he was making a certain effort to assume, '... but I don't think that would help. If we start to go we'll go backwards, so I don't foresee any rush to leave by the rear exit.'

He was right, of course, Macomber thought pessimistically; they were totally boxed in – by the wall, the abyss, and by the danger of the vehicle starting to slide backwards. Their options were also critically limited in another direction which Prentice probably hadn't grasped yet: Macomber dare not risk braking – stopping on this glass-like surface – because once he stopped they would face the almost inevitable peril that when the half-track tried to move forward again the caterpillars would revolve uselessly over the ice, the first stage in the final slip-back. Boxed in, unable to stop, compelled to move up and up whatever faced them, Macomber began easing the vehicle round the shallow curve, his eyes switching constantly from one point to another – from the curving wall to the extension of the road ahead in case it narrowed even farther. He sat very still behind the wheel, his mind filled with the clanking sound of the turning metal, the curve of the sheer wall which went on and on, the sharp edge where the road ended and the blurred abyss began.

Behind him Prentice sat motionless on the bench in the position nearest to the drop, with Ford in the middle and Grapos seated close to the wall, a wall the Greek viewed with increasing disenchantment as it insidiously moved nearer to his right shoulder: the ledge was contracting. Perched above the brink, Prentice's gloved hand gripped the side of the vehicle as though attached to it and he felt the vibrations of engine and tracks passing up his arm, felt the freezing air numbing his cheeks, felt the tremble of the half-track when it wobbled as it passed over an ice-coated unevenness. The crackling sound, the thinly-iced layer crumbling under the weight, came to him above the engine's purr like the sputtering of a log fire, the symbol of warmth while he slowly froze into a state of immobility, and he couldn't take his eyes off the ribbon of ascending ledge which gradually unwound as the road climbed higher and higher. How much more of this could Mac stand? An audacious gamble – like the reversing of the half-track down the slope to hit the Germans on the bridge – he had grasped this side of the Scot's character; but this murderous, mind-killing creep up the ice-bound mountain, this was something else again, something which made him regard the Scot with far greater awe. And he must be nearly asleep over that wheel ... He pushed the thought out of his head quickly. It frightened him too much. Glancing at the others, he saw Ford's hands clasped rather tightly in his lap, his face woodèn, whereas Grapos was leaning forward, watching the road intently as though expecting a fresh hazard any second. To take his mind off watching the road Prentice pulled out the looped rope from under the bench, saw that at one end a grappling hook was attached, and when he opened the Alpenkorps satchel he saw more climbing equipment – another rope, pitons, a hammer. As he shoved satchel and rope back under the bench something damp flaked his face, dropped into his lap. It had started snowing.

The snow started falling heavily as they navigated a fresh turn in the road and a rising wind met them, a bitter wind which blew the flakes into a turmoil so they danced above the ledge, driven this way and that in disconcerting flurries. For Macomber the coming of the snow was the final straw, the ultimate hazard. He had kept the half-track on the ledge, maintaining an even space on either side as it narrowed, as he found himself increasingly compressed between wall and brink; maintaining an even speed as it balanced itself delicately on the solid ice, but he had accomplished this gruelling task with a reasonable visibility. Now this only asset was taken away from him as blinding snow fogged his vision, pasted itself over the windscreen, blurred wall and precipice edge to mere silhouettes whose exact location he could no longer rely on. He switched on the lights and they sent out short-lived swathes penetrating only a few yards inside the frenzy of the snowstorm which was growing rapidly more violent as the wind rose to a moaning howl and the men on the bench seat behind him bowed their heads to shield themselves against the onslaught of the elements. Grapos, his chin dug into his chest, was peering warily to his right where the rock face seemed to be closing in; if they collided with that at the wrong moment it could veer the vehicle outwards and over the drop, and Macomber, seated on the other side of the half-track was less able to judge their distance from the wall than from the brink. In the faint hope that he might be able to issue a warning in time, the Greek lifted his head, ignored the whipping snowflakes which stung his skin and stared ahead through half-closed eyes. No doubt about it – they were appreciably closer to the wall.

This slight change of position was not a mistake on the Scot's part as Grapos feared; it was a deliberate act to try and reduce a little the overwhelming danger they now faced. Unsure from moment to moment of the precise position of the abyss edge he had turned in nearer to the mountain, knowing that if they struck the rock face he at least had a chance to recover, and knowing that if the tracks tipped over the edge there would be no chance of survival at all. Macomber had seriously considered halting, but they were still passing over solid ice and they were still moving up a steepish incline, so if he could keep going until the storm died away the hazards were probably a fraction less dangerous than the hazards of stopping – to say nothing of the fact that somewhere not too far behind them Burckhardt's force must already be making its own way up the mountain road. And the possibility of finding himself stationary on the ice-bound ledge as armed men, more than likely men equipped with mortars, came round a corner in his rear was not a contingency which appealed to him. He turned his head slightly, shouted to make himself heard above the howling wind. 'Any idea how much farther, Grapos?'

'One kilometre beyond the big bend.'

'How far to this ruddy bend?'

'Soon – very soon now.'

'How do you know in this stuff?' Macomber bawled out sceptically.

'Because of the gash.'

Gash? The Scot glanced quickly to his right and saw for the first time a break in the endless mountain wall, a fissure scarcely wider than the breadth of a man, and beyond the gyrating snow he had a glimpse of a narrow tumble of water which fell almost vertically and which was frozen solid in mid-air. Then it was gone. Jesus, the temperature must be low up here. As he looked ahead again the road began to turn round the mountain, and it went on turning, which forced him to keep the wheel swung over permanently to the right, but at least this was an improvement on the zigzags he had encountered lower down, hairpin bends he doubted he could even have attempted if the snow had come then. He drove on, up and up, following the continuing curve of the wall, peering from underneath his Alpenkorps cap brim as his gaze switched from brink to wall and back again to brink, and so great was his concentration that it was a few minutes before he realized there had been a change in the weather. It was still snowing but the wind had dropped, fading away to a chilling stillness as the curtain of snow floated down almost vertically in the windless atmosphere. For the hundredth time he brushed his hand over the windscreen to clear the snow: the wipers had packed up some time ago and his hand was equally effective for removing some of the freezing snow which was steadily adhering to the glass at either end of the screen. And now the headlights penetrated farther, giving him a safer view of what was coming up – and they were only about one kilometre from safety according to Grapos. The thought had barely passed through his head when he stiffened, felt his hands grip the wheel more tightly. A short distance ahead a boulder rested against the inner wall, a boulder rounded and partly covered with snow, and as the headlights moved nearer he saw its massive size, that it was only partly protruding from a ravine similar to the one they had recently passed, that it must have tumbled down the ravine and then become jammed in the exit immovably just before it crossed the ledge and swept down into the abyss. The dream of safety receded as every turn of the tracks took them closer to the emergency. Macomber weighed up the chances quickly – the boulder appeared firmly jammed inside the ravine, they were within a kilometre of easier going, there appearing to be just sufficient room for them to squeeze past, but it would take them to the edge of the precipice.

'You'll never make it, Mac...' It was Prentice's strained voice which spoke, but the Scot maintained the same even pace as he called back to them.

'Prentice, get to the back and watch the tracks – the outside one. If I'm going over, signal Ford by waving your hand. Ford! You warn me by clapping a hand on my left shoulder – damned quickly, too!' He heard feet moving back along the floorboards. Someone slipped in the snow and swore as they saved themselves. On his own initiative Grapos went back to watch the inner track which had to pass the boulder. Macomber reduced speed to a point where he feared the engine might stop altogether and the snow-covered obstacle crept closer and seemed to magnify itself hugely as he steered away from the mountain wall to give himself maximum clearance, which involved placing the left-hand track on the very edge of the precipice.

The half-track crept forward through the deepening gloom, because now the snow drifting down had made it seem almost like night, and his headlights reflected weirdly off the ice covering which had formed over the mountain wall. It was like living through a bad dream, Macomber thought wearily – the drifting snow which he no longer brushed away from the windscreen, from his weighted coat; the uncanny silence, the muffled throb of the engine, the creak of the turning tracks, the blurred cones of the headlights, and now that frozen gleam off the rock wall. Inside his gloves his hands had hardly any feeling left, his feet were losing contact with the rest of his body, the dull ache in his forehead was fogging his mind, and he had the strange sensation that he was disembodied, that his limbs belonged to someone else, that he was reacting like an automaton. Perhaps his judgement had gone, he was attempting the impossible, and they would end up plunging into that abyss which could easily go down for a couple of thousand feet. He blinked, bit his lip, pushed the defeatist thoughts out of his mind and glared ferociously ahead as the trapped boulder moved closer and closer and the outer track revolved along the rim of the ledge. They were within yards of the obstacle now, would attempt to slide past it within seconds.

At the rear of the vehicle Prentice was leant half over the side as he followed the progress of the caterpillar which was starting to inch out over the precipice as they began to pass the boulder. It was a frightening sight – a portion of the moving belt suspended over the drop – and he was on the verge of signalling to Ford when he decided to wait a few seconds longer, to see whether the position deteriorated. On the far side, mid-way along the half-track, Grapos was gazing down at the boulder with equal intensity while the inner track churned slowly forward, drew alongside it and shaved snow from its encrusted surface. Glancing over his shoulder towards Prentice he frowned at the lieutenant's precariously poised position and then looked down at the boulder again. The main section of track was beginning to slide past it. Prentice, leaning over the

212

outer edge, was supporting himself with one hand only to give himself the best possible view of what was happening, and the fact that his head was almost upside down probably brought on the attack. He was in the same position, staring intently as an inch of track revolved in mid-air, when the dizziness swept over him and he knew he was going to faint. Muddled, disorientated, he felt the quick movement of his right foot slipping over a patch of snow at the same moment as he heard the first grind of the vehicle against the boulder. His balance went completely, both feet sliding under him as Grapos lurched across the half-track, grasped his right arm and jerked him backwards. Prentice fell heavily, caught the back of his head on the bench and sprawled on the floorboards.

Macomber was concentrating on the precipice brink, his hands gripping the wheel, his foot ready to apply a little pressure, when he heard the scraping sound of the inner track contacting the boulder. He waited, his nerves strung up to fever pitch, waited for the hand to descend on his shoulder warning him to brake, and when nothing happened – confident that Prentice was still checking the outer caterpillar – he continued forward. The vehicle was shuddering unpleasantly as the scraping developed into a grinding sound and he suppressed the urge to glance back. His job was driving, not observation, but again he was obsessed with the mounting fear of what would happen if the caterpillar disengaged from the vehicle, leaving it with only two wheels and a single track, which must cause a state of fatal disequilibrium within seconds. The half-track shuddered again and the vibrations travelled up the steering column while he resisted the temptation to steer the front wheels, which were now well past the boulder, in towards the mountain wall. Then the shuddering and grinding noise ceased at the same moment. He drove a few yards farther forward and turned the wheel, taking the half-track away from the edge. Within minutes the road was fanning out, becoming wider as the weather began to clear and the snow drifted down more slowly, soon to stop altogether. To his right the mountain wall moved away from him, the road followed it at a distance, and on his left the precipice faded away where the ground sloped more gradually. He increased speed, experiencing a sense of exhilaration.

'Soon we shall see the monastery.' It was Grapos who spoke with hoarse confidence as he stood behind the Scot and stared over the windshield. 'We go down, pass a big rock, and there it is.'

'How are the others?'

'Prentice fell down and struck his head, but he is conscious again and Ford is helping him.'

Macomber glanced over his shoulder and saw Prentice seated on the rear bench with his head between his hands and Ford beside him. The lieutenant looked up, caught the Scot's frowning expression and waved back encouragingly. 'I'll be OK in a minute – how much farther before we see something?'

'Not far. Take it easy while you can.' Macomber looked up at Grapos. 'That rock you mentioned – I seem to remember it hangs out over the road, doesn't it?'

'Yes. We pass it – we see the monastery.'

They were travelling downhill but the view to the south was obscured by a snowbound slope as they lost altitude rapidly, descending into a bowl with wintry hills sweeping down on all sides. Along the ridges the wind whipped up the snow in flurries which eddied briefly and then vanished, but the sky above was a clear cold blue and the sun shone palely and without warmth. Macomber thought he had never seen such a bleak landscape, a wilderness where savage rocks reared up in strange shapes which reminded him of the wastelands of Arizona. They were close to one of these weird rock formations – the only one which towered above the road – when Grapos' hand gripped his shoulder tightly. 'There is someone up there – up on the crag.' Macomber looked up a second too late and they were already moving into the faint shadow the rock cast across the road. He slowed down, braked under the lee of the rock, and followed Grapos out of the half-track, flexing his stiffened fingers which had become almost locked to the wheel.

They had climbed only a few feet when the Greek pulled the Scot close to the rock and whispered. 'I go up this side – you take the other and wait. If he hears me coming he will go down your side – you wait and he meets you.' Macomber nodded, scrambled stiffly back down through knee-deep snow to the road, gestured to the other two men to stay where they were, and made his way under the looming rock. The far side was a steep slope covered with harder snow where the east wind had blown over it, and he had climbed less than fifty feet before he came up behind a large boulder which provided a perfect ambush point. With his Luger in his hand he settled down to wait, and while he waited he stared out at the panoramic view.

The monastery was in sight. Mount Zervos, remote above the vagaries of the weather was fully exposed to view. Crouched behind his boulder, Macomber saw that it was as he remembered it – the huge bluff shouldered out from the mountain, hanging over the sea on one side while on the other it plunged hundreds of feet to the lake below. The walls of the monastery rose vertically from the summit of the bluff; four windowed slabs like giant watch-towers linked together by battlemented walls. They seemed to grow up out of the rocky bluff as they sheered upwards and were silhouetted against the sea with the mainland beyond, the most remote and ascetic hermitage in all Europe – and the ultimate objective of Colonel Burckhardt.

The sea was grey and choppy but comparatively calm as the last of the snowstorm crossed the gulf. Macomber doubted whether the snow had even reached the bluff this time, so once again the monastery had retained its unimpaired view across the sea to the mainland supply road. Below where he waited the ground receded away to the lake, a stretch of water at least half a mile wide, a lake frozen solid. The road went down to the eastern shore, turned along the northern edge of the ice-sheet, and then vanished before reappearing at the far end, close to the sea at the point where it began its unseen ascent to the bluff. A good half mile of the road was lost, blocked completely by an immense mass of snow heaped up against the slope below Macomber. This was drift snow, probably anything up to thirty feet deep, snow blown there recently by the high wind and which would strangle any type of powered vehicle attempting to drive through it. He stared down at the frozen lake, a sheet of water which must have frozen steadily thicker throughout the long winter. Was it solid enough to support half-tracks and mountain guns? A rattle of disturbed stones beyond the boulder warned him that someone was coming.

'Do not shoot! Please!'

Grapos' voice. Macomber lowered his Luger, stood up and saw the Greek leaning against the rock face with his rifle hoisted harmlessly over his shoulder. 'What's wrong?' he asked sharply.

'He is dead. Come, you must see.'

'Who's dead?'

But the Greek had turned back and was scrambling up again through the snow, using one hand to lever his limping foot more rapidly up past the rock. Macomber swore at his ambiguousness and went up after him. When he arrived at the top, receiving the full blast of the wind in his face, Grapos was staring down at a flattened projection just below which spurred out over the road, and Macomber found he could see down past the spur into the half-track where Ford still sat on the rear bench while Prentice stood in the road gazing up at them with his machine-pistol at the ready.

The uniformed figure on the spur lay sprawled over a machine gun. His attitude was that of a soldier watching the road from the north, the road they had just driven down in the half-track, but despite the presence of the two men above him he remained in his life-like posture until Grapos reached down and prodded him with his rifle tip. The uniformed figure went over sideways and ended up on his back with his face staring at the sky, a face with a rigid look and an unnatural bluish tinge. The poor devil had frozen to death at his post. Macomber gazed down at the Alpenkorps, uniform, the stiffened Alpenkorps cap which still clutched the head, the weapon which still stood mounted in position, the barrel encased in ice and frozen snow so that it had the appearance of a glass gun. The Germans were already on Zervos, had already penetrated the monastery.

CHAPTER TWELVE

Sunday, Zero Hour

The attack on the monastery was planned, agreed in detail, and each man knew the part he had to play. The plan was Macomber's, a plan which relied on audacity, on an eruptive breakthrough into the heart of the sanctuary, and it was based on the unproven assumption that only a small number of Germans had taken over the place in preparation for the arrival of Burckhardt's army. It was also based on Grapos' intimate knowledge of the interior of the monastery, knowledge which Prentice had transferred to his notebook as a series of ground-plans which showed the layout. It was the basic assumption which still worried Prentice as he closed the book and tucked it inside his pocket.

'If there are more men up there than we think, we haven't a hope,' he warned.

'I agree,' Macomber replied briskly, 'but it's logical. They must have arrived as civilians – the only safe way they could travel before war was declared – and in that case a large party would arouse suspicion. They only faced the monks, so a few of them could do the job.' He checked his watch. 'And we've spent twenty-one minutes working this out, so we'd better get moving before Burckhardt lands on our tail. God knows there's enough to do in the time . . .'

He had kept the engine ticking over during their discussion; now he released the brake and the half-track began moving down towards the lake. Behind him the others were seated on the floor of the vehicle, their backs against its sides and their heads crouched forward, so from a distance it appeared that only Macomber, still wearing his Alpenkorps cap, occupied the vehicle. As they rumbled downhill at a steady pace the caterpillars whipped up the soft snow and cast it into the ditches on either side, and within a few minutes they had driven past the point where the road entered the massive snowdrift, had crossed a stretch of uneven ground and were pulling up at the eastern end of the lake to give Macomber a chance to study the ice. He would have liked to conduct a reconnaissance, to attempt walking out over the ice, but time was short. He had little faith in the Germans being held up for long by that boulder on the mountain ledge: with their manpower and the equipment they carried they would soon shift it higher up the ravine, and since he had negotiated the formidable road the weather had improved. German luck again. The wind, bitter and penetrating, whined eerily across the frozen sheet and he could see snow powder blowing over the dulled surface, but was Grapos right – right in his conviction that the prolonged winter had solidified the ice to a depth which would support the enormous weight of a half-track? He turned in his seat as though looking back up the road and saw Prentice's anxious face staring up at him. 'You think we might make it?' the lieutenant inquired.

'Only one way to find out.'

'I have told you,' Grapos repeated hoarsely. 'In winter the monks take their ox-wagons over the lake when the road is blocked.'

'As late in the year as this?' Macomber asked critically.

The Greek hesitated and Ford, disliking the hesitation, looked at him quickly. Grapos cleared his throat before speaking again, but his voice was confident. 'It is not usual – but five years since we also have the bad winter and then they take the wagons across in April. That was also the time of the great landslide – the avalanche. Much snow had fallen all through the winter and when the spring comes the mountain comes alive ...'

Macomber lit his last but one cigar, then interrupted the Greek's flow of words. 'Let's hope it's as thick as it was five years ago, then. And now I'd appreciate it if the League of Nations debate could be adjourned – this is going to take a little concentration.' He released the brake, exerted a little foot pressure and they were moving out over the ice.

He kept his speed down to a crawl, to less than ten miles an hour as the tracks rumbled hollowly over the ice sheet and

218

their treads ground into the surface with a brittle sound which tingled his nerves. It was almost spring, the time of the year when the ice would imperceptibly begin to thin, to lose that extra inch of solidity which might make all the difference to whether they crossed safely or plunged through shattered ice into the depths below. And the depths were something which didn't repay thinking about. During their discussion the Scot had asked Grapos about the depth of the lake and his answer had not exactly raised anyone's morale. 'Fifty metres. More deep in places,' had been the answer. Fifty metres. More than one hundred and fifty feet of sub-zero water below the frozen floor they were crossing. The right-hand track wobbled gently as it mounted an area of unevenness in the ice and then there was an unpleasant crushing sound as the track squashed the tiny ridge. Inside the vehicle Prentice, with his back against the right-hand side, felt the slight incline, followed by the trembling fall. His heart leapt, his hands locked round his machine-pistol and his eyes met Ford's. The staff-sergeant had an opaque look but Prentice saw the flicker of fear as Ford observed the brief contraction of the lieutenant's eyebrows. Then the half-track was rumbling forward smoothly again while Prentice flexed his fingers and let out his breath, breath expelled like a small puff of steam in the chilled temperature inside the vehicle.

The ordeal was probably more mind-wracking for the men concealed on the floor than for Macomber, because hidden away inside the half-track they couldn't see where they were going or how far they had come, and they experienced everything by feel alone, leaving their imaginations free to conjure up the most frightful possibilities. At least Macomber had a task to accomplish, a vehicle to steer; but for him the pressure built up in other ways. He had intended keeping close to the shore, driving past the immense snowdrift as he followed the line of the invisible road, but shortly after moving onto the lake he had taken an irrevocable decision, plagued by the desperate shortage of time. So he had changed his mind and was now heading on a course which would take them along the diameter of the circle – straight over the centre of the lake.

The half-track was rumbling smoothly on, wobbling only

occasionally, a wobble which was probably only the natural sway of the unwieldy vehicle, although for Macomber it had an unpleasant similarity to the bowing of weakened ice under a great weight, when he noticed the paler colour of a huge area of ice towards the centre of the lake. His lips tightened – he was on course to cross directly over this strangely discoloured section. In early winter, when ice had formed, it must have formed first at the fringes along the shore before creeping inwards until eventually it had encompassed the entire lake. So the ice in the centre was the freshest, the youngest, probably the thinnest. The wheels were close to this distinctive section when he changed direction, steering a curve which would take him beyond this possibly treacherous zone. He only hoped to God he had turned in time, that he wasn't already moving over ice only a fraction of the thickness of what they had already crossed. With an effort he resisted the urge to reduce speed – the advantage now might lie in crossing this area as swiftly as possible – but he also resisted the succeeding temptation to increase his speed over ten miles an hour, since faster movement might intensify the danger.

The distant shoreline crawled nearer with agonizing slowness. The huge snow-covered bluff to their left where the rock rose vertically from the lake slid behind them as they drew level with the rampart walls of the monastery. And now Macomber saw that there was someone at the summit of the lofty tower which overlooked lake and sea, a tiny, faceless figure too minute to be identified as monk or German soldier, and the Scot blessed his foresight in arranging for the others to conceal themselves on the floor. The sun was low, casting the interior of the half-track in deep shadow, so even a lookout with field-glasses would see only a German half-track driven by one man, a man in a nondescript coat with an Alpenkorps cap rammed down over his head. You see what you want to see, Macomber told himself, so with luck a German lookout would see one of his own vehicles sent ahead to test the stability of the ice. He sucked in a deep breath of chilled mountain air to revive his flagging reserves. God he was tired, he was so damned tired! Within the next few seconds he was stirred into petrified alertness.

He was within two hundred yards of safety, coming closer to the shoreline where the road emerged from the snowdrift, when he felt the vehicle begin to tremble, saw the ice sheet ahead of him tilt and quiver prior to the moment of fracturing fatally, realized that the huge weight under him was beginning to drop ... His hands tightened on the wheel, his foot pressed down on the accelerator – reflex actions he was unaware of – and the sagging motion of the half-track quickened. He was speeding forward over the ice when he grasped what was happening – happening to him rather than to the vehicle: he was suffering a violent attack of giddiness. He leaned back hard against the seat, sucked in quick gulps of the pure air, felt his lungs expanding, his head clearing, and then he was closing the gap between lake and road, keeping his foot pressed down regardless and with only one idea in his mind – to get clear of this bloody lake come hell or high water. The wheels bumped over rock-hard ruts, the half-track drove forward through frosted grasses which broke off and scattered like pine needles as it moved onto the road, and it was soon ascending until it was lost from the view of the monastery under the leaning overhang of the bluff towering above them. Macomber pulled up, left the engine running and rested on the wheel. His eyes were still open when Prentice scrambled to his feet and laid a hand on his snow-covered shoulder.

'You've made it! Are you all right, Mac?'

'Give me a minute ... Look down there ...'

The words came out in gasps and while he struggled to get a grip on himself Prentice extracted the Monokular from his coat pocket and focused it out over the gulf. In the distance to the south a lean grey vessel was approaching with smoke streaming from its stack and a clear wake to stern. A British destroyer was heading for the peninsula. Her deck was crammed with troops and Prentice fancied he recognized the individualistic hats the Australians wore – Australians and some New Zealanders probably, steaming directly for Cape Zervos where the tortuous track led up the cliff face.

'It's packed with troops,' Prentice said quickly. 'Aussies and Kiwis. God, if only they'd get here in time.'

'They won't!' Macomber was recovering and he clambered

221

unsteadily out of the vehicle to stand by the lieutenant. 'Burckhardt should make it within the hour and . . .' He looked back at Grapos who was seated on a bench beside Ford. 'How long do you reckon it would take a man to come up that cliff track?'

'Three or four hours. It would depend on the man. Mules find it difficult.'

'There you are,' Macomber said grimly. 'And they haven't even landed yet – won't for a while. That's always assuming they're heading for the cape – they could easily be bound for Katyra.'

'Lord, no!' Prentice was appalled. 'If only we had a Verey pistol – or even a mirror.' He turned to the others. 'It would be just too damned convenient if anyone had a mirror, I suppose?'

It was too damned convenient; no one possessed a mirror. Macomber brushed snow off his leather coat and began walking stiffly downhill the way they had come, and every step jarred his cramped body, cramped with sitting behind the wheel, cramped with the tension of crossing the lake. Feeling as though at any moment he might keel over and fall in the snow, he reached the point where the road turned under the bluff to continue along the shore, and with Ford at his heels he came round the corner. He stopped abruptly, holding back the sergeant with his hand. 'There you are – that shows how much time we've got. Sweet Fanny Adams.' The bluff loomed above them, and above that rose the sheer climb of the monastery wall, terminating in the high tower which reared like a pinnacle in the sunlight. But it was across the lake where Macomber was staring, his face bleak as his lips chewed briefly. Round the flank of the snow-covered slope on the distant shore a small dark bug-like object was crawling forward. The first half-track had arrived already.

'You were right,' Prentice said tersely as he peered over their shoulders. 'Those chaps on the destroyer will never make it.'

Macomber turned round, talking as he started back towards the half-track, his weary feet scuffling through the snow. 'We'll go ahead with the plan exactly as we arranged. We've got to find some way of warning that destroyer – if they land men and start them up that track with Jerries in position at the top of it there'll be a massacre.'

'Burckhardt will know he can cross that ice when he sees our track marks,' Prentice called out, panting up behind him. The Scot had temporarily recovered his vitality, spurred on by the sight of Burckhardt's arrival, and he was moving uphill with rapid strides as he shouted over his shoulder. 'He'll see nothing. The wind has practically obliterated the marks we made, so he'll have to make his own recce. Which gives us extra time. Not bloody much of it, though.'

Taking a last quick look at the oncoming destroyer, he climbed back into the half-track, glanced to his rear to make sure they were all on board, and then began driving uphill. For a short distance the road fell away steeply to the west – to their right – where the mountain slope sheered down towards the wind-ruffled Aegean far below, while on their left the toppling wall of the bluff leaned over them. The road was deep with snow, soft snow from the recent fall, and streaks of whiteness smeared the bluff's wall. Across the gulf Macomber could see the ship-wrecking chain of rocks extending towards him from the mainland, ending in the saw-tooth which had so nearly destroyed the *Hydra*, and beyond the rocks he could see the mainland itself where Allied troops would be moving up the vital supply road. Then another rock wall closed off the view and they were ascending a narrow, twisting canyon on the last lap of their long journey to the monastery.

He had ascended perhaps two hundred feet, confined between the narrowing walls of the canyon which climbed vertically above them, when he saw a trail of cloud creeping over the road ahead, blotting out what lay beyond. Switching on his headlights, he reduced speed as they slipped inside the vaporous mist; ice-cold drizzle chilled his face and there was a sudden drop in temperature as he crawled round a bend and went up a steep incline. The headlights penetrated the cloud just sufficiently for him to see what was happening, to see where the road turned yet another bend as it spiralled up towards the summit of the bluff, and now water was starting to run down the snow-packed road and the snow itself was melting to slush.

He drove on up through the drifting cloud, feeling his clothes grow heavier as the damp clung to him, feeling the tracks slither once and then recover stability as they ground patiently upwards while he grew cold and miserable and sodden and it seemed as though the elements were flinging one final ordeal in his path almost within sight of their objective. Behind him the others had taken up position. Grapos stood at the rear of the vehicle, the Alpenkorps rope looped over his shoulder, while Prentice and Ford huddled on a bench close to him, their weapons gripped between their hands as they watched the Greek who stood facing the way they were going. Macomber turned another bend, saw the road levelling out, switched off his headlights, and heard the hammering of Grapos' rifle butt. The signal to halt.

He braked, left the engine running, and the tang of salt air was strong in his nostrils as the cloud began to thin and pale sunlight percolated through the haze. Grapos dropped off at the rear between the tracks and was followed by Prentice and Ford who went after him and vanished in the cloud. Behind the wheel, Macomber was wiping moisture off his watch-face while he timed five minutes exactly. The mistiness, which would have masked his onslaught until the last moment, was receding rapidly as the cloud left the peninsula and floated out over the gulf. He grimaced, saw ahead the final rise in the road which hid him from the monastery, checked his watch again. At four minutes and thirty seconds the cloud had dispersed completely, but again that would have been too damned convenient. Now for the break-in, the final effort – with everything staked on one vicious surprise attack.

With the cloud gone he was bathed in the cold bright sunlight of winter and he could see the Aegean to his right, but rising ground shielded the destroyer from view; he could see the stark triangle of Mount Zervos, a peak of whiteness where the light caught the snow crystals, but the monastery was still invisible; and he could see the deep, trench-like gulley along which Grapos had led the other two men, but they had disappeared. He checked his watch: ten seconds to go. Reaching inside his pocket he dragged out the Luger from the sodden folds and laid it on the seat beside him. Five seconds left. His hand clutched the brake, waited, released it. He was off.

He accelerated rapidly, mounted the rise, crested it. The road ran straight to the monastery which rose up less than two hundred yards away. He took in the impression in a flash. The towers and the wall linking them were lower on this side. The greenish shell of a dome, which he remembered was the church, showed beyond the wall-top. The ancient gatehouse, a tumble-down wooden structure which appeared to lean back against the stone for support, was in the centre of the wall. Three or four storeys up wooden box-like structures were attached to the stonework, protruding from the wall like giant dovecotes, each structure faced with tall shutters which led out to a small balcony. The ground between the crest and the monastery was bare and level with huge boulders strewn close to the left-hand section of the monastery. Mid-way to the gatehouse he swerved off the road, crossing open ground in a sweeping half-circle, which brought him back on the road again with the half-track's rear presented to the monastery. So far he had seen no sign of life and the place had a derelict look. He changed gear, began reversing towards the closed gate which barred his way, twisting round in his seat as he kept one eye on the road, another on the gateway rushing towards him as he built up speed and the monastery came closer and closer.

He saw out of the corner of his eye movement on the roofed-in, railed walk which spanned the first floor of the gatehouse, the movement of a field-grey figure steadying himself as he took aim, and he knew something had gone fatally wrong. The Alpenkorps cap was not enough to make the German pause, or had he spotted one of the others at the last moment – Macomber had no idea which – but he knew that within seconds the German would open fire, that he must ignore the threat of almost certain death, that the rifle would be discharged at point-blank range if the man had the sense to wait only a few seconds longer when he couldn't possibly miss, firing down from his elevated position at a target moving rapidly closer under his gunsight.

During the final rush up to the closed gates Macomber became aware of everything around him – the snow-covered ground where rocks poked up through the whiteness, the shabbiness of the small balconies where decrepit paint exposed the mellow woodwork, the open-necked collar of the Alpenkorps soldier on the gatehouse who was steadying himself against the wall as he aimed his rifle, the rotting timbers of the large double gates, the mildewed-looking dome of the church vanishing from view as the wall rose up and screened it, the high-powered throb of the engine, the metallic grind of the whirling tracks . . .

He heard the report of the rifle above these sounds, a sharp crack, the first shot fired in the coming encounter – the shot fired by Grapos from behind a large boulder. The German on the balcony was stood immediately over the roadway and he staggered forward as the bullet penetrated, reached out a hand to steady himself on the frail balcony rail, sagged forward with his full weight, which was too much for the support, and he fell through it at the moment the half-track smashed through the gates, tearing both loose from the upper hinges so they toppled inwards and the vehicle stormed over them and continued reversing under the archway and into the vast courtyard beyond. Macomber blinked with relief, heard something thud down behind him, glanced back swiftly and saw the dead German folded over the second bench. The half-track roared on inside a stone-paved square which was larger than he remembered it, a square with a plane tree in the centre, the church to the right, an ancient stone well beyond the tree – a square large enough to accommodate a small army, overlooked on all sides by windows and arcaded walks which ran round the inner walls at each floor level. The vehicle was charging towards the tree when he reduced speed, changed gear, went forward and began thundering round the square, turning the wheel erratically as though the half-track had gone berserk. His Alpenkorps cap was prominently on view, as was the German soldier behind him, a soldier impossible to identify from his crumpled position. Macomber completed one circuit, heard the sound of shots, described a wild S-bend tour round the church and reappeared suddenly from the other side as he headed into the square again and accelerated afresh. For anyone inside the monastery the speeding half-track had become a hypnotic focal point – a focal point to divert their attention for vital seconds from what might be happening elsewhere.

When Grapos jumped from the stationary half-track as the cloud dispersed from the bluff he plunged straight into the gulley leading away from the road and towards the monastery, a ravine seven feet deep which hid the hurrying men from any possible observation from the monastery walls. He ran forward in a crouch, his rifle between his hands, the rope looped from his shoulder. He was heading for one of the towers which protruded out from the wall, so that the side farthest from the gatehouse formed a right-angled corner which couldn't be seen from that direction. Behind him came Prentice with Ford close at his heels. The staff-sergeant's shoulder still throbbed with a dull ache but he could use the lower part of his arm and, more important still, he could use his machine-pistol if he held it awkwardly.

Close to the wall, Grapos paused and lifted himself half-out of the gulley at a point where a large boulder hid him from the gatehouse. This was the position he must take up to cover Macomber when he had arranged the ascent of his companions. Dropping back into the gulley, he ran forward again and clambered out where the ravine ended at the base of the wall. They were now hemmed in by the corner, invisible from the farther extension of the wall unless someone came out onto a balcony. Ford took up a position where he could observe the receding wall while the lieutenant gazed upwards, his machine-pistol hoisted. It took Grapos less than a minute to prepare the rope for throwing, a rope weighted at the tip by the metal hook, and when he hurled it upwards and inwards the hook trapped itself on the floor of the projecting side-balcony twenty feet above them. Taking a long breath, Grapos jumped up the rope, held on, swayed briefly like a pendulum as he tested its resistance, then dropped to the ground again and glared at Prentice.

'It is good – but you must be quick. You remember the way?'

'Perfectly!' Prentice glanced at his watch, looped the machine-pistol over his shoulder, began to climb the rope hand over hand, his legs stiffened, his boots pressed against the roughened stonework as he half-hauled, half-walked himself up towards the balcony. The shaky structure trembled a little under his progress, but he ignored the warning of its instability, climbing faster as he got the hang of the ascent. If the bloody thing came down, it came down. Neck or nothing now. His face eased up to balcony level and he saw the hook firmly embedded between the open floor-boards. One final heave and he was clutching the shaky rail, hauling himself over the top, standing on the floor with the closed shutters behind him. He propped the machine-pistol against a post where he could reach it easily, looked over, saw that Ford had already tied the rope round his body and under his armpits. As he started to haul up the sergeant Grapos was slipping back inside the gulley and running along it to take up position behind the boulder.

Hauling up Ford proved strenuous: the sergeant tried to help by splaying his feet against the wall, but he was unable to lift himself by his hands which were concentrated on gripping the rope, so the lieutenant had to haul up his full weight length by length, the rope taut over the balcony rail which was shuddering under the pressure, the floor quivering under his feet as Grapos' warning flashed through his mind. 'The balcony has not been used for many years because it is dangerous...' Sweating profusely, his arms almost strained from their sockets, his legs trembling with the arduous exertion, Prentice saw a tangle of dark hair appear, a hand grasp the floor edge, and then the railing gave way, collapsed inwards like broken matchwood. He jerked in more rope, his back pressed hard into the shutters, his feet driving into the floor as he heaved desperately and Ford was half-dragged, half-scrambled his way through the smashed rail and ended up on his knees on the balcony. The sergeant was still recovering his breath, blood was still oozing from his left hand where the wood had gashed it, while Prentice untied the rope, released him from it, and then dropped the rope end down to the ground for Grapos to use later. 'All right, Ford?' he croaked, leaning against the shutters as he reached out for the machine-pistol.

'Just like the obstacle course at Chester, sir.' He stood up

228

cautiously and unlooped his own weapon. 'But maybe I need a refresher course. We'd better get inside – I can hear Mac coming.'

The clattering rattle of the approaching half-track was in their ears as Prentice dealt with the process of getting in. He used his machine-pistol butt to club the latch and the woodwork splintered swiftly under his third blow. Without realizing that the shutters opened outwards, he used his shoulder to go through them, head tucked well in as he rammed his body against and through the breaking shutters with such force that the impetus took him half-way across the room before he could pull up. He hardly saw the room: faded religious murals on the stone walls, a cloth-covered table, an ikon; then he reached the varnished door and opened it with great care. The musty odours of the unused room were in his nostrils as he peered both ways along a deserted corridor and from beyond the balcony he heard the grumble of the oncoming half-track. They'd cut the timing pretty fine. Beckoning to Ford, he ran down the passage to his left. It was like running through a cloister – wooden archways at intervals and large windows to his right which looked down on the square below – and the only sound in the monastic silence, now the walls had muffled the half-track's approach, was the sound of his clumping boots as he ran full tilt for the staircase at the end. He paused briefly when he arrived at the corner, looked to his right where another deserted corridor ran along the second side, glanced up the empty staircase and ran up it, turning at a landing before running up the second flight. On the second floor an identical view faced him – corridors stretching away from the corner in two directions. To his right, at the far end, Ford, who had just emerged from his own staircase, raised a thumb. Prentice returned the signal and went over to the nearest window, hid himself behind a section of the wall and waited.

In less than thirty seconds he saw the half-track coming backwards into the yard, but gave the vehicle only a brief glance as his eyes searched the windows across the square at different levels. His waiting time was very short – the half-track had entered the square, had reversed direction and started driving forwards round the square below them when a window opposite opened and two German soldiers leaned out to stare down at the half-track's mad career round the square. Prentice raised his machine-pistol, thrust the muzzle sharply through the glass, and the shattering noise was lost in the long burst as he sprayed the window steadily, saw the Germans crumple and disappear as movement higher up caught his eye. Through an open window on the top floor another German was aiming his rifle downwards at Prentice when Ford's machine-pistol opened up with a murderous rattle, one much shorter burst, short but lethal. The German with the rifle lost his weapon and followed it down into the yard below as Macomber sped towards the church. A burst of answering fire from farther along the top floor hammered Prentice's shattered window as he jumped back behind the wall. He heard Ford's weapon replying as something moved behind him. He swung his gun round, knowing the magazine was almost empty, and the muzzle pointed at Grapos who froze at the top of the stairs. He must have come up the rope like a charge of electricity.

The explosion came as Prentice, inserting a fresh magazine, was grinning crookedly at Grapos. The grenade landed midway along the corridor between Ford and the lieutenant, but Grapos had seen it fly in through a window and was sheltered behind the staircase. 'Jesus, this is getting rough,' Prentice muttered half to himself. He knocked a shard of glass from his sleeve, staring down at the Greek who stood with his rifle and the rope looped afresh over his shoulder, and started to move round the corner into the next corridor. Ford, protected by a section of wall, was firing again across the yard as the German on the top floor opposite changed tactics. He must have assumed that there were men spread along the side corridor because suddenly a stream of bullets began shattering every window along the passage Prentice was about to move into. Glass was strewn over the floor, bullets scarred the inner wall while the lieutenant, safe behind the wall in the next corridor he shared with Ford, waited for the barrage to cease. The next grenade landed closer to Ford, sent a fresh shock wave in both directions, and for the first time Prentice grasped what was happening.

A German had entered the corridor below them. Knowing the enemy was on the floor above, he hadn't risked coming up a staircase: instead he was leaning out of a lower window while he tossed grenades upwards and inside the second-floor windows. It was only a matter of time before he chose the right aperture for his deadly missiles. Prentice hesitated, reviewing the situation. Macomber couldn't fire on the German while he was driving the half-track round the square at that pace, and the plan called for him to keep up this diversion whatever happened. The fusillade along the next corridor ceased briefly and Grapos called out, 'I will deal with him...' He gestured along the corridor and then downwards, took out his knife and ran down the passage before disappearing inside a room mid-way along the building.

The room which the Greek had entered also had a balcony, and it was towards this he ran after closing the door as a precaution against a grenade landing in the entrance. Thrusting open the shutters, he went into the sunlight and the firing in the square was muffled to a quiet rattle. It took him a matter of seconds to jam the hook down between the floor-boards, to throw the rope over the edge, then he was slipping down the rope which dangled past the first-floor balcony below. His boots scraped the rail, felt their way inside it, and he slithered the last few feet on to the balcony. Inserting his knife blade between the ill-fitting shutters, he forced up the latch, fingered open the left-hand shutter gently and went inside the half-darkened room. The inner door was closed and he listened with his ear pressed against its panel for several seconds before gripping the handle with his left hand. The right hand held the knife ready for throwing as he eased the handle to the open position, stood to the opening side of the door and flung it back against the wall. When he went into the corridor he saw that the lone German had changed his position and was standing by the window below where Prentice was sheltering. The German had a grenade ready for throwing when he saw Grapos, changed his mind instantly, and hoisted it for a throw straight down the corridor. The knife left Grapos, sped along the passage, struck the soldier a second before he threw. He staggered, dropped the grenade, crashed into a window,

231

one hand clutching his arm. The grenade detonated at his feet.

Macomber, hearing bullets ricocheting off a bench behind him, had driven the half-truck behind the church. His role as a diversion was over and it was time to give a hand with his Luger, so he drove out once more, pressed his foot down and headed for the ramp leading up into the arcaded walk on the eastern side of the square, the side where most of the Germans had appeared earlier. The half-track surged forward at an angle across the square and he was turning the wheel as he went up the ramp, swung round into the corridor, and realized too late it was a fraction narrow for the passage of the vehicle he had intended driving the full length of the arcade. The ground floor was enclosed from the square by a railing only and it was the left-hand caterpillar which encountered this railing, churning it to pieces as it rasped its way forward. The first stone pillar it met was the obstacle it refused to overcome; instead the track parted company with the vehicle, disengaged itself completely and whipped across the square as an intact ring. Macomber had braked at the moment of impact and he jumped over the windscreen, landing on the bonnet and sliding off on to the floor as the vehicle settled at a drunken angle. The engine sputtered and died. He wondered why there was no more shooting.

After waiting a minute, he hobbled slowly along the corridor and stopped at a short flight of steps leading down into the square at a point half-way along the arcade. Shattered windows everywhere, some starred with pieces still intact. And no sound of gunfire. The silence which had descended on the monastery seemed uncanny as he saw Ford peering out from the second floor, risking a quick look-round before withdrawing his head with equal abruptness. Macomber waited a little longer, but there was no sign of the enemy except for the crumpled figure in Alpenkorps uniform which had toppled from the fourth floor early in the battle. The German in the half-track had long ago been thrown to the floor by one of the Scot's wilder swerves. Still cautious, he made his way along the arcade, turned the corner at the bottom, and walked along

232

the second side. Grapos met him at the foot of the staircase and nodded towards an impressive figure standing a few steps up. A man as tall as Macomber, a vigorous seventy-year-old, he was dressed in the long robes and the flat-topped hat of a dignitary of the Greek Orthodox Church. It was the Abbot of Zervos.

'I found him locked inside his room on the second floor,' Grapos whispered as Prentice appeared on the stairs behind the Abbot.

Macomber spoke in English, remembering from his visit five years earlier that the Abbot understood this language, and he wanted the lieutenant to hear what was said. 'We need information quickly, Father. How many Germans are there here?'

'There were ten men,' the Abbot began crisply. 'They arrived by car yesterday evening disguised as civilians, but they had their uniforms with them. There were three cars...'

'Just a moment, please.' Macomber held up his hand and looked at Prentice. 'Any idea how many you've accounted for yet?'

'Seven,' the lieutenant replied. 'I've been round the building with Ford and checked...'

'Eight then, including that frozen lookout – or nine with the man on the gatehouse...'

'*Seven*,' Prentice repeated firmly. 'I've included both those Jerries in my count...'

'There are three men on the north tower,' the Abbot intervened urgently, crossing himself. 'Captain Braun, who commands this unit, spends a lot of time up there with two other men. They have organized an observation post on the roof of the tower and I think they are watching the mainland road. They have a telescope, a wireless transmitter and a mortar gun...'

'A mortar!' Macomber looked up the staircase at Ford who had come round the corner with his machine-pistol tucked under his good shoulder. Despite his wound he looked the coolest man in the group as he stopped and listened to the Scot's question. 'Ford, could a mortar on that high tower cause the destroyer any trouble?'

'It depends. If it's an 8-cm job like the ones I saw on the plateau things could get pretty sticky. Mind you, the range would have to be right and the mortar man would have to be good – but being in the Wehrmacht he probably is. If he's damned lucky and drops a bomb down the stack into the boiler-room – well, you saw what happened to the *Hydra*...'

'We'd better get up there bloody quick,' Macomber snapped. He turned to Grapos. 'You know the way up, so get us up there...'

The Abbot intervened again, fingering the crucifix suspended from his neck. 'This is a holy place and should never have become a battlefield, but the Germans have only themselves to blame and they have invaded my country. Captain Braun has taken over my bedroom on the fourth floor as his office – Grapos will show you the room I mean – so he may be inside there rather than on the tower.'

'I doubt it – after all this shooting.' Macomber frowned and thought for a moment. 'On the other hand none of you have been seen in the square since the firing stopped, so Braun may just have assumed we've all been wiped out.' He looked again at the Abbot and spoke quietly but firmly. 'And now I want you to go back to your room on the second floor and stay there, whatever happens.' He was following Grapos up to the first landing when he turned for a final word with the Abbot. 'What's happened to all the monks who live here?'

'They have been locked up inside the refectory – across there.' The Abbot pointed across the square towards the church. 'There is plenty of room for them...'

'So it's best they stay there for the moment,' Macomber broke in briskly. 'Wait here until we've gone and then go to your room, please.' He turned to Grapos. 'There are only three of them but this could be the most dangerous job of the lot. Let's get going.'

They ascended to the third floor without incident and Macomber led the way with the Greek one step below him. The Scot was desperately worried about what might happen if the destroyer came within range before they reached the tower, but he still went up cautiously, pausing at each landing to listen carefully, climbing the stairs like the others on the soles of his boots, so they made very little sound as they approached the fourth floor. Macomber had reached the landing, was about to peer round the corner, when he heard footsteps coming along the top floor. Gesturing to the others below, he waited. The footsteps arrived at the top of the staircase, then faded. Macomber ran up the last flight, saw an empty corridor stretching away, a short passage to his left, an iron-studded door in the stone wall at the end of the passage, a door which must lead to the tower and which was open. He went silently down the short passage and listened at the open door, looking up a stone spiral which vanished round a corner in the gloom. He arrived just in time to hear someone hammering sharply on a wooden surface in a certain way, a signal which doubtless identified the new arrival. Metal scraped over metal as a bolt was withdrawn, nailed boots climbed the last few steps, a trap-door slammed shut and the bolt rasped home again.

'Who was it?' Grapos whispered in his ear while Prentice and Ford kept a watch on the corridors. Macomber waved a hand to make the Greek shut up and started up the spiral, feeling his way in the darkness with his hand on the roughened wall. The steps were dangerously narrow, fading into nothingness at the inner edge, and when his head touched something he knew he was at the top. He retreated down several steps and switched on his torch. The trap-door was a massive slab of wood, so close-fitting that no hint of daylight had shown through in the darkness. We'll never break through that, he thought, and went back down the spiral.

'We can't shoot our way up on to the roof,' Macomber informed them quietly, 'there's a trap-door like a piece of teak up there. Prentice, let's take a quick look at the Abbot's bedroom and see what drags the brave captain – if it is Braun – out into the open. Ford, you stay here while Grapos watches the lower stairs. If someone starts coming down this spiral, join Grapos, and we'll take care of ourselves.'

They approached the bedroom tentatively in case a guard had been left inside, but the room was empty. The windows looked out over the mountain and the only furniture was an austere bed, a wooden table and a chair. A wireless transmitter rested on the table with a pair of headphones laid neatly behind it close to the chair. 'So that's it,' Macomber commented. 'He's transmitting to Burckhardt from here now. He must have found the roof inconvenient. I'm damned sure he thinks we've all been killed – he hasn't even locked the door.'

'Couldn't,' Prentice pointed out laconically. 'There's no keyhole. Do you think he'll be back?' He was looking out of the window but the wall of the tower cut off any view down to the lake.

'I hope so. It's our only chance of getting up to that tower roof. I'd give anything now for a ten-kilogram demolition charge. Placed under that trap-door it would blow the whole roof into the lake. We'll have to work something simple out in case he does come down again. I expect he might – those headphones look as though he's expecting to use them again in the near future.'

This time Macomber let Prentice make arrangements for Braun's reception because he wanted to hold himself in reserve for what he proposed to attempt if Braun came down again. While Ford watched the staircase, Prentice and Grapos took up ambush station on either side of the doorway leading up to the spiral. Macomber waited at the end of the stone passage with his Luger ready for an emergency. It was a simple-seeming operation like this which could so easily go wrong. They waited and the minutes passed as Macomber wondered whether Braun was now permanently stationed on the roof, whether having radioed a warning of the attack on the monastery he was now going to sit tight until the first half-tracks poured into the square below. Or would he venture once more down the spiral to send a further message about the destroyer's progress? In the silence he heard his wrist-watch ticking and then he heard something else.

Something which thudded hollowly from the interior of the spiral. The trap-door had been opened very quietly this time, had then been closed with less sound than previously. Macomber stared down the passage to where Grapos waited pressed against the wall, his knife held by his side, to where Prentice waited on the other side of the doorway, his forehead moist although the temperature was low inside the stone passage. There was a long pause when they heard nothing and Prentice

236

began to think it was a false alarm, but the Scot thought differently and could almost sense the presence of someone listening inside the spiral before he came out. Then a boot scraped over stone, the muzzle of a machine-pistol stabbed out of the doorway and a uniformed captain of the Alpenkorps came out behind it. Prentice grabbed with both hands as Grapos lunged with the knife, but the German swung round with a swift reaction which made Macomber take a step forward. The lieutenant had one hand pressed over his mouth, the other locked round his throat when the German swung so unexpectedly, tearing the hand free from his throat. Grapos had little better success when his knife hit the wrong target, was deflected along the barrel of the machine-pistol and skidded over the German's hand, which made him let go of the weapon but had no disabling effect. The German flung his whole weight on Prentice, catching the freed hand between himself and the bare wall, and the lieutenant thought his knuckles were broken as Grapos lunged a second time and the knife went home. Braun sagged, collapsed on the floor, and when Macomber checked his pulse he felt nothing. Captain Braun had become a permanent casualty.

'I'm going straight up,' Macomber said quickly. 'We're running out of time and they may think Braun's forgotten something if I go up now. Grapos, if I can get that trap opened, can get even half-way on to the roof, you follow...'

He was mid-way up the spiral when the pain caught him across the back, a sharp stabbing pain which locked him immovably for several seconds: he must have twisted something when he'd leapt out of the half-track. He suppressed a groan, felt Grapos bump into him, and forced himself up the last few steps. With the Luger in his right hand, his fingers felt the trap-door to check his whereabouts, then he rapped confidently on the underside of the lid in a certain way, the way Braun had rapped. There was a pause, long drawn-out moments when he thought the stratagem hadn't worked, followed by a rattling sound as the bolt was withdrawn.

It went wrong at once. The trap-door opened slowly and there was no one to shoot at as daylight flooded down into the spiral.

When the gap was wide enough he ran up the last few steps, aware of an unforeseen handicap – the trap was being opened from behind him by someone he couldn't see. He reached the stone-paved roof and half-turned round, only to find himself again temporarily immobilized in that position by the fierce pain which seared his back and cramped his movement, making it impossible for him to aim the Luger at the kneeling corporal who slammed down the trap and pushed the bolt home. The falling slab of wood had struck Grapos on the shoulder, leaving Macomber isolated on the roof with the two Germans. The corporal, still on his knees, was reaching for a pistol lying on the stones beside him when Macomber threw his Luger. The weapon smashed into the corporal's temple and he fell over sideways, his fingers still closed over the pistol as he lay still, facing the sky with his eyes open. The other soldier had been standing by the wall looking out over the gulf when Macomber came onto the roof, his body crouched as he pressed his eye to a powerful field-telescope mounted on a tripod, while close by a short, squat-barrelled mortar was set up on its own tripod near a pile of snub-nosed shells. Heavily built, the German's open collar exposed a thick neck, and he was only taken by surprise for a few seconds, then he dropped to his knees and began tugging furiously to free something caught under the canvas which cushioned the mortar bombs. It came free as Macomber wrenched himself into action and reached him.

The German, still on his knees, swung round with the machine-pistol and the Scot grabbed at the muzzle in midswing. Instead of pulling at the weapon, which the German expected, he pushed viciously and the soldier lost balance, letting go of the gun as he fell over backwards, but his elbows saved him from sprawling over the floor. Still in pain, Macomber made a mistake, thinking he had enough time to reverse the weapon and get a grip on it. He was still fumbling when the German came to his feet and went for his throat, and the momentum of his charge carried Macomber back against the waist-high tower wall. He couldn't even attempt to use the gun which was compressed between their bodies as they grappled fiercely and Macomber felt himself being pushed remorselessly backwards over the brink. The soldier was a few inches shorter but he was in prime condition and ten years younger, and the Scot was very close to the end of his physical resources. With the gun penned between them, the German had both hands locked tightly round Macomber's throat and now, as his back arched over the wall screamed with pain, he felt his air supply going. A momentary panic gripped him as he started to tip over the drop, the rim of the wall hard against the small of his back and acting as a fulcrum for the German to lever him down to the lake far below.

Knowing that he was winning, the soldier ignored the gun, squeezing his hands tighter and tighter as Macomber's face changed colour. The Scot's hands still held the machine-pistol and he managed to force it sideways, but he still couldn't use it. Had the German continued his pressure he would have sent Macomber over the edge within seconds, but he saw the gun come loose and released his right hand to grab at it, confident that the Scot was done for. And Macomber was almost done for – the German was holding his throat with only one hand but he had quickly inserted his thumb into the Scot's windpipe and his victim began to choke. Get rid of the gun! The message raced through Macomber's brain and he jerked feebly but with just sufficient force to snatch it out of the hand clutching the dangling strap. He let go and the machine-pistol disappeared over the edge.

As the thumb pressure increased reddish lights sputtered in front of his eyes and he felt his last remaining strength ebbing away. This was it. Nothing else left. His right hand fluttered, felt hair at the moment when the German's nailed boot ground down his instep. Pain shrieked up his leg like an electric shock and he was seized with a spasm of blind fury which sent fresh adrenalin through his veins. He grabbed a large handful of hair, clawed his hand, twisted it and dragged it sideways with all the energy he could muster, hauling at the hair as though to tear it out by the roots. The thumb pressure slackened, was released. Macomber sucked in a gasping lungful of cold mountain air, knowing that within seconds the brawny German would recover. Releasing the hair, he clawed his hand again and, as the soldier's face reappeared, he struck. The savagery of the onslaught unnerved the German and he propelled himself backwards away from the wall to save his face, catching the heel of his boot on an uplifted stone. He was fighting to restore his balance when Macomber's bull-like charge, head down, punched into his stomach, driving him headlong across the roof. The Scot was following him when his right foot tangled with a leg of the telescope's tripod and he crashed forward on his chest as the telescope toppled, broke away from its tripod and rolled over the roof. Macomber had hauled himself up on all fours, his chin sticky with blood where it had grazed the stones, when he saw that the wall had saved his opponent. The German had slapped his hands hard down on the wall-top to halt his momentum when Macomber, close to him, whipped a hand round his right ankle and lifted. The German made his second mistake. Acting by reflex, still off-balance, still groggy from the pile-driving blow in the stomach, he lifted his other foot to kick Macomber in the face. Elbow hard into the roof, the Scot hoisted as high as he could, no more than a few inches, but a fraction more of the German's weight was now poised over the brink than over the roof. The imprisoned foot jerked upwards out of Macomber's grasp of its own volition and the soldier was propelled outwards and downwards as the Scot climbed to his feet. The scream came up as a fading wail and he was just in time to see the minute spread-eagled figure strike the ice hundreds of feet below.

Using the wall for support, he made his way over to the trapdoor, kicking out of the way an opened notebook, the book they had used to record the passage of Allied supplies up the mainland road. Stooping painfully, he pulled back the bolt, but he let them open it, and when the lid lifted it was being raised by Grapos, with Ford below and Prentice bringing up the rear. It was the staff-sergeant who made the first comment. Seeing the crumpled corporal lying on his back he stared curiously at Macomber. 'We didn't think we'd see you alive again, but I thought there were two of them.'

'One went over the side ... you'd better look down here quick.' He was still holding on to the wall support and he looked haggard as he gently massaged his throat and stared down at the lake. 'Burckhardt's nearly here ...'

Burckhardt had moved with great speed: his force was already arrayed and moving far out onto the lake, so that as the Scot gazed down from the great height of the tower he had the sensation of watching a diorama in a war museum. Six half-tracks, spread out widely over the ice like toy models, led the advance, followed by Alpenkorps and parachutists on foot. Farther back more half-tracks crawled forward and each of the weird vehicles carried only its driver – to minimize casualties if the ice broke at any point Burckhardt had shrewdly emptied the half-tracks of all superfluous passengers. Several light ack-ack guns and 75-mm mountain howitzers, unlimbered from the half-tracks which had hauled them up the mountain road, were being drawn bodily over the ice, two men to a gun, and Macomber noticed that round all the vehicles and guns there were unoccupied areas of frozen lake – the men on foot were nervous of the weight this equipment was imposing on the lake's surface. The sense of looking down on a scale model was heightened by the heavy silence which had fallen over the mountain as the wind dropped, and no sound of the advancing army reached the watchers on the tower. Macomber looked at the staff-sergeant who was also gazing down at the threatening spectacle.

'Any hope at all, Ford – by using the mortar? It is an 8-cm, isn't it?'

'Yes. You mean break the ice under them? We can try, but I can't feed the mortar with this shoulder.' He looked across at Prentice who was nursing his swollen right hand. 'And neither can he. Grapos' shoulder is temporarily numbed from the blow it took from that trap-door.' He looked doubtfully at Macomber, who instinctively straightened up from the wall. 'Can you cope?'·

'I'll have to. And we'd better get moving.'

Macomber looked back out to sea. The mounting crisis was of the worst possible magnitude. The destroyer had turned to come in closer, to steam directly for the cape, and within a matter of minutes it would have vanished under the lee of the peninsula prior to commencing landing operations. If Burckhardt reached the monastery he would not only have achieved his objective – he would be in a position to slaughter those troops as they wound their way up the cliff-face track. What on earth had warned Athens that something was wrong? He dismissed the question as academic and began a quick count of the snub-nosed shells lying half covered with canvas while they waited to service the mortar. Thirty bombs. It didn't seem many, not nearly enough. He rammed his last cigar into his mouth and chewed at it as Ford, the calmest man on the roof, stood by the parapet, turning his face sideways to gauge the strength of the fading breeze, screwing up his eyes against the sun as he estimated distances and trajectories. While they waited for the staff-sergeant to complete his calculations Macomber helped Prentice to fix his hand in a makeshift sling with the aid of his scarf, a hand which was swelling ominously, and he watched Burckhardt's progress tensely as he attended the injury. The half-tracks were crawling steadily forward like mechanical bugs – bugs which were now almost two-thirds of the distance across the lake as they approached the road up to the monastery. And even from the great height he looked down on them, Macomber could at last hear a faint purring sound travelling up through the cold mountain air, the purr of engines and caterpillar tracks grinding over the ice.

'That must be Burckhardt – in that car.' Prentice had looked up after testing the sling, and Macomber focused his glass quickly to where the lieutenant had pointed with his good hand. A compact open car, strangely shaped, was driving over the ice slowly as it reached a position mid-way between the distant shore and the leading half-tracks. Ford left the wall, lurching unsteadily towards the mortar as he made his comment.

'It will be a Kubelwagen. The car, I mean. Looks a bit like a squashed bucket close up – they'd bring that in by glider. Now, I need your help, Mac.'

First, they had to move the mortar, to drag it round away from the sea so that its muzzle aimed out over the lake, and then Ford, with considerable difficulty, cradled a bomb in his arms and showed Macomber what he must do. 'There are three basic things to remember – don't put a bomb down the barrel nose first, or else we can all say good-bye; slide it in – don't push; and keep your hands out of the way afterwards if you want to hang on to them. I'll try and give you a demonstration, and then you're on your own – I've got to be by the wall to see what's happening ...'

'They're going up the mountain, too!' Prentice, who had again borrowed the Scot's Monokular, was focused on a point beyond the bluff as he shouted out. Colonel Burckhardt was proving himself an excellent tactician and was leaving nothing to chance: the greater portion of his force was assembled on the lake, but beyond the distant shore two straggled lines of dots were ascending the lower slope of Mount Zervos itself as ski troops made for the monastery by a different route. Seeing those two lines climbing higher, already disappearing behind the bluff, Macomber guessed the route they would follow. The southern shore of the lake was blocked by the bluff climbing vertically from the water's edge, but ski troops could ascend to a point above the bluff and then cross the mountain slope above it, until they reached a position where they could ski downwards over a slope which ended close to the monastery entrance. The snowbound mountain had an overloaded look above the bluff and Grapos, who also guessed at their route, spoke grimly.

'They will need care and luck up there.'

'Why?' demanded Macomber.

'The thaw is coming – the time for the mountain to move.'

'You mean an avalanche?'

'Yes.'

'We'll worry about them later.'

Ford completed his demonstration for the Scot's benefit. Replacing the bomb on the canvas, he then crouched down to make a careful adjustment to the angle of fire, went quickly back to the wall to check the target, and returned to the mortar to adjust it again. Macomber, in a rising fever of impatience to get the thing firing, also went briefly to the wall for a final appraisal. The Kubelwagen was moving closer to the front line, halting frequently for a few seconds, presumably while Burckhardt had a word with his troops. The six half-tracks in front were now three-quarters of the way across the lake and within minutes they would have reached firm ground. Feeling automatically for a match to light his cigar, he brought out his hand empty; this was going to be tricky enough as it was without smoke getting in his eyes. He went back to the mortar, checked to make sure that the blood on his hand was dried, wiped both hands briskly on his handkerchief, and then stooped to lift the first bomb as Ford took up position by the parapet and warned Prentice and Grapos to stay in their corners.

Prentice had the best view, squeezed into the north-east corner where he looked down on the entire lake. The first bomb went away seconds later, soaring out over the wall, diminishing rapidly in size as it described an arc and landed on the ice ahead of the leading half-tracks. Prentice's teeth were clenched with anxiety as he watched its fall. He saw a brief spurt of snow where the projectile hit. Then nothing happened. Nothing. His eyes met Ford's as the sergeant pressed his hands harder on the wall, his face expressionless.

'It didn't go off,' said Prentice bitterly.

'No. It must have been a dud. Let's hope the whole batch isn't. I hear there's a lot of sabotage in German factories.' He looked over his shoulder at Macomber who stood ready with a fresh bomb, gave a brief order. 'Fire!' The second bomb was away, vanishing to a pinhead. It landed close to the dud, followed by the sound of detonation, a burst of snow, Prentice swore out loud. The ice had remained intact. Was it too solid for penetration? The fear was in all their minds and Prentice's hopes hadn't been high from the beginning. 'Fire!' Ford had rushed to the mortar to make a fractional adjustment before returning to the wall and giving the order. The third bomb soared through its parabola, curved to its descent. It landed close to the leading half-tracks and the distant thump echoed back to the tower as snow flew in the air with the burst of the bomb. An area of black shadow fissured the lake as ice cracked and disintegrated and water opened up under three half-tracks. 'Fire!' The fourth bomb spread the fracturing process as the three half-tracks disappeared almost simultaneously. One moment they were there and then they were gone, swallowed up as a new lake spread, a lake of ice-cold water. Over fifty metres deep, Grapos had said. So the half-tracks were now settling one hundred and fifty feet below the lake's surface. 'Fire!' Ford had made a further minor adjustment before he rushed back to the wall, his head thrust forward as he scanned the whole lake and Macomber, already drenched in sweat, fed in a fresh bomb. At this stage even Prentice, who could see everything happening, had not grasped the magnitude of the plan the precise Ford had devised for the destruction of the entire German force.

The fifth bomb sped out over the wall, almost too fast for the eye to follow, descended, struck the lake in the middle of the three surviving half-tracks closest to Zervos. Another spray of snow flashed upwards, another thump reached the distant tower, and then a huge area of ice cracked. Prentice gazed in astonishment as a sheet of ice became a temporary island separated from the rest of the frozen lake, a sheet supporting the three half-tracks and a group of Alpenkorps gathered behind them. The island's existence was momentary. The sheet fissured in all directions, broke up and sank. With the Monokular screwed hard against his eye, Prentice saw one half-track at the outer edge of the ice go down, wheels first, the tracks tilting upwards into the air, and then the whole vehicle slid out of sight under the ink-dark water which had appeared. The chances of a single man surviving in those sub-zero waters was nil. 'Fire!' The next bomb landed farther to the right, just reaching the ragged rim of the still-intact ice, detonating while still above the water-line. Figures beyond the rim were thrown into confusion, some falling and some scattering in a hopeless search for safety. The whole ordered array on the lake was beginning to change, to falter, to break up into a vast disorganized chaos as Ford increased the rate of attack, frequently adjusting direction or angle or both as Macomber, the pain in his back now stabbing at him non-stop, his clothes sodden with sweat, his bruised body protesting with growing aches, worked away methodically stooping, grasping, lifting, feeding the barrel.

'Fire!' This bomb travelled much farther, the zenith of its parabola far higher above the lake, the descent point more distant. Prentice pressed the Monokular into his eye, focusing it on the Kubelwagen. He heard the thump and saw the snow

dust at almost the same moment – dust which immediately
rose behind Burckhardt's vehicle. The whiteness surrounding
the car dissolved, became pitch-black water, and as the vehicle
went straight down Prentice saw there were still four people
inside. Burckhardt was drowning, surrounded by his own men.
The fresh area of sinking ice stretched out towards the monastery road, tilting as men on top of it ran in all directions trying
to escape. Prentice saw one man run straight off the edge into
the water and as he took the glass away from his eye the ice
sheet went under. A huge channel of dark water, perhaps a
hundred yards wide, separated the frozen area of the lake from
the road on the western shore leading up to the monastery.

'Fire!'

Ford had again made an adjustment and Prentice saw that
the mortar's barrel was pointing at an extreme angle, saw also
the bomb cradled in Macomber's arms nearly slip as the Scot
forced his wearied body to further effort. The bomb coursed
out over the lake, became a tiny dark speck against the whiteness below, and landed close to the distant eastern shore on the
far side of the scattering troops. The thump was fainter. A
fresh channel of water opened up, starting at the shoreline and
spreading inwards towards the centre as three more bombs
landed and black dots scurried over the diminishing white surface. Two mountain guns vanished. A half-track driving to the
rear to escape the cannonade drove straight over the edge.
More than a third of the attacking force on the frozen lake had
disappeared and for the first time Prentice grasped the pains-
taking cleverness of Ford's plan. He had quartered the lake
systematically in his mind and was destroying it section by
section in such a way that he inflicted the maximum amount of
damage, commencing with the vital section near the road up to
the monastery, working backwards, and then over-leaping to
destroy the ice near the far shore. His ultimate objective was
to compress the surviving Wehrmacht force on a huge island of
ice caught between water to east and west, the snow-drifted
road to the north, and the sheer wall of the bluff to the
south.

'Fire!' The bomb landed uselessly in clear water. 'Fire!'
Prentice's glass was focused just beyond the most recent drop-

ping point and he saw two puffs of snow as the bomb bounced across the ice and detonated in the midst of a crowd of German troops fleeing towards the bluff. At this point some of the more quick-witted Alpenkorps were escaping. Using their climbing ropes, they had begun to scale the precipitous bluff face, realizing that only suspended in air would they be safe from the rain of missiles pouring down on them. Ford now turned his attention to the section of frozen lake which bordered the snow-drifted road. A large number of troops and a mountain gun were heading for the drift zone when the falling bombs began to shatter their escape route, driving them back on the huge remaining sheet of ice which covered perhaps a third of the lake. 'Fire!' Prentice removed the Monokular, dropped it into his pocket. The fatigue of staring through the glass made him rub his eyes and then dab them with his handkerchief, and all the time the bombardment was continuing as Ford concentrated on the huge island of ice covered with marooned Germans. 'Fire!' 'Fire!' 'Fire... !' Prentice lost count of the number of bombs Macomber slipped down the barrel, and the rate was increasing as Ford built up the barrage and Macomber, wiping his hands frequently on his trousers for fear of dropping a bomb, summoned up his last reserves of energy and went on feeding the mortar with fresh ammunition.

When Prentice looked out across the lake again he was astounded at the changed scene. The lake, which had so recently been a white plain, was now a dark sheet spattered with what, from that height, looked like slivers of snow, but which were really large spars of floating ice. The central island had almost disappeared and there was only a handful of men still marooned on a small patch of whiteness. Macomber fed in more bombs, surrounded the ice islet with five fountainheads of spurting water. Five misses. The next bomb landed dead centre on the remaining floe, fragmented it, tipped the survivors choking, drowning, sinking into the chill water. Perhaps a dozen Alpenkorps men still clung to the bluff which they were ascending slowly, but the invasion force on the lake had been annihilated.

'Like a target range,' Ford said. 'Unique.'

'Not quite,' Macomber reminded him. 'There was also

Austerlitz.'* In response to the shake of the sergeant's head, he replaced the bomb he was holding on the near-empty canvas and went stiffly over to the parapet. 'And now we've got to face that lot.'

There were three bombs left on the tower roof when Macomber made his grim remark and pointed out over the wall. Unlike the others, whose whole attention had been concentrated on the lake below, the Scot had been observing with increasing anxiety the ski troops' progress. They had now climbed the slope to an altitude well above the bluff and were coming forward in a line which curled over the flank of the mountain. The leading man was less than a quarter of a mile away as he sped closer towards the monastery. Grapos hobbled out from his corner and gripped Macomber's arm.

'You make avalanche,' Grapos said urgently. 'Where the dark hole is . . .'

'He means that hollow in shadow,' Prentice interjected. 'Why there?' Macomber had already gone back to the mortar, was helping Ford to shift the weapon's position, then waiting, cradling another bomb in his arms as the staff-sergeant checked the mountain slope and changed the angle of fire.

'Because,' Grapos explained, 'that is where the Austrian ski man started the avalanche. We had warned him not to go – but he laughed at us. I was standing on this roof watching him. He comes down over the hole and the avalanche begins. The mountain comes alive.'

'We'd better try it, Ford,' Macomber said quickly. 'It's a gamble, but it's the only one we've got. A hundred bombs could miss them all considering the speed they're moving at.'

He waited, still cradling the bomb, while Ford reconsidered the angle of fire and made a further adjustment. The reaction was setting in, his arms and legs felt like jelly, and he knew he might collapse on the roof at any moment. For God's sake stop fiddling with that mortar, man, and let's get on with it! Ford nodded – to indicate he was satisfied – and Macomber let the first one go. Because the mountain slope rose above the tower he was now able to see what was happening and he saw the

* At Austerlitz Napoleon destroyed a Russian army by firing at a frozen lake and drowning the enemy crossing the ice.

bomb hit the snow some distance above the hollow.

'Damn!' It was the first display of emotion Ford had shown since they had begun firing the mortar. The shot was wide and he knew it was his fault – not enough care taken over the initial preparation. And there were no bombs to waste this time on ranging shots. He adjusted the angle of fire as Macomber picked up the second bomb. The missile went away. Macomber saw this one land below the hollow, close enough to the Alpenkorps column to provoke a sudden swerve in the well-spread line – the section leader had not overlooked the lesson of what had happened on the lake – but no more than a swerve. Ford bit his lip as Macomber encouraged him. 'Third time lucky.' The staff-sergeant looked dubious – too high last time, too low this time. And only one more to go. But he kept his nerve: the first two shots had bracketed the target above and below, so now they must drop one mid-way between the two points. He took a deep breath, adjusted the barrel very carefully, then nodded to Macomber. The final bomb burst on the mountain a short way above the hollow.

It was very quiet on the tower and the four men stood perfectly still while they waited. Behind them the sea was empty, the destroyer had disappeared; below them the lake was still and lifeless; above them rose the peak of Zervos, crisp-edged against the palest of skies. The mortar barrel gaped upwards, as harmless now as a piece of old scrap iron, something they might as well tip over the wall so that at least the Alpenkorps would never use it. Probably it was imagination, but the Scot fancied he heard the swish of oncoming skis as he stood with his eyes fixed on Mount Zervos. He blinked and looked again, unsure whether his eyes had played him a trick. He had been watching the hollow but now he transferred his gaze higher up the mountain to a point near the summit where something had attracted his attention. Was there a gentle ripple of movement, so gentle that his eye might never have noticed it but for his fading hope? There seemed to be a trembling, a hazy wobble close to the peak. Slowly, like the rolling back of a sheet, the snow began to move in a long wave, the wave stretching the full width of the slope as it surged downwards, gathering height as it swallowed up more snow. And now Macomber heard something – a faint growl which gradually swelled and deepened to a sinister rumble as he saw fresh signs of something terrible happening. The slope was shifting downwards at increasing velocity, a moving slope at least a mile wide as the wave mounted higher, picked up momentum and thundered down on the Germans like a tidal wave. The mountain had come alive.

The slope seemed like a living thing as it seethed and rolled towards the lake far below, a whole mountain erupting sideways, the wave curling at the crest, the snow-slide roaring down, the rumble a tremendous sound in their dazed ears, a sound like the eruption of a major volcano, blowing its lava flow up from the interior of the earth. The Alpenkorps tried to scatter at the last moment – some ski-ing downhill, some whipping across the slope, all trying to race the wave which bore down on them and for a brief moment in time they were like a disturbed nest of ants scurrying away from catastrophe. Then the wave arrived, swept over the broken line, engulfing them, burying them, carrying them down the slope and over the bluff face where it cascaded down the precipice like a vast waterfall and washed away the men still ascending it before it plunged down into the depths of the lake. Prentice shouted his frantic warning as the wave reached the bluff's brink – the leading skier, not yet overwhelmed by the avalanche, had stopped, unlooped his rifle from his back, was taking aim at the roof of the tower. Macomber, his gaze fixed on the bluff, heard the shout too late. He was dropping to the floor when the bullet thudded into him and he was unconscious before he sprawled over the stones.

The Australian doctor had underestimated Macomber's vitality, so he came out of the drugged state at the wrong moment, the moment when they started to take him down the nose of Cape Zervos, strapped to a stretcher, powerless to move, but conscious enough to think, to remember, to experience to the full the unnerving ordeal of being transported in the prone position down a track a mule might jib at. The track, no more than a rather broad path, was the route from the cliff summit to the base of the cape where the Allied troops had landed. It

250

was a fine morning, the sun was shining, there was not a trace of sea mist, so his downward view was unobscured as his life balanced in four hands – two holding the rear of the stretcher, two supporting the front. The stretcher tilted downwards at an angle of forty-five degrees as the two men carrying him found the way increasingly dangerous – ascending a precipitous zig-zag can be difficult, descending it may prove impossible. The Scot thought the unobscured view was impressive – a sheer drop seaward to the ruffled waters of the Aegean far below, a glimpse of a lower level of the zigzag, perched on another brink. And in his invalid state, Macomber had lost his head for heights.

He watched the uncertain gait of the man in front through half-closed eyes, half-closed because he was determined they shouldn't realize he had come awake – even a small surprise like that at the wrong moment could make a foot stumble, a hand lose its grip, could cause the stretcher to leave them and send him vertically down to his grave as the stretcher turned over and over in mid-air before it mercifully reached the sea and the waves closed over him. Cursing his over-vivid imag-ination, he tore his mesmerized gaze away from the trembling distant waters and tried to concentrate his mind on what had happened, on what Prentice had told him when he first re-covered consciousness. 'He got you in the shoulder ... the bullet's out now ... the quack says you'll be all right ... they'll be taking you to Athens.'

Macomber wasn't sure what day it was as he went on staring at the back of the man below him, but he remembered other things the lieutenant had told him. The Australians had come up this hellish track like demons. With the New Zealanders. They had dragged up dismantled twenty-five-pounder guns by brute strength, had reassembled them on the heights, were now in full command of Zervos. The blowing up of the *Hydra* had warned them something was seriously wrong; the great cloud of black smoke rising over Katyra had forced a quick decision – the sending of a destroyer laden with troops. I wish I had one of those bloody German cigars, Macomber thought as the man behind him tripped and the stretcher wobbled uneasily. They should have let Grapos take the rear. But at least the bearer had held on firmly, had regained his balance quickly. They went slowly down another section, then another, poised over sheer drops, the only sound a slithering of boots over the treacherous ground. Time stopped for the Scot, went into a state of suspension, so that it seemed to go on for ever. They were close to the half-ruined jetty at the base of Cape Zervos, but still a hundred feet above the sea, when the man in front stumbled over a hidden rock, fell sideways onto the track, saving himself by cannoning against a boulder and completely losing his grip on the stretcher. Macomber's legs hit the earth with a bump. He braced himself for the long spiralling fall.

The rear of the stretcher sagged a foot, then steadied and was held there by two hands only until the other man climbed to his feet, started to apologize, then stopped as he saw the look in the eyes of the man holding Macomber. He lifted the stretcher again and they went on down the track to where the launch moored by the jetty waited to transport the Scot to the destroyer anchored farther out. Macomber delayed his official awakening until he was rested on the jetty wall, then he twisted his head round to say thank you. Grapos' whiskered face stared down at him. 'I come with you,' he said simply. 'Now they take me in the Greek army. Yes?'

Double Jeopardy

For Jane

CHAPTER 1

Sunday May 24

After the murder it was assumed that Charles Warner — always so vigilant — had let down his guard because of the atmosphere. When he left the harbour at Lindau, Bavaria, and took his powerboat out on to Lake Konstanz it was a sunny, peaceful afternoon.

'And it was a diabolically clever and audacious killing,' Tweed commented to Martel two days later in London.

The powerboat, with Warner as its sole occupant, moved slowly as it passed through the harbour exit, flanked on one side by the stone statue of the Lion of Bavaria; on the other by the towering lighthouse. Conforming to regulations, he sounded his hooter.

A lean, agile man of forty, Warner was wearing a German suit. On the seat beside him lay a Tyrolean hat. For his secret crossing to his landfall on the Swiss shore he had substituted a peaked, nautical cap which merged into the holiday scene.

There was nothing ahead of him on the huge lake to arouse suspicion. In the glare of the afternoon sun a fleet of yachts with coloured sails drifted like toys. Beyond rose the jagged, snow-bound peaks of Liechtenstein and Switzerland. To his right one of the many white steamers which ply the lake disappeared towards the German town of Konstanz.

To his left a group of wind-surfers was using the light breeze to skim over the glassy surface of the water. He counted six of them as they moved across his bows.

'Kindly get out of the Goddamn way,' he muttered as he throttled back his engine.

They were all young, fine physical specimens, clad only in bathing trunks as they propelled their strange craft in an enclosing arc. Two of them were blond. Warner was about half a mile from the shore when he realised they were playing games, circling round to stop him opening up the throttle.

'Go and play elsewhere,' Warner growled.

He had a damned good mind to open up and scare them — but they were so close he might run them down. The tallest blond waved and brought his craft alongside the powerboat. He held the sail steady with his left hand while his right gripped the sheath knife strapped to his thigh. Too late a flicker of alarm alerted the Englishman. The wind-surfer abandoned his sail and jumped into the powerboat. He wielded the blade with speed and lethal efficiency, plunging it into his victim at varying angles.

The other five wind-surfers formed a screen of sails, masking the powerboat from anyone who might be watching them through glasses onshore. And the *Wasserschutzpolizei* — Water Police — had a unit and a launch at Lindau.

They maintained the screen while the tall blond completed his butchery. Then he left the powerboat, slipped into the water and upended his own sail. They resumed formation, heading for the deserted shore between Lindau and the Austrian border at the end of the lake.

'Multiple stab wounds — like the work of some maniac . . .'

Sergeant Dorner of the Water Police stood up from his examination of the body in the drifting powerboat. He looked at the launch with *Polizei* painted in blue letters on the hull drawn up alongside. The youngest policeman aboard who had been watching the examination began to retch over the side. Baptism of fire, Dorner thought.

He frowned as he noticed something gleaming by his foot. When he picked it up and saw what he had found he slipped it quickly into his pocket. A triangular-shaped badge very like the Greek letter *delta*. He glanced down at the body again; it was a pretty grisly mess. He opened the passport extracted from the corpse's jacket together with a wallet.

'He's English. Funny, the wallet is stuffed with money . . .'

'Maybe those wind-surfers panicked . . .' From his high point on the bridge of the launch, Busch, Dorner's deputy and the third man in the team, shielded his eyes and stared east. 'No sign of the bastards. They moved off fast ...'

'It takes only seconds to snatch a man's wallet,' Dorner persisted. 'This is the strangest killing I've come across ... Christ!'

Sifting through the contents of the wallet he had found a small card made of plastic rather like a credit card. But this was no credit card Dorner thought grimly as he studied the green and red stripes, the embossed number – which identified the owner – and a five-letter code reference which meant London.

'What's the matter?' Busch called down.

Something in his chief's expression warned him they had found trouble. Dorner slipped the card back inside the wallet and beckoned Busch to leave the bridge and come close to the powerboat. He kept his voice low when Busch faced him over the narrow gap between the two vessels.

'This has to be kept quiet. First we inform the BND at Pullach immediately ...'

'You mean he's ...'

'I don't mean anything. But I think there are people in London who will want to know about this before nightfall ...'

Sergeant Dorner was very silent as he stood on the bridge of the police launch, leaving the handling of the vessel to his subordinate as they approached the harbour of Lindau. Attached by a strong rope, the powerboat with its ghastly cargo was being dragged at the stern, the body carefully concealed by a sheet of canvas.

It was the macabre condition of the corpse's back which worried Dorner, a fact he had not mentioned even to Busch. And the horror of what he had discovered seemed such an appalling contrast to the holiday atmosphere of Lindau where visitors strolled in the sun along the short harbour front.

Keep close watch for group six wind-surfers possibly approaching your shore now. If seen apprehend and hold in close custody. Proceed on basis group armed and dangerous.

This was the top priority signal Dorner had told the young

radio operator to send before they began the return trip to Lindau. By then the latest addition to his crew had fortunately recovered from his bout of vomiting. And the signal had been sent to police headquarters at Bregenz on the Austrian shore as well as to Dorner's home base.

'I thought I saw some weird markings carved on his back,' Busch remarked as he sounded the siren prior to entering the harbour. 'Almost like some kind of symbol – but there was so much blood ...'

'Keep your mind on your job,' Dorner told him tensely.

With the sun blazing down on their necks they entered the small harbour and turned east to the landing-stage where the launch always berthed. Dorner was most concerned about how to smuggle the body the short distance from harbour to head-quarters without anyone seeing it. He need not have worried. The early discovery of Charles Warner's body was already being observed.

The ancient town of Lindau with its medieval buildings, nar-row, cobbled streets and even narrower alleys stands on an island at the eastern end of Lake Konstanz. There are two quite separate routes to reach this geographical oddity.

Coming by car you drive over the Seebrücke – the road bridge. Travelling to Lindau by international express from Zürich, you cross a rail embankment further west. The train stops at the Hauptbahnhof perched by the waterfront; it then moves back over the embankment and proceeds on to München.

The pavement artist was located outside the Bayerischer Hof, the most luxurious hotel on Lindau which faces the station exit. From here he could easily observe arrivals by train or boat.

A lean, bony-faced man in his early twenties, he wore a faded windcheater and jeans. The clothes were spotlessly clean. There are few beggars in Germany but those who exist preserve a respectable appearance. Only in this way can they hope to obtain money from passers-by.

His work was a picture of the Forum in Rome drawn in

crayon on the stones of the sidewalk, a small cardboard box by its side for coins. At frequent intervals he paused while he walked up and down slowly, hands clasped behind his back.

He was now watching the police launch entering the harbour. As it swung round, broadside on, heading for its berth, he saw the powerboat being towed in its wake. Turning away, he made sure no one was watching him and checked his watch strapped well above the wrist. Then he strolled across the road, pushed open a door and walked into the Hauptbahnhof.

Before he entered the phone booth he checked to make sure no one was coming out of the office marked *Polizei*. Once inside the booth he called the number and waited. From an apartment block in Stuttgart a girl's voice answered.

'Edgar Braun,' he replied.

'This is Klara. I'm just going out so I only have a minute ...'

'A minute is all it will take ...' He paused. The agreed opening had confirmed to each the other's identity. 'I thought that you would like to know the expected consignment has arrived ...'

'So quickly?'

She sounded startled. The man who called himself Braun frowned. It was most unlike the girl to lose her detachment. Whoever's body was inside the powerboat had clearly been found much earlier than expected.

'Are you sure?' she demanded.

'Of course I'm sure.' He bridled. 'You want the details?' he suggested nastily.

'That won't be necessary.' Her voice had resumed its normal cold tone. 'Thank you for calling ...'

'And my fee?' Braun persisted.

'Waiting to be collected at the Post Office in the usual way two days from now. And continue in your present job. Remember, jobs are not so easy to get at the moment ...'

He was left staring at the phone. The bitch had broken the connection. He shrugged, left the booth and returned to his pitch on the pavement. Braun knew what he had to watch for but beyond phoning a girl called Klara he had never met – and the fact she had a Stuttgart number – he knew nothing about the organisation he was spying for.

In the luxurious penthouse apartment in Stuttgart Klara stared at herself in the dressing-table mirror. An ex-model with a superb figure she was twenty-seven years old. Her sleek black hair was attended to weekly by the city's top hairdresser and there was a small fortune in her wardrobe of clothes.

She had dark, sleepy-looking eyes, fine bone structure and was a chain-smoker. She was hesitating before she picked up the white telephone and called the man who owned the apartment. She lit a fresh cigarette and dialled the number in southern Bavaria.

Inside the moated *schloss* many miles north-east of Lindau a firm, leathery hand picked up the receiver. On his third finger the man wore a large diamond ring. Beneath his strong jaw he wore a solid gold tie-slide. Attached to his left wrist was a Patek Philippe watch.

'Yes!'

No identification, just the single curt word.

'Klara calling. It is convenient to talk?'

'Yes! You received the fur I sent? Good. Anything else?'

The voice had a gravelly timbre, a hint of impatience that they must go through this identification rigmarole before they could get to the point. Like Klara earlier, he sounded startled when she relayed Braun's message.

'You say the consignment has arrived *already*?'

'Yes. I knew you would be relieved ...'

The sixty-year old man she was talking to was not relieved. He concealed his reaction but he was alarmed at the speed with which the police had discovered the body of the Englishman.

The reference to the 'consignment' confirmed that Warner had been liquidated on schedule as planned. The further reference to 'has arrived' told him the corpse was already in police hands. He repeated almost the same words Klara had used to Braun.

'Are you quite certain? It is very quick ...'

'I wasn't there to witness the collection,' she said, her voice tinged with sarcasm. 'I'm reporting what our observer told me less than five minutes ago . . .'

'Remember who you're talking to,' he told her. He replaced the receiver, took a Havana cigar from a box on his desk, clipped off the end and lit it with a gold lighter.

In her Stuttgart apartment Klara was careful to replace her own receiver before she used the four-letter word. He might share her bed, pay the rent, buy her clothes but he didn't bloody well own her.

She lit a fresh cigarette, studied herself in the mirror and began manipulating an eye pencil. The trouble was Reinhard Dietrich was a millionaire industrialist, a considerable land-owner and a well-known politician. And she never let herself forget that she was consorting with one of the most dangerous men in West Germany.

CHAPTER 2

Tuesday May 26

Tweed sat behind his desk in the first floor office of a house which overlooks Regents Park in the distance. Through thick-lensed spectacles he gazed at the pile of relics taken by the Lindau Water Police off the dead body of Charles Warner.

The hub of Britain's Secret Service is not – as has been reported – in a concrete building close to Waterloo Station. It is situated inside one of many Georgian buildings in a crescent, most of which are occupied by professional institutions.

The location has a number of advantages. On leaving the building there are different directions one can take. To check whether anyone is following you the simplest route is to walk straight into Regents Park. In the open parkland it is impossible for a shadow to conceal his presence.

Only a few paces away is the entrance to Regents Park Underground. Unlike most other stations you descend in a lift to reach the platforms. Again, anyone following has to show himself by stepping into the same lift.

'Pathetic what a man carries about with him,' Tweed remarked.

Keith Martel, the only other occupant in the room, lit a cigarette and wondered whether Tweed was criticising the relics because they offended his sense of order or commenting on the poverty of what a man left behind. He decided it was the latter.

There was about twenty years' difference in the ages of the two men. Martel, tall, well-built, dark-haired and with an air of supreme self-confidence, was twenty-nine. His most prominent feature was his Roman nose. His most outstanding characteristic was insubordination.

He chain-smoked, using a black holder. He spoke German, French and Spanish fluently. He was a first-rate pilot of light aircraft and helicopters. He swam like a fish and hated team sports.

No one knew Tweed's age. Five feet eight inches tall, wiry and with a ramrod back, he had the appearance of an ex-Army major – which he was – and his grey moustache matching his thatch of hair was neatly trimmed. Behind the spectacles his eyes bulged and held a haunted look as though expecting the worst.

'It usually happens – the worst. Count on it,' was his favourite maxim.

Events had an uncanny habit of proving him correct. It was this fact – his reputation for solving problems – and his caustic manner which had persuaded the new head of the department to sidetrack him into the post of Chief of Central Registry. Also the new supremo, Frederick Anthony Howard, had taken an instant dislike to Tweed when they first met in some mysterious past.

'What do you make of it all, Keith?'

Tweed gestured to the possessions of Warner spread in a gap on his desk he had cleared amid tidy piles of dossiers. Martel picked up several slips of paper and tickets extracted from the dead man's wallet.

Warner had been a squirrel, stuffing his wallet with odd items other agents would have thrown away. But Martel knew it was not carelessness: Warner had worked on the basis that if ever anything happened to him while on an assignment he should leave his successor clues.

'What was he doing in Germany?' Martel asked as he examined the collection.

'On loan from me to Erich Stoller of the *Bundesnachrichtendienst*. I owe Erich and he needed an outsider who could pass for a German to infiltrate this Delta outfit in Bavaria – neo-Nazis, as you well know. They cleverly keep just inside the law so they can't be banned.'

The *Bundesnachrichtendienst* – the BND – was the German Federal Secret Service with discreet headquarters near München. There was a dull *clink* as Tweed took something from his pocket and dropped it on the desk. A triangular-shaped silver badge like the Greek letter *delta*.

'That's their latest version of the swastika,' Tweed remarked. 'The badge was found under Warner's body. The killer must have dropped it without realising he'd lost it ...'

'How *was* he killed?'

'Brutally.' Tweed took off his glasses and leaned back in his swivel chair, settling himself on his favourite cushion. 'The BND pathologist reports that Warner was struck with some kind of knife twenty-five times. Twenty-five! And they completed the job by carving their trademark on his naked back – the Delta symbol.'

'We're relying on that to identify it as a Delta killing?'

'We're relying on an impartial eye-witness – whose name Stoller won't reveal even to me. Some German tourist was sitting on an elevated terrace above the harbour at Lindau ...'

'Sounds like the Romerschanze,' Martel interjected.

'Of course, I'd forgotten. You know Lindau. Rum-looking sort of place – I checked it up on the map. From the air it must look like a raft linked by a couple of planks to the mainland. As you know, it's an island linked to Bavaria by two bridges ...'

'One road bridge and a separate rail embankment with a cycle and pedestrian track running alongside the railway.'

'Nice to have an eye for detail,' Tweed commented with a hint of sarcasm. Martel appeared not to notice: the reaction showed Tweed was concealing considerable anxiety.

'As I was saying,' Tweed continued, 'this German tourist using his binoculars watched Warner take his powerboat out on to the lake. He saw a crowd of wind-surfers – six to be precise – get in Warner's way so he had to stop his boat. When they pushed off he saw Warner's boat was drifting – with Warner slumped over the wheel. He thought he must have been taken ill so he immediately contacted the Water Police who berth their launch just below that Romer-what-not terrace ...' He consulted Stoller's report. 'Chap called Dorner went out to have a look-see ...'

'And the rest is history – past history, unfortunately.'

'Except that I want you to go out and replace Warner for me.' Tweed said quietly.

Frederick Anthony Howard came into the office without knocking. It would be more accurate to say he *breezed* in. It was the essence of Howard's personality that you dominated a room the moment you entered it.

He was accompanied by Mason, a new recruit. Mason had restless eyes and a lean and hungry look. He said nothing and stood behind his chief like a commissionaire.

'Tweed, I suppose you know we need all *active* personnel mustered for the protection of the PM during her trip to the summit conference in Vienna?'

He invested the word 'active' with a significance which included Martel and specifically excluded Tweed. Florid-faced and with a choleric temper, Howard was a well-built man of fifty who had an unruly shock of grey hair and a brisk manner. He had a reputation for being a devil with the women, a reputation he relished.

The fact that his wife, Cynthia, lived at their 'small manor' in the country and he rented 'a pied-à-terre' in Knightsbridge could not have been more convenient. Tweed's privately expressed comment had been rather devastating.

'Pied-à-terre? I've been there once. When he has a girl with him it must be standing room only ...'

'What's all this bumf?' Howard demanded, picking up the wallet from the desk. Martel had palmed the slips of paper he was perusing and slipped them into his pocket as Howard entered the room.

'That *bumf*,' Tweed said grimly, 'happens to be the personal effects of the late Charles Warner. The BND kindly flew them straight to London from Münich so we can begin our investigation at the earliest moment.'

Having delivered his statement in a calm, cold voice Tweed put on his spectacles. Without them he felt naked, especially in the presence of people like Howard. And he was well aware that wearing the glasses made it impossible to judge his expression.

'Getting touchy in our old age, are we?' Howard enquired lightly, trying to bluff his way through what he now realised had been the height of bad taste.

'The man is dead,' Tweed replied, giving no quarter.

'I don't like it any more than you do.' Howard strolled over to the heavily net-curtained window and gazed through the armoured glass. He clasped both hands in a theatrical pose before making his pronouncement.

'I simply must insist that all active personnel are available to travel aboard the Summit Express from Paris to Vienna one week from today. Tuesday June 2 ...'

'I do have a calendar,' Tweed commented.

Howard looked pointedly away from Tweed and at Martel who said nothing, his cigarette holder in his mouth – which to Howard was insubordination. He had made it very clear he preferred no one to practise the filthy habit in his presence.

'Well?' he pressed.

Martel stared back at Howard, puffing away, his expression hard and hostile. 'I'm otherwise engaged,' he said eventually, still clenching the holder. Howard turned to Tweed and erupted.

'This is too damned much. I'm taking Martel and attaching him to my protection group. He speaks good German ...'

'Which is why he's going to Bavaria,' Tweed told him. 'We were suspicious something strange is going on in that part of the world. It looks as though we were right. Otherwise why was Warner killed?'

Howard glanced at Mason who still stood by the door like a commissionaire. Time to assert his authority. '*We*?' he repeated in a supercilious tone. 'May I enquire the identity of "we"?'

'Erich Stoller of the BND and myself,' Tweed said tersely. Time to get rid of Howard. 'I have a minute from the Minister — authorising me to investigate the Bavarian enigma and full powers to use my staff in any way I see fit. May I also point out that the route of the Summit Express carrying the four top western leaders to Vienna to meet the Soviet First Secretary passes through Bavaria?'

They were alone again. Howard had stormed out of the office on hearing of the existence of the special ministerial minute. Mason had followed, closing the door carefully behind him.

'He was memorising my appearance,' Martel said.

'Do let's get on. Oh, all right, who was?'

'The new boy, Mason. Who brought him in off the street?'

'Ex-Special Branch, I gather,' Tweed replied. 'And it was Howard who recruited him — interviewed him personally, I heard. I think he'd been angling to join us for a while ...'

'We don't take people who apply,' Martel snapped.

'We do now, apparently. How are you going to pick up Warner's trail? And since you've had your breakfast your stomach should be strong enough to study these pictures taken by Stoller's man — two show clearly the triangular symbol of the Delta Party carved out of Warner's back ...'

'Delta being the neo-Nazis,' Martel ruminated as he studied

the glossy blow-ups. 'Delta is run by that millionaire electronics industrialist, Reinhard Dietrich. He's also running for office in the Bavarian state elections which take place ...'

'On Thursday June 4 – the day after the Summit Express crosses Bavaria,' Tweed interjected. 'Which is something else Howard may have overlooked. You know, Keith, I have the oddest feeling the whole thing interlocks – the Bavarian crossing by the express, the state elections, and the murder of Warner before he could reach us.'

Martel dropped the glossy prints back on the desk and extracted from his pocket the pieces of paper he had secreted while Howard was in the room. He showed Tweed one particular piece of paper.

'I'll start in Zürich to try and find out what got Warner killed.'

'Why Zürich? I did notice a first-class ticket from München by train to Zürich – and another from Lindau to München, but ...'

'This little scrap of paper. Go on, have a really good look at it.'

Tweed examined it under a magnifying glass. It was some kind of ticket which carried the printed legend *VBZ Zuri ... Linie*. The words *RENNWEG/AUGUST* had been punched in purple on the ticket together with the price *0.80*.

'From the last time I was in Zürich I'm sure you're holding a tram ticket,' Martel explained. 'A tram whose route takes it along Bahnhofstrasse – Rennweg is a side street running off Bahnhofstrasse. Warner travelled about inside the city. Why? Where to? He never wasted time.'

Tweed nodded agreement, unlocked a drawer and brought out a file. From inside he produced a tiny black notebook and thumbed through the pages. Then he waved the key he had used.

'I suppose you know Howard waits until everyone has gone home in the evening and then prowls – hoping to find something he hasn't been told about? He spends more time spying on his own staff than on the opposition. Still, it will help to keep his hand in ...'

'You're just about to play your strongest card,' Martel observed. 'You're enjoying the anticipation. Could I now see what you hold in the way of aces?'

'It came with Warner's possessions Stoller flew to me with such commendable speed.' Tweed riffled the pages of the tiny notebook. 'Only I know Warner carried two notebooks – a large one inside his breast pocket, which is missing. Presumably filched by the swine who mutilated him. That was full of meaningless rubbish. This little fellow he kept in a secret pocket Stoller himself found when he flew to Lindau – or the nearest airstrip – when he heard from Dorner of the Water Police.'

'Am I to be allowed to see it?'

'You have a viper's tongue, Mr Martel.' Tweed handed over the notebook. 'The trouble is the jottings in it don't make sense.'

Martel went through the pages. The references seemed disjointed. *Hauptbahnhof, München ... Hauptbahnhof, Zürich ... Delta ... Centralhof ... Bregenz ... Washington, DC, Clint Loomis ... Pullach, BND ... Operation Crocodile.*

'Charles ...'

They had always called him Charles. Warner was the kind of man they would never dream of calling Charlie; he would have resented it.

'Charles,' Martel repeated, 'seems to have been fixated on the main stations – the Hauptbahnhofs in München and Zürich. Why? And if the note sequence means anything Delta is somehow linked with Zürich, which is odd, wouldn't you say?'

'Delta is the official neo-Nazi party with candidates standing in the coming Bavarian state elections,' Tweed remarked. 'But it also works underground. Rumour has it Delta cells are operating in north-east Switzerland between St. Gallen and the Austrian border. Ferdy Arnold of Swiss counter-espionage is worried ...'

'Enough to give us support?' Martel enquired.

'At arm's length. You know the Swiss – policy of neutrality so they feel they have to be careful ...'

'With that bunch of thugs? Look what they did to Warner. And who is Clint Loomis – Washington, DC?'

'I can't fathom that reference.' Tweed leaned back and swivelled his chair through small arcs. 'Clint is an old friend of mine. *Ex*-CIA. Kicked out by Tim O'Meara, now chief of the Secret Service detachment which will protect the US President aboard the Summit Express to Vienna. Makes no sense ...'

'Who provides most of the funds for this link-up with the BND if Howard is against it?'

'Erich Stoller of the BND – and he has plenty of money at his disposal. Delta is scaring Bonn ...'

'So Charles, being the secretive type he was, could have flown on a quick trip to Washington from München without your knowing?'

'Yes, I suppose so.' Tweed sounded dubious. 'I don't see why.'

'But we don't see anything yet, do we? Least of all what Warner found out that provoked his cold-blooded murder.' He checked the notebook again. '*Centralhof*. That rings a bell.'

Tweed stirred in his chair and the expression behind his spectacles went blank. Which meant, Martel knew from experience, he was going to be told something he wouldn't like. He lit another cigarette and clamped his teeth on the holder.

'You at least have some help on this thing, Keith,' Tweed said cheerfully, 'Ferdy Arnold put his best operative at the disposal of Warner and that operative may have more to tell you. Outside of his killers, she may have been the last person to see Warner alive ...'

'*She*?'

'The pronoun denotes a woman. Claire Hofer. Her mother was English, her father Swiss – and one of Ferdy's best men, which is how she came to join the Swiss Service. She lives at Centralhof 45 in Zürich. Hence the reference, I presume ...'

'Except that Warner seems to have used his secret notebook for suspect factors ...'

'You may need all the help you can get ...'

'All the help I can *trust* ...'

'She could be a major asset,' Tweed persisted.

'You do realise,' Martel began vehemently, 'that Warner was

betrayed by someone who *knew* he was making the crossing to Switzerland — by someone he *trusted*. And tell me again why Stoller asked for outside help.'

'Because he thinks the BND may have been infiltrated. You will find an atmosphere of suspicion everywhere you go. And with the Summit Express leaving Paris at 2335 hours on Tuesday June 2 you have exactly seven days to crack this mystery.'

CHAPTER 3

Wednesday May 27

Will Mr Keith Martel bound for Geneva please report immediately to the Swissair reception desk ...

Martel was inside Heathrow on his way to the final departure lounge when the message came over the Tannoy. He went back down the stairs slowly and paused where he could see Swissair. Only when two more passengers had called at the reception desk did he wander over.

The Swissair girl told him he was wanted urgently on the phone and left him as he picked up the receiver, fuming. It was Tweed. His voice held that quality of detached control which meant he was alarmed. They went through the identification routine and then Martel quietly exploded.

'What the hell do you mean broadcasting my name so everyone in the bloody terminal can hear ...'

'I did change the destination to Geneva. Didn't they ...'

'They did. Thank you for that small consideration. I now have ten minutes to board my flight ...'

'My office was bugged — while we were talking yesterday. About Delta, the lot ...'

'Where are you calling from.'

'A phone booth at Baker Street station, of course. You don't imagine I'm such a damned fool as to call from the building, do you? I found the bloody thing purely by chance. The cleaning woman had left a note that my main light bulb had gone. I checked it – the bug was inside the shade ...'

'So anyone could have overheard our conversation, could have taped it, could know where I'm going and why?'

'I thought you ought to know – before you boarded the plane.'

Tweed sounded genuinely concerned. Unusual for Tweed to display any emotion.

'Thanks,' Martel said shortly. 'I'll keep my eyes open ...'

'Probably it's the Zürich end you should watch. A reception committee could be waiting for you ...'

'Thanks a million. I must go now ...'

The Swissair flight departed on time at 1110 hours. In London it had been 50°F. As they lost height over Switzerland Martel, who had a window seat, watched the saddleback ridge of the Jura mountains which he felt he could reach down and touch. The plane had come in over Basle and headed east for Zürich.

As the machine tilted the most spectacular of views was framed in a window on the other side of the plane, a sunlit panorama of the snowbound Alps. Martel picked out the savage triangle of the Matterhorn, a shape not unlike Delta's badge. Then they landed.

At Kloten Airport, ten kilometres outside Zürich, a wave of heat enveloped him as he disembarked. 50°F in London; 75°F in Zürich. After Heathrow it seemed unnaturally quiet and orderly. When he had passed through Customs and Passport Control he started looking for trouble.

He was tempted to take the train from the airport's underground station to the Hauptbahnhof, the second location recorded in Warner's notebook. Instead he took a cab to the Baur au Lac.

He was staying at one of the top three hotels in Switzerland and the room tariff would have caused Howard to have apoplexy. But Howard was not paying the expenses. Before Martel left London a large amount of deutschemarks had been telexed to Tweed for the trip from Erich Stoller.

'The Germans are paying, so enjoy yourself,' Tweed had commented. 'They're conscious of the fact that the first man I sent to help is no longer with us ...'

'And that I may be next?' Martel had replied. 'Still, it's good cover – to stay at the best place in town rather than some grotty little *pension* ...'

Good cover? He recalled the remark cynically as the cab sped along the two-lane highway into the *centrum* of Zürich. It had been made in Tweed's office which they now knew had been bugged. He could change his hotel – but if the opposition sought him out at the Baur au Lac it might present him with a golden opportunity.

Just so long as I see them first he thought as he lit a fresh cigarette.

It was good to be back in Zürich, to see the blue trams rumbling along their tracks. The route the driver followed took him down through the underpass, sharp right across the bridge over the river Limmat and into the Bahnhofplatz. Martel stared at the massive bulk of the Hauptbahnhof, wondering again why the place had figured in Warner's notebook.

To his left he caught a glimpse of the tree-lined Bahnhofstrasse, his favourite street in his favourite European city. Here were the great banks with their incredible security systems, their underground vaults stacked with gold bullion. Then they were driving down Talstrasse, the street where the Baur au Lac was situated at the far end facing the lake.

A heavy grey overcast pressed down on the city and, as was so often the case when the temperature was high, the atmosphere was clammy. The cab turned in under an archway and pulled up at the main entrance. The head porter opened his door and Martel counted five Mercedes and one Rolls Royce parked in the concourse. Beyond the entrance the green lawns of the mini-park stretched away towards the lake.

From the airport to hotel he had not been followed. He was quite certain. The fact somehow did not reassure him as he followed the porter inside. The hotel was almost full. On the phone he had accepted a twin-bedded room overlooking the park. When the porter left he checked bedroom and bathroom for hidden microphones and found nothing. He was still not happy.

He went down the staircase after checking his room — avoiding the lift because lifts could be traps. The atmosphere was luxurious, peaceful and disturbingly normal. He strolled over the concourse to where tea and drinks were being served under a canopy near the French Restaurant. He ordered coffee, lit a cigarette and waited, watching the world's élite arrive and depart. He was looking for a shadow.

His appointment with Claire Hofer at her apartment was eight in the evening, an odd hour which he had wondered about. Normally he would have scanned the area in advance but the bugging of Tweed's office changed his tactics. He was good at waiting and he counted on the impatience of the opposition.

By 7.30 he was swimming in coffee and people were starting their evening meal in the nearby restaurant. He suddenly scribbled his signature and room number on the bill, stood up and walked out under the archway. Crossing Talstrasse, he turned left up Bahnhofstrasse away from the lake. He had spotted no one but could not rid himself of a feeling of unease.

Stopping by a machine in the deserted street, he inserted four twenty-centime coins obtained from the Baur au Lac cashier, took his ticket and waited for one of Zürich's 'sacred cows'. These gleaming trams had total right-of-way over all other traffic — hence the Zürichers' irreverent description.

The ticket gave him a slight twinge. Inside his breast pocket was an envelope which contained the contents of Warner's wallet — including the tram ticket with the destination RENNWEG/AUGUST inscribed. This stop was not far away and the ticket could have been used by Warner when he called on Claire Hofer. A tram glided up the street, streamlined and freshly-painted. Martel climbed aboard and sat down near the exit doors.

From the hotel it would have taken him five minutes to walk

to Centralhof 45, Claire Hofer's address. Taking a tram and travelling only one stop he hoped to flush out anyone following him. He played it deviously at the next stop. Standing up, he pressed the black button which would automatically open the double doors when the tram stopped.

The doors opened, he checked his ticket and stared about in a perplexed manner as though uncertain of his destination. People left the tram, came on board. Still he waited. The doors began closing. Martel *moved* . . .

He knew how the tram worked. He stepped down on to the outside footboard just when it began to elevate in conjunction with the closing of the automatic doors. As a safety device, when there is weight on the footboard, the doors remain open – or open again if they are closing. Reaching the sidewalk he paused to light a cigarette, to see if anyone rushed out after him. The doors shut, the tram moved off.

Centralhof is a square enclosed by buildings. One side overlooks Bahnhofstrasse. There are four entrances under archways at the centre of each side of the square – one leading off Bahnhofstrasse – to the interior garden beyond.

Martel crossed the street, walked down Poststrasse, turned right and continued along the third side of the block. Walking under the archway he saw the trees and the fountain he remembered. Nothing had changed. He sat down on a seat.

He had never visited this apartment in Centralhof before – but on an earlier visit he had used exactly the same tactic to entice a shadow to show himself. On that occasion it had worked.

The only sounds in the semi-dark were the chirruping of invisible sparrows in the foliage of the trees, the gentle splash of fountain water. It was impossible to imagine a more peaceful scene. He looked up at the windows masked by net curtains and the silence was almost a sound.

No one had followed him into this oasis of peace. He began to think he had evaded detection. He got up and headed for the archway Tweed had shown him on a street plan which contained the entrance to the apartment.

There was only one name-plate, a bell-push by its side. *C. Hofer*. He pressed the bell and a woman's voice responded through the metal grille of the speakphone almost immediately. In German – not Swiss-German, which he would not have understood.

'Who is that?'

'Martel.'

He kept his voice low, his mouth close to the grille. The other voice sounded disembodied, filtered through the louvres.

'I have released the catch. I am on the first floor ...'

He went into a bare hall and the spring-loaded hinge closed the door behind him. An old-fashioned lift with open grille-work enclosing a cage faced him. He ignored it and ran lightly up the staircase to arrive a few seconds before she would expect him.

Height: five feet six inches. Weight: nine stone two pounds. Age: twenty-five. Colour of hair: black. Colour of eyes: deep blue.

This was the description of Hofer Tweed had supplied to Martel in London. It was typical of Ferdy Arnold's consideration and efficiency that he should supply the girl's vital statistics in this terminology: he knew Tweed's detestation of the Common Market and the metric system.

Martel was not armed with any weapon when he reached the first floor. He expected Hofer to supply a hand-gun. A closed door faced him on the deserted landing and he noticed that – blended in with the grain of the highly-varnished woodwork – was a spy-hole. At least she took *some* precautions when strangers arrived.

'Welcome to Zürich, Mr Martel. Please come in quickly ...'

The door had been opened swiftly and the girl examined him as she ushered him inside, closed the door and double-locked it. Martel had stubbed out his cigarette as he waited inside the archway below. He held the black holder between his fingers and studied her without any show of enthusiasm.

She was wearing dark-tinted glasses with the outsize exotic-shaped lenses so many girls affected these days. Her hair *was* very black, her height *was* about five foot six and he calculated

27

she *would* turn the scales at around nine stone. She was also very attractive and wore a flowered blouse and a pastel-coloured skirt which revealed shapely legs.

'Satisfied?' she demanded in a waspish tone.

'You can't be too careful,' he told her and walked out of the tiny hall into a living-room whose windows overlooked the garden inside Centralhof. His manner was off-hand and he inserted a cigarette and lit it without asking her permission.

'Yes, you may smoke,' she told him.

'Good. It helps my concentration ...'

He looked round the room which was filled with heavy leather arm-chairs and sofas and the usual weighty sideboard. The German Swiss went in for solid furniture which was probably a reflection of their sturdy character. He thought he knew what Hofer was thinking. *Hell, do I have to work with this bastard?*

'I'm just making some coffee,' she said in a more friendly voice.

'That would be nice ...'

He went towards the window and changed direction as she vanished through a swing-door into a kitchen. From a quick glimpse it looked expensively equipped. Quietly he turned the handle of a closed door and eased it open, peering inside.

The bedroom. Large double bed. Large dressing-table with a few cosmetic articles neatly arranged. A pair of large double doors which presumably led to a large built-in wardrobe or dressing room. Everything spotless. He left the door half-open.

She had the percolator bubbling away when he walked uninvited into the kitchen. On a wing counter there were plates of half-eaten food, an unwashed glass, unwashed cutlery and a pair of scissors with a piece of sticking-plaster attached to one of the blades. She swung round, her mouth tight.

'Make yourself at home, Martel ...'

'I always do ...' He smiled briefly, the cigarette-holder still clenched between his teeth. 'Did Warner sleep here often?'

It threw her. She almost caught the percolator with her hand and knocked the whole thing over. He waited, watching her, smoking his cigarette. She unplugged the percolator, which had stopped bubbling, went to a wall-cupboard and opened it.

'Spring-cleaning – that's when I change things around to stop life getting boring ...'

She took coffee-cups from another cupboard next to the one she had first opened and Martel was relieved to see they also were large. He drank coffee by the gallon. He said no cream and she poured two cups of black coffee, put them on saucers and looked at him.

'You're in my way ...'

'Allow me ...'

He picked up both cups and carried them into the living-room where he placed them on mats on a low table. She followed him, talking as she came through the swing-door.

'You're agile – I can't get through that swing-door with two cups. I have to take them one at a ...'

He looked up as she stopped in mid-sentence. She was staring through her dark glasses at the half-opened bedroom door. It was impossible to see the expression in her eyes but her mouth compressed into a bleak gash.

'You've been in the bedroom ...'

'I like to be sure I really am alone with someone ...'

'You've got a bloody nerve ...'

She started towards the bedroom but he reached forward, caught her arm and sat her down on the sofa beside him. Still gripping her arm with one hand he reached up towards the outsized tinted glasses. She clawed her other hand and struck at his face with talon-like nails. He had to move fast to grab her wrist to protect himself: she had moved like a whip-lash.

'Martel, I've had you in a big way,' she hissed through perfectly formed teeth. '*If* we are going to work together we have a few things to get straightened out ...'

'You never answered my question about you and Warner ...'

He had released her and picked up his cup of coffee, sipping at it while he watched her. She got herself under control very quickly, picking up her own cup before she replied.

'That's one of the things. First, it's none of your damned

business. Second, the answer is no — he didn't even make a pass at me in all the time I knew him. It was strictly a business relationship — like ours is going to be ...'

'Oh, that you can count on, Claire. When did you last see Warner before he was murdered? And I may call you Claire?'

'I suppose so. I last saw Charlie three days before he went off on a trip to Lindau. He was frustrated — said he felt he wasn't getting anywhere ...'

'With Delta?'

She paused. Martel sat thinking and guessed if she could have read his thoughts they would have surprised her. He was recalling Tweed's comment that the dossiers never lied.

'If the facts conflict with your expectations, always believe the facts,' was a maxim Tweed had hammered into Martel. Hofer had worked out her reply.

'You're referring to their neo-Nazi background?'

'I'm referring to Delta's underground organisation he was tracking.'

Martel's attitude now was one of complete relaxation but inside his nerves were tingling as he forced himself to lean back and cross his legs. Hofer drank more coffee and then stood up. When she had followed him in the kitchen she had brought with her a shoulder bag which she left on a chair behind the sofa close to the window. She went round the back of the sofa, talking while she moved.

'He did leave a notebook with me. There's a lot in it but I'd have remembered any reference to Delta ...'

Martel was like a coiled spring. There was a faint thumping sound which came from beyond the half-open bedroom door. Hofer continued talking as she undid the clasp of her bag.

'The workmen next door are a nuisance — they're making alterations to the apartment before redecorating. The people cleared out to Tangier until it's all finished ...'

Martel had chosen the sofa to sit on because it faced a large mirror over the fireplace. There were vases of flowers on the ledge but between them he could watch Hofer behind him. He had made a bloody awful mistake when he was so careful to check that he was not followed to Centralhof. He had got it the wrong way round. The danger had been in front of him, not behind. *The enemy was waiting for his arrival at the apartment* ...

'I'm sorry if I was uptight when you arrived,' Hofer continued, 'but the news of Charlie's death shook me ...'

He heard the click, watched her coming up behind him through a gap in the flowers in front of the mirror. He swung round suddenly, grasped Hofer's right hand by the wrist. The hand held an object like a felt-tip pen.

The click had occurred when she pressed something and a blade shot out from inside the handle, a blade unlike any he had ever seen, a blade like a skewer with a needle-thin tip. She had been pushing the needle-point towards the centre of the back of his neck.

He twisted the wrist brutally and she yelped as she dropped the weapon and he hauled her bodily over the back of the sofa and sprawled her along its length. Her skirt was dragged up to her thighs exposing a superb pair of legs. She arched her supple body in a sexual movement, using her free hand to try and pull him down on top of her.

'Bloody cow ...'

He hit her a hard blow on the side of the jaw and she went limp. Standing up, he undid his leather belt and tightened the adjustable fasteners on either hip. When he bent down to turn her over on her face she suddenly came awake and jabbed two stiffened fingers towards his eyes. He became rougher, gave her a tremendous slap.

'Start struggling and I'll break your Goddamn neck ...'

For the first time he saw her mouth go slack with fear and she remained passive as he turned her over, pulled the upper part of her body towards him, then used the belt to strap her ankles to her wrists.

It was the most uncomfortable position anyone can be forced into: if she struggled she would suffer excruciating pain. He tightened the belt to the limit of his strength. Soon the circulation would start to go. He left her on the sofa after using his handkerchief as a gag.

31

'It's not too clean,' he assured her.

Then he walked into the bedroom where the faint thumping was repeating itself. He opened both doors of the built-in wardrobe cupboard and looked down. The dark-haired girl on the floor had been trussed up like a chicken and her mouth was sealed with a band of sticking plaster.

'Hello, Claire Hofer,' he said. 'Thanks for the warning. Now let's make you comfortable. You have got guts ...'

CHAPTER 4

Wednesday May 27

Hofer was emerging from the state of shock brought on by her ordeal inside the cupboard. She had cleared up the mess in the kitchen and was making coffee for herself and Martel.

'How did you know that girl was impersonating me?' she asked.

Their prisoner was lying on the living-room floor. Martel had released her from his belt and replaced it with the ropes used to bind up Hofer. Her mouth was sealed with a fresh strip of sticking-plaster Hofer had provided from the kitchen.

'She made a lot of mistakes,' Martel explained. 'Although her physical description fitted the one I had been given she wore dark-tinted glasses – in a room where the light was dim anyway. Now we know why – her eyes are brown ...'

'There must have been more ...'

'When I peered into the bedroom your cosmetics were neat and tidy on the dressing-table – one hell of a contrast with the food remains and dirt in here. The bit of sticking-plaster stuck to the scissors intrigued me. She had no visible injury. The normal one is when a woman cuts her hands in the kitchen. There were other things, too ...'

'Such as?'

'More damning was the fact she didn't know which cupboard held the coffee cups. She denied Warner had ever made a pass at her – he always made one try for an attractive woman. And she called him Charlie. He always insisited on Charles.'

'You really are observant. Coffee in here?'

'No, in the living-room. I have questions to ask our imposter. She also over-reacted to my leaving the bedroom door half-open. Plus her elaborate explanation to cover your thumping the inside of the cupboard. You took a chance there ...'

'I heard a man's voice and guessed you had arrived. I felt such a fool that I'd let her overpower me I had to warn you. Was she going to kill you?'

They had moved back into the living-room where their prisoner was rolled on her side in front of the fireplace. Martel lowered his voice so she couldn't hear him.

'Was she going to kill me?' He picked up the needle weapon he had earlier rescued from the floor and placed on a table. 'I think so. This ingenious little toy is very like a hypodermic. When I grabbed her she was about to ram it into the back of my neck. Press this button a second time and I'd say it injects the fluid. Let's test her reaction to her own medicine ...'

Holding the weapon out of sight he knelt on the floor and rolled the girl on her back. With the other hand he took a grip on the plaster and ripped it off her mouth. She screamed. He placed a hand over her lips.

'No more noise. I'm going to ask questions. You're going to answer. Your real name?'

'Go stuff yourself ...'

'What would happen if I jab this into you and press the button?'

He showed her the needle weapon. He moved the point close to the side of her neck. Her brown eyes glared up at him with a mixture of hatred and apprehension.

'For God's sake, no! *Please* ...'

'She says *please*,' Martel observed sarcastically. 'And yet she

33

was about to give me the same treatment. Oh, well, here we go ...'

'Gisela Zobel ...'

'Where is your home base?'

'Bavaria ... Münich. For pity's sake ...'

'Pity?' Martel glanced up at Hofer who was staring intently, wondering how far he was prepared to go. 'She wouldn't know the meaning of the word, would she?'

'Not from the way she treated me ...' Hofer responded with deliberate callousness. 'You decide ...'

She lit a cigarette and the girl on the floor watched her with bulging eyes. Sweat beads were forming on her forehead. Martel moved the needle closer as he asked the question.

'Who do you work for?'

'He will kill me ...'

'How could he? If you don't give the reply – the right reply – and we have certain information Warner sent by a secret route, you will be dead anyway. That is, unless I'm mistaken about what this instrument you were going to use on me contains. So, once again, here goes ...'

'*Reinhard Dietrich* ...'

Then she fainted from terror – whether from uttering the name or because of Martel's threat to use the weapon he was not sure. He looked into Hofer's deep blue eyes, shrugged and withdrew the needle tip from the proximity of Zobel's neck.

'Get me a cork to protect this damned thing,' he suggested and while she fetched one from the kitchen he gazed at the weapon. He was convinced that the contents injected into the victim would be lethal, that Gisela Zobel *had* planned to kill him. He would hand it to the counter-espionage people: Forensic could then check it.

At ten o'clock night had descended and Martel decided they could safely leave the apartment. Hofer packed a bag and Martel arranged with the police to send a plain-clothes man to the Baur au Lac to pay his bill and collect his suitcase. The bag was now standing in the small hall outside the apartment.

'We take a train to St. Gallen,' Martel told the Swiss girl in the living-room. 'We have to pick up Warner's trail there . . .'

'We have very little to go on,' the girl reminded him. 'Only that he stopped off there on his way here from Bavaria . . .'

'So we make use of what little we have got . . .'

The evening had been packed with activity. Hofer had looked up the number in her pocket diary and Martel had phoned Berne. While he was talking to her boss, Ferdy Arnold, he had studied her in the mirror.

Her description fitted the one provided by Tweed perfectly but he was puzzled by her passive personality. She was a nice girl with long dark hair, a soft voice and graceful movements. Already he liked her. But he had expected someone more dynamic.

The Swiss counter-espionage chief had flown by private plane to Zürich. The atmosphere changed the moment he entered the place. A small, serious-faced man with rimless glasses, Ferdy Arnold resembled a banker. He took immediate decisions.

'We smuggle her out in an ambulance,' he announced, indicating Gisela Zobel who was now propped up in one of the deep arm-chairs. 'She will be taken to a special hospital. She will be kept under heavy guard. She will be intensively interrogated.'

He looked at Martel, ignoring Hofer. 'Phone me at this number at ten in the morning . . .' He scribbled a number on a small pad, tore off the sheet and handed it to the Englishman. 'I've left off the Zürich code in case you lose the paper . . .'

Arnold, smartly dressed in a dark blue suit, looked at Martel with a wry smile. 'It isn't that I don't trust you . . .'

'But one English agent, Warner, was spotted – even posing as a German – so you're playing it to cover all angles. And why do I phone at ten in the morning? Surely you'll only just have started Zobel's daily interrogation . . .'

'On the contrary, we shall just have *finished* since she will be interrogated throughout the night without a break . . .'

Martel was not happy. There was an atmosphere which did not ring true. Something in the relationship between Ferdy Arnold and his 'top operative', Hofer. He was damned if he could detect why he sensed he was being tricked — but his instincts had never let him down yet.

'Come into the bedroom,' Arnold suggested, glancing at Gisela Zobel, who sat motionless watching and listening. 'Keep an eye on her,' he told Hofer. When he had closed the bedroom door he accepted a cigarette from Martel.

'All that I said in there was strictly for Zobel's ears. It can help the breaking-down process if they worry about what is in store for them.'

'She admitted she was working for Reinhard Dietrich,' Martel told him.

'I see.'

Arnold showed no interest in the statement. Martel recalled a remark Tweed had made in London. *At arm's length ... you know the Swiss. Policy of neutrality ...* It was understandable — that the Swiss counter-espionage should not want an open war with a German neo-Nazi movement. Understandable but unhelpful. Arnold was, he suspected, maintaining a watching brief.

'Berne,' Arnold commented, 'is disturbed about rumours that an underground organisation has spread its tentacles into northern Switzerland ...'

'St. Gallen?'

'What made you mention that place?' Arnold enquired.

'Because it is one of the chief towns in north-eastern Switzerland,' Martel replied casually. 'I find the choice of the word *delta* interesting — the Rhine delta is located just beyond your border with Austria. The Vorarlberg province ...'

He watched Arnold's reaction closely. One of the references in Warner's tiny notebook had been to *Bregenz*. This was the only port Austria had on its narrow frontage of lake shore at the eastern end of Lake Konstanz.

'We've been in touch with Austrian counter-espionage,' Arnold commented vaguely. 'Nothing has come of it so far. Berne is sensitive about the recent unprecedented student riots here in Zürich. It is suspected they are organised by a secret Delta cell.' He checked his watch and seemed disinclined to linger. 'I must go now.'

He left without saying a word to the girl except for a brief exchange before walking out. Martel frowned as he looked round the living-room. Gisela Zobel had disappeared. Hofer explained before he could ask.

'A team dressed like ambulance men came. They took her away on a stretcher.'

'Arnold doesn't waste much time, does he? By the way, as he was leaving he said something to you. Did you mention that we are on our way to St. Gallen?'

'No.' She looked surprised. 'Is something wrong? I'm beginning to know your intonations . . .'

Martel passed it off lightly as he picked up both bags in the hall. 'When you get to know me better you'll realise I often ask random questions. We board one of the trams for the Hauptbahnhof?'

'It will be quicker – the tram goes straight to the station. A number eight. And it's an unobtrusive way of travelling . . .'

'Warner thought that, too . . .'

The brutal assault – the insane shock – commenced as soon as they closed the street door to the apartment and emerged from the archway leading into Bahnhofstrasse. Ten o'clock at night. Illuminated by the street lights, the trees lining one of the most famous thoroughfares in the world cast patches of shadow on the wide pavement. It was very quiet and few people were about.

One essential addition to Martel's equipment since he arrived at the Centralhof apartment was the Colt .45 he now carried in a spring-loaded shoulder holster. Hofer had provided this, taking it from a secret compartment in the floor of the wardrobe cupboard where she had been imprisoned. She had also given him ammunition.

Martel was committing a strictly illegal act carrying the gun but they would cross no frontiers on their way to St. Gallen. He had asked her not to mention to Ferdy Arnold the fact that he was now armed. He was not sure why he made this request.

'The ticket machine is over here,' Hofer said and he followed her with the two cases. 'I'll take my own case once we're on the tram.'

He watched her inserting coins. Light from a lamp shone down directly on her. She really was a very beautiful girl and he wondered why she had ever joined the service. He'd try to find out when he knew her better ...

A tram was coming in the distance from the lake direction so, if it was the right number, it would take them to the top of the street which faced the Hauptbahnhof. That was the reason he stood with a case in each hand, ready to board the tram – which put him at an initial disadvantage.

He was listening to the rumble of the approaching tram, the faint hiss of the traction wires, when the huge six-seater Mercedes appeared and charged like a tank. It came out of nowhere and swung up on to the sidewalk alongside the ticket machine, alongside the girl ...

The shock hit Martel like a physical blow. Men were pouring out of the Mercedes, men dressed in respectable business suits and wearing dark glasses. He saw two of them grab Hofer, one of them pressing a cloth over the upper part of her face. Beneath the glare of the street light they had another common denominator – a triangular silver badge like the Greek letter *delta* in their coat lapels.

He heard the oncoming tram ringing its warning bell – the car was positioned diagonally, its front on the sidewalk, its rear in the street, blocking the tramline. A second car appeared, a Rolls Royce, and swung across the tramline blocking it completely. The tram's bell continued clanging as the driver jammed on his brakes and stopped a few feet from the Rolls Royce.

Martel had dropped his bags and was moving. The Colt .45 was in his hand as the Rolls turned slightly and swivelled the glare of its undipped headlights full on him. Shielding his eyes with one hand he snapped off two shots. There was a tinkling of glass and both lights died. One of the men from the Mercedes

38

produced an automatic and aimed point-blank at Martel. The Englishman shot him and the gunman sagged back against the Mercedes, blood cascading from his forehead.

Martel ran towards the two men still grappling with Hofer. She had torn the cloth away from her face and in the clammy night air a waft of chloroform reached Martel's nostrils. The first man was turning towards Martel when the Englishman lashed out. The savage kick reached its target – the assailant's kneecap. He screamed and dropped in a heap. More men appeared from the far side of the Mercedes and now Hofer was screaming at the top of her voice.

Martel found it a nightmare. This was anarchy, violence, kidnapping on the main street in Zürich. Another attacker levelled an automatic at Martel who fired in a reflex movement, still trying to reach the girl. The man clutched at his chest and his hand came away covered in blood as he toppled forward.

More men were appearing – from inside the Rolls. Martel ducked and weaved, never still for a moment, lashing out with the barrel of his Colt, catching one man a terrible blow on the side of his face, raking him from his ear to the tip of his jaw.

The arrival of reinforcements distracted Martel. He was fighting for his life. He went on using the Colt as a club, preserving his remaining bullets. He took refuge with his back to the ticket machine so they could only come at him from the front – and something very hard struck his skull, blurring his vision. As his sight cleared he saw an appalling sight. Hofer was being dragged head first inside the rear of the Mercedes, her legs kicking until another man grabbed her ankles and twisted them viciously over each other. She looked as though she were being sucked inside the maw of a shark.

And now there was smoke. One of them had thrown a smoke bomb – probably several – in the direction of the tram. The street began to fill with fog. A car engine started up. A man grappling with Martel let go and tried to flee. They had Hofer inside the Mercedes. *He had to reach the Mercedes*! As the man ran Martel shot him and he sprawled with a crash on the flagstones.

The Mercedes backed off the sidewalk. The injured and the

dead had been collected and taken inside the two cars – except for the man on the flagstones. The Rolls Royce also was moving. With the Mercedes leading both cars sped off up Bahnhof-strasse, then turned left at the Paradeplatz.

It was suddenly very quiet and the stationary tram was still hidden in drifting smoke. Martel slithered in a pool of blood. He stumbled back to the man they had abandoned, the one who had grappled with him.

The body was lying on its face and Martel quickly felt the neck pulse, cursing when he realised the man *was* dead. As he would have been had Hofer not given him the Colt. He shoved the weapon back into the holster, bent down and heaved the man over on his back. Yes, he also wore the silver badge in his coat lapel. Martel ripped it free and dropped it in his pocket.

A ten-second search of the man's pockets revealed they were empty. No means of identification – except for the badge. He had no doubt all clothing identity such as maker's tabs had been removed. He straightened up and looked around, frustrated and dazed.

The tram was still hidden in the smoke but its silhouette was becoming clearer. No sign of the driver. Sensibly he had remained inside his cab. Martel felt sure he had kept the automatic doors closed to protect his passengers. Nearby was a pathetic sight – two cases standing on the pavement.

At any moment the tram driver was going to emerge from his cab. Martel scraped his shoes back and forth on the edge of the kerb to remove blood from the soles. Then he picked up the two suitcases and left the scene of the nightmare as he heard the distant scream of a patrol-car siren.

The blast from the explosion sent a shock wave down the funnel of Bahnhofstrasse which thumped Martel in the back. He turned down a side street towards the Old Town, taking a roundabout route to the Hauptbahnhof. He didn't think any-one aboard the tram had seen him but a man carrying two suitcases at that hour was conspicuous.

What had caused the explosion he had no idea. He wasn't too

interested. At that moment he had three objectives. To hide Hofer's suitcase in a left-luggage locker at the station. Next, to book himself temporarily into a hotel near the station – if he returned to the Baur au Lac he could walk straight into the arms of the opposition. Finally, to phone Ferdy Arnold's head-quarters in Berne.

Martel felt he was on the edge of a whirlpool. He could hardly credit what had happened in Bahnhofstrasse. And Swiss security was renowned for its ruthless efficiency. What the hell had gone so horribly wrong?

When a woman replied to his call to the Berne number Arnold had given him he opened with the identification phrase and she didn't react.

'What was that you said? Who are you calling? You know what time of night it is . . .'

'I'm sorry,' Martel replied. 'I was calling . . .' He repeated the number Arnold had provided him and risked it: after all, Arnold was a common name.

'No one here of that name – you have the wrong number. This is the number you said you were calling but – for the second time – there is no one here of that name. *Good night!*'

Martel sat staring at the receiver and replaced it. He was inside a third-floor bedroom he had booked at the Schweizer-hof – which faced the Hauptbahnhof. Hofer's suitcase was parked in one of the station lockers, the key for which he had in his pocket. Why had Ferdy Arnold given him a meaningless phone number when he visited the apartment in Centralhof? The obvious conclusion was that *he was not the real Ferdy Arnold* – whom Martel had never met.

If this same man had organised the savage onslaught on himself and Hofer it explained his anxiety to leave the apart-ment urgently. *He had known what was waiting for them outside.* So he had to be well clear of the place when Martel came out with Hofer. But in that case why had Hofer accepted him as Arnold? Martel felt the sensation of being swept inside a whirlpool growing.

Leaving his room, he went down the staircase, again instinctively ignoring the lift. Crossing the street to the station he found a row of phone booths, went inside one and dialled the Ferdy Arnold number Tweed had given him in London.

He *had* realised 'Arnold' had provided a different number, but he had assumed it was a security precaution and Tweed had not been immediately informed of the change. This time the reaction at the Berne number was different. He used the code-phrase, a girl asked him to wait just a moment.

'Who is this?'

The voice was crisp, almost curt, and had a ring of competence, of no nonsense about it. Martel identified himself.

'Where are you calling from?' Arnold demanded.

'That doesn't matter at the moment,' Martel replied. 'I have regretfully to report that your assistant, Claire Hofer, has been kidnapped by Delta ...'

'You were part of that massacre in Bahnhofstrasse in Zürich?'

'Massacre?'

'Delta – if it was Delta – bungled a major bank raid. A limpet mine was attached to the main door of a certain bank. It detonated and some people alighting from a tram which had been stopped were badly injured. What was that about Claire Hofer? And I'd still like to know where you're calling from ...'

'Skip that. This call is going through your switchboard ...'

'That's crazy.' Ferdy Arnold's voice reflected indignation and disbelief. 'Our security ...'

'You said something about a bungled bank raid.' Martel was bewildered. 'I'm limiting this call to two minutes so talk ...'

'I've just told you – a bomb, presumably with a quick-acting timer, was attached to the entrance to a bank. It blew the door but no one followed it up. The driver of the tram which was stopped saw nothing because smoke bombs were used ...'

'What about the Rolls Royce that stopped him by driving across his bows?'

'I don't know anything about that. On the pavement we found a small silver badge shaped like a triangle – or a delta ...'

'Send out an all points bulletin alarm for Claire Hofer.'

42

Martel was checking the length of the call by the second-hand on his watch. 'I'm very worried about her . . .'

'You can stop worrying.' Arnold paused and there was something in his tone Martel didn't like. 'We know what happened to her – part of the story anyway.'

'Then for Christ's sake tell me – and fast. In the short time we were together I came to like – admire – the girl . . .'

'Her body was discovered floating down the Limmat less than half an hour ago. She had been brutally and professionally tortured before they dumped her in the river. I want you to come in, Martel. I want you to come to an address in Berne . . .'

Arnold stopped speaking. Martel had broken the connection.

CHAPTER 5

Wednesday May 27

If Arnold had kept the conversation going so his tracers could locate the source of the call Martel was confident he had rung off in time. He was no happier about the real Arnold knowing his whereabouts than he was for the fake Arnold to obtain the same information. And the news of Claire Hofer had hit him hard.

Leaving the booth he walked round the huge Hauptbahnhof, stopping to study the departure board like a man waiting for his train. This great station – along with its counterpart in München – had fascinated the murdered Warner. Why?

Martel made a swift inventory of the place. *Gleise* 1–16: sixteen platforms, all of the tracks ending here. The long row of phone booths for communication and, he realised as he strolled round the hushed concourse, numerous exits. There was a *kino* – cinema – the *Cine-Rex*, and a Snack-Buffet.

He walked down one of the broad aisles leading away from the platforms past a large luggage storage counter facing a door marked *Kanton-Polizei*. Two men emerged dressed in blue uniforms with berets, their trousers tucked into boots. They had the look of paratroopers.

He passed *Quick*, a first-class restaurant which provided two more exits and came out into the street. The Hauptbahnhof was a place you could get out of swiftly – a place you could linger inside for a long time unobtrusively. An idea formed at the back of his mind and receded. He crossed two roads and gazed down into the back water of the Limmat river. Dizzying reflections from street lamps danced in the night.

These were the waters which within the past hour had carried the mutilated body of poor Claire Hofer. Martel was not a sentimental man but he decided someone was going to pay for that barbaric act.

Glancing round he noticed the huge greystone bulk of a four-storey building to his right on the Bahnhofquai. The *Stadtpolizei* – police headquarters. The working quarters of a friend, David Nagel, Chief Inspector of Intelligence. He checked his watch. 2245 hours.

While at the Hotel Schweizerhof he had borrowed a rail timetable and found that the last train from the Hauptbahnhof left at 2339, reaching St. Gallen at 0049 hours. He had less than one hour to catch that train – to get out of Zürich which was becoming a death-trap.

He entered police headquarters through the double doors in Lindenhofstrasse. The receptionist, a stocky policeman in shirt sleeves, confirmed that Chief Inspector Nagel was in his office. He asked Martel to fill in a printed form.

'Just tell him I'm here, for God's sake,' Martel snapped. 'If you keep me waiting you won't be popular. This is an emergency.'

'Even so . . .'

'And he's expecting me,' the Englishman lied. 'My name is all he will need . . .'

Within minutes he was inside Nagel's third-floor office

overlooking the Limmat. The windows were wide open, letting in dense clammy air. There were the usual heavy net curtains, the usual neon lighting, harsh and uninviting, the usual filing cabinets along one wall.

'I've been hoping you would contact me,' Nagel said when they had shaken hands. 'Tweed called from London and warned me you were coming in. He said you might need help . . .'

'I think I do . . .'

David Nagel was a well-built Swiss with a thick moustache, humorous eyes and a mass of dark hair he kept well-brushed. Some of his colleagues dismissed him as a bit of a dandy whose greatest interest in life was women.

'No, that is my second greatest interest,' he would correct them when they hinted as much. 'My first is my work – which is why I'm not married. What wife could stand the hours I keep? So, being normal, my second greatest interest is . . . Now get the hell out of here.'

Martel liked him. Tweed said he had the most acute brain in the Swiss police and security system – and Intelligence had one foot in both camps. Nagel came straight to the point – as he always did.

'You didn't fill in a form before you came up here, I hope?' He looked worried as he asked the question, and Nagel rarely showed anxiety no matter how critical the situation. 'You were dressed like that?' the Swiss continued, speaking rapidly. 'And not using that blasted cigarette holder . . .'

'No to all your questions – and yes I was wearing these glasses.' Martel removed a pair of horn-rimmed glasses fitted with plain lenses. 'I had to give my bloody name to get through to you. Are you going to nag about that . . .'

'Please, please, Keith . . .!' Nagel held up a restraining hand in a pacific gesture. 'But from *your* point of view your whereabouts might be best left unknown. Ferdy Arnold's security mob is moving heaven and earth to locate you.'

Martel lit a cigarette and indulged himself in the luxury of employing his holder. He knew that Nagel disliked Arnold, that he had once told Tweed it 'was purely a political appointment'. The Swiss continued talking.

'Your name doesn't matter. When you have gone I shall tell the man at reception you are one of my key informants, that you used a code-name – that officially you never entered these premises. With no written record you will be safe from Arnold's hard men.'

'That's reassuring at any rate . . .' Martel was about to refer to the debacle in Bahnhofstrasse when Nagel again went on speaking.

'I have a number here you must phone urgently. She called me only ten minutes ago – knowing we are good friends. Despite my reservations about her chief, I like and trust Claire Hofer . . .'

Martel felt himself spinning, the whirlpool whipping him round faster.

CHAPTER 6

Wednesday May 27

Stunned, Martel's teeth clenched tight on the cigarette-holder. To mask his reaction he took the holder out of his mouth and readjusted the position of cigarette in holder. *She called me only ten minutes ago.*

What the hell was wrong with the timing? Thirty minutes earlier Arnold had told him on the phone that 'less than half an hour ago' her body had been found in the Limmat. That meant Hofer had been found about one hour from this moment. And now Nagel – the most precise Swiss – had clearly stated the call from Claire Hofer had come through 'ten minutes ago'. On the scrap of paper Nagel had handed to him was written a St. Gallen phone number.

Nagel would know the girl's voice well. Being Nagel he would have wanted proof of the identity of his caller. *Irrevocable* proof. Martel began to consider whether he could be going out of his mind.

'Something wrong?' Nagel enquired softly.

'Yes, I'm tired.' Martel folded the scrap of paper and put it in his wallet. 'What sort of a night are you having?'

'Routine so far.'

Again Martel was stunned. David Nagel, chief of police Intelligence, *had no knowledge of the traumatic event which had taken place in Bahnhofstrasse.* There was no reason for him to conceal such knowledge – Martel felt certain of this. He had to tread damned carefully.

'Why do you mistrust Ferdy Arnold?' he asked.

'It was a political appointment – not a professional one ...'

'And why does Claire Hofer – who works for Arnold – call *you* when she has a message for me?'

'Because she knows you and I are close friends.' The Swiss paused. 'I also employed her before she transferred to counter-espionage ...'

'You said you've had a routine night so far,' Martel probed.

'Except for the explosion aboard some tourist's launch out on the lake. Some poor idiot who obviously knew nothing about engines or boats – so he had an accident and lost his life. We did hear the faint boom of the detonation ...' He pointed towards the open windows behind curtains which hung motionless in the airless night. 'The sound came up the Limmat from the lake ...'

No, it didn't, Martel thought. It came straight up the funnel of Bahnhofstrasse and then down Uraniastrasse, the side street leading towards police headquarters. He was watching Nagel and the extraordinary thing was he was convinced the Intelligence man was not lying. Someone was trying to cover up the incident, to pretend it had never happened.

'Good to see you, David,' Martel said and stood up. 'And I'll call Claire Hofer soon but there's something I have to attend to, and you don't want to know about it ...'

'That is a direct line which bypasses the switchboard,' Nagel suggested, pointing to one of three phones on his desk. 'I can leave you on your own ...'

'It isn't that, David. I'm just short of time.'

'Enjoy yourself while you're in Zürich ...'

It was 2310 hours when Martel left police headquarters. He had half an hour to catch the 2339 train to St. Gallen, but he still had things to deal with. He walked past a patrol car parked outside, a cream Volvo with a red trim. Two uniformed men sat in the front with the windows open. Where the devil had they been when all hell broke loose in nearby Bahnhofstrasse?

And he *had* lied to Nagel he recalled as he hurried back to the Hauptbahnhof. He felt certain he could rely on the Swiss but he had mistrusted the offered phone which passed through no switchboard. He was now gripped by a feeling of insecurity and determined to take no chances.

'Maybe I'm getting paranoid,' he told himself as he slipped inside one of the empty phone booths in the station. *These* were safe. Again he remembered the dead Warner who apparently had also haunted Hauptbahnhofs. As he dialled the number Nagel had given him he began to sympathise with Charles Warner. Martel himself felt *hunted*.

The receptionist at the Hotel Hecht in St. Gallen confirmed that Claire Hofer was staying with them. She asked him to hold while she tried her room. A girl's voice came on the line – decisive, sharp and wary.

'Who is this?'

'Our mutual friend, Nagel, passed on your message and I want you to take certain action very fast. Can you get to an outside payphone? Good. Get there immediately and call me at this number.' He read out the booth number from the dial. 'It's Zürich code,' he added tersely. 'I'm very short of time ...'

'Goodbye!'

Martel found he was sweating. The atmosphere inside the booth was oppressive. He felt both exposed and trapped in the confined space. The phone rang in an astonishingly short time.

He snatched up the receiver. The same voice asked the question crisply.

'Is that . . .? Please confirm name of our mutual friend . . .'

'Nagel. David Nagel . . .'

'Claire Hofer speaking . . .'

'Again do what I tell you without questioning my judgement – as fast as you can. Pay your bill at the Hotel Hecht – make up some plausible reason why you have to . . .'

'All right, I'm not stupid! What then?'

'Book in at another hotel in St. Gallen. Reserve a room for me. Warn them I'll arrive about one o'clock in the morning . . .'

'You need parking space for a car?'

'No. I'm coming in by train . . .'

'I'll call back in minutes. I have to find accommodation and tell you where to come. Goodbye!'

Martel was left staring at a dead receiver. More precious time was being consumed. But she sounded good, damned good. He had to give her that. The whirlpool was gyrating faster. He felt he had been talking to a ghost. Claire Hofer had just been dragged out of the Limmat – according to Arnold . . .

Despite the growing heat inside the kiosk he inserted a cigarette into his holder, cursed, removed the cigarette and placed it between his lips minus holder. While talking he had turned round with his back to the coin box so he could watch the deserted concourse. He took several deep drags and the phone was ringing a second time. Her voice . . .

'Is that . . .? Good. Our mutual friend . . .'

'Nagel. Martel here . . .'

'I got lucky. Two twin-bedded rooms on the first floor. Hotel Metropol. Faces the station exit. Staring at you as you come out. I'll leave a note at the desk with just my room number inside the envelope. O.K.?'

'Very . . .'

'Goodbye!'

In the next few minutes Martel moved very fast. He bought his rail ticket for St. Gallen. At the Hotel Schweizerhof he paid for the room he no longer needed. He did his best to make the cancellation seem normal.

'I'm a consultant – medical – and I'm urgently needed in Basle by a patient . . .' *Consultant* was the word he had filled in on the 'occupation' section of the registration form when he had arrived. The term was impressive and totally vague.

He had not unpacked his bag – a precaution he always took when arriving at a fresh destination – so all he had to do was to shove his shaving kit and toothbrush inside and snap the catches. Running down the stairs – the night clerk would see nothing odd now in his speedy departure – he hurried across to the first of the taxis waiting outside the station.

'I want you to take me to Paradeplatz. Can you then wait a few minutes by the tram stop while I deliver something? Then drive me straight back here?'

'Please get in . . .'

He was using up his last few minutes before the St. Gallen train departed but – knowing Zürich and the quietness of the streets at this hour – he believed he could just manage it. *Because he had to check the state of Bahnhofstrasse where shots had been fired, blood spilt all over the sidewalk, and a bomb detonated against a bank.*

He began chatting to the driver. All over the world cabbies are plugged in to a city's grapevine.

'Did you hear that terrific explosion not so long ago? Sounded like a bomb going off.'

'I heard it.' The driver paused as though picking his words with care. 'Rumour is some fool of a tourist blew himself and his boat up on the lake . . .'

'It sounded closer . . .'

Martel left the query mark hanging in the air, wondering why the driver sounded so cautious. They were near Paradeplatz: soon all conversation would cease.

'Sounded closer to me,' the driver agreed. 'I was with a fare in Talstrasse and that was one hell of a bang. Now it could have come up the street from the lake . . .' He paused again. 'Anyway, that's what the police told us.'

'The police?'

'A patrol car stopped at the Hauptbahnhof rank. The driver got out to chat. He told us about this fool tourist blowing himself up on the lake.'

'Someone you knew? The policeman?' Martel asked casually.

'Funny you should say that.' Their eyes met in the rear-view mirror. 'I thought I knew every patrol car policeman in the city. I've been driving this cab for twenty years – but I never met him before ...'

'Probably a new recruit fresh out of training school.'

'He was fifty if he was a day. All right if I wait here?'

It suited Martel admirably. The cabbie had parked well inside Paradeplatz – which meant he wouldn't be able to see where Martel went after he turned down Bahnhofstrasse. He lit a fresh cigarette and walked quickly. He was going to catch – or lose – the train by a matter of seconds.

The street was deserted and the only sound was that of his own footfalls on the flagstones. He crossed over to the other side and then stopped in sheer bewilderment. The whirlpool was spinning again.

There was no sign of the bloody incident Martel had witnessed and participated in two hours earlier. And there was no mistaking the location. He could see the archway where he and the girl had come through into Bahnhofstrasse. And there *was* a large and important bank in just the right position – opposite where the tram had been stopped, a bank with double plate-glass doors. But *the glass was intact*.

There was not a sliver of shattered glass in the roadway that Martel could see. The Swiss were good at clearing up messes, at keeping their country neat and tidy – but this was completely insane.

Now he was checking the sidewalk for blood, the blood he had slipped in, the dried blood still staining the soles of his shoes. *The sidewalk was spotless*. He had almost given up when he saw it. The fresh scar marks where bark had been torn and burnt by explosive from a tree. Even the Swiss couldn't grow a new tree in two hours.

51

CHAPTER 7

Thursday May 28

It was just after midnight at the remote *schloss* in the Allgau district of Bavaria. Reinhard Dietrich stood by a window in his library, looking out at the lights reflected in the moat. In one hand he held a glass of Napoleon brandy, in the other a Havana cigar. A buzzer began ringing persistently.

Sitting down behind a huge desk he unlocked a drawer, took out the telephone concealed inside and lifted the receiver. His tone was curt when Erwin Vinz identified himself.

'Blau here,' Dietrich barked. 'Any news?'

'The Englishman has left Zürich. He caught a train departing at 2339 hours from the Hauptbahnhof.' The wording was precise, the voice hoarse. 'Our people just missed getting on board after he jumped inside a compartment ...'

'*Left Zürich!* What the hell do you mean? What happened at the Centralhof apartment?'

'The operation was not a complete success ...' Vinz was nervous. Dietrich's mouth tightened. Something had gone wildly wrong.

'Tell me exactly what happened,' he said coldly.

'The girl has taken a permanent holiday and she was unable to tell us anything about her job. We gained the impression she had no information to pass on. You don't have to worry about her ...'

'But I do have to worry about Martel! Goddamnit, where is he now? Which train?'

'Its final destination was St. Gallen ...'

Dietrich gripped the receiver more firmly, his expression choleric. In clipped, terse sentences he issued instructions, slammed down the receiver and replaced the instrument inside the drawer. He emptied his glass and pressed a bell.

A hunchback padded into the room. His pointed ears were

flat against the side of his head so they almost merged with his skull. He wore a green beize overall and smelt of cleaning fluid. His master handed him the glass.

'More brandy! Oscar, Vinz and his special cell bungled the job. It looks as though Martel has arrived in St. Gallen, for God's sake ...'

'We dealt with the previous English,' Oscar reminded him.

Reinhard Dietrich, a man of sixty, had a thatch of thick silver hair and a matching moustache. Six feet tall, he was well-built without an ounce of excess fat. He was dressed in the outfit he preferred when at his country *schloss* – a London-tailored leather jacket and cavalry twill jodphurs tucked inside hand-tooled riding boots. Dietrich looked every inch the man he was as he stood savouring the Havana – one of post-war Germany's richest and most powerful industrialists.

He had entered the electronics field in its infancy, shrewdly judging this to be the product with the greatest development potential. His headquarters was in Stuttgart and he had a second large factory complex at Phoenix, Arizona. He sipped at his refilled glass, watching Oscar's unblinking eyes.

'We shall certainly deal with this fresh meddler from London. Vinz is flooding St. Gallen with our people. Martel will be tracked down by nightfall. They have eliminated that Swiss bitch, Claire Hofer.' His voice rose, his florid face reddened. 'Nothing must interfere with Operation Crocodile! On June 3 the Summit Express will be crossing Germany. On June 4 the Bavarian state elections will be held – Delta will sweep into power!'

'And Martel ...'

'The order is – kill him!'

Martel left the night train at St. Gallen confident that no one had followed him. At Zürich he had caught the train seconds before it departed. Once aboard he had waited by the window to see if there were any other last-minute passengers. No one appeared and he made his way through an almost-empty train to a first-class compartment. With an overwhelming sense of relief he sank into a corner seat.

At St. Gallen he took his time getting off the train. As he carried his suitcase slowly towards the exit the platform was deserted. There is no more depressing place than a station in the early hours. As Claire Hofer had told him, the Hotel Metropol faced the station.

The night porter confirmed his reservation and Martel asked him the room rate. He counted out banknotes, talking as he did so to distract the man, adding a generous tip to keep him distracted.

'That's payment for two nights – this is for you. I'm so tired I can hardly stand up. I'll register in the morning. Are there any messages for me?' he asked quickly.

'Just this envelope ...'

It had worked – the delay in filling in the registration form which is obligatory for a guest to complete on arrival at any Swiss hostelry. The form is in triplicate. During the night the police tour the hotels to collect their copy. By not filling in the form immediately Martel had delayed knowledge of his presence in St. Gallen by twenty-four hours.

Inside his twin-bedded room he opened the sealed envelope. In a neat feminine script were written the words 'Room 12'. It was the room next to his own. He knocked very lightly on the door and she opened it immediately. She didn't say a word until she had closed and locked it. Over her right hand was draped a towel.

'The mutual friend?'

'David Nagel, for God's sake ...'

'I saw you from my window which looks across to the station – but you can't blame me for checking ...'

'I'm sorry. I *want* you to be careful. It's just that I last ate before noon on the plane. I'm tired ...'

'You look exhausted.' She removed the towel, exposing a 9-mm pistol she had been concealing and which she slipped under her pillow. 'You must be thirsty. It's a hot night. I'm afraid I only have Perrier water ...'

'I'll take it from the bottle.'

He sank on to the bed furthest from the window and forced himself to study her as he drank. She was the right height, correct weight, and her dark hair was cut with a heavy fringe over her forehead and shoulder length at the back. In the glow from a bedside light her eyes were a deep blue. 'You'll want proof of my identity ...' He hauled out his passport, gave it to her and finished off the Perrier.

She tried to show him her own identity card but he was so weary he waved it aside. What bloody difference did it make? Delta had put in a substitute – Gisela Zobel – in Zürich. He had rescued another girl – whose description also matched – trussed up in a cupboard at the Centralhof apartment. The whirlpool began spinning in his head again ...

But this girl *felt* right. It was his last thought before he lay back on the pillow and fell fast asleep.

He woke with a sensation of alarm. It was dark, the air heavy like a blanket pressing down. He wasn't sure where he was – so much had happened in so short a period of time. He was lying on his back on a bed. Then he remembered.

He was just relaxing when he experienced a second tremor. He kept his breathing regular. Someone had taken off his tie, undone the top buttons of his shirt, taken off his shoes. What alerted him was the lack of weight under his left armpit. The shoulder holster was still strapped to him but *his Colt had been removed.* He turned his head carefully, not making a sound, and reached out with his right hand. The fingers of another hand touched his own, grasped his hand. A girl's voice whispered before the bedside light came on.

'You're all right. You're in St. Gallen at the Hotel Metropol. I'm Claire Hofer. It's four o'clock in the morning so you've only had two hours' sleep ...'

'I can get by on that.'

Martel was wide awake now, his throat feeling like sandpaper. He sat up and propped the pillow behind him. Claire Hofer was still wearing her pale grey two-piece suit and like himself, sat propped against a pillow. In the light glow he noticed she had made herself up afresh. No blood-red nail varnish, thank God!

'Your Colt is in your bedside table,' she told him. 'Not very comfortable sleeping with that. The door is double-locked – and as you see I've tipped a chair under the handle ...'

'You seem to have thought of everything ...'

Martel, who never accepted anyone at face value, set about discovering every facet of Claire Hofer. She was remarkably like the second girl he had encountered in the Zürich apartment, the girl he had rescued – only to let her be kidnapped and ... Martel found it hard to push the atrocity to the back of his mind.

'What are you thinking about?' she asked.

'This ...'

He extracted from his jacket pocket the silver Delta badge he had ripped from the lapel of a dead would-be assassin in Bahnhofstrasse. Casually, he tossed it on her bed. She moved away from it as though it were alive, staring at him, her eyes wide with fear.

'Where did you get that?'

She was quick and clever. During the few seconds while she was talking her right hand, which was furthest away from him and in shadow, slipped under her pillow and reappeared holding the 9-mm pistol which she aimed point-blank at his stomach.

'The badge frightens you?' he asked.

'*You* frighten me now. I shan't hesitate to shoot ...'

'I believe you.'

He was careful to keep his hands folded in his lap, well away from the bedside table drawer. There was no softness in her voice now, in her expression, in the posture of her well-developed body. If he miscalculated the Swiss girl would pull the trigger.

'I took that badge off the body of a man I shot in Bahnhofstrasse last night. They were waiting for us when we came out of the apartment – Delta. None of your men with stocking masks or Balaclava hoods. Men in business suits! And each wearing a badge in his lapel. There was a lot of blood split – but an hour later the place was nice and tidy for tomorrow's tourists ...'

'You said blood was spilt. You said "us" ...'

'Why didn't *you* keep our appointment at Centralhof?' he snapped.

'Arnold was going to take me off the Delta investigation after Warner's murder – so I went underground. Lisbeth was supposed to bring you here, to make sure you weren't followed. Unlike you, she knows some of Arnold's trackers ...'

'And she knows Ferdy Arnold himself?'

'No, she has never met him. Why?'

'Let me describe Arnold,' he suggested. 'A thin, wiry man in his late thirties. Brown hair brushed back without a parting. Slate-grey eyes ...'

'That's not a bit like him ...'

'I thought so. Someone impersonating him turned up while we were at the apartment. I was even suspicious of Lisbeth because she had to look up his number in her notebook – she should have known that backwards if she had been you. The fake Arnold must have phoned her before I arrived and made some excuse as to why she should use that number if the need arose. Who is ...' He was very careful still with his use of tenses '... the girl who impersonated *you*?'

'Before she got married we both worked for David Nagel in police Intelligence. We once played a joke on him – we dressed in exactly the same clothes and went into his office separately, one after the other within the space of ten minutes. He didn't grasp there was any difference and was furious when we told him. It's no wonder you were fooled.'

She showed her renewed confidence in him by slipping her pistol back under the pillow. Smiling by way of apology, she leaned forward and asked the question he had been dreading.

'Where is Lisbeth? Did she wait in the station here to catch a train back to Zürich? As you'll have gathered, she does look terribly like me – although we aren't twins. You realise she is my sister?'

In London Tweed was still at his desk studying a file when he received the frightening news. Rubbing his eyes, he glanced wistfully at the camp-bed he had had set up 'for the duration' as he termed it. Miss McNeil, his faithful assistant, brought in the signal.

A handsome, erect, grey-haired woman – men in the street turned their heads when she passed them – no one knew her age or even her first name, except Tweed, who had forgotten. She was just McNeil – who was always on hand when needed at any hour of the day or night. She also possessed a shrewd brain, a caustic tongue and an encyclopaedic memory.

'This just came in from Bayreuth ...'

Bayreuth. Alarm bells began ringing. Tweed unlocked the steel-lined drawer containing his code-book. At the moment the signal read like a perfectly normal business enquiry about the despatch of certain goods.

Bayreuth was in *Bavaria.* Lindau, the last place Charles Warner had set foot in before being murdered, was in Bavaria. Delta, the neo-Nazi Party, had its power base in Bavaria. He busied himself with the decoding, using a piece of thick paper clipped to a metal sheet so there could be no imprint of what he was writing.

'Would you prefer me to leave you alone?' McNeil suggested.

'Of course not! Just let me concentrate, woman ...'

It was a compliment – that she should be asked to stay, because Tweed felt that when the decoding was completed he might welcome company. She sat down, crossed her shapely legs and watched. It was fortunate that – like Martel – she could manage on two or three hours' sleep. As he finished his task Tweed's expression became blank – which told McNeil a great deal.

'Bad news?'

'The worst, the very worst.'

'You will cope. You always do ...'

'I'm not the one who has to cope. Manfred has just crossed the border into Bavaria from East Germany. Oh, Christ ...'

Manfred!

Tweed was appalled as he re-read the signal. It had travelled to him along a most devious route he could see in his mind's eye. First, his agent planted inside the Ministry for State Security in Leipzig, East Germany, had radioed the message from his mobile transmitter. The message had then been picked up by Tweed's station in Bayreuth.

From Bayreuth a courier had driven at breakneck speed to the British Embassy in Bonn. There the signal would have been handed personally to the security officer. He, in his turn, had radioed it to Park Crescent. The decoded signal was deadly and un-nerving in its implications.

Manfred today Wednesday May 27 crossed East German border near Hof into West Germany. Ultimate destination unknown.

He handed the signal to McNeil without a word, stood up and went to examine the wall-map of Central Europe he had pinned up when Martel had left for the airport. Tweed was quite familiar with the map. In his head he carried a clear picture of the geography of the whole of western Europe. But he wanted to verify which route Manfred might have taken.

From the Hof area an autobahn ran due south via Nuremberg to the Bavarian capital of München. That was the most likely route. And Warner had spent a lot of time in München, paying special attention to the Hauptbahnhof for some unknown reason. He went back to his swivel chair, adjusted his glasses and sagged into his cushion.

'We don't know much about Manfred, do we?' McNeil ventured.

'We know nothing – and we know too much,' Tweed growled. He tapped a file. 'I must be getting psychic in my old age – I was looking at his dossier when you brought that signal.'

'He's a top East German agent, isn't he? Some query about his nationality and origins. A top-flight assassin – and a first-rate planner. An unusual combination ...'

59

'But Carlos is an unusual man,' Tweed said and pushed his spectacles back over his forehead.

'You really think he is Carlos? Nothing has been heard of him for ages ...'

'The Americans assume so. But there is something very peculiar going on which I don't understand. Delta is the neo-Nazis. Manfred is a free-lance Communist expert on major subversive operations. So who is behind Operation Crocodile – whatever that might be? And *Crocodile* – that reminds me of something I have seen ...'

'You look really worried. Shall I make coffee?'

Tweed stared at the silent phone on his desk. He spoke half to himself. 'Come in, Martel, for God's sake! I must warn you – before it's too late. You're up against both Nazis and Communists. It's double jeopardy ...'

In a darkened apartment in a large building near München police headquarters in Ettstrasse a gloved hand lifted a telephone. The man wearing nylon gloves was the sole occupant. The only illumination came from a shaded desk light. He dialled a number. It was 4 a.m.

'Who the bloody hell is this? Don't you know the time ...'

Reinhard Dietrich had been woken at the *schloss* from a deep sleep and his voice reflected his fury. If it was Erwin Vinz again he would blast him to ...

'Manfred speaking.' The tone of voice was creepily soft and controlled. 'We hear you have a problem and that we find most disturbing.'

Dietrich woke up very quickly, thrown off balance by the identity of the caller, by his words which suggested he knew something about the Zürich débacle. He sat up in bed and his tone of voice became polite and cooperative.

'Nothing we can't handle, I assure you ...'

'But in Zürich, it was *mis*handled, so what may we expect next in St. Gallen?'

Dietrich, a man accustomed all his life to issuing commands, dreaded the sound of Manfred's sleepy voice. When Manfred had first approached him at his Stuttgart office with his offer to supply arms and uniforms at cut-rate prices he had jumped at the chance. Now he half-regretted the decision – when it was too late.

'You don't have to worry about St. Gallen.' He spoke in a bluff confident tone. 'I have already made arrangements to deal with the situation ...'

'We are very pleased to hear it. More arms and uniforms are available for immediate collection at the same warehouse. Where and when will you store this consignment?'

Dietrich told him. There was a click and the industrialist realised Manfred had gone off the line. Arrogant bastard! And he detested his caller's habit of using the plural 'we' – as though Dietrich was taking orders from some all-powerful committee. At least more arms were on the way – God knows they had lost enough. How Erich Stoller of the BND tracked down the locations he had no idea.

In München Manfred switched off the desk light. Wherever he was staying in the West he always wore gloves – there would be no fingerprints to trace when he left the apartment. There was a thin smile on his face. Operation Crocodile was proceeding according to plan.

In the bedroom at the Hotel Metropol Claire Hofer was enduring a state of delayed shock after Martel told her of Lisbeth's murder. He omitted reference to the fact that she had been tortured. When she reacted she caught him off guard.

'And you let them take her? *Bastard!*' She hit him across the side of the face with the flat of her hand. When she raised her hand a second time he grabbed her wrist and pushed her down on the bed, his face inches from hers as she glared up at him. Their position reminded him of when he had pinned his would-be assassin, Gisela Zobel, down on the sofa in the Centralhof apartment and she had attempted to distract him with sexual games.

But this girl was different. Tough as whipcord, but vulnerable, a vulnerability she covered up with an outwardly controlled manner. The deep blue eyes seemed larger than ever in the light from the bedside lamp. He kissed her gently on the forehead and felt her whipcord muscles relax.

'There were at least a dozen armed Delta soldiers in the assault,' he told her softly, still gripping her wrist. 'They piled out of two cars. I shot three men. I saw them hauling Lisbeth inside a large Mercedes which drove straight off. I blew it ...'

'A dozen armed men!' Her eyes gazed into his. 'But how could you have saved Lisbeth against such odds? And why did they do this thing – take her away?' Her body had gone limp. He relaxed his grip on her wrist.

'They thought they were taking you ...'

'Me? Why me?'

'Something big is coming up.' He perched on the edge of her bed and lit a cigarette. 'So Delta is eliminating every agent who might get in their way. First Warner, then the attempt on yourself. I'm their next target. Incidentally, why didn't Warner use the train to get from Lindau to Switzerland – why that business of the boat?'

'He was an ex-Navy man and mistrusted confined spaces – a train could be a trap he'd say. There was nowhere to run. Can't we hit back at these people?'

'We're going to. That's why I'm in St. Gallen. There's a rare embroidery museum here, isn't there? The receptionist at the Baur au Lac said so ...'

'There is.' She was sitting up now, using a hand-mirror and a brush to tidy her dishevelled hair. 'And that's the place Charles used as a rendezvous to meet his contact inside Delta. How do you know about it?'

'We'll come back to that. Do you know how far Warner had gone with his attempt to infiltrate Delta?'

'He had this contact I've just mentioned. I've no idea what he looks like. Charles went to great lengths to protect his identity, but his code-name is Stahl. Incidentally, you've seen the latest news about Delta?'

She reached for a newspaper and handed it to him. It was dated the previous day. The headline jumped out at him and beneath it was the main article.

New Cache of neo-Nazi Arms and Uniforms Found in Allgau.

The text was padded out but the message was simple. Acting on information received the Bavarian police had raided an isolated farmhouse just before dawn and found the arms dump. The farmhouse had shown traces of recent occupation but was deserted at the time of the raid ...

'That's the seventh Delta arms dump they've found in the past four weeks,' Claire remarked. 'They don't seem to be all that efficient ...'

'Odd, isn't it?'

'What are you thinking about?' she asked. 'You've got that look again ...'

He was staring at the wall, recalling his conversation with Tweed. Fragments of that conversation kept beavering away at the back of his mind.

The badge was found under Warner's body. The killer must have dropped it without realising ... And they completed the job by carving their trademark on his naked back – the Delta symbol ...

'I think there's something we're missing – it's just too damned obvious.' He checked his watch. 0430 hours. 'But we can trap the bastards. In the Embroidery Museum here in St. Gallen. In less than eight hours from now.'

CHAPTER 8

Thursday May 28

'This is what we're talking about – I hope ...'

They were sitting at a secluded breakfast table in the hotel dining-room. Martel produced from his wallet an orange-coloured ticket and handed it to Claire. The ticket bore a number, several words printed in German and no indication of a town. *Industrie und Gewerbemuseum ... Eintritt: Fr. 2.50.*

'Warner had that in his own wallet when he was killed,' Martel continued. 'I have my fingers crossed ...'

'You can uncross them,' she said cheerfully. 'It *is* an entrance ticket to the St. Gallen Embroidery Museum. The building is in Vadianstrasse – near the Old Town. Not ten minutes' walk away ...'

'Look at the back.'

Claire turned over the ticket and saw words written in a script she recognised. Charles Warner's. She was probably looking at the last words he wrote before he had embarked on his fatal boat trip from Lindau.

St. 11.50. May 28.

She looked at Martel and he detected a hint of excitement in her expression as he drank his eighth cup of coffee. He had already consumed seven croissants, three slices of ham and a large piece of cheese. He was beginning to feel better.

'May 28 – that's today,' she said and checked her watch. 'Nine o'clock. *St.* must stand for Stahl. In less than three hours we shall be talking to him ...'

'*I* shall be talking to him,' Martel corrected her.

'I thought I was part of the team ...'

'You told me Warner never let you attend these meetings. And if whoever turns up sees you he may take fright ...'

'He won't recognise *you*,' she persisted stubbornly.

Martel quietly blew up. 'Now listen to me, Claire Hofer. You're not going to like this but there's no nice way to get the message across. I work alone – because then the only person I have to worry about is me. And me is all I've got – so I worry about me quite a lot.'

'I don't have to come inside the museum ...'

'I haven't finished yet, so kindly shut up! Ever since I landed in Zürich nothing has been what it seemed. At the Centralhof apartment Delta had put in a girl to take me out. I find another girl in a cupboard – sorry about this, but it's necessary – and I'm led to think she's Claire Hofer ...'

'I told you why we arranged it like that, damn it!'

Her face flushed with rage and her eyes blazed. He admired

her spirit – he might even be able to use it – but he had to get his point across.

'Next thing,' he went on patiently, 'is a holocaust in Bahnhofstrasse – and within one hour all signs of it disappear ...'

'Ferdy Arnold's wash-and-brush-up squad,' she said shortly.

'Come again?'

'You said yourself earlier you thought they had cleaned up the carnage to keep it quiet – to avoid worrying tourists. Arnold has this special team of engineers, glaziers, builders – you name it – standing by in case of a riot or terrorist outrage. They seal off the area temporarily and their motto is "as good as new within thirty minutes". They even have experts who fob off the press with some phoney story if necessary ...'

'That's what I mean,' Martel said as he buttered another croissant. 'Nothing is what it seems. Delta – for some reason I have yet to fathom – advertises its outrages. Arnold pretends nothing has happened. He even spreads some lying story which fools Nagel of Intelligence. You really expect my meeting with this Stahl will turn out to be straightforward? Damned if I do.'

'And yet you're walking headlong into it?'

'I'll arrive at exactly 11.45. After breakfast you show me the place ...'

'The rendezvous is 11.50,' she reminded him.

'So I arrive five minutes early and wait to see who does come into that room. Warner could have been followed.'

'He was always extremely careful,' she observed.

'He is now extremely dead ...'

In Münich the wide avenue of Maximilianstrasse leads straight as a ruler from Max-Joseph-Platz to the Bavarian state Parliament on an eminence overlooking the river Isar. To reach the east bank it passes over two bridges as it crosses a large island. The body was found trapped on the brink of one of the giant sluices below the first bridge.

It was discovered about two hours before Martel sat down to fortify himself at the Metropol in St. Gallen with a considerable breakfast. A lawyer on his way to work glanced over the parapet as he crossed the bridge. In the river a series of giant steps like four great weirs carried the swift flow of the water. At each step there is a series of square cement pillars at intervals. The corpse was folded round one of these pillars, snagged by chance.

The *Kriminalpolizei* arrived with a doctor to supervise retrieval of their evidence when a frogman had reported the man had been shot in the head. A preliminary examination was carried out inside an ambulance by the riverside. Chief-Inspector Kruger looked at the doctor after a few minutes.

'Surely you can tell me something? I have a pile of work on my desk a mile high and my wife is beginning to ask questions about my secretary when I arrive home.'

'Get a less attractive secretary,' the doctor suggested. 'Shot three times in the head. Powder burns visible. Likely time of death – but don't hold me to it – within past twelve hours. And no signs of rope abrasions on the wrists so they didn't tie him up to murder him ...'

'I can at least check through his clothes for identification? That really is most kind of you, Doctor.'

Kruger searched quickly with expert fingers while his deputy, Weil, carefully said nothing. He could tell from his chief's expression that he was not pleased. He completed the search without producing one single item from the water-logged body's pockets.

'No means of identification,' Kruger announced. 'That's just what I need. I can see what kind of a day this is going to be ...'

'His watch,' replied Weil.

He lifted the corpse's left arm which seemed to weigh a ton and unstrapped the watch which had stopped at 0200 hours. He showed Kruger the back plate of the watch which was made of steel and had a single word engraved on it.

'One hell of a lot of help,' commented Kruger.

The word engraved in the plate was *Stahl*.

On their way to the Embroidery Museum Martel and Claire walked arm in arm. It was Martel who had made the suggestion. 'A couple is far less conspicuous,' he commented.

'If you say so ...'

He bridled. 'Use your head. Two groups may be hunting for us. Delta for me – so they will search for a single man. Arnold's mob for you – so they'll look for a single girl ...'

'Logical, I suppose,' she said indifferently.

'And never let emotion cloud your judgement. I make it 11.30, fifteen minutes before I have to be inside that museum. That wallplate says Vadianstrasse ...'

'The Embroidery Museum is at the far end on the left-hand side – and I've decided, I'm coming with you ...'

'Not inside the place. I'll find somewhere nearby to park you.'

'I'm not a bloody car!' she flared up. She played her part well, hugging his arm and staring up at him with lover's eyes as she hissed the words. 'You're expecting trouble – you brought a silencer for your Colt.'

'I told you – nothing so far has been what it seemed and I have an idea the trend will continue.'

During their walk Martel had observed that St. Gallen was located inside a deep notch or gulch. Hemmed in on two sides by vertical hill-slopes, the shopping area had been built on the floor of the gorge. Stepped up on the hillsides, one above another, were large solid-looking villas erected in the previous century.

The weather was again clammy with a heavy overcast and there was a hint of a storm in the air. Martel walked more slowly as they came closer to the entrance, his eyes scanning the area for signs of danger. He stopped again to look in a shop window but no one followed his example. On the surface the area was clean – only women shoppers, smartly dressed, strolling along the street.

'The police station isn't near, is it?' he murmured.

'As a matter of fact it is. *Stadtpolizei* is at Neugasse 5 – the first turning off to the left from that street over there ...'

'Great! How far away on foot – walking fast? The Swiss police can walk fast.'

'Less than five minutes – two if they use a car. Why?'

'I like to know where all the pieces on the board are – in case of emergency.'

They had left the shop and walked the full length of the building containing the museum. Claire pointed to where the Old Town started while Martel searched for a convenient café to leave her. They should have allowed more time.

'Looking for somewhere to park the car?' she enquired. 'Well I've found the ideal place – and I can watch the entrance to the museum without anyone seeing me ...'

She was pointing across the wide street to an orange booth with a black curtain pulled back revealing a metal stool. In large letters over the booth were the words PRONTOPHOT PASS-FOTOS.

'I'd better grab the seat before someone else decides they want a passport picture,' she said. 'Good luck. Don't forget to collect me on your way out. I don't want to sit there all day taking my picture – the results are lousy ...'

Martel took one final look-round. He couldn't rid himself of the feeling something was wrong about the atmosphere. Shrugging his shoulders, he crossed Vadianstrasse, opened the door and went inside.

It was exactly as Claire had described: a wide flight of steps leading up into a large entrance hall. At a ticket window he paid a woman two francs fifty for a ticket like the one he had in his pocket, the one Warner had purchased. While buying it he held a handkerchief over his face and blew his nose incessantly. The woman behind the window would never be able to identify him later.

A notice indicated that the museum was on the first floor. He climbed two longer flights of steps. There was no one else about, the atmosphere was hushed. He could see why Warner had chosen this place and this time for meeting his Delta contact. On the wall outside the front entrance a plate had given the opening hours. *10.00 – 12.00* and *14.00 – 17.00*. When the place closed at midday who else would arrive at 11.50?

To his left along the wide landing were a pair of double doors leading to the library. Very quietly, his soft-soled shoes making no noise, he walked to the library and tried the door. It was locked. He crossed back over the landing quickly and tried the Embroidery Museum door. It gave way under his pressure. He stepped inside, closed it and scanned the silent room.

The exhibits were in glass cases standing in various positions in a large room with windows overlooking Vadianstrasse. Before he was convinced the place was empty he checked several alcoves. Then he extracted the Colt from his shoulder holster and screwed on the silencer. His watch registered precisely 11.50 when he saw the handle of the door turning slowly.

He watched, fascinated, the Colt held behind his back, as the turning handle completed its revolution and then remained in that position without the door opening. It was a good ten seconds before the door began moving slowly inwards. Martel stepped back out of sight.

Because his hearing was acute he heard the slight click – the release of the door-handle after closing. He controlled his breathing. The silence in the museum room was so complete the patter of a mouse across the wood-block floor would have been heard.

Soon the new arrival, Stahl, would come into view. Was he checking to make sure he was alone? Or did he – as Martel would have done in his place – sense a presence in that silent archive of the ages, the repository of craftwork by people who had died centuries earlier . . .?

It was a man in a light overcoat and smart trilby. Very like a businessman. Like the men who had flooded out of the Rolls and the Mercedes in Bahnhofstrasse. Under the hat a bleak white bony face. In his lapel a silver triangular badge, the symbol of Delta.

In his right hand he held an object like a felt-tip pen – the needle-blade was already projecting ready for action. The click Martel had assumed to be the door-handle had been the pressing of the button which projected the blade.

When he appeared the bony-faced man was only a few feet from Martel. Stiffening his hand, he lunged forward, the needle-point aimed at Martel's stomach. The Englishman remained exactly where he was, jerked up the Colt and fired twice in rapid succession. The *phut-phut* of the silenced gun sounded unnaturally loud in the hushed atmosphere.

The bony-faced man dropped his hypodermic weapon and reeled backwards. He slammed into one of the display cases, flopped sideways and his head crashed down through the glass lid. As his legs gave way he slithered to the floor, his heels making runnels across the polished surface. A stream of blood gushed from his torn face.

Martel left the museum without being seen. As he slipped past the ticket window he glimpsed a woman's back. She was drinking from a cup. The Colt was rammed inside his belt. They closed in less than five minutes. He had to get out on the street. But they were waiting for him out there. *Delta.*

They had sent in a single man to do the job but they would have people outside as back-up. It was that kind of thorough organisation. Martel had not forgotten the nightmare in Bahnhofstrasse. The audacity, the ferocity. He opened the door and stepped out into Vadianstrasse.

Everything seemed normal. Housewives out shopping, singly or in couples. A man wearing yellow oil-skins and a cap, carrying some kind of bag, leaned against a wall on the opposite side. He was trying to light a cigarette: the lighter seemed to be defective.

Claire! He had to protect Claire, to lead them away from her. Already one Hofer – Lisbeth – had been killed. And they were out here somewhere. He could see Claire's legs below the closed curtain inside the photo booth. He began walking.

He timed it carefully. Taking out his holder to make himself conspicuous he inserted a cigarette. He stopped alongside the booth and cupped his hand to use the lighter, to conceal the fact that he was talking. The curtain was open a fraction of an inch. He didn't look towards the booth as he spoke.

'They sent a Delta operative. He's dead inside the museum. I am giving you an order. Stay there, give me two minutes to lead anyone out here away, then get to hell back to the Metropol and wait till I contact you . . .'

Then he was moving away, heading into the Old Town where the road surfaces were cobbled, the buildings ancient, the shops new. He turned into Neugasse and followed the curve of the street.

Neugasse 5, Claire had said. Police headquarters. Five minutes' walk, two or less by car. He had to pinpoint the opposition and this should give him more time. The bastards could hardly start something in close proximity to a police station. He stopped to look in a window.

He had no idea what the shop sold. He was concentrating on a reflection. The man in yellow oil-skins had stopped on the other side of the narrow street. He was staring into another window, holding a large carrier bag and puffing at his cigarette. His lighter had conveniently worked as soon as Martel began moving.

The Englishman sucked at his holder. Something was wrong. Something more than the fact that it appeared he was being shadowed by Yellow Oil-skins. He resumed his walk. *Stadtpolizei.* Walls a muddy grey roughcast, grey shutters almost merging into the walls. An archway entrance wide enough for a single car. He walked on.

He was approaching an intersection, a more spacious area which, he remembered from the street map Claire had shown him, was the Markt-Gasse. He turned left and stopped to drop his half-smoked cigarette which he stubbed under his heel. The possibility of a coincidence ended. Yellow Oil-skins was looking in yet another shop window. Something was very wrong indeed.

It was too damned obvious: using as a shadow a man clad in an outfit which could be picked out hundreds of yards away. It was as though he were making his presence as conspicuous as possible – to divert Martel's attention from someone else. *The danger was going to come from another quarter.*

He stood on the kerb gazing at a curious spectacle. In the middle of the street stood a small train for children made up of wooden, open-sided coaches with canvas canopies. At the front was a black railway engine with a gold trim and the driver, a man, was operating a whistle to signal imminent departure. Each of the coaches carried four children, two facing each other. A couple of coaches were occupied by mothers sitting with their offspring. The trolley-car train was large enough to carry adults.

Yellow Oil-skins remained staring into a window displaying ladies' underwear, for God's sake! Martel moved quickly, leaving the train still stationary. If there was to be havoc — Zürich-style — it must not happen near those children. Ahead he saw a buff-coloured building which was the Hotel Hecht — where Claire had originally been staying. Crossing the road, he concentrated his attention on everyone except Yellow Oil-skins.

The attack came from the least-expected quarter at a moment when his alertness was briefly distracted by an astonishing sight. He was walking past the Hecht when he heard a piercing shriek, the train's whistle. It had followed him as it proceeded confidently amid the traffic to pass alongside the Hecht. In the last coach on the side nearest to him sat Claire Hofer.

The seat next to her was occupied by a small girl and two more children faced them. They were all looking away from the Hecht while Claire stared straight at him. Under cover of her handbag, the flap open, she was holding her pistol, the barrel aimed towards him.

He sensed rather than felt someone close to his left. Glancing away from the train he saw a tall woman wearing a dark hat with a veil concealing her face. Her shoulder-bag was supported by her left arm. In her right hand she held a familiar object — the needle-pointed hypodermic weapon.

This was the back-up Yellow Oil-skins had tried so very hard to conceal from him. Martel had a vague memory of seeing this veiled, elegantly-dressed woman in Neugasse and for a second he was taken off guard. He almost put out a hand to ward her off, which would have been his last movement since she would have jabbed the weapon into his hand and injected its contents.

Somewhere close by a car backfired, a sound cut off by the blare of a car's horn. The elegant woman wore a dress with a deep V-cut which exposed a generous portion of her bosom. Another distraction? Then she leaned back against the wall of the hotel. A small hole had appeared in the V of her bosom, as though drilled by a surgeon. The hole began to well redness as she sagged to the ground.

In falling her hat had tipped sideways, removing the veil from her face. Martel forced himself to walk on, threading his way among the morning shoppers. The face now exposed to view was not unfamiliar. It was the dead face of Gisela Zobel.

He saw the train moving on towards an ancient gateway in a wall which had probably once protected the town. Claire was still on board, clasping her closed handbag as she chatted to the girl next to her. The Swiss girl had shot his would-be killer from a moving vehicle. Marksmanship of that order he had never encountered before. And Yellow Oil-skins had now vanished as a crowd began to gather in front of the Hecht, huddled over something lying on the ground.

CHAPTER 9

Thursday May 28

In her bedroom at the Metropol Claire was shaking with fright. She held herself in check until Martel arrived back a few minutes after she had returned. Now reaction set in and she broke down. He sat on the bed beside her and she pressed her face into his chest and quietly sobbed. He stroked her soft black hair, saying nothing until he felt the tremors easing.

'You disobeyed orders,' he said harshly. 'While you were in the photo booth I told you get to hell back here. The next thing I see is you riding on that kids' train . . .'

'A bloody good job for you I did!' she flared up, then her expression changed to one of consternation. 'Oh, my God – are you saying that woman wasn't trying to kill you – I distinctly saw a knife in her hand . . .'

'It wasn't a knife – it was one of those hypodermic weapons Delta favour. You saved my life,' he went on in his normal blank monotone to help quieten her. 'How the devil did you follow me? I never saw you . . .'

'I wouldn't be much good if you had done,' she snapped back and blew her nose. 'Sorry if I fouled it up.'

'If shooting an assassin accurately from a moving vehicle comes under the heading fouling it up then please make a habit of it.'

'Did I kill her?'

'You killed the bitch,' he said shortly. 'It was Gisela Zobel, the girl who impersonated Lisbeth at Centralhof. There seems to be no end to the ruthless ingenuity of Delta. First they send in a man to keep the appointment inside the museum – a man wearing the Delta symbol in his lapel . . .'

'You left him there – with the badge?'

'Yes. Odd, isn't it, the way they flaunt that badge. Almost as though someone wants to advertise their role as murderers. I am beginning to get an idea about that. Then they have a back-up team. A very obvious man in yellow oil-skins follows me while a very unobvious woman in hat and veil waits her chance to finish me off . . .'

'I spotted both of them through the gap in the booth curtain. That's why I came after you . . .'

'And thank God you did,' Martel replied as he stood up. 'You haven't unpacked your case?'

'You told me not to – so only my toilet things are in the bathroom . . .'

'Pack them. We're catching the first train out of St. Gallen.'

'Why? I'm exhausted . . .' she protested.

'You can rest on the train. We're heading east for Bavaria ...'

'What's the Goddamn rush?'

'The Goddamn rush is the police. They'll soon realise they have two murders on their hands. *Two!* The man I killed in the museum, the woman you shot outside the Hecht. Then they'll be watching every train leaving St. Gallen ...'

Martel concealed one fact from Claire as they sat in a first-class compartment which they had to themselves aboard the München express. He was convinced they were moving into the zone of maximum danger – Bavaria. Somewhere in that scenically glorious part of Germany Delta had its headquarters.

Switzerland, the most neutral, stable country in Europe had almost been a death-trap. But the risks encountered in Zürich and St. Gallen were nothing compared with what lay ahead of them.

While waiting for the train in St. Gallen station Martel had called Tweed in London. This was one of the many advantages of Switzerland: its superb telephone system enabled you to dial abroad from a payphone where no one could intercept the call.

Martel had used his usual technique when speaking to Tweed – knowing his call would be tape-recorded. He had spoken in a kind of shorthand – shooting random facts at Tweed, every scrap of information he had picked up. Later Tweed, remote from the battlefield, would try to fit the fragments of data into some kind of pattern.

'Thursday calling,' he said as Tweed came on the line and waited for the answering code identification.

'Two-Eight here ...'

It was Thursday May 28. Martel used the *day* of the week while Tweed responded with the *date* of the month. Martel began to pour out data.

'*Delta very active inside Switzerland ... agents wear businessmen suits ... Delta symbol openly displayed in lapels ... strange lack of cooperation from locals ... dummy Claire waiting Centralhof tried to kill me ... arrested by fake Arnold ... imprisoned Hofer waiting Lisbeth*

*Hofer ... Claire's twin-like sister ... Lisbeth kidnapped during blood-
bath in Bahnhofstrasse ... repeat in Bahnhofstrasse ... Ferdy Arnold
later reported her body found in Limmat ... Nagel denied all knowledge
events in Bahnhofstrasse ... now with genuine Claire Hofer St. Gallen
... leaving immediately with her to investigate scene Warner murder ...
Claire reports Warner made three mentions Operation Crocodile ...
something phoney about Delta neo-Nazis ... must go ...'*

'Wait!' Tweed's tone was urgent. 'Bayreuth reports Manfred
has crossed the border near Hof into West Germany. Manfred
– got it?'

'Christ!'

Martel had slammed down the receiver, grabbed his suitcase
and run across the platform to the compartment door Claire
had left open. Boarding the express, he hauled the door closed
behind him as the train began moving east, dumped his case on
a seat and sat down.

Even in the early afternoon the third-floor apartment in the
sombre München apartment block was so dim the occupant had
turned on the shaded desk-lamp. He had entered the apartment to find the phone ringing. His gloved hand lifted the
receiver.

'Vinz – calling from Lindau ...'

'We are here,' Manfred replied in his soft, calm voice. 'You
are calling to confirm that a successful deal was concluded in St.
Gallen?'

'Regrettably it was not possible to conclude the deal ...' Erwin
Vinz forced himself to go on. 'Kohler has reported from
there ...'

'And why was the deal not concluded?'

'The opposition's negotiator proved uncooperative ...' Vinz
was sweating, his armpits felt damp. 'And the services of two of
our people were terminated ...'

'T-e-r-m-i-n-a-t-e-d?'

Manfred repeated the word with great deliberation as
though he were sure he had misheard. There was a pause and
the light from the desk-lamp was reflected in the lenses of the

large dark-tinted glasses Manfred wore. In Lindau Vinz made the effort to continue.

'The Englishman is now aboard an express bound for München. It is due here in about half an hour ...'

'So,' Manfred interjected smoothly, 'you have made all preparations to board the express at Lindau to continue negotiations with this gentleman.' Now it was Manfred's turn to pause. 'You do, of course, realise it is imperative you conclude the deal with him before the train reaches München?'

'Everything has been arranged by me personally. I just thought I should check with you ...'

'Always check with me, Vinz. Always. Then, as a matter of courtesy, you keep Mr Reinhard Dietrich informed ...'

'I will report progress ...'

'Passengers have been known to fall out of trains,' Manfred purred. 'You will report *success* ...'

Cooped up inside his payphone on the Bavarian mainland Erwin Vinz realised the connection had been broken. Swearing, he pushed open the door and hurried away through a drift of grey mist.

The medieval town of Lindau – once an Imperial city – was blotted out in the fog coming in off the lake. The Old Town is a network of cobbled streets and alleyways which at night only the most intrepid venture down. Not that there is normally any danger – Lindau is a most law-abiding place.

Shortly after Manfred received his phone call three cars proceeded over the road bridge and headed for the Hauptbahnhof. The station is another curious feature of Lindau. Main-line expresses on their way from Zürich to München make a diversion at this point. The line takes them across the embankment to the west on to the island. They stop at the Hauptbahnhof next to the harbour.

If you alight from an express at Lindau you pass through *Zoll* – the customs and passport control post – because you have crossed the border from Austria into Germany. But boarding a train at Lindau for München you do not pass through *Zoll* – since you are already in Germany.

This factor was important to the eight men led by Vinz alighting from the three cars at the Hauptbahnhof. The drivers took the cars away immediately. Dressed like businessmen, two of the eight passengers carried suitcases containing uniforms. These would be donned aboard the Münich express as soon as it began moving out of Lindau.

The uniforms were those of a German State Railways ticket inspector and a German Passport Control official. It was the latter – travelling rapidly through the train and explaining there was a double-check on passports – who expected to locate Keith Martel. The plan was simple. Erwin Vinz, thirty-eight years old, small, thin and with hooded eyelids, was in charge of the execution squad.

Vinz would wear the Passport Control uniform. Vinz would locate the target. If Martel were travelling alone in a compartment it would be invaded when the express was travelling at speed by four men. The outer door would be opened and the Englishman would be hurled from the train. The whole operation, Vinz calculated, would take less than twenty seconds.

If Martel had fellow-passengers in his compartment Vinz would ask him to accompany him because there was a query on his passport. He would be guided to an empty compartment and the same procedure would be followed. Vinz knew that this particular express was always half-empty on this day of the week.

The platform marked for the arrival of the express was deserted as the eight men arrived separately from the concourse. The fog created a hushed atmosphere and the men moved in it like ghosts. Vinz checked his watch. They were in good time. The express was due in twenty minutes.

CHAPTER 10

Thursday May 28

'You'll like Lindau, Keith,' Claire said as Martel peered out of the window from the fast-moving express. 'It is one of the most beautiful old towns in Germany . . .'

'I know it.' He had his mind on something else. 'I shall want to contact Erich Stoller of the BND as soon as we can – to let him have a look at this . . .'

Unlocking his case, he produced something rolled up in a handkerchief. A blue, shiny cylinder like a large felt-tip pen. There were two press-buttons: one on the casing, the second at the base.

'I rescued this little Delta toy from the floor of the Embroidery Museum where the killer dropped it. This button half-way along the casing ejects and retracts the needle. I imagine the one at the base injects the poison. Ingenious – you can use the full force of the palm of your hand to operate the injection mechanism. Stoller's forensic people will tell us what fluid it contains . . .'

'That woman I shot outside the Hecht . . .'

'Was going to use the duplicate of this. Intriguing that Reinhard Dietrich runs an electronics complex – which involves fine instrumentation . . .'

'You mean *he* manufactures that horrible thing?'

'Damned sure of it.' He replaced the weapon inside his case and looked again out of the window. Up to now the view had been one of green cultivated fields and rolling hills – one of the most attractive and least-known parts of Switzerland. Well clear of the tourist belt.

The landscape was changing. They were crossing flatlands dimly visible in swirling mist which hid nearby Lake Konstanz. They saw few signs of human habitation and there was something desolate in the atmosphere. Martel concentrated on the view as though he might miss something important.

'This is the Rhine delta, isn't it?' he queried.

'Yes. We cross the river soon just before it runs into the lake.'

Delta. Was there significance in this geographical curiosity at the extreme eastern end of the lake? The southern shore was Swiss except for a weird enclave of land occupied by the German town of Konstanz away to the west. The northern shore was German. But at this eastern tip a few miles of lake frontage was *Austrian*.

Martel adjusted the horn-rimmed spectacles with plain glass he wore to change his appearance. He lit a fresh cigarette, being careful not to use his holder. He seemed to have relapsed into a dream.

'We shall soon be in Lindau,' Claire said exuberantly, trying to drag him out of his dark mood. 'Surely we must find something – it was ...' Her voice wavered and then she had herself under control. 'It was the last place Warner was seen alive.'

'Except that we are getting off at the stop before – Bregenz in Austria.'

'Why?'

'Bregenz could be important. And it will be the last place Delta will expect us to leave the train ...'

Hauptbahnhof, Münich ... Hauptbahnhof, Zürich ... Delta ... Centralhof ... Bregenz ... Washington, DC, Clint Loomis ... Pullach, BND ... Operation Crocodile.

These were the references the dead Charles Warner had written in the tiny black notebook hidden in a secret pocket, the notebook Erich Stoller of the BND had discovered on the body and flown to Tweed in London.

Bregenz.

As the express slowed down Claire caught a glimpse of Lake Konstanz through the corridor windows – a sheet of calm grey water. The express stopped and when Martel opened the door at the end of the coach he found no platform – they stepped down on to the track. He dumped his suitcase, took Claire's and held her elbow while she ᴜ₌scended the steep drop. She shivered as she picked up her case and they made their way across rail tracks to the station, an old single-storey building.

'You shivered ...'

'It's the mist,' she said shortly.

A cold clammy dampness moistened her face and she felt it penetrating her light raincoat. She had lied. It *was* the mist partly – but mainly it was the atmosphere created by the drifts of greyish vapour. You saw things, then they were gone.

Behind Bregenz looms the massive heights of the Pfänder, a ridge whose sides are densely forested. As they crossed to the station Claire saw a gap appear in the mist pall exposing the dripping wall of limestone, then it too was gone. There was no ticket barrier to pass through – tickets had been checked aboard the express. They deposited their cases in the self-locking metal compartments for luggage and walked into Bregenz.

The place seemed deserted, as though it were a Sunday. A line of old block-like buildings faced the station. Martel paused, puffing his cigarette as he glanced round searching for anything out of place. Claire gazed at him.

'Those glasses make you look studious – they change your whole personality. And you're walking more ponderously. You're just like a chameleon. Incidentally, what are we going to do here?'

He extracted two photos of Charles Warner obtained from Tweed before leaving Park Crescent and handed her one of the prints. She looked at the picture of the man she had worked with for over six months, the man who had been brutally murdered on the lake behind them – only a short distance from where they stood.

'The story is we're looking for a friend – Warner,' Martel told her. 'His wife is seriously ill and we think he's somewhere here. We'll buy a street map, divide up the place into sections – then meet up at an agreed place in two hours' time ...'

'It sounds a hopeless task,' she commented when they were studying a street plan bought at a kiosk.

'Warner was here – he made a reference to the place in his

81

notebook. Concentrate on anywhere selling cigarettes – he smoked like a chimney. He had a strong personality, made an impression on anyone he talked to. Now, we'll decide which district each of us is going to tackle. Half this job is legwork ...'

In the München apartment the phone began ringing and Manfred, who was expecting the call, picked up the receiver with his gloved hand. It was Erwin Vinz. Manfred, a teetotaller, poured Perrier water as he listened intently.

'I am speaking from München Hauptbahnhof,' Vinz began after giving the identification code. 'I got off the train a few minutes ago ...'

Manfred knew immediately something was wrong. Vinz was rambling, reluctant to come to the point. Manfred introduced into the conversation his often-used ploy.

'Excellent! We assume all went well. Appointment kept and deal concluded!'

'The Englishman was not on the train. There is no doubt – I can vouch for the fact personally. *If* he got aboard at St. Gallen he must have got off at Romanshorn or St. Margarethen in Switzerland.'

'Kohler saw him closing the compartment door after he boarded the express at St. Gallen ...'

Manfred's voice was gentle and delicate, concealing his livid rage. Vinz's insolence in emphasising *If* cast doubt on Kohler's competence. Not that Manfred cared a damn about Kohler – but Vinz was trying to shift the blame and that he would not tolerate.

'Kohler would have known,' Manfred continued, 'if our friend left the train while it was moving through Switzerland ...' Manfred saw no reason to explain that Kohler would have had men with a clear description of Keith Martel waiting at each Swiss stop. He continued to make Vinz sweat.

'Your sector began at the Swiss border. You got on the train at Lindau ...'

'The bastard must have got off at Bregenz,' Vinz interjected. 'It was the only place left uncovered ...'

'Left uncovered by *you* ...'

Bregenz! Manfred's hand gripped the receiver tightly. The one town he did not want Martel poking around in was Bregenz. He felt like screaming at Vinz, but the sensitivity of the situation must at all costs be hidden.

'I can have a team in Bregenz in one hour,' Vinz volunteered, disturbed by the silence at the other end of the line.

'We would like your team to keep its appointment with the client in half an hour. I hold you personally responsible for bringing about a successful conclusion to this transaction ...'

Inside the payphone at Münich Hauptbahnhof Vinz swore again. Once more Manfred had abruptly terminated the conversation. And now he had to fly his bloody team back from Münich to the airstrip nearest Bregenz. This time they had to eliminate the Englishman.

In London Tweed had left his office for his flat in Maida Vale after receiving the St. Gallen call from Martel. Mason, Howard's new deputy, had tried to delay him. Looking leaner and hungrier than ever, he arrived as Tweed was leaving.

'The chief would like to see you in his office, sir. He says it is extremely urgent ...'

'It always is – to him. I'll see him when I get back.'

Tweed took a cab to the flat. He also took Miss McNeil and she carried the Martel tape concealed in a hold-all. While in the cab he asked his question.

'That new recruit, Mason. Is he any good at anything?'

'He'd make a good bodyguard,' McNeil replied in her crisp Scots accent. 'He's an expert at judo, karate. A marksman with handguns. Special Branch were happy for Howard to take him.'

'Why?'

McNeil had a finely-tuned ear on the grapevine. Probably due to her gift for listening with attentive concentration and unlimited patience.

'He was too physical – always resorted to heavy handling of

any suspect at the drop of a hat. A lot of hats – and clangers – were dropped, I gather.'

At the flat McNeil played back the tape of Martel's conversation on the machine kept there permanently, making notes in neat loops and curls. She had offered to make the tea but Tweed insisted only he could make it the way he liked it. You would imagine he had been a lifetime bachelor, McNeil thought, as she went on making her notes. Tweed arrived with the tray of tea as the tape came to the end of the recording.

The block of flats Tweed lived in was self-service. He had a Sicilian woman who came in to clean the place and often complained she was 'illiterate in three languages'. There was a restaurant on the ground floor. Here Tweed, now on his own, led a self-contained existence. He poured the tea as he asked the question.

'Anything strike you about Martel's data?'

'Two things. Delta seems to be acting in a frenzy – as though they're working against a deadline. *Bloodbath.* That's strong language from Martel in a report. And another reference – *something phoney about Delta neo-Nazis.* I don't understand what he's driving at ...'

'McNeil, you're a treasure. You always spot the salient facts. Makes me feel redundant. I'm pretty sure the deadline is June 2 when the Summit Express leaves Paris – because by morning it will be crossing Bavaria ...'

'You're thinking about the Bavarian state elections?'

'Exactly. Three main parties are competing for power – to take over the state government. Dietrich's Delta – the neo-Nazis – the government party under Chancellor Kurt Langer, and the left-wing lot under Tofler, the alleged ex-Communist. If something dramatic happens on June 3, the day before the election, it might swing the election result – into Tofler's hands. For the West it would be a major disaster.'

'What dramatic event could happen?'

'I only wish I knew.' Tweed sipped his tea. 'I'm convinced Delta has some secret plan – hence the frenzy to eliminate anyone digging into their affairs.'

'What about the reference to *something phoney*?'

McNeil sat quite still, watching Tweed gazing owlishly through his spectacles into the distance. He was, she knew, capable of sudden flashes of intuition – a leap into the future he divined from just the sort of ragbag of facts Martel had provided.

'It has the feel of a separate cell operating secretly inside Delta,' Tweed said slowly. 'That's the only explanation for some of their actions which seem to be designed to ensure they *lose* the election ...'

'Now you've *lost* me,' McNeil commented tartly.

'Where *have* you two been?'

Howard was waiting for them when McNeil and Tweed returned to the latter's office. Standing stiff-backed he had the window behind him –so his own face was in shadow while the new arrivals were caught in the full glare of the light from the curved window. He clasped his hands over his stomach which was decorated with the double loop of a gold watch-chain.

Very militant in mood as well as stance, Tweed observed as he sat behind his desk. He knew the type only too well. An inferiority complex as large as Everest – so they compensated by periodic assertions of authority, just to make sure they still held it.

'Went for a walk in Regent's Park,' Tweed lied blandly.

'You're working on a problem?' Howard pounced.

The SIS chief was in a nervous state of mind, McNeil decided. She was carrying the empty hold-all inside which she had smuggled out Martel's tape to the flat in Maida Vale.

'What's inside that hold-all?' Howard demanded.

'Cheese sandwiches – Cheddar, if you must know,' Tweed interjected. 'It's better than the Cheshire – more flavour ...'

'Could you very kindly find something to do elsewhere?' Howard asked McNeil, who promptly left the room, still carrying the hold-all.

'Have you heard from Keith Martel?' Howard barked as soon as they were alone.

'I thought you were concentrating on security for the PM on her trip to the forthcoming Summit Conference in Vienna. So why interest yourself in Martel ...'

'It's a waste of personnel. Just when I need every man ...'

'So you told me. If you want it on record send me a minute and I can show it to the Minister.' Tweed perched his glasses on the end of his nose and peered over the rims at his visitor, a mannerism which he knew infuriated Howard. 'By the way, I suppose the normal people are in charge of security for the others – the Presidents of America and France, and the German Chancellor?'

'Tim O'Meara in Washington, Alain Flandres in Paris and Erich Stoller in Bonn. Does it really concern you?'

'Not really. I just wondered if all my old friends were still in their jobs.' Tweed looked at his chief. 'These days so many get the chop just when they least expect it ...'

Howard left the room, his mouth tight, his stride almost that of an officer route-marching. He would be incensed for days over the exchange which had taken place – and would therefore keep well away from Tweed, which was what the latter intended. McNeil peered round the door.

'Has he gone?'

'Yes, my dear, the British lion has roared. It is now safe to return.' He opened a copy of *The Times* atlas. 'Crocodile – I'm sure the meaning of that codeword is under my nose ...'

Erwin Vinz took his execution squad back into the new search area – Bregenz – by the fastest possible route. Flying from a private airstrip outside München he landed his men at another airstrip close to Lindau. From here the eight men piled into three waiting cars and were driven at speed to the border and Bregenz beyond. It was three o'clock when they pulled up in front of the station.

'I think Martel got off the train here,' Vinz told the two men in the rear of his car. 'He may well still be in Bregenz. You stay here. The rest of us will quarter the town and drive round until we locate him ...'

'And if we do see him board a train?' one of the two men asked as he alighted from the car.

'He has a fatal accident, of course!' Vinz was irritated by the man's stupidity. 'Whatever happens he must not reach Münich ...'

Vinz held a brief conference with the other five men. 'There are twenty thousand deutschemarks for the man who locates Martel. You have his description. You tell people he escaped from a home for the mentally disturbed, that he is dangerous. Rendezvous here two hours from now. Turn over this backwater!'

Martel picked up the spoor Charles Warner had left behind in Bregenz at his twelfth attempt. The contact was a bookseller, an Austrian in his early forties with a shop at the end of Kaiserstrasse. Outside was the pedestrian underpass where Martel had arranged to meet Claire in half an hour's time. He told his tale, showed Warner's photo and the reaction was positive.

'I know your friend. Grief seems to be his companion ...'

'Grief?' Martel queried cautiously and waited.

'Yes. His closest friend died here while on a visit. It was during the French military occupation of the Vorarlberg and the Tyrol after the war. His friend was buried here so he thought he would pay his respects.'

'I see ...'

Martel did not see at all and was careful to say as little as possible. The bookseller broke off to serve a customer and then continued.

'There are two Catholic cemeteries in Bregenz and one Protestant. This man's friend had a curious religious history. Born a Protestant, he was converted to the Catholic faith. Later he appeared to lose his faith. Under the peculiar circumstances the man who came into my shop asked for the location of all three cemeteries. I showed them to him on a street map.'

'How recent was his visit to you?'

'Less than a week ago. Last Saturday ...'

87

'Can you sell me a street map and mark the three cemeteries?'

The bookseller fetched a map and ringed the areas. 'There is the Blumenstrasse, the Vorkloster – both are Catholic. And here is the Protestant burial-ground ...'

Claire was waiting when Martel descended the steps into the otherwise deserted subway. She stood gazing at a scene behind an illuminated window set into the wall. The glass protected relics of an archaeological dig which had unearthed the ancient Roman town which once stood on the site of present-day Bregenz.

'Spooky, isn't it?' Clare remarked and gave a little shudder. 'All that time ago. And today in this mist the whole place seems creepy – and I haven't found a trace of Warner ...'

'Last Saturday he was standing not a hundred feet from where we are standing now ...'

She listened while he summed up his interview with the helpful bookseller. As he completed his résumé she was frowning. 'I'm not grasping the significance ...'

'Join the club – except that one thing's almost frighteningly certain. He was here last Saturday. Sunday he's murdered out on the lake. Whatever he found in Bregenz probably triggered off that murder ...'

'But how long ago was the French military occupation of Austria, for God's sake? This goes back to just after the war ...'

'Not necessarily. The Allied occupation of Austria ended May 15 1955 – so whatever Warner dug up could have happened close to that date ...'

'It's still over a quarter of a century ago,' she objected, 'so what could have happened then that's relevant to today?'

'Damned if I know – that's what we have to find out. That yarn Warner spun about his closest friend dying here was eye-wash, but he had his teeth into something. The period – the time of the French occupation might mean something ...'

'So how do we find out, where do we start?'

'We hire a car first at a place I saw near here. Then we visit the three cemeteries Warner was enquiring about. The secret has to lie in one of them. Literally ...'

Erwin Vinz walked into the bookseller's shop in Kaiserstrasse. Despite his later arrival in Bregenz he had, without knowing, an advantage over Martel: six men were scouring the town. He spoke first to a girl assistant and asked for the manager. She went upstairs to find the proprietor who had talked to Martel.

'I'd better go down and see this man myself,' the bookseller decided.

On the ground floor he listened while Vinz told his story. The verbal description Vinz gave was graphic. Take away the glasses and add a cigarette holder and the bookseller recognised that this man was describing his earlier visitor. The Austrian studied Vinz and was careful not to interrupt.

'You say that this man has escaped from a mental asylum?' he enquired eventually.

'Yes. A very violent patient. Unfortunately he can give the impression he is completely normal and this makes him even more dangerous. You have seen this man?'

CHAPTER 11

Thursday May 28

IN GOTTES FRIEDEN   ALOIS STOHR   1930–1953

In God We Trust ... Inside the mist-bound cemetery known as the Blumenstrasse three people stared at the headstone. Martel and Claire were bewildered. Alois Stohr? The name meant nothing to either of them. Martel turned to the gravedigger who had brought them to this spot. Again he showed him Warner's photo.

'Look, you're quite certain this was the man who asked to see this particular grave?'

The old gravedigger wore an ancient cap and his moustache dripped moisture globules from the grey vapour swirling amid the headstones. So far as Martel could see — which was not very far — they were the only visitors. It was not a day to encourage sentimental journeys.

'This is the man.'

The gravedigger, Martel noted, spoke with the same conviction of recognition as had the bookseller when viewing the photo. And he had identified Warner previously before Martel gave him a sheaf of schilling notes.

'When did he come here?' Martel asked.

'Last week. Saturday.'

The same story that the bookseller had told. It was maddening. Martel no longer had any doubt that Charles Warner had visited this particular grave only a short time before he was murdered. But where was the link-up — what made Alois Stohr so important he must remain undisturbed at all cost?

'Did he say anything else, anything at all?' Martel demanded.

'Simply asked me to show him the grave of Alois Stohr ...'

Watching on the sidelines Claire had an overpowering impression the gravedigger was withdrawing into his shell under the impact of Martel's interrogation. The Englishman continued.

'Did he give the date of Stohr's death?'

'Only said it was near the end of the French occupation ...'

Warner had used a similar phrase while talking to the bookseller in Kaiserstrasse. *It was during the French military occupation* ... Why pinpoint the time like that instead of giving an approximate year?

Claire had remained silent, studying the gravedigger, and she spoke suddenly, her voice confident as though she knew the reply and was interested only in confirmation?

'Who else visits this grave?'

'I don't know as I should talk about such things,' the old boy said after a long pause. Martel almost held his breath: Claire, by a flash of intuition, had put her finger on something they would otherwise not have been told. She kept up the pressure.

'My friend gave you a generous sum so we expect complete frankness. Who comes here?'

'I don't know her name. She comes every week. Always on a Wednesday and always at eight in the morning. She lays a bunch of flowers, waits a few minutes and then goes ...'

'How does she get here?' Claire persisted. 'By car? By cab?'

'She comes in a cab – and keeps it waiting till she leaves ...'

'Her description? Colour of hair? Her age – roughly. How is she dressed? Modestly? Expensively?'

The barrage of questions reinforced the gravedigger's obvious reluctance to say more. He handed Warner's photo back to Martel and picked up his shovel, prior to departure.

'Expensive – her clothes ...'

'Colour of hair?' Claire went on relentlessly.

'Can't say – she always wears a head-scarf ...'

'And you passed on the same information to the man in this photo when he came here?' Martel asked.

The gravedigger, shouldering his shovel like a soldier, was moving away, vanishing into the mist shrouding the head-stones. His voice came back like that of a ghost.

'Yes. And I think he found out where she lived. While she was here I saw him talking to her cab-driver. Money exchanged hands ...'

Have you seen this man?

The bookseller who had talked to Martel adjusted his glasses and gazed at Erwin Vinz. He took his time before replying.

'You have some form of identification?' he enquired.

'You *have* seen the escaped patient then?' Vinz pressed eagerly. 'As to identification – we're not police, we don't carry cards ...'

'Your description means nothing to me. I have never had anyone in my shop remotely resembling this man. If you will excuse me, I have a shop to run ...'

He watched Vinz leave, shoulders hunched, his mouth a thin

line. He climbed into a car outside, said something to the driver and the vehicle disappeared. The girl assistant spoke tentatively.

'I thought we did have a man in here earlier ...'

'You think that man who just called had anything to do with an asylum?' There was a note of contempt in the Austrian's voice.

'For one thing he was a German so he would have approached the authorities if his story were true ...'

'You think he was ...'

'Lying in his teeth. You have just met a neo-Nazi – I can smell the breed, to say nothing of the badge he flaunts in his coat lapel. If he returns, tell me and I will call the police ...'

The sun had burnt off the mist and it was now a brilliant afternoon. When Vinz arrived and left two men to watch the railway station there remained a team of six – including himself – and he had divided them up into pairs. Each couple took one of the three cars to explore the district allocated to them.

One couple was driving up Gallus-strasse, a prosperous residential area, while Vinz was making his abortive visit to the bookshop. Vinz's men had just enquired at yet another hotel and again drawn a blank. The car descending Gallus-strasse towards them contained Martel and Claire. Both vehicles moved at a sedate pace as they closed the gap between them.

Vinz's men, in a BMW, were keeping down their speed so they could check the sidewalks for any sign of Martel. Behind the wheel of the Audi they had hired, Claire drove slowly through the unfamiliar district while Martel, beside her, gave directions as he studied the town plan.

'At the bottom – to avoid going past the railway station – we turn ...'

'Oh, my God! Keith – inside that BMW coming towards us. I saw the sun flash off something shiny in the lapel of that man beside the driver, I'm sure it's a badge. It's Delta ...'

'Don't speed up, don't look at them, don't change anything – just keep going as you are doing ...'

'They'll have your description . . .'

'Good luck to them!'

Inside the BMW the man in the front passenger seat carried a Luger inside his shoulder holster. He studied the two people in the oncoming Audi. It was second nature for him to overlook no-one. Imprinted in his memory was the detailed description of Martel every member of the squad had been provided with.

Gallus-strasse was exceptionally quiet at this hour. Claire was suddenly aware she was gripping the wheel tightly and forced herself to relax – *not to look at the BMW driver who had lowered his window which would allow his passenger to fire at her point-blank.*

'Steady now . . .!'

Martel spoke softly, his lips scarcely moving as he studied the street map spread out on his lap. The two cars, still slow-moving, drew level. The passenger inside the BMW stared hard at the man next to the girl driver. Then the cars were moving away from each other.

'Something about that Audi?' asked the man behind the wheel.

'Just checking. Not a bit like him . . .'

At the bottom of Gallus-strasse Martel directed Claire to keep them away from the lake front – and the railway station. She gave a sigh of relief.

'Not to worry,' he remarked. 'I wonder how they got here while we were still in town . . .'

'They were Delta . . .'

'I saw the badges out of the corner of my eye as they passed us. In any case, I was prepared . . .' He lifted a corner of the street plan and she saw his right hand gripping the butt of his .45 Colt. 'Any sign of hostile action and I could have blown them both away. There was no one else about. And how did you expect them to recognise me?'

She glanced at him. He wore a Tyrolean hat with a feather in the band purchased while she arranged the hire of the Audi. Clamped between his teeth was a large, ugly-looking pipe he had bought in another shop. On the bridge of his Roman nose perched horn-rimmed glasses. The transformation from his normal hatless appearance with cigarette-holder at jaunty angle was total.

'God,' she said, 'I'm a fool not to have your confidence ...'

'Your reaction was correct,' he rapped back. 'The day you're not nervous in a situation like that is likely to be your last. Now, let's head for the border and the whirlpool – Lindau.'

In the late afternoon Vinz phoned Reinhard Dietrich from Bregenz. He was exhausted. So were his men. By phoning the *schloss* he also avoided reporting to the man he most feared. Manfred.

'Vinz speaking. We were asked to undertake a commission ...'

'I know.' Dietrich sounded irritable. 'I was informed by the agent who placed the commission. I take it you have earned your keep?'

In the payphone near Bregenz station Vinz gazed out at the dense fog rolling in from the lake. 'From the beginning it was an impossible task,' he said. 'We ran ourselves into the ground. The Englishman is not here ...'

'What! He must have got off that express at Bregenz. Don't you see – he chose that stop because he guessed the competition might be waiting for him at Lindau. And Bregenz is a small town ...'

'Not all that small,' Vinz snapped. He was so tired he answered back. 'The layout is complex – and the fog has returned. The whole place is blotted out ...'

'Get back here at once! All of you! We'll discuss our next move the moment you arrive. And don't stop anywhere for a drink or anything to eat ...'

'We haven't eaten all day ...'

'I should bloody well hope not! Straight back here! You understand?'

Dietrich slammed down the receiver. He was red in the face. He ran his hands through his silver hair and gazed round the library. Vinz would never know his outburst had been promoted not by rage but by *fear*. He rang for Oscar and when the hunchback arrived told him to pour a large brandy.

'They haven't found the Englishman,' he said savagely.

'He must be clever. The first spy, Warner, was clever — but he revealed himself in due course. This new Englishman will make the same mistake ...' He handed the brandy to Dietrich who took a large gulp and shook his head.

'He eludes every trap. He has been on the continent less than two days and is getting closer to Bavaria, to Operation Crocodile, every moment. In six days' time the Summit Express will be crossing Bavaria!'

'So we have six days to find him,' Oscar said reassuringly, refilling his master's glass.

'God in heaven, Oscar! Don't you see you can turn that round? *He has six days to find us!*'

Close to the main entrance to Dietrich's walled estate there was a small forest by the roadside. The entrance was guarded by wrought-iron gates and a sentry lodge. It was early evening when a large bird swooped over the gates and all hell broke loose.

Behind the gates ferocious German shepherd dogs appeared, huge brutes which leapt at the gates, barking and snarling, eager to tear any intruder to pieces.

Inside a Mercedes parked out of sight on the edge of the trees Erich Stoller, chief of the BND, listened to the sound of the dogs, his slim hands lightly tapping the wheel. Forty-three years old, Stoller was six feet tall and very thin, his face lean and sensitive.

His chief assistant, Otto Wilde, sat beside him clasping a cine-camera equipped with a telephoto lens. Small and plump, Wilde was terrified of fierce dogs. He glanced at his chief.

'Supposing they open the gates ...'

'Oh, we can deal with that.' Stoller opened the glove compartment, extracted the gas-pistol nestling inside and handed it to his companion. 'A whiff of tear-gas up their nostrils should discourage their ardour ...'

'They know we're here — they have picked up our scent ...'

'Nonsense! They were startled by that large bird which swooped past the entrance. When we develop your film it will be interesting to see if any old friends are present. I think I recognised one – the driver of the first car ...'

Parked out of sight they had witnessed the recent return to the *schloss* of a cavalcade of three cars. Erwin Vinz had been driving the leading vehicle. What Vinz did not know was that when they pulled up at the entrance – waiting while the dogs were locked up in their compound – Otto Wilde had been busy with his camera.

This was Stoller's first visit to the area of the *schloss* owned by Dietrich. By chance Vinz's team, returning from its fruitless search for Keith Martel, arrived while the BND chief was surveying the target area. Stoller was persisting in his efforts to locate Delta's main base.

'I'm convinced, Otto,' he remarked as he reached for the ignition, 'that Delta could have its headquarters here.'

'Why?'

'Because it is the home of Reinhard Dietrich who has put himself forward in the state elections as the next Minister-President of Bavaria, because you say the estate is vast ...'

'I showed you on the map. Look at the distance we drove round the perimeter to get here ...'

'So, it could fit. You can't see the *schloss* from any point from the road. It is remote, secluded – ideal for concealing a horde of rabble-rousers. And God knows they are rousing – look at the riots recently. Almost as bad as in England ...'

'They're opening the gates!'

Stoller had started the engine and was already driving into the open and on to the road leading past the entrance to the *schloss*. It was the direct route to Münich and Stoller was not prepared to go the other way for some millionaire thug who employed killer dogs.

'Raise your window,' he ordered Wilde, using one hand to shut his own. The dogs were out in the road, rushing towards the unmarked police car. Faces appeared at either window, fangs bared, mouths slavering, the heads huge, paws clawing desperately to get beyond the glass to ravage the men inside. Stoller put his foot down.

The car leapt forward. Two of the beasts appeared briefly in front of the radiator. The occupants felt the thuds of speeding metal colliding with animal bodies. Then they were hurtling past the open gates where men were pouring out led by a tall, well-built blond giant. Wilde looked back.

'They're going to follow us in a car ...'

'That damned bird started it,' Stoller said calmly. 'The dogs kicked up, Dietrich's guards became suspicious – and sent out the hounds. Did you notice the blond Adonis who appeared to be their leader? That was Werner Hagen – a keen wind-surfer. We have to evade them – on no account must they know they're under surveillance ...'

'Evade them? How?'

They moved at manic speed round bends in the country road and Wilde braced himself. He was almost as terrified of Stoller's driving as he was of fierce dogs: his chief had the reputation of being the fastest driver in Bavaria. Stoller gave a fresh order.

'When I stop at the next intersection stay in the car – and get well down out of sight. I'll need the gas-pistol – I'm going to block the road. Look, this will do ...'

Wilde glanced over his shoulder and saw only deserted roadway. Stoller had gained a temporary lead – but Wilde knew the road ahead would be empty and for miles there were long straight sections. It couldn't be done ...

Ahead a farm-track led off to the right. Stoller jammed on the brakes. There was a screech of rubber and he turned through ninety degrees, ending up a short distance along the track. Wilde was saved from being hurled through the windscreen by Stoller's insistence that he always wore his seat-belt. It was not over yet.

Stoller was now backing rapidly until his vehicle blocked the road. Grabbing the gas-pistol handed to him by Wilde who was already hunching himself below window level, he left the car, slamming the door shut. He ran towards a large tree near the roadside and hid behind the massive trunk.

The pursuing car – driven by Werner Hagen with two men accompanying him – came round a nearby bend. Hagen found himself confronted by a Mercedes broadside on and which appeared to be empty. He braked, stopped, reached for the gun under his armpit and told the two men to wait in the car.

Leaving his door open he looked cautiously round while the man in the back lowered his window to see what was going on. Stoller used the tree trunk to steady himself, aimed the gas-pistol and pulled the trigger. The missile exploded on the driver's seat – a bull's eye which spread fumes in all directions, smothering Hagen who dropped his gun and staggered, coughing, unable to see anything.

The man in the front passenger seat was choking, his vision blurred. In a matter of seconds Stoller reloaded and took fresh aim. The second missile passed through the open rear window and exploded in the rear of the car. Stoller ran back to his own vehicle.

Minutes later he was miles away, driving along one of the endless stretches with no sign of any other vehicle in his rear-view mirror. Wilde saw that his chief was frowning.

'You pulled that off beautifully. Why the scowl?'

'I was thinking about Martel. Tweed warned me he was coming – but he's a loner ...'

'So, like Warner, no cooperation?'

'On the contrary, he'll contact me when he needs me. Excellent judgement. I just wonder where he is at this moment ...'

CHAPTER 12

Thursday May 28

Martel drove the hired Audi across the road bridge linking the mainland of Bavaria with the island of Lindau. He no longer wore the Tyrolean hat nor was he smoking the pipe used to disguise his appearance in Bregenz.

Hatless, his profile prominent with its strong Roman nose, the Englishman smoked a cigarette in his holder at a jaunty angle. It was as though he wished to draw attention to his arrival to any watchers who might be stationed in Lindau.

'What do you think you are doing?' Claire had demanded when he discarded his disguise as soon as they had crossed the border into Germany.

'Showing the British flag,' replied Martel. 'If I had a Union Jack pennant I'd be flying it . . .'

'Delta will spot us soon enough . . .'

'Sooner, I hope.'

'You're setting yourself up as a target?' she protested. 'You must be mad – have you forgotten Zürich, St. Gallen . . .'

'The point is I have remembered them – and we're working to a time limit. You said the Bayerischer Hof is the top hotel on the island?'

'Yes, and it's next to the Hauptbahnhof . . .'

'Then we must rig it so it looks as though you've arrived on your own by train. We'll register separately, eat separately in the dining-room. We don't know each other. That way you can guard my back. And put on those dark glasses which transform your appearance . . .'

'Would sir like anything else?'

'Yes, guide me to the hotel,' he said. 'This place is a rabbit warren and I've forgotten the burrows. Use the map.'

They had a taste of the beauty of the island when they drove over the bridge and past a green park which ran to the lake edge. The mist had lifted temporarily and the sun was a luminous glow. She checked the map and gave directions. Within minutes she laid a hand on his arm.

'We're almost there. Better drop me here. Turn left at the end. The Bayerischer Hof is on your left, the Hauptbahnhof on your right, the harbour straight ahead. Where do we meet?'

'At the terrace elevated above the harbour, the Romer-schanze – the place where a tourist looking through binoculars witnessed the killing of Warner without realising it . . .'

She left the vehicle, carrying her suitcase. Only two or three tourists were in this quiet section of the old street but she took no chances, calling out in German.

'Thank you so much for the lift. Now I shall catch my train.'

'My pleasure . . .'

The pavement artist, Braun, spotted Martel as soon as he drove round the corner.

Today Braun's picture drawn in crayon on the flagstones was an impression of the amphitheatre at Verona. The small card-board box for coins lay beside the picture. Again wearing a windcheater and jeans he was patrolling back and forth, hands clasped behind his back as though taking a rest from his labours.

He was actually watching the exit doors from the Haupt-bahnhof. A main-line express from Switzerland was due. He turned round at the precise moment Keith Martel appeared and recognised him immediately. It was no great feat of obser-vation.

Thick black hair, early thirties, tall, well-built, clean-shaven, promi-nent Semitic-like nose, habitually smokes cigarettes in holder at slanting angle . . .

The pavement artist was so thrown off-balance by Martel's sudden appearance, by the accuracy of the description pro-vided, that he almost stopped in mid-stride – which would have been a blunder since it might have drawn the target's attention to himself. He strolled on as the Audi passed him and he heard it pull up. He sneaked a glance over his shoulder so he would be able to recognise the Englishman *from behind.*

'I wonder, you curious sod . . .'

Martel muttered the words to himself as he stared in his wing mirror, still seated behind the wheel. It had been a reflex action – to make one final check before he got out of the car with his suitcase. The swift glance of the pavement artist over his shoulder showed clearly in the mirror.

He got out of the car and saw the mist beginning to roll in

from the lake, invading the harbour. He walked inside the hotel's spacious, well-furnished reception hall and up a few steps to the desk. The girl behind the counter was helpful and brisk. Yes, they had an excellent double bedroom on the third floor overlooking the lake. Certainly it would be acceptable for him to pay for his room in advance as he might have to make a sudden departure on business.

'And if you would fill in the registration form, sir?'

The conversation had been carried on in English — Martel was booking in under his own name and nationality. Under the heading *Occupation* he wrote *Consultant*.

Escorted upstairs in the lift by the porter, he was shown into a huge room with a large bathroom. Martel liked to travel well and Erich Stoller was paying. As soon as he was alone he went to the side window which, as he expected, overlooked the Hauptbahnhof and hotel entrance. He saw Claire coming out of the station.

Her performance had been a model of skilled evasion. Wearing her dark glasses and a head-scarf, she had crossed the road immediately Martel had turned the corner. The pavement artist had not even seen her. He was not *looking* for a girl, only a man, Martel ...

Once inside the Hauptbahnhof Claire had waited for someone else to walk out. A couple staying at the hotel had gone across to check the timetable board. Claire emerged with them, having heard a brief snatch of their conversation in German.

'I'm looking for the Bayerischer Hof,' she said to the elderly man who was beside her. It was his wife beyond who answered.

'My dear, it is just across the road. We're staying there ourselves. You'll find it an excellent hotel ...'

'Let me have your case,' the German said and took it, grasping the handle.

It was perfect cover for anyone who might be watching. Claire appeared to belong to the couple who had gone to the Hauptbahnhof to meet her. The pavement artist never even noticed her as the trio vanished inside the hotel entrance.

From the open third floor window in his bedroom Martel

stared at the sidewalk immediately below where his car was still parked. The pavement artist held a tiny notepad in the palm of his hand and he was noting down the vehicle's registration number.

Seen from street level, the pavement artist's action was carried out with such skill no one noticed what he was doing. He never gave a thought to the possibility that he might be observed from above.

'Got you, you bastard . . .'

Martel muttered the words as he ran to his case, snapped open the locks and pulled out from under neatly folded clothes a small instrument. He shoved it inside his jacket pocket, left the room and descended in the waiting lift.

At ground floor level he ignored Claire who was completing the registration form after reserving a single room with bath. Walking to the exit, Martel peered out and strolled into the street. As he expected, the pavement artist was casually crossing the road on his way to the Hauptbahnhof.

The watcher had to have some quick means of communication with his employers – what could be more convenient than the public telephone booths he would undoubtedly find inside? The double doors closed in Martel's face as the pavement artist entered ahead of him. The Englishman pushed a door open slowly and walked into a large booking-hall. The row of phone booths was to his left.

The pavement artist had entered a booth in the middle of the row, the only one now occupied. Martel paused. Shoving his hand into his jacket pocket he waited until his quarry picked up the receiver and commenced dialling. Then Martel entered the booth to the right and slammed the door shut.

The noise attracted the pavement artist's attention. Out of the corner of his eyes, his head bent over a notebook he appeared to be consulting, Martel sensed the man's shocked disbelief. For the next few seconds he held his breath. It was a question of psychology.

The pavement artist turned his back on Martel and continued making his call. It was the reaction Martel had prayed for. The man was *not* a top-flight professional. Had Martel been in his place he would have continued dialling the first figures which came into his head, listened for a moment as though getting the wrong signal, slammed down the receiver and left the booth.

He knew exactly what had happened instead. Startled to find his target in the next booth, the man had experienced seconds of indecision. *But because he had started dialling — and because he was certain Martel could not possibly suspect him —* he continued what he had been doing.

Martel raised his own receiver with one hand while the other performed a quite different action. Extracting the instrument taken from his suitcase, he pressed the rubber sucker at waist-level on the glass window separating his booth from the next one. He then inserted the hearing-aid in place, using his upper left forearm to conceal the wire from the sucker to the ear-piece.

The Englishman was gambling on the second-rate calibre of the pavement artist — that he would keep his back to Martel to hide his features. The instrument was working perfectly. Every word of the conversation in the next booth was transmitted to him with great clarity.

'Is that Stuttgart . . .?'

Martel memorised the number, although unable to hear the other end of the conversation.

'Edgar Braun speaking,' the pavement artist said formally. 'Is that Klara . . .'

'*Cretin!* You have already made *two* mistakes!' the girl told him venomously. 'No number or name at this end to be transmitted. You want someone to keep an appointment with you?'

'S-orry . . .' Braun mumbled the words. He has been badly thrown off balance by Martel's sudden appearance in the next booth. His fervent wish now was that he had broken off the call — but he dare not do that at this stage because Klara would guess something was wrong, that he had blundered. The only thing was to press on.

'The second consignment you were expecting has arrived,'

Braun continued. 'It has been delivered safely to the Hotel Bayerischer Hof a few minutes ago ...'

'Where exactly is that?' Klara demanded, her tone icy.

'Facing both Hauptbahnhof and harbour. The following car registration number is linked with the consignment ... I stay on duty?'

'Yes! We shall react at once. And I shall have to report your indiscretion ...'

'Please ...'

But the Stuttgart connection had gone dead. Behind Braun's back Martel had pulled the rubber sucker from the glass, hauled the earpiece free and thrust the whole contraption in his jacket pocket. The change in Braun's tone had warned him the conversation was ending.

Martel performed a pantomime as Braun sneaked out of the booth without a glance in his direction. He spoke loudly in English about nothing into the receiver. When Braun disappeared through the exit he left the booth. He now had solid data for Stoller to check.

Inside the luxurious tenth-floor apartment in a building less than a mile from the headquarters of Dietrich GmbH, Klara Beck slammed down the receiver. Tearing open a fresh pack with nails painted like red talons she lit her forty-first cigarette of the day.

'Braun must be losing his marbles,' she said to herself.

The cigarette was necessary to calm her nerves – and her voice – before she phoned Reinhard Dietrich. Although sexually attractive she knew it was her outward coolness which most appealed to the Bavarian millionaire, which made her his mistress. Her apparent calm in all situations was such a contrast to Dietrich's choleric temperament – and to that of his whining wife.

Taking several deep drags, she expelled smoke from her lungs, her bosom heaving with the relaxation afforded by the nicotine. It was time to make the call. She dialled the number of the *schloss*. Dietrich himself answered.

'Yes!'

Just the single, curt word.

'Klara calling. It is convenient to talk?'

'Yes! You received the emerald ring? Good!'

They had performed the ritual of positive identification. During alternate calls Dietrich would refer to sending her a fur or some item of jewellery – which secretly infuriated her since few of these desirable gifts were ever given to her. She hurried on.

'The second consignment has been delivered. I have just heard – it has arrived at the Hotel Bayerischer Hof in Lindau . . .'

'Meet me there this evening!' Dietrich responded instantly. 'Get the executive jet to fly you to the airstrip nearest Lindau. Then take a hired car. A room will be reserved for you. Your help may be needed . . .'

'There is a car registration number. Here it is . . .'

Dietrich repeated the number and broke the connection without a goodbye. Klara Beck replaced the receiver slowly, preserving her self-control. Despite her annoyance she was impressed. She had just told Dietrich in an oblique manner that Keith Martel – the man they had scoured Switzerland, Austria and Bavaria to track down – had been located. Dietrich had reacted decisively to the news, taking only seconds to plan his next move.

One phrase intrigued her. *Your help may be needed* . . . It conjured up one possibility – Dietrich was considering asking her to seduce Martel. She went into the bedroom, slipped out of her dress, the only item of clothing she was wearing in the clammy atmosphere, and studied her full-bodied nude form in a full-length mirror.

It could be fun – playing with the Englishman. Before – at the appropriate moment – she rammed the needle between his ribs and pressed the button which released the lethal injection.

At the *schloss* Dietrich had ordered Oscar to bring one of his packed suitcases for an overnight stay. A series of cases were packed and unpacked daily by the attentive Oscar.

There were cases for a short trip, cases for more prolonged journeys, cases for hot climates and cases for countries like Norway in the depths of winter. The system meant Dietrich was ready for departure anywhere at a moment's notice. On the intercom he summoned Erwin Vinz who had recently returned with his team from Bregenz. He did not mince his words.

'Someone else has done the job for you! A woman at that! I am leaving at once for the Bayerischer Hof in Lindau – Martel has just arrived there. Choose your best men, follow me and book in at the same hotel ...'

'This time we should get him ...' Vinz began.

'This time you *will* get him, for God's sake! Before morning – he will be tired after his recent activities ...'

'Peter has the car waiting,' reported Oscar who had returned with a Gucci suitcase.

Wearing a suit of Savile Row country tweeds Dietrich left the library, crossed the large hall and Oscar held open one of the two huge entrance doors. Dietrich ran down the steps and climbed into the rear of a black, six-seater Mercedes. The uniformed chauffeur closed the door as his master pressed a button and lowered the window to give the order.

'Lindau. Drive like hell ...!'

Inside Lindau Hauptbahnhof Martel paused outside the phone booth, inserted a cigarette into his holder and lit it. Braun had vanished through the exit doors but Martel waited to see whether the German was smarter than he appeared to be – whether he would dodge back into the station to check up on the Englishman. He did not reappear.

Martel strolled towards the exit doors, opened one a fraction and peered out. On the sidewalk outside the Bayerischer Hof, Braun was on his knees with his back towards Martel, adding to his drawing. The Englishman walked out and got inside one of the taxis waiting under a huge tree.

'The Post Office,' he said. 'Quickly, please – before it closes.'

'It is no distance ...'

'So you get a good tip for taking me there . . .'

At the post office Martel explained he wanted to call London and gave the girl behind the counter the Park Crescent number. He was gambling that Tweed was waiting for his call. Within two minutes the girl directed him to a booth.

'Thursday calling,' he said quickly as Tweed came on the line.

'Two-Eight here . . .' the familiar voice replied.

Martel began pouring out data to be fed into the recording machine.

'Warner seen in Bregenz . . . visited cemetery, grave of Álois Stohr . . . headstone 1930–1953 . . . references to time of French occupation . . . expensively dressed woman, identity unknown, visits grave each Wednesday morning . . . Warner contacted her . . . Delta active everywhere . . . two men in car in Bregenz . . .'

'Did they see either of you?' Tweed interrupted urgently.

'We sighted them . . . no reverse sighting . . . now staying Bayerischer Hof Lindau . . . Delta watcher pavement artist Braun sighted and reported me – repeat me . . . Stoller should check Stuttgart phone number . . . Stuttgart contact woman named Klara . . . closing down . . .'

'Wait! Wait! Damn! He's rung off . . .'

Tweed replaced the receiver and stared at McNeil who switched off the recording machine. A very thrifty, Scots type, McNeil. Tweed was certain she had never taken a taxi in her whole life. Buses and the Underground were her sole means of transportation.

'The maniac is setting himself up as bait to flush Delta into the open,' he snapped. 'I know him . . .'

'He's a loner. He gets results,' McNeil said placidly.

'He's in the zone of maximum danger,' Tweed replied grimly. 'Get me Stoller on the phone. Quickly, please. I sense an emergency.'

Thursday May 28

The signal had been arranged between Martel and Claire before they made separate entrances into the magnificent dining-room as though strangers. The Englishman had a single table next to a picture window which looked out on to the fog-bound harbour.

The signal was that if anyone significant entered the dining-room while they ate their separate meals Claire would light a cigarette. In the middle of her dessert she was doing just that, lighting a cigarette.

A most dominant personality had made his entrance – and he came into the room in precisely this fashion, like an accomplished actor making his entrance on stage. There was a sudden hush in the conversation: eyes turned and stared towards the entrance. The new arrival paused and surveyed the people at their tables.

He ran a hand through his thick, silver-coloured hair, tugged gently at his moustache, his ice-blue eyes sweeping the assembled guests. Other eyes dropped as they met his gaze. His skin was tanned and leathery. He had changed into an immaculate blue bird's-eye lounge suit.

The maître d'hôtel escorted Reinhard Dietrich to another window table at the opposite end of the room from Martel. And since his arrival there had been a subtle change in the atmosphere. The conversation was now carried on in murmurs. Handsome women glanced at the table where the millionaire sat, which amused Martel.

There's no glamour like a lot of money, he thought.

Two or three minutes after Claire had vacated her table he left the room. Wandering along a wide corridor he found her standing at the reception desk, waiting her turn while a fresh arrival – (an attractive brunette in her late twenties with a full-bodied figure) was completing the registration form.

The reception hall opened out into a well-furnished and spacious lounge area with comfortable armchairs. Martel chose one of these chairs, settled himself and picked up a magazine. He inserted a cigarette into his holder, lit it and waited.

The attractive new guest had gone up in the lift to her room with the porter. Claire was asking the receptionist about train times to Kempten – the first thing which came into her head. The receptionist was being very helpful, checking a rail timetable and noting times on a slip of paper.

'Thank you.' She turned away and then turned back. 'I thought I recognised the girl who just arrived. She stays here often?'

'Her first visit as far as I know, Madame . . .'

Claire had her handbag open, slipping the piece of paper inside as she wandered into the lounge area. As she passed Martel's armchair she deliberately tipped her bag and the contents spilt over the floor. Her 9-mm pistol remained safely inside the special zipped-up compartment.

'Let me help you,' Martel said, gathering up objects.

'I'm so sorry . . .'

Their heads were close together. The receptionist was a distance from where Martel sat. They carried on their brief conversation in whispers.

'That girl who just arrived,' Claire told him. 'I saw the name on the registration form. *Klara* Beck – from *Stuttgart* . . .'

'The hyenas are gathering. And the man in the dining-room who arrived as though he owned the damned world – Reinhard Dietrich?'

'Yes – I've seen pictures in the paper . . .'

The spilt contents had been collected up. Claire, who had been crouching with her knees bent, her back to the receptionist, stood up and raised her voice.

'That really was most kind of you – and most clumsy of me . . .'

Claire wandered to the far side of the room and chose a chair where she could see everything and had her back to the wall.

She opened her handbag, unzipped the compartment, slid out the pistol and left it inside the bag where she could reach it swiftly. She had just completed this precaution when Erwin Vinz and his associate, Rolf Gross, walked into the reception hall, each carrying a small case.

Claire *froze* — then slid the gun out of her handbag and covered it on her lap with a newspaper. *Rolf Gross had been the driver of the Delta car they had encountered in Gallus-strasse in Bregenz.*

Both men glanced into the lounge area as they crossed to the steps leading to the reception counter. Claire thought Gross stared at Martel who was reading a newspaper and smoking a cigarette in his holder. Vinz appeared to notice nothing and neither man showed any interest in the girl at the back of the room.

Slipping the gun inside her handbag, she closed it, stood up and wandered over to the reception desk where both men were filling in their registration forms. She waited patiently, looking at a picture on the wall.

'We require two single rooms with baths,' Vinz said in the tone of voice used for addressing serfs. 'If you haven't singles, two doubles will do. And we want dinner ...'

'I have two single rooms ...' The receptionist was not looking at Vinz although his tone of voice remained polite. 'And I would suggest you hurry to the dining-room which stops serving ...'

'Inform them of our arrival! We both require steaks, plenty of potatoes. The steaks rare — and a very good bottle of red wine. We'll be down as soon as *we* are ready ...'

'Understood, sir. The porter here will show you your rooms.'

With obvious relief he turned to Claire with a smile. She asked for a street plan of Lindau and he explained that a section of the Old Town was a 'walking-only' zone. At that moment Reinhard Dietrich, smoking a large cigar, came down the corridor from the dining-room. Continuing past the reception desk he marched into the lounge and eased his bulk into the armchair next to Martel.

*

'Reinhard Dietrich at your service. You are English?'

Martel looked at the leathery hand extended in greeting, made a movement as though about to clasp the hand – and ignored it, inserting a fresh cigarette in his holder.

Dietrich overlooked the insult. His extended hand grasped the glass of cognac a waiter had just placed on the table, making it appear that had been his original intention. He raised the glass.

'Yes,' said Martel.

'I beg your pardon?'

'Yes, I am English.'

'Oh, of course! Taking a holiday in our beautiful Bavaria?'

Martel turned and looked straight at the industrialist, switching to German, which momentarily threw him off balance.

'You are a Nazi. They need wiping off the face of the earth.'

'Unless we inherit the earth,' Dietrich replied harshly. 'In the coming state election someone has to make sure Tofler does not win. How would you enjoy a Communist controlling the largest state in Germany – geographically speaking? The West's main bulwark against the Soviets would be shattered ...'

'I could never see the difference. Both are inhuman dictatorships. Both rule through secret police – KGB or Gestapo. They are interchangeable – as are the systems. I prefer Chancellor Langer's party. And now, if you will excuse me ...'

'Take a cigar with you – they are Havanas ...'

'From Cuba?' Martel was standing, his expression ironical as he stared down at the German. 'Thank you – but I smoke only cigarettes. It has been most illuminating meeting you. Goodnight.'

It has been most illuminating meeting you ... The words disturbed Dietrich because he sensed a hidden meaning. He watched the Englishman stroll to the lift, his eyes narrowed as he recalled the conversation word for word, trying to decide whether he had made a slip.

A girl who had been talking to the receptionist had reached

the lift first and was entering it when Martel called out, asking her in German, please could she hold it? The lift ascended out of sight with both passengers aboard.

The third floor landing was deserted as Martel escorted Claire out of the lift. Unlocking the door of his own room, he ushered her inside, closed the door and gripped her arm. She remained quite still in the darkness while Martel checked the bathroom. He then closed all the curtains and turned on the bedside lights which gave out a shaded glow. She began reporting at once.

'I worked the same trick when those two werewolves arrived. I saw their registration forms and the one who seems to be boss is Erwin Vinz. His sidekick—the driver of the car in Bregenz ...'

'I know ...'

'He goes under the name Rolf Gross. Both registered as coming from Münich ...'

'Which is probably a lie. They're trained killers. Things are developing as I hoped—but faster than I expected. The enemy is here in force. My guess is Dietrich is here to see they don't botch the job of eliminating me as they did in Zürich, St. Gallen and Bregenz. Vinz and Gross do the job. Klara Beck provides back-up ...'

'She's a reptile,' Claire commented savagely. 'You should watch out for her — *the others* may be diversions. And why did you set out to provoke Dietrich? I heard every word both of you said — it was like a duel ...'

'It was a duel. He was weighing me up—I was doing the same with him. I thought he was a stiff-necked has-been, but he's no fool. He believes in what he's doing. He's ruthless and he's decisive. We have to be very careful ...'

'He might take action tonight?'

'No — because he's staying at the hotel. He won't risk being present when his dirty tricks squad goes into action. We'll still take precautions. You stay here for the night and we'll take turns—one sleeping, one in a chair with a gun handy.'

'And tomorrow?'

'First thing we approach this Sergeant Dorner of the Lindau

Water Police – the man who brought in Warner's body.'

'And the second thing?' she asked, watching him closely.

'Lay a trap for Delta.'

'I'm still not happy about tonight,' she persisted. 'In this hotel we have two men who are almost certainly killers – and one woman who is pure poison. You said Dietrich was decisive – I've the strongest feeling he'll move faster than you expect …'

CHAPTER 14

Thursday May 28

At eleven o'clock at night Martel realised Claire had been right. He had underestimated Reinhard Dietrich. The bedroom was in darkness, he was taking the first turn on guard and Claire was lying on the bed fast asleep. He heard sounds of activity at the entrance to the hotel.

Pulling aside the curtain over the side window he looked down. Below, outside the hotel entrance, a black, six-seater Mercedes was parked by the kerb, its engine gently ticking. A uniformed chauffeur stood by the rear door in the mist, a mist blurring the street lights which were vague haloes in the drifting vapour. A familiar figure emerged from the hotel, the rear door was opened and Reinhard Dietrich climbed inside.

Within a minute the large vehicle had driven away and a hushed silence descended. From the harbour direction came the mournful moan of gulls, like the sirens of ships at sea destined never to reach a port. A distant foghorn sighed. And there was a third sound – the creak of a door opening or closing from the Hauptbahnhof.

He moved to his suitcase, felt inside, extracted a light raincoat and slipped it on. The bedsprings stirred and Claire called out, no more than a whisper.

'Something has happened, Keith?'

He went over to the bed where she lay fully dressed and placed a reassuring hand on her shoulder. He could smell the faint aroma of perfume. What was it about women that never made them forget their personal impact when they were exhausted – when they were living on their nerves?

'You were right,' he said. 'Dietrich has tricked us. He gave the impression he was staying the night and now he has left in a chauffeur-driven limousine. Something is going to happen ...'

'What do we do?' she asked calmly.

'One trump card is they don't know there are two of us – they think I'm on my own ...'

'So?'

'Slip back to your own room – be careful no one sees you.'

'And what are you going to be doing?'

'Contacting the local police. It's late but I want to talk with Sergeant Dorner. My guess is he's the only man in Lindau we can trust ...'

'You're going out in this fog? It is still foggy?'

'Thicker than ever. Which is helpful. More difficult for anyone to see me leaving and where I go. It's only a short distance – you showed me on the map ...'

'I'm coming with you!' She sat up in bed and felt for her shoes on the floor. 'I can watch your back ...'

'Go to your room before I belt you ...'

'You are a very stupid man and I don't like you much. Bloody well take care ...'

He waited until she had gone before venturing out. And he had deliberately not mentioned the creaking door. If she had known about that he would never have got rid of her.

The atmosphere of menace hit Martel the moment he walked out into the night. Mist globules settled on his face. The damp chill penetrated his thin coat. He could just make out the bulk of the Hauptbahnhof as he turned right and headed for Ludwigstrasse, a narrow, cobbled street which was the direct route to police headquarters.

There was no one visible but he heard it again, the sound he had detected from his bedroom window three floors up – the *creak* of one of the station doors being opened. He was careful not to glance in that direction as he turned right again and proceeded along the centre of Ludwigstrasse – as far away as possible from the darkened alcoves of doorway recesses.

His rubber-soled shoes made no sound on the cobbles although he had to place his feet firmly on their surface – the street was slimy with dampness. He wore his grey-coloured raincoat, which merged with the atmosphere, unbuttoned. Anyone grabbing him would find themselves holding only the fabric of the coat. And he had easy access to the Colt in his shoulder holster. He stopped.

The sound of the foghorn out on the lake. But his acute hearing had caught a second sound – the whispering slither of a padded sleeve moving against a coat, something like Gannex material. Behind him.

The watcher waiting inside the Hauptbahnhof had heard nothing, he was convinced. But even in the mist he could have seen Martel's silhouette outlined for a few seconds against the glow of lights in the lounge as he left the hotel.

He stood motionless in a shadowed area and the whispering stopped. Somewhere behind him his follower realised that Martel had also paused. The trouble was the bastards probably knew every inch of Lindau. *Their* problem was they could not be sure of his destination.

He started walking again suddenly, sensing there were several men somewhere in the mist. There *would* be several: Delta operated in strength. He had not forgotten Zürich where men had poured out of the two cars. He had been counting side-turnings and came to a street light, a milky globe supported by a wall-bracket. *Krummgasse.*

Martel had no option. To reach the main street, Maximilianstrasse, he had to leave the dubious safety of the narrow Ludwigstrasse and make his way along the even narrower alley of Krummgasse. Moving away from the blurred glow of the light he stared into the well of darkness. Once he negotiated Krummgasse he was within shouting distance of the police station.

Behind him he heard again the slither of sleeve against cloth. They were moving in. Reinhard Dietrich would be miles away — his previous presence totally unlinked with the murder of a second Englishman in the Lindau area. Martel went inside Krummgasse — taking longer strides to confuse the man behind him, accustomed to his earlier, slower pace.

Martel's vision was exceptional and he was peering ahead. For the moment he had out-distanced the follower behind. He stopped again and heard no whispering slither. His tactic was to get to the more open Maximilianstrasse and then sprint for police headquarters. *Ahead of him* he heard the squeak of a shoe.

The mouse in the trap. Himself. A man — men? — coming up behind. And the enemy also in front just when he was close to the end of Krummgasse. Delta had planned well. The moment he entered Ludwigstrasse they had guessed his destination — or assumed the one place he must never be allowed to reach. The police station.

So at the end of each alley leading from Ludwigstrasse to the parallel street, Maximilianstrasse, they had positioned a soldier. The squeaking shoe suggested the man in front was advancing down Krummgasse towards him, closing the pincer movement. Martel darted into the shadowed recess of a doorway and prayed that Squeaky Shoe would arrive quickly.

Something solid emerged from the swirling mist, right hand projected forward like a fencer about to lunge. With his left hand Martel extracted a Swiss five-franc coin from his pocket and tossed it across the street. *Clunk!*

In the hushed silence the sound was surprisingly loud and the man, who seemed familiar — something about his marionette-like movements — stopped next to the Englishman's doorway, glancing the other way. There was still no repetition of the slither — so the follower behind was a distance away. Martel moved.

The man sensed danger, turned and held his right hand ready to ram it forward. The barrel of Martel's Colt crashed down on the would-be assassin's head with tremendous force. Martel felt the barrel hammer through a hat, strike the skull and reverberate off it. The attacker slumped and lay in a twisted heap on the cobbles like a pile of old clothes.

Martel ran. Reaching the end of the alley he turned right and by the glow of a street lantern read the legend *Stadtpolizei* on a wall-plate. The entrance was round the corner in Bismarck-platz. He shoved open the door and stopped in front of a counter behind which a startled policeman gazed at him.

He slammed down a piece of plastic like a credit card on to the counter and slipped the Colt back inside its holster as the policeman surreptitiously unbuttoned his hip holster. Still short of breath, he gasped out the words.

'Sergeant Dorner! And bloody quick! If he's at home get him out of bed. There's my identification. And send a couple of men to Krummgasse. There should be a body for them to trip over ...'

'We've had an alert out for you, Martel – they should have seen you when you crossed the Bavarian border ...'

Martel was impressed by Sergeant Dorner. A short, burly man in his early forties, he had sandy hair, shrewd grey eyes with a hint of humour, and a general air of a man who knew what he was doing, a man not frightened to take decisions.

Martel was seated across a table from the police officer on the second floor of the building overlooking Bismarckplatz, drinking a cup of strong coffee. It was very good coffee.

They had found the body lying in Krummgasse, the body Martel had identified as Rolf Gross, the second man who had arrived late at the Bayerischer Hof. They had found more than that. Underneath the corpse – Martel's powerful blow had split Gross's skull – was lying what Dorner called a 'flick hypodermic'. He held up the weapon with the needle projecting inside a plastic bag.

'You were lucky,' Dorner commented. 'And this clears you. The fingerprint boys checked Gross's against those on the handle. It must look like a felt-tip pen before this button is pressed and the needle shoots out. Forensic were dragged out of bed to tell me what it contains ...'

'And what is inside it?'

'Potassium cyanide in solution. It's the kind of weapon you'd expect the Soviets to have dreamt up ...'

'Maybe they did ...'

'But these people are Delta – neo-Nazis. I've never seen any weapon like it before ...'

'I have. It's a Delta special,' Martel replied with grim humour. 'So how do you account for the fact that neo-Nazis are using it?'

'I don't,' Dorner admitted. 'Nothing makes sense about what is going on. We're finding the caches of their weapons and uniforms with Delta badges too easily ...'

'*Too easily?*'

'Yes. Erich Stoller of the BND is on his way here. I got him out of bed, too ...' Dorner lowered his voice. 'When Stoller flew here after Warner's body was found he told me he has an informant who regularly passes on the location of these arms dumps. Always in an uninhabited place – an abandoned farm building, an empty villa.'

'In other words you get the arms, the uniforms – the *news* in the press – but you never grab a single person?'

'Weird, isn't it?' Dorner stood up and lit a cheroot, staring out of the window he had closed against the mist. 'We get no individual, no record of a property owner we can trace. Just as we've been unable to locate any colleague of Gross's ...'

'I told you Erwin Vinz is staying at the Bayerischer Hof ...'

'Paid for his room and left ten minutes before my men got there. Said an urgent business message had called him away. I've put my best man on guard outside Claire Hofer's room – dressed as a porter, he's whiling away the night cleaning shoes.'

'Thanks.' Martel, almost dropping from lack of sleep, was beginning to approve of Sergeant Dorner more and more. 'And as I told you, Reinhard Dietrich was staying at the same hotel ...'

'Not *staying*,' Dorner corrected him. 'He arrives in that bloody great Mercedes, has a leisurely dinner, a chat with you – and then leaves. What do I charge him with? Eating too large a dinner and smoking Havana cigars?' He eased his large buttock on to the edge of his desk. 'Bloody frustrating . . .'

'So we set a trap – make them an offer they can't refuse.'

Dorner took the cheroot out of his mouth and frowned. 'Just what are you proposing?'

It took Martel one hour, the arrival of Erich Stoller, eight cups of coffee and four cheroots to obtain their backing for his plan.

CHAPTER 15

Friday May 29

Claire reports Warner made three mentions Operation Crocodile . . .

While Martel was finally catching up on his sleep at the Bayerischer Hof after the key meeting with Stoller and Dorner, Tweed – in his Maida Vale flat – was playing the same section of the tape-recording of Martel's report from St. Gallen over and over. It was the fifth time he had listened to the recording, he was alone and tired.

During the day there had been another row with Howard who was about to fly to Paris. There he was attending a meeting of the four security chiefs responsible for the security of the VIP's who – in only five days' time –would start their journey from Paris aboard the Summit Express bound for Vienna.

The British Prime Minister would fly to Charles de Gaulle Airport and from there would be driven direct to the Gare de l'Est. At about the same time the French President's motorcade would be on its way to the same destination.

The head of the French Secret Service in control of security for his President was Alain Flandres, an old friend of Tweed's. And the American President, flying the Atlantic direct to Orly

Airport in Air Force One, would be driven from there at high speed to join the others.

The security chief – head of the American Secret Service – responsible for his chief of state was Tim O'Meara, a man Tweed had met only once. It was a recent appointment. The fourth VIP – Chancellor Kurt Langer of West Germany – was scheduled to board the express the following morning at München. Erich Stoller of the BND would lose sleep watching over his master.

'Why this bloody train lark?' Tweed had asked Howard during the confrontation in his office. 'They could all fly direct to Vienna to meet the Soviet First Secretary. It would be a damned sight safer ...'

'The French President,' Howard had explained tersely. 'Hates flying. The excuse given is they'll all take the opportunity to coordinate policy at leisure before the train reaches Vienna. I do need every man possible and Martel ...'

'What's the route?'

'The direct one,' Howard had replied stiffly. He implied Tweed's knowledge of geography was limited. 'Paris to Strasbourg ...'

'Ulm, Stuttgart, München, Salzburg – then Vienna ...'

'Then why ask?' Howard rasped.

'To check no diversion is planned ...'

'Why the hell should there be one?'

'You tell me,' Tweed had replied, watching with some satisfaction as Howard stormed out of the office.

But Howard had cause to worry, Tweed thought later in the early hours in his flat. *The Times* atlas was open in front of him with the double-page spread of Plate 64 – South-West Germany including the northern tip of Switzerland. On it he followed a large section of the route from Strasbourg across Bavaria to Salzburg.

Operation Crocodile ...

What the hell could that be? He took off his glasses, rubbing his eyes. Without them everything -- including the map -- was blurred. You saw everything in simplified shapes. He raised a hand to close the atlas and then stopped, rigid, like a man unable to move. *He could see the crocodile!*

In the morning after breakfast Martel made an elaborate pantomime about hiring a launch from a man in Lindau harbour – the same harbour from which Charles Warner, also in a hired launch, started out on his last journey.

There was a lot of waving of hands. There were discussions about the merits of one vessel compared with another. There was debate as to how long he wanted to hire the craft for. Finally, there was lengthy argument about the price.

From a distance two women watched this carefully staged charade. Perched on a seat on the Romerschanze terrace over-looking the harbour, Claire played the role of tourist. And Martel had warned her again there must be no sign to tell a watcher that they knew each other.

She swivelled her field-glasses at apparent random. Lake Konstanz was living up to its unpredictable reputation. Fog-bound the previous evening, the new day was crystal clear with a vault of Mediterranean-like sky. To the south across the placid lake was a superb panorama of snow-tipped mountain peaks including the Three Sisters of Liechtenstein. A handful of tourists trudging round the waterfront added to the peaceful scene.

Klara Beck, also equipped with binoculars, sat on a seat on the front with the hotel behind her. She had not been forgotten by Martel who had reported her presence to Sergeant Dorner and Stoller the previous night.

'My men report Klara Beck is apparently staying the night at the hotel,' Dorner relayed to Martel after receiving a phone call.

'That I would expect,' Martel had commented.

'Why, may I ask?' enquired Stoller.

'Because Delta don't realise I know she belongs to them. She's had no contact with Dietrich since she arrived, no contact with Erwin Vinz or Rolf Gross – so she's the ideal person to leave behind as a spy. And in the morning I can use her ...'

Martel was using Beck now, Claire decided as she trained her lenses on the girl. Like Claire, Beck was using her binoculars and they were aimed in the direction of Martel.

'I think, dear, you're going to move soon,' Claire said to herself.

She left her seat, strolled down the steps to the harbour front and wandered slowly towards the hotel in the warming glow of the sun. Her timing was perfect. She was close to Beck's seat when the German girl got up and began walking rapidly back towards the Bayerischer Hof entrance. On the mole Martel had just ostentatiously shaken hands with the man he was hiring the launch from.

But when she turned the corner it was not the hotel Beck headed for. Instead she crossed the road, passed under the large tree where taxis waited and disappeared inside the Hauptbahnhof. Her shadow followed.

Pushing open a door, Claire glanced to her left and saw what she had expected. Beck was inside one of the telephone booths, making a call. Claire drifted over to a bookstall and started to look at paperbacks. The new development worried her.

Inside the phone booth Beck dialled a local number, cradled the receiver on her shoulder and looked towards the station exit. No one was there. At the other end of the line a man's voice responded as though waiting for her call.

'Hagen here ...'

'Werner, this is Klara ...'

'We are ready. Any joy?'

'The goods are aboard a grey launch. Departure imminent ...'

She broke the connection and left the station, crossing over to the hotel at a leisurely pace, drinking in the delight of the sun's warmth. On the steps she paused close to a pavement artist as he began drawing a fresh picture, taking out her cigarette pack.

'Watch for the police bringing back that grey launch,' she murmured.

She lit the cigarette and went into the lounge. She had just triggered off the execution of the second Englishman.

Sergeant Dorner was not looking where he was going as he walked down Ludwigstrasse towards the harbour. He crashed into the girl and would have knocked her over except for his swift grab round her shoulders with both hands. Claire Hofer, who had timed her arrival as agreed earlier, stood quite still. Dorner, wearing civilian clothes, spoke loudly.

'I do apologise. My own clumsy fault ...' His voice dropped, his lips scarcely moved. 'Everything is organised. Fifteen minutes from now the island is sealed ...'

Dorner left Claire who walked rapidly after checking her watch. Minutes – seconds – counted if the trap were to be successfully sprung. She turned down a short cut to the harbour front. Martel was aboard his launch, reached by climbing down a steep ladder attached to the side of the mole.

Claire glanced to her right, saw the pavement artist, Braun, as he strolled into view, hands clasped behind his back. Taking a brilliant red head-scarf out of her shoulder-bag she wrapped the covering round her head.

Aboard the launch Martel saw the flash of brilliant red cloth – the signal that everyone was in position. He caught a glimpse of Sergeant Dorner strolling round the harbour to where the large police launch was berthed. Lighting a cigarette, he watched Claire out of the corner of his eye. She was hurrying now towards the open-air bathing-pool walled off from the lake below the Romerschanze terrace.

Reaching the pool, she used the entrance ticket purchased earlier and entered one of the changing cubicles. With the door locked she stripped off her synthetic jersey dress, revealing the bikini she wore underneath. Slipping the rolled-up dress and her pistol inside a water-proof bag, she attached the bag to her wrist with a leather thong.

She left the shoulder-bag which was now empty inside the cubicle, locked the door, checked her waterproof watch and walked along the outer wall. At that time of day there was hardly anyone about. She dived off the wall into the lake.

Slipping loose the mooring rope, Martel went inside the cramped wheel-house of the launch and checked his watch – which earlier he had synchronised with Claire and Sergeant Dorner. Two minutes to go. He inserted a cigarette into his holder and lit it.

The only lingering traces of the mist which had shrouded Lake Konstanz the previous day covered the Austrian shore. The forecast promised a warm sunny day. It was a major factor Martel had taken into account when finalising his plan with Dorner and Stoller. And at this moment the BND chief was controlling operations from an office at *Stadtpolizei*.

Martel was careful not to look towards the eastern side of the harbour. Moored to its berth by the Lion Mole lay the two-decker launch of the Water Police commanded by Sergeant Dorner. The German was already below-decks, changing into official uniform after slipping aboard unnoticed. Martel double-checked his watch, took a deep breath and began to leave harbour.

Inside his office at *Stadtpolizei* Erich Stoller stood looking out of the window into the main street. It was just another day for the townspeople. Tourists sat at tables outside Hauser's drinking coffee and consuming cream cakes. Behind him on a heavy table were the transceiver and its operator – the key to Stoller's control.

With the use of the transceiver he could instantly communicate with police cars discreetly stationed near the road bridge, with other vehicles strategically placed on the mainland near the end of the rail embankment.

The transceiver also kept him in direct touch with Sergeant Dorner aboard the police launch still berthed in the harbour. A signal came over the transceiver.

'Siefried is riding ...'

Dorner had reported that Martel was on his way.

At a remote point on the misty shore five wind-surfers ran down the shallow beach to board their waiting craft. They were stationed midway between Lindau and the Austrian town of

Bregenz. Their leader, Werner Hagen, a six-foot blond giant, was running towards them, gesturing at the lake. He had been waiting by a telephone inside a deserted warehouse, waiting for the call from Klara Beck.

'He's leaving Lindau harbour,' he shouted as he ran to his own sail. 'A grey launch. Martel alone is aboard ...'

They wore swimming trunks as they manoeuvred their sails into the gentle breeze. Round each man's wrist was a belt from which hung a sheath encasing a large throwing knife. A silver triangle, the Delta symbol, was attached to the side of their trunks. The team of executioners, led by Werner Hagen, headed for a position about half a mile outside Lindau harbour.

'Thank God I found you – it was difficult in this mist ...'

Claire leaned against the hull of the launch where Martel had hauled her aboard. With her legs stretched out and her bosom heaving with the recent effort she let Martel untie the leather thong and place the waterproof bag beside her.

The launch was stationary. Martel had taken it out through the harbour exit moving slowly, sounding his siren – according to regulations for ships entering or leaving – for longer than necessary to help Claire locate him. A wind was blowing up, making a low whining sound which got on Claire's nerves.

'You think they'll come?' she asked.

'Damned sure of it ...'

She extracted from the bag her dress and the 9-mm pistol. He looked at the dress and picked it up to take it inside the wheelhouse. 'This won't be much good for you to wear ...' He came out checking the action of his .45 Colt and slipped it back inside the shoulder holster.

'It's synthetic jersey cloth,' she told him. 'I chose it since it's practically crease-proof ...'

She broke off, realising his attention was elsewhere. He still had the engine switched off as he peered eastward into the grey, thinning mist. The light wind was dispersing it slowly.

'You think they're coming from over there?' Claire asked.

'It's the shortest distance from a shoreline where they're least likely to be detected. In a minute you put on this face-mask – if one of them gets away I don't want you recognised ...'

'And that thing?' She pointed to a bulky instrument on the small chart-table in the wheelhouse. 'Is it radar?'

'It's a tape-recorded signal which does two things – it signals Stoller at his headquarters when I press a button – warning him we're under attack. It also sends out a continuous signal which Dorner in his police launch can pick up to home in on where we are.'

'You worked this out pretty well,' Claire commented.

'Because from the Warner killing I know we're up against a first-class brain who thinks out *his* plans well ...'

'Reinhard Dietrich?'

'No. An international anarchist called Manfred.' Martel was inside the wheelhouse, about to start up the engine. 'And I should never have agreed to your coming ...'

'But you did!'

'So put on your face-mask and shut up,' he told her brusquely, then fired the engine.

The mist had cleared in the west where the vast waters of the lake stretched away like an oil blue sheet. On the eastern mole of Lindau harbour the Lion of Bavaria was a massive silhouette as they got under way.

Claire had adjusted the face-mask and after checking her pistol tucked the weapon inside the top of her pants. Martel's instructions – given to her earlier in his room at the hotel – had been precise.

'If they come – as they came for Warner – I need one man alive so I can work on him. After what they did to Warner, the rest can drown ...'

Martel kept down the launch's speed, heading out direct across the lake towards the distant Rhine delta. That, he was convinced, was the lonely country where Warner had intended to make his landfall.

One thing bothered him. The grey pall to the east between the launch and the Austrian shoreline was persisting. How could anyone moving in from that direction locate him? And if they did they would be on top of the launch almost before he saw them. Looking again towards Austria he saw movement in the mist.

Werner Hagen gripped his sail with one hand while he checked the compact device attached to the mast. It was a miniature radar set designed at Dietrich's electronics factory in Arizona. Martel's launch showed clearly on the screen.

He's following Warner's route, Hagen thought.

He made a gesture to the other five wind-surfers who were closer together than would be their normal tactic: it was vital they did not lose sight of each other. The gesture told them the target had been sighted. And the mist was lifting as they glided across the rippled waters of the lake.

Hagen timed it nicely, keeping one eye on the radar screen, the other on the dispersing wall of vapour ahead. He held on to the sail with his left hand and dropped his right, unsheathing the razor-edge knife which had carved out of Warner's back the crude outline of Delta's symbol. Then he saw the launch, made a fresh gesture and the team curved in a semi-circle to force Martel to stop.

It happened too fast for comfort. One moment the views from the wheelhouse showed a vague disturbance in the wall of mist, shapes which could have been a mirage. Then six wind-surfers appeared, three of them steering their sails across the course Martel was following, compelling him to stop the engine.

'They're here,' he yelled to Claire and pushed the signal button.

'I've seen them!'

She knelt with her back to the wheelhouse, holding the pistol out of sight, gripping the butt with both hands.

'They're under attack!'

Crouched inside the wheelhouse of the police launch Sergeant Dorner watched the winking bleep which had suddenly appeared on his specially adapted radar screen.

Standing up in full view, he switched on the powerful engine which flared with a roar.

Dorner knew that at this moment there would be no lake steamer approaching the entrance but he obeyed regulations, sounding his siren as the launch rushed from its berth – the mooring rope had been surreptitiously slipped free when he sneaked on board.

Parallel to the exit, he stopped the forward rush and swung his wheel well over, turning the craft through ninety degrees, thrashing up a wake which transformed the harbour into a turmoil of waves and froth. With his bow aimed between the two moles he opened the throttle, his siren screaming non-stop. The launch shot forward as he increased speed, checking the blip on his screen.

'Get me there in time,' Dorner prayed.

Klara Beck had decided not to leave the excitement to Braun so she had occupied the same seat on the front. Confident, now that she had made her vital telephone call, she had been relaxing and gazing round like a tourist. The sudden departure of the police launch appalled her.

She hurried along the promenade, dashed across the street and into the Hauptbahnhof. She was half-way to the row of telephone booths when she stopped. Across the window of each booth a gummed sticker carried the legend *Out of Order*. A uniformed policeman strolled up to her and she fought down a moment of panic.

'You wished to use the phone?' he enquired.

'They can't *all* be out of order,' she protested.

'The notice is clear enough,' he replied less politely. 'They are working on the fault now.'

'Thank you …'

She made herself walk out of the Hauptbahnhof slowly. Her pace quickened as she went across to the Bayerischer Hof. Once in her room she picked up the receiver to dial a number. A girl's voice came on the line.

'I am very sorry but there is a temporary breakdown in the

phone system. Would you like to give me a number and I will call you as soon as ...'

'It's not important ...'

Exerting her exceptional self-control Klara Beck put down the receiver and lit a cigarette. God, would she be blamed for not warning Dietrich. What the bloody hell was going on?

'Cut all the lines to the mainland ...'

At the police station Erich Stoller gave the order immediately he received Martel's signal. In the same room with him a policeman sat with the phone to his ear – the line held open to the exchange where they were waiting for precisely this order. The turning of three switches isolated Lindau island from all telephonic communication with the outside world.

On hearing the order a second policeman left the room and ran to the radio-control office. A signal went out to patrol-cars strategically placed in advance. The road bridge to the mainland was blocked. Other patrol-cars appeared at the mainland end of the rail embankment, closing off the cycle track and footpath.

A 'fault' developed in the signal box controlling rail traffic to Lindau, stopping all trains. Only a man with Stoller's authority could have achieved this result. Now his main worry was what might be happening out on the lake.

Werner Hagen was supremely confident as he led his team of wind-surfers to encircle and engulf the launch. The element of surprise was everything. The blond giant was the first to reach the port side of the stationary launch and he placed one bare foot over the side prior to temporarily abandoning his sail. His right hand held the large-bladed knife ready for the first lunge.

He was surprised to see a girl, her features concealed behind a face-mask, and then he was otherwise occupied. Martel came out of the wheelhouse wielding a boat-hook. He had guessed Hagen was the leader – it was written all over him.

The swing of the boat-hook ended as it struck Hagen a vicious blow at the side of the head. He sprawled full-length inside the launch, lifting his head in time to meet the carefully calculated thud of Martel's gun barrel. He collapsed unconscious.

A second man was coming aboard, knife in hand, when Claire aimed her pistol and shot him three times in the chest. Blood spurted and formed a pool below the deck-planks. Martel looked round and summed up the situation. Four killers left. Three still forming a crescent round his bow, another coming up behind the stern. He heaved Claire's target overboard, dashed back inside the wheelhouse and opened up full throttle.

The trio blocking his passage could not react in time. The launch moved too suddenly, too fast. One moment it was stationary, then it was a projectile hurtling towards them, its bow smashing their frail craft, weathered wood hammering into pliable flesh.

One man, giving a final scream, was literally keel-hauled as the launch beat his already-broken body to pulp. The other two men lay floating close together in a patch of lake which suddenly became red, their bodies crumpled like the relics of their sails.

'There's the man behind us,' Claire called out.

Martel was already taking appropriate action as he put the engine into reverse and moved backwards at speed, steering by glancing over his shoulder. The stern of the launch struck the surviving killer, he fell and the propeller passed over him.

'We'll run for it,' he told Claire. 'I think I see Dorner on the way ...'

Friday May 29

It was a sunny, hot, sweaty day in Paris when Howard flew in to Charles de Gaulle. He was attending the conference to finalise security aboard the Summit Express. Typically he travelled alone. Typically he wore country tweeds.

From the airport a car sent by Alain Flandres drove him to No. 11, rue des Saussaies, official headquarters of the Sûreté. This narrow, twisting street, only a few minutes' walk from the Elysée, is rarely noticed by tourists. Inside an archway uniformed policemen watch the entrance.

Flandres often chose the complex of sombre old buildings for a clandestine meeting. The place was well-guarded, there was much coming and going by plain-clothes detectives – so the arrival of three civilians in separate cars was unlikely to attract attention. The head of the French Secret Service was waiting to greet Howard in a second-floor room equipped with a table, chairs and little else.

'Good to see you, Alain,' Howard said tersely.

'I am delighted to welcome you to Paris, my friend,' Flandres replied enthusiastically as he shook hands and turned to a man already seated at the table.

'You know Tim O'Meara, of course? Just in from Washington ...'

'We had the pleasure of meeting once,' the American interjected. He shook hands without rising from his chair and resumed smoking his cigar.

They sat round the highly polished table while Flandres poured drinks. Howard fiddled with the new pad and pencil in front of him, sitting stiff-backed. O'Meara did not improve on further acquaintance he was thinking. Heavily built, in his early fifties, the American had a large head, was clean-shaven, wore rimless glasses and exuded self-confidence. He did not behave as the 'new boy'.

The fact was Tim O'Meara had only been chief of the American Secret Service detachment which guarded his President for a year. In his loud check sports jacket – he also was obviously playing the tourist – he settled his bulk in his chair as though he had been a member of the club for a decade.

As he poured the drinks Alain Flandres observed all this with a hint of Gallic amusement. Short and of slim build, Flandres was impeccably dressed in a lounge suit despite the heat. Also in his early fifties, the Frenchman's features were finely chiselled and he sported a trim, pencil-style moustache the same colour as his well-brushed dark hair.

'Erich Stoller from Germany is due any moment,' he announced as he settled in his own chair and lifted his glass. 'Gentlemen – welcome!'

He sipped at his cognac, noted that Howard took a big gulp while O'Meara swallowed half his glass of neat Scotch. There was tension under the surface, Flandres observed. This was a gathering of nervous men. Who was the catalyst?

The door opened and Erich Stoller was ushered into the room. His tall, thin figure was in extreme contrast to the other three, as was his manner. He tended to listen, to say very little. He apologised for his late arrival.

'An unexpected problem required my urgent attention ...'

He left it at that. It was mid-afternoon and he had no wish to reveal that in the morning he had been in Lindau, sealing off the island while Martel took his launch on to the lake. He'd had the devil of a rush to reach Paris – involving a helicopter flight to Münich airport where a plane had waited for him.

'Only some beer,' he told Flandres, sitting bolt upright in his chair. An excellent psychologist, he proceeded to throw Howard completely off Martel's scent by irritating him. 'And how is my friend, Tweed?' he enquired. 'I expected to see him here ...'

'Tweed is home-based these days,' Howard said curtly, his face very bony. 'Getting on in years, you know ...'

'Really? I thought you were both the same age,' Stoller remarked blandly and drank some beer.

'This isn't his territory,' Howard snapped. 'Maybe we can get on with the subject which brought us to Paris?'

'But, of course!' Flandres agreed, even more amused by this exchange. 'I have the route of the Summit Express ...' He proceeded to unroll a large-scale map of Northern Europe with the route marked in red. He sat back in his chair and lit a cigarette watching the others study the sheet.

Alain Flandres, whose handsome features and easy charm proved so irresistible to women, also had a flair for the dramatic. He made the remark casually and three heads bent over the map jerked up.

'A sighting of Carlos – Manfred – call him what you like, was reported in London this morning – in Piccadilly to be precise ...'

'*Manfred!* How the hell do *you* know what's happening in London? And will someone tell me whether he really is Carlos?'

It was Howard who had exploded. Flandres noted he was edgier than he had realised. Why, he wondered? In a casual tone of voice the Frenchman explained.

'A girl operative of mine, Renée Duval, is working at the French Embassy for the moment. This telex just came in from her with an extract from your midday paper.' While Howard read the strip the Frenchman handed him, Erich Stoller commented on Carlos.

'Carlos has no known base. Manfred has no known base. No one is sure of the real appearance of Carlos. The same applies to Manfred. Carlos has been known to take temporary refuge behind the Iron Curtain – as has Manfred. Both are independants who cooperate with the KGB only when it suits them ...'

'So there *are* two of them?' Howard broke in.

'Or,' O'Meara intervened in his gravelly voice, 'has Carlos *invented* two of them – if so, which is the real one? You omitted, Erich, to add that both men – *if* two exist – are brilliant assassins

Flandres studied the American more closely. That is a most telling point you have made, my friend, he was thinking. Howard coloured with annoyance at Stoller's next question.

'Could you be more precise about this sighting in London? How was he dressed? Why was he recognised so easily?'

'His usual "uniform",' Howard murmured reluctantly. 'Windcheater, jeans, his dark beret and very large tinted glasses.'

'Can you elaborate on this incident?' the German persisted.

'He was recognised by a policeman patrolling on foot. Carlos – if it was Carlos – vanished up Swallow Street leading to Regent Street. The policeman pursued him and lost him in the crowds. Later, one of the assistants in Austin Reed, a nearby man's outfitter, found on a chair the windcheater with the beret and glasses on top. Underneath the windcheater was a loaded .38 Smith & Wesson . . .'

'A *patrolling* policeman,' Stoller continued. 'He was walking up and down a particular section of this street?'

'I imagine so, yes. Probably keeping an eye open for IRA suspects. Where is all this leading to?' Howard demanded.

'Someone dressed in this manner could have made sure the policeman did see him and then disappeared?'

'I suppose so, although I hardly see the point . . .'

O'Meara relit his cigar. 'A Havana,' he explained. 'I have to get through this box before I return to the States where, as you must know, they are contraband.'

Stoller, after his unusual burst of conversation, lapsed into silence and Flandres had the eerie impression the German was studying one particular person. But he could not identify which man had for some unknown reason aroused the BND chief's interest.

They proceeded with the main business in hand – planning security for their respective political heads attending the Vienna Summit. The rail journey was broken down into sectors. The division into sectors was marked on the map.

Paris to Strasbourg – French. From Strasbourg via Stuttgart and Münich to Salzburg – German. The last stage, Salzburg to

Vienna – American, with nominal cooperation from the Austrians. Alain Flandres, in sparkling good humour, did most of the talking.

Howard was allocated a 'mobile' role – his team would cover all three sectors. Flandres went over his sector in detail, pointing out potential danger points from terrorist attack – embankments, bridges. O'Meara, puffing his cigar, decided the Frenchman knew his job.

Then it was Erich Stoller's turn and again O'Meara was impressed. The German paused as he reached a certain point on the map and was silent for a short time. Something in his manner heightened the tension inside the airless room as he prodded with his finger.

'Here the express crosses into Bavaria. There is a certain instability in this area. It is unfortunate the state elections take place the day after the train crosses this sector ...'

'The neo-Nazi business? Delta?' Howard enquired.

'Tofler,' O'Meara said with great conviction. 'His support is growing with each fresh discovery of more Delta arms and uniforms. And Tofler is a near-Communist. His programme includes plans for detaching Bavaria from West Germany and making it a "neutral" province or state like Austria. That would smash NATO and hand Western Europe to the Soviets on a platter ...'

'Chancellor Langer is fully aware of the problem,' Stoller said quietly. 'His advisers tell him Tofler will not win ...'

Flandres arranged for excellent food and drink to be brought in and they continued going over the route untile late in the evening. The Frenchman sipped at his glass of wine as he looked round at his colleagues, all of whom were now in shirt-sleeves. The evening was warm and clammy. The bombshell fell after he made his remark.

'I am beginning to think, gentlemen, that the main requirement for our job is stamina ...'

He broke off as an armed guard entered the room and handed him a message. He read it, frowned and looked at Howard. 'This says the British ambassador is outside with an urgent signal which he must pass to you at once.'

'The *Ambassador*?' Howard was shaken but nothing showed in his expression. 'You mean he has sent a messenger . . .'

'I mean the Ambassador in person,' Flandres said firmly. 'And I understand he wishes to hand you the signal himself while you are present at this meeting.'

'Please ask him to come in,' Howard requested the guard.

A tall distinguished man with a white moustache entered the room holding a folded slip of paper. Everyone stood, brief introductions took place, and Sir Henry Crawford handed the folded slip to Howard.

'Came direct to me, Anthony – in my personal code. No one except myself knows about it. It was accompanied by a request that I came here myself. Reasonable enough – when you read the contents.' He looked round the room. 'A pleasure to meet you all and now, if you will excuse me . . .'

Howard had unfolded the slip and read it several times before he sat down and gazed round the table. His expresssion was unfathomable but the atmosphere had changed. The Englishman spoke quietly, without a trace of emotion.

'This signal is from Tweed in London. He makes an assertion – I emphasise he gives no clue as to his source. Only the gravity of the assertion compels me to pass it on to you under such circumstances . . .'

'If Tweed makes an assertion,' Flandres commented, 'then we can be sure he has grounds for doing so. The more serious the assertion the less likely he is to reveal the source. It might endanger the informant's life . . .'

'Quite so.' Howard was aware that his armpits were stained with dampness. He cleared his throat, glanced at each man and read out the contents of the signal.

Reliable source has just reported unknown assassin will attempt to eliminate one – repeat one – of four VIP's aboard Summit Express. No indication yet as to which of four will be target. Tweed.

Friday May 29

On the morning of the day when the four security chiefs met in Paris for their afternoon conference, Martel's launch headed for a remote landing-stage on the eastern shore of Lake Konstanz.

Werner Hagen, sole survivor of the wind-surfer execution squad, lay helpless in the bottom of the launch. His mouth was gagged, wrists, knees and ankles were bound with strong rope and a band of cloth was tied round his eyes. All he could hear was the chugging of the engine, all he could feel was the compression of the ropes and the glow of the sun on his face.

Inside the wheelhouse Martel steered the craft closer to their objective, guided by Claire who stood alongside him. The mist had dispersed, the shoreline was clear, and he slowed down until they were almost drifting as he scanned the deserted stony beach, the crumbling relic of a wooden landing-stage.

'You're sure we won't run into someone – campers, people like that,' he checked as the momentum carried them forward in a glide.

'Stop fussing,' she chided. 'I told you – I know this area. I used to meet Warner here when he came down from München. And last night I parked the hired Audi among those trees before I walked to the nearest railway station to catch a train back to Lindau.'

'I don't see the Audi . . .'

'You're not bloody meant to see it!' she exploded. 'When are you going to give me credit for being able to cope on my own? You know your trouble, Martel?'

'If I don't do a job myself I start worrying about it . . .'

'Right! So have a little faith. And – before you ask me – I do know the way to that old water-mill I mentioned, which is another place where Warner and I used to meet. Although why we're driving there I don't understand . . .'

'To interrogate Blond Boy . . .'

He had carried Werner Hagen to the car and dumped him on the floor in the rear, folding him up like a huge doll so no part of him protruded above window level. Then he had relaxed while Claire took the wheel and drove them some distance to another crumbling relic – the water-mill, located at a remote spot in the Bavarian countryside.

Everything was exactly as Claire had described it. There was no way of guessing the purpose the mill had once served – but the huge wheel still turned ponderously as foaming water from the rapids behind the structure revolved the wheel. Martel studied the wheel, watching the blades dip below the surface before they emerged dripping to commence another revolution.

'Yes,' he decided, 'it will work . . .'

'What will work?'

'My new version of the old Chinese water torture. Blond Boy has to talk . . .'

It took their combined strength to manhandle the German into the required position. Before they started Martel told Clair to don her face-mask again. 'To scare the living daylights out of him he has to *see* – which means removing his blindfold. Tuck your hair up inside the back of your mask. You're wearing the slacks left in the car – he'll think you're a man . . .'

With her face-mask adjusted she helped Martel as he stood on the platform above the slow-turning wheel. They spread-eagled Hagen over a part of the wheel clear of the water and moved rapidly – whipping more rope round his recently-freed ankles and attaching them to one of the huge blades.

To make it worse, Martel had laid the German with his head downwards so it submerged under the water first while the upper part of his body was still above the surface. It took them ten minutes to secure Hagen's splayed body to the wheel and then the blindfold was removed. He glared with hatred at Martel and then a look of doubt crossed his handsome face as he caught sight of the sinister figure of Claire.

Standing very erect, wearing Martel's jacket to conceal her bosom, she stared through the face-mask at the German with her arms crossed, her pistol in her right hand. She looked the epitome of a professional executioner.

Then the wheel dipped again and Hagen took a deep breath for when he went under the water. The trouble was the slow revolution of the wheel kept him submerged for longer than he could hold his breath. He surfaced spluttering water, his lungs heaving. He knew there was a limit to the period of time he could survive the ordeal.

There was another factor Hagen found increasingly difficult to combat. The circular rotation was disorientating and he was becoming dizzy. His great fear was he would lose consciousness, taking in a great draught of water while submerged.

Martel made a gesture that they retreated from the platform to the river bank. He inserted a cigarette into his holder and lit it as the wheel continued its endless revolutions. Away from the shade of the water-mill the sun beat down on them out of a sky like brass.

'We can talk now without him hearing us,' he remarked. 'He is, of course, slowly drowning . . .'

'Let him,' Claire said calmly, her face-mask eased up clear of her mouth. 'He's probably the one who carved up Charles . . .'

'The female of the species . . .'

'How long are you going to leave him?' she enquired.

'Until I gauge his resistance is broken. When we release him he has to talk immediately. I just hope he knows something . . .'

They waited until Hagen was on the verge of losing consciousness, until he was swallowing huge quantities of water each time he went under. Claire re-adjusted her face-mask and they ran to the platform. They had the devil of a job freeing Hagen: constant immersion in water had made the ropes impossible to untie. Martel used a knife he kept inside a sheath strapped to his left leg.

When he carried the water-logged man to the river bank Martel had to work on him, kneading his body to eject water. Claire sat on a rock a short distance away, her pistol aimed at the German. The first question Martel fired was an inspired guess.

'Who are you?'

'Reinhard Dietrich's nephew and heir . . .'

Only the face-mask concealed Claire's astonishment at the reply. They had hit pure gold. She remained still and menacing as Martel continued the interrogation.

'Name?'

'Werner Hagen — you know these things . . .'

'Just answer the questions.' He waited while Hagen coughed and cleared his lungs. 'What is the Delta deadline for Operation Crocodile?'

'June 3 — the day before the election . . .' He paused and Claire sensed his powers of resistance were returning. She raised her pistol in her right hand, used her left arm as a balance and took deliberate aim.

'Oh God, stop him!' Hagen pleaded with Martel. 'I'm answering your questions. I want out of the whole bloody business. Something's wrong. Vinz's . . .'

'You said June 3. You were going to add something,' Martel prodded.

'The key is the Summit Express will be moving across Bavaria . . .'

'All this we know,' Martel lied. 'Warner got the information to London.' He puffed at his cigarette to let his statement sink in. 'I simply want confirmation from you about Delta's flashpoint for June 3 . . .'

'You know that!' The surprise was apparent in Hagen's tone. He was still in a state of disorientation.

'So why not tell us what is worrying you — something to do with the Summit Express? Yes?'

'One of the four western leaders aboard is going to be assassinated . . .'

The statement sent Martel into a state of shock although nothing in his expression betrayed the reaction. His teeth clenched on the holder a fraction tighter and he continued the interrogation.

'Who is the target?'

'I don't know! *God in heaven, I really don't know . . .!*'

Hagen's shout — caused by Martel's glance towards the revolving wheel — was convincing.

'How do you know any of this? You — a mere lad,' Martel jibed, 'but a murderous thug at that . . .'

'Because I'm Reinhard Dietrich's nephew!' Hagen flared. 'I'm regarded as his son, the son his wife never provided. He confides in me . . .'

'You said earlier "I want out of the whole bloody business. Something's wrong." Don't think about it! Tell me quickly — what is wrong?'

'I'm not sure I know,' Hagen replied sulkily.

'I'm waiting for a reply,' Martel reminded him. 'The trouble is, I'm not a patient man.'

'My uncle is supposed to take over Bavaria in the coming election. The people are turning to us because they fear the party of Tofler, the Bolshevik.' He was recovering rapidly, sitting with a frown on his face. 'But as soon as we build up a store of uniforms and arms for the militia to be formed when we win, the BND discover them — as though someone is informing the BND . . .'

'And who is going to assassinate one of the western leaders?'

Martel threw the question at him. Hagen stood up slowly. 'I have the cramp . . .' He bent down and massaged the calf of his left leg, then straightened up, flexing his hands.

'I told you I'm not a patient man,' Martel snapped.

'The assassin — again I swear I do not know his identity — is one of the four security chiefs supposed to be guarding the western leaders . . .'

The reply threw Martel completely off guard for the fraction of a second. It was all Hagen needed. He rushed forward, aiming a blow at Claire which knocked her off the rock she had perched on. She could have pulled the trigger but knew Martel wanted the German alive.

Hagen's headlong rush was intended to carry him to cover behind the water-mill before either captor could react. It carried him forward as he intended but he stumbled over a protruding outcrop of rock close to the water-mill.

He screamed, hands outstretched to save himself. Claire heard the horrid sound of his skull striking one of the descending metal blades and the scream faded to a gurgle. He lay motionless, head and shoulders in the river. A gush of blood welled, mingling with the peaceful sound of tumbling water.

Claire ran forward, steadied herself on the slope and checked Hagen's neck pulse as Martel came up behind her. Standing up she looked at the Englishman, shaking her head.

'He's dead. What do we do now?'

'Get him back to civilisation and contact Stoller or Dorner at once. I have to find a safe phone to call Tweed.'

They reached police headquarters in Lindau with the body concealed in the back of the car under Martel's raincoat. Dorner gave them the news without preamble.

'Erich Stoller left a message strictly for your ears – he flew to Paris for a security conference. I will make arrangements about Hagen – Stoller will want him sent by special ambulance to a morgue in München. As to making a phone call to London which can't be intercepted, the answer is the Post Office . . .'

Dorner drove them there himself. They were closing the doors when the German gently pushed them open and escorted his two companions inside.

A few words from Dorner persuaded the switchboard operator to call the London number. Martel first tried the Maida Vale flat and was relieved when he heard Tweed's voice which sounded weary. The voice changed pitch when Tweed realised who was calling. He activated the recording machine, rushed through the identification procedure and spoke before Martel could say any more.

'Operation *Crocodile*, Keith. You're standing in the middle of it. Look at a map of southern Germany through half-closed eyes – concentrate on the shape of Lake Konstanz. The damned thing is just like a crocodile – jaws open to the west with the two inlets, Uberlingersee and Untersee ...'

'That confirms my data – something is scheduled to happen in Bavaria. Reinhard Dietrich's nephew, Werner Hagen, talked before he left us permanently ...'

Crouched over the table in his flat Tweed gripped the receiver more tightly. Events were piling on top of each other – always the most delicate and dangerous phase in an operation. He listened as Martel continued.

'One of the four VIP's aboard the Summit Express is scheduled for assassination on the train. Do you read me ...'

'Of course I do.' Tweed's voice and manner had never been calmer. 'Give them numbers – starting geographically from west to east. Which number is the target ...'

'Informant didn't know ...'

'At least we're alerted. Aboard the train – I've got that. Identity of assassin?'

The question Martel was dreading. Would Tweed think he had gone off his rocker? He took a deep breath, thankful that Dorner had stayed with the switchboard operator so no one could overhear this call.

'I'm convinced – and so is my colleague – that this next bit of information provided by Hagen is genuine. You have to trust my judgement ...'

'Get on with it, man ...'

'The killer is one of the four security chiefs who will be guarding the VIP's. And, before you ask, not a damned clue as to who is the rotten apple. I'd better get off the line, hadn't I?'

'I consider that a sensible suggestion ...'

Tweed had the devil of a time, almost the worst few hours he could remember. He found a cab quickly to take him to Park Crescent, but then his problems were only beginning. That supercilious careerist, Howard, had flown to the security meeting in Paris without telling anyone where the conference was being held. Supercilious *careerist?* It suddenly occurred to him that Howard was one of the four prime suspects ...

Never averse to using unorthodox methods, Tweed was careful to follow protocol on this occasion. He knew Sir Henry Crawford, the British Ambassador in Paris, but his first move was to call a friend at the Foreign Office.

'... an emergency,' Tweed explained. 'I have to send a signal and it must reach the Ambassador within two hours ...'

'Why not phone the Embassy first to make sure he will be there to receive the message,' his friend had suggested.

Had Tweed put forward this suggestion he had no doubt it would have been stiffly rejected as a breach of protocol – but it was all right providing the idea came from the Foreign Office.

He made the call, spoke to the Ambassador, who assured him there was no problem. He would wait for the arrival of Tweed's coded signal and, since the matter was so delicate, deliver the decoded message himself.

'Yes,' he concluded, 'I do know where the conference you are concerned with is taking place ...'

Crawford was cordial – and discreetly uninformative as to where the conference was being held. It was the reaction Tweed had anticipated. He took another cab to meet his contact at the Foreign Office.

'I have spoken to Sir William Crawford,' he announced when he was seated in an uncomfortable armchair. This statement formed a bridge between the Ambassador in Paris and his contact – across which the contact was compelled to walk.

'What is the message?' the other man in the room enquired.

'It was agreed I should present that in isolation to the cipher clerk on duty. I hope you don't mind?'

Tweed was at his meekest, most concerned with not offending the august institution inside whose portals he had been privileged to enter. This was unusual – for someone outside the Foreign Office to use its private code. Tweed employed the weapon of silence, adjusting his glasses while the other decided whether he could see any way out. He couldn't.

'Come with me,' he said, a chilly note infusing his tone.

Ten minutes later the signal was on its way to Paris. Other than Tweed, the only person who knew its contents was the cipher clerk. *He* would reveal it to no one. Tweed sighed with relief as he hailed yet another cab in Whitehall, gave the Park Crescent address and sank back into the seat.

Low cunning had won the day. The Ambassador himself would know the contents – should any witness ever be needed that the signal had been sent. And the Ambassador was personally delivering the message to Howard *in the conference room*. That would force Howard to read out the warning to the other three security chiefs.

'I wish I could be there to study their faces when that message is read out,' Tweed reflected as the cab proceeded up Charing Cross Road. 'One of those four men will be shaken to the core ...'

'It could be any one of the four. You'll have to track through their dossiers back over the years ...'

Tweed gave the instruction to McNeil as they strolled together in Regent's Park after the clammy heat of the day. It was still light, the trees were in full foliage, the grass had a springy rebound which Tweed loved. Everything was perfect – except for the time-fuse problem he must solve.

'O'Meara, Stoller and Flandres ...'

'Don't forget Howard,' Tweed said quickly.

'What am I looking for ?' McNeil enquired with a note of sharp exasperation.

'A *gap*.' Tweed paused under a tree and surveyed the expanse of green. 'A gap in the life – in the records – of one of those four trusted men. Maybe as little as two months. Time unaccounted for. He will have been trained behind the Iron Curtain – I'm sure of that. This man was planted a long time ago ...'

'Checking Howard's dossier will be tricky ...'

'You'll need cover – a reason why you're consulting all these files from Central Registry. I'll think of something ...'

He resumed his walk, his shoulders hunched, a faraway look

in his eyes. 'The funny thing, McNeil, is I'm certain we've already been given a clue – damned if I can put my finger on it ...'

'Tim O'Meara won't be any easier than Howard to check – he's only been head of the President's Secret Service detachment for a year.'

'Which is why I'm taking Concorde to Washington tomorrow if I can get a seat. I know somebody there who might help. He doesn't like O'Meara. A little prejudice opens many doors ...'

'Howard will want to know why,' she warned. 'The expense of the Concorde ticket will be recorded by Accounts ...'

'No, it won't. I'll buy the ticket out of my own pocket. There is still something left from my uncle's legacy. I'll be away before Howard returns. Tell him I've had a recurrence of my asthma – that I went down to my Devon cottage ...'

'He'll try and contact you ...'

'About my signal via the Ambassador?' Tweed was amused. 'I've no doubt when he returns his first job will be to storm into my office. Make it vague – about my trip to the cottage. I felt I just had to get out of London. It will all fit,' he remarked with an owlish expression. 'He'll think I'm dodging him for a few days. He'll never dream I've crossed the Atlantic.'

McNeil stared straight ahead. 'Don't look round – Mason is behind us. He's pretending to take that damned dog of his for a walk ...'

Tweed paused, took off his glasses, polished them and held them up as though checking his lenses. Reflected in the spectacles was the image of Howard's lean and hungry-looking deputy recently recruited from Special Branch. He also had stopped by a convenient tree which his Scottie at the end of a leash was investigating.

'I prefer the dog to the man,' Tweed commented as he replaced his glasses and started walking again. 'Add him to the list. If anyone can find the vital discrepancy in the dossiers you can ...'

Howard had reserved a room for the night at the discreet and well-appointed Hôtel de France et Choiseul in rue St. Honoré.

While he waited for his guest he put in a call to Park Crescent. When the night duty operator answered he identified himself and continued the conversation.

'I want a word with Tweed,' he said brusquely.

'Just a moment, sir. I will put you through to his office.'

Howard checked his watch which registered 2245 hours. He was disturbed: Tweed was still inside Park Crescent when the building would be empty. It was later than he had realised when he made the call. He had another surprise when McNeil's voice came on the line. He spoke quickly to warn her it was an open line.

'I'm talking from my hotel room. I'd like an urgent word with Tweed ...'

'I'm afraid Mr Tweed has been taken ill. Nothing serious – a bad attack of asthma. He's gone down to the country for a few days ...'

'It's not possible to get him on the phone?'

'I'm afraid not, sir. When can we expect you back?'

'Impossible to say. Goodnight!'

Howard ended the call on a stiff note: he never liked questions about his future movements. Sitting on his bed he frowned while he recalled the conversation. That was an odd departure from McNeil's normal behaviour – asking a question she knew he would disapprove of.

In the Park Crescent office Miss McNeil smiled as she replaced the receiver. She had been confident the final question would get Howard off the line before he probed too deeply. She returned to her examination of the dossier in front of her. It carried a red star – top classification – on the cover, and a name. Frederick Anthony Howard.

In the Paris bedroom Howard was pacing impatiently when there was an irregular knocking on his locked door, the signal he had agreed with Alain Flandres. Despite the signal he extracted from his case the 7.65-mm automatic Flandres had loaned him and slipped it inside his pocket before opening the door. Flandres walked into the room.

'*Chez Benoit, mon ami!*'

The slim, springy Flandres was a tonic; always optimistic, his personality *fizzed*. He walked round the room smiling, his dark eyes everywhere.

'Chez What?' Howard enquired.

'Benoit! Benoit! They serve some of the best food in all of Paris. The last serving is at 9.30 in the evening – but for me *le patron* makes the exception. The Police Prefect often eats there. You are ready? Good ...'

Flandres had a cab waiting at the entrance to the hotel. The journey took no more than ten minutes and the Englishman, sunk in thought, remained silent. Normally voluble, Flandres also said nothing but he studied his companion until they arrived and were ushered to a table. They were examining the menu when Flandres made his remark.

'My telex from London about the Carlos sighting this morning in Piccadilly has disturbed you? You wonder who he went there to meet? You were in London this morning?'

Howard closed the menu. 'What the bloody hell are you driving at, Alain?' he asked quietly.

'I have offended you?' Flandres was astonished. 'Always it is the same – I talk too much! And Renée Duval, the girl who sent me the telex – I have withdrawn her from London. She was only on routine assignment. Now, the really important subject is what we are to select for dinner ...'

Flandres chattered on, steering the conversation away from the topic of the telex. He was now convinced something else was disturbing the Englishman, something he was carefully concealing from his French opposite number.

Saturday May 30

Washington, DC, Clint Loomis ...

The extract from the secret notebook discovered on Warner's dead body had linked up with nothing so far, Tweed reflected.

Concorde landed on schedule at Dulles Airport. Tweed was not among the first passengers to alight, nor among the last. He did not believe in disguises but before disembarking he removed his glasses. This simple act transformed his appearance.

Clint Loomis was waiting outside. He ushered him straight into a nondescript blue sedan. The American, in his late fifties, had not changed since their last meeting. Serious-faced, his dark eyes penetrating and acutely observant, he wore an open-necked blue shirt and pale grey slacks. His hair had thinned somewhat.

'We can say "Hello" when we get there,' he remarked as he drove away from Dulles. 'Maybe you'd better take off your jacket ...'

The sun was blazing, the humidity was appalling. It was like travelling inside a ship's boiler room.

'Is it always like this in May?' Tweed enquired as he wrestled himself out of his jacket, turned to cast it on the seat behind and looked through the rear window, studying the traffic.

'In Washington nothing is "always",' Loomis replied. 'In the US of A we're a restless lot – so we change the weather when we can't think of anything else to change. We'll talk when we get there – and no names. O.K.?'

'The car could be bugged?'

'They're bugging everything these days – even clapped-out old CIA personnel. Just to keep someone in a job. You have to file a report to show the boss you're still in business.'

'Why the rush at the airport? My bag slung on the back seat ...'

'We could be followed, that's why. By the time we get where we're going we'll shake any tail ...'

'Like arriving in Moscow,' Tweed said drily.

The signposts told him they were heading for Alexandria. Tweed looked through the rear window again and Loomis glanced at him with a frown of irritation.

'We're *not* being followed if that's what's bothering you ...'

'When we get to a place where you can stop, could I take the wheel for awhile, Clint?'

'Sure. If that's the way you feel ...'

This was one of the many things Tweed liked about Loomis – if he trusted you he never asked questions. He did whatever you requested and waited for explanations.

Later, as they stood outside the car prior to changing places, the Englishman glanced back up the highway. A green car had also pulled in to the side and one of the two male occupants got out to lift the bonnet. A blue car cruised past which also contained two men – neither of them spared the stationary sedan a glance, Tweed observed. He got in behind the wheel and began driving.

'What make is that green car behind us – the one behind the truck? You'll see it as we go round this curve ...'

'A Chevvy,' Loomis replied. 'It pulled up when we did ...'

'I know. And that blue car ahead of us – which was cruising and is now picking up speed to keep ahead. They have a sandwich on us, Clint. Those two cars have been with us since we left Dulles. They keep changing places – one in front, one behind ...'

'Jesus Christ! I must be losing my grip ...'

'Just the fresh eye,' Tweed assured him. 'Better lose our friends one at a time, don't you think?'

They were coming up to traffic lights at an intersection and the green Chevvy was still one vehicle behind them when Tweed performed. To his right was one of those damned great trailer trucks which transported half of America's freight coast to coast. He rammed his foot down ...

'*Look out – the lights ...!*' Loomis yelled.

There was a scream of rubber as Tweed shot forward like a torpedo. He swerved crazily to avoid the trailer which was coming out with the lights in its favour. A second scream – of airbrakes being jammed on. Loomis looked back and then at Tweed who had returned to his correct lane. To the American he looked so bloody unruffled.

'You nearly got us killed back there ...'

'I don't see the green Chevvy any more,' Tweed commented with a glance in his rear view mirror.

'Like hell you don't – it just rammed its snout into the side of that trailer. It was overtaking as you hit the lights ...'

'To change places with the blue job ahead of us. Now ...' Tweed tapped his fingers on the wheel. '... we lose him and we're on our own, which will be more comfortable ...'

'Not the same way. *Please!* I thought you Brits were sober, law-abiding types. You realise what would have happened had a patrol-car been nearby ...'

'There wasn't one. I checked.'

The meeting place was a white power cruiser moored to a buoy on the Potomac river. Tweed had followed signposts to Fredericksburg and then, guided by Loomis, turned off down a minor road to the east. By now he had lost the blue car in an equally hair-raising performance which had ended in their tail skidding off the highway. It was very quiet and deserted as Tweed switched off the engine, climbed out and savoured the breeze coming off the water.

'That's yours?' he asked, pointing at the cruiser.

'Bought it with my – severance pay, don't you call it? – when I left the Company. Plus a bank loan I'm damned if I'll ever pay off. It gives me safety – I hope ...'

'Safety?'

Tweed concealed his sense of shock. His trip to Washington was developing in a way he had never expected. First they had been followed from Dulles by an outfit which had money at its disposal. It cost a lot of dollars to employ *four* men to do a shadow job. And ever since he had arrived Clint Loomis, retired from the CIA, had shown signs of nervousness.

'The Company doesn't like people who leave it alive.'

Loomis was dragging a rubber dinghy equipped with an out-board which had been hidden among a clump of grasses down to the river's edge. He gave a lop-sided grin as the craft floated and he gestured to his visitor to get aboard. 'I suppose it comes from all those dumbos who got out and wrote books, revealing all as the publishers' blurbs say.'

'You're writing a book?' Tweed asked as he settled gingerly inside the vessel and Loomis started up the outboard.

'Not me,' Loomis said with a shake of his head. 'And when we get to the *Oasis* ...' He pointed towards the power cruiser, '... that's when we shake hands.'

'If you say so,' Tweed replied.

They crossed the smooth stretch of water and Loomis slowed the engine to a crawl as the hull loomed up. Aboard the *Oasis* a huge Alsatian dog appeared, running up and down the deck, barking its head off. Then it stopped at the head of the boarding ladder and stared down, jaws open, exposing teeth which reminded Tweed of a shark.

'Now we shake hands,' Loomis explained. 'That shows him you're a friend and you don't get chewed up.'

'I see,' said Tweed, careful to make a ceremony of the display of friendship. The dog backed off as he mounted the ladder without too much confidence while Loomis tied up the dinghy and followed him on deck.

'Over the side!' Loomis ordered.

The dog dived in, swimming all round the boat until it completed one circuit. Loomis stretched over the side down the ladder, hooked a hand in the dog's collar and hauled it aboard as the animal pawed and scrambled up the rungs. It stood on the deck and shook itself all over Tweed.

'Shows he likes you,' Loomis said. 'We'd better go below now that everything is safe. A beer?'

'That would be nice,' Tweed agreed, following his host down

the companionway where the American handed him a towel to dry himself. He was beginning to have serious doubts as to whether he had been wise to cross the Atlantic.

'What was all that business about the dog?' he enquired.

'The swim in the river?' The American settled himself back on a bunk, his legs stretched out, his ankles crossed. For the first time he seemed genuinely relaxed. 'Waldo has been trained to sniff out explosives. So, we get back and find him alone on deck. Conclusion? No intruders *aboard* the cruiser – or one of two things would have happened. Waldo would be dead – or a man's body would be lying around with his throat torn out. O.K.?'

Tweed shuddered inwardly and drank more beer, 'O.K.,' he said.

'Next point. Waldo is trained to stay aboard no matter what. So the opposition uses frogmen who attach limpet mines with trembler or timer devices to the hull – devices which detonate with the vibration of a grown man's weight walking on deck. I send Waldo overboard and he swims round once without a pause. Conclusion? If there were mines Waldo would be yelping, kicking up one hell of a row when he gets the sniff of high-explosives. Now we know we're clean ...'

'What a way to live. How long has this been going on? And who is going to attach the limpet mines?'

'A gun hired by Tim O'Meara who kicked my ass out of the Company when he was Director of Operations – before he transferred to become boss of the Secret Service.'

'And why would O'Meara do that?'

'Because I know he embezzled two hundred thousand dollars allocated for running guns into Afghanistan.'

In his München apartment Manfred concentrated on the long-distance call. His main concern was to detect any trace of strain in the voice of his caller. Code-names only had been used.

'Tweed knows there is a selected target,' the voice reported.

'He has identified the target?'

Manfred asked the question immediately, his voice calm,

almost bored, but the news was hitting him like a hammerblow. He might have guessed that in the end it would be Tweed who ferreted out the truth. God damn his soul!

'No,' the voice replied. 'Only that there is one. You might wish to take some action.'

'Thank you for informing me,' Manfred replied neutrally. 'And please call me tomorrow. Same time . . .'

Replacing the receiver, Manfred swore foully and then comforted himself with the thought that he had detected no breaking of nerve in the voice of the man who had called him. Checking in a small notebook, he began dialling a London number.

This incident took place on the day before Tweed departed for Washington, late in the evening on the day the four security chiefs attended the conference at the Sûreté building in Paris.

Tweed realised he had walked into a nightmare. The question he couldn't answer to his own satisfaction was whether Clint Loomis was paranoid, suffering from a persecution complex which made him see enemies everywhere. Hence the obsession with security aboard the *Oasis*.

Against that he had to weigh the fact that they *had* been followed by four unknown men in two cars when they left Dulles Airport. It was Loomis who changed the subject – much to Tweed's relief.

'Charles Warner came to see me two weeks ago – he was interested in O'Meara. Have you also flown to the States just to talk to me? I'd find that hard to believe . . .'

'Believe it!' Tweed's manner was suddenly abrupt. 'When O'Meara was CIA Director of Operations he manipulated your retirement?'

'Bet your sweet life . . .'

'You know his history. What is that history?'

'He was an operative in the field early on. I was the man back home who checked his reports . . .'

'After a period of duty at Langley he was stationed in West Berlin for several years? Correct?' Tweed queried.

'Correct. I don't see where you're leading, Tweed. That always worries me ...'

'*Trust me!*' The Englishman's manner had a quiet, persuasive authority. He had to keep Loomis talking, to concentrate his mind on one topic. O'Meara's track record. 'You say you checked his reports from West Berlin. He speaks German?'

'Fluently. He can pass for a native ...'

'Did he go under cover – into East Berlin?'

'That was strictly forbidden.' There was a very positive note in Loomis' reply. 'It was written into his directive ...'

'Anyone else with him in this unit?'

'A guy called Lou Carson. He was subordinate to O'Meara ...'

'And all the time O'Meara was in West Berlin you're convinced he obeyed the directive – under no circumstances to go over the Wall?'

He was watching Loomis closely. The American had swung his legs off the bunk and was opening another can of beer. Tweed shook his head, his eyes fixed on Loomis who was staring into the distance.

'Maybe that was when the bastard first started to dislike me,' he said eventually.

Tweed sat quite still. He had experienced this before with interrogations – you *sensed* when pure chance had played into your lap. There was a time to speak, a time to preserve silence.

Loomis stood up and stared through a porthole across the peaceful waters. The craft rocked gently, scarcely moving. Tweed looked round the neat cabin. The American kept a tidy ship. He had kept a tidy desk at Langley, Tweed recalled – which was where he should still be. Loomis started talking.

'This particular unit in West Berlin was just these two guys – keeping tabs on the East German espionage set-up. It was one time Carlos was reported as being in East Berlin ...'

'Really?'

'We had a system of identification codes,' Loomis continued, 'so I always knew when a signal came from O'Meara and when it was from Lou Carson – without either man knowing the other had his personal call-sign. We started playing it pretty close to the chest after the débacle ...'

'Let me get this clear. Each man had his own identification signal so you knew who was sending a report. But both O'Meara and Carson thought the system applied only to them – not to the other?'

'You've got it. You know, Tweed, you get a feeling when something is wrong. Signals were coming through from O'Meara but the wording didn't sound like O'Meara – although they carried his sign. So I hopped on a plane and arrived in West Berlin unannounced. Lou Carson was pretty embarrassed. I'd caught him with his pants down. He was on his own ...'

'And where was O'Meara?'

'He surfaced two days later. Swore he had gone underground to another base for a couple of months because our normal one had been blown to the East German security people ...'

'You believed him?' Tweed pressed.

'No, but that was only a gut feeling. You don't go to the Director with gut feelings. He likes solid evidence ...'

'How had O'Meara got round the identification system?'

'Simple – he'd handed Lou Carson his identification log book so Lou could send messages and it would look as though they came from O'Meara. Carson cooperated because O'Meara told him to ...'

'What happened next?' Tweed asked while Loomis was still wound up.

'Both men were recalled to Washington and others took their place. O'Meara had done a good job in West Berlin, he knew the right people, he can charm the birds out of the trees. Before I know it, he's promoted over my head and he's sending me to Bahrain with two hundred thousand dollars in a case aboard a special flight ...'

'You said he embezzled the money.'

'Let me finish, for Christ's sake! When the people with the guns for Afghanistan checked the money I handed over they

156

said it was counterfeit. They had a bright Indian who had worked for currency printers ...'

'The counterfeit was good enough to deceive you?'

'I'd have accepted it without question. O'Meara had the case locked in his office safe, he took it out and handed it to me. He levered me out of the Company over that incident,' Loomis blazed. 'They let me go quietly because there had been too many scandals and they were worried about their image ...'

'O'Meara just cleaned you out? No one else?'

'Lou Carson went. There were others. He was bringing in his own people. When he'd wrecked half-a-dozen lives he joins the Secret Service and walks away from the wreckage. There are guys like that everywhere ...'

'It happens – but it's not pleasant,' Tweed murmured, then he changed the subject. Best to leave a pleasant atmosphere behind when he boarded Concorde for London the following day.

The second long-distance call to Manfred came duly at the agreed hour the following day while Tweed was aboard the *Oasis*. It was Manfred who opened the conversation.

'You have nothing to worry about. Tweed is in Washington.'

'The devil he is! How do you know that?'

'Because I have people everywhere. The problem is a small one. Measures have already been taken to deal with it ...'

'You mean you're going to have Tweed ...'

'*Enough!* And the answer to your question is no. It would be bad policy. Crocodile will proceed on schedule. Now I must go – I have matters to attend to ...'

It would be bad policy ... Manfred stood quite still, staring into space. He had not been quite frank with his caller, but Manfred was often anything but frank. He was certainly not going to admit that the killing of Tweed would be an extremely difficult operation. The Englishman was equipped with a sixth sense where danger was concerned.

Instead there was a better way of dealing with the problem. He picked up the phone again to call a Washington number.

It was Sunday May 31. Tweed had spent the night aboard *Oasis* – which the American had moved to a fresh mooring. This action confirmed the nervousness Tweed had detected on his arrival.

'Never stay in the same place for long,' Loomis remarked as he tied up the cruiser to a fresh buoy. 'And always move after dark without lights.'

'Illegal, isn't it?' Tweed enquired. 'To sail without navigation lights?'

'Bet your sweet life it is . . .'

Over a meal which the American cooked in the galley they talked about old times. Loomis remarked he had heard Tweed was being held in reserve for 'the time when Howard trips over his big feet. Then they bring you back to clean up the mess. No, don't protest,' he admonished, waving his spatula, 'my grapevine is good.'

Just prior to his departure for Dulles, it was Tweed who noticed two incidents which disturbed him. He was on deck with his suitcase, waiting for Loomis to climb down the ladder into the dinghy, when he observed movement onshore.

'Loan me your field-glasses, Clint,' he called out.

Something in his guest's tone made Loomis react quickly. Tweed raised the glasses to his eyes, adjusted the focus and studied the shoreline briefly. Then he handed them back, his lips compressed.

'Bird-watching?' Loomis enquired.

'There were two men in the trees over there. One of them had a camera with a telephoto lens – bloody great piece of equipment. I think he was photographing the *Oasis* . . .'

'Probably just a camera nut. They shoot anything.'

They had climbed down into the dinghy and the dog, Waldo, stood at the top of the ladder keening, when a helicopter appeared, flying from the Chesapeake Bay direction down the centre of the channel. As they left the cruiser Tweed craned his neck to get a look at the machine.

'That's the third time that chopper has over-flown us since I arrived,' Tweed commented.

'You see them all the time in this part of the world. Coastguard machines, private jobs . . .'

Loomis was concentrating on steering the dinghy to where they had parked his car. Tweed, hunched in the stern, continued staring up at the helicopter. The sun was reflecting off the plexiglas, making it impossible to see inside the pilot's cabin.

'I think it was the same machine each time,' he insisted.

Loomis was unconcerned. 'It's O.K. – we left Waldo on board.'

At Dulles they repeated their performance of the previous day – wasting no time. Tweed got out of the car and walked rapidly into the building without a glance back. Behind him he heard Loomis already driving away.

Aboard Concorde after lift-off it seemed to Tweed he might never have visited America – it had all happened so quickly. He was so absorbed in his thoughts he never noticed when they passed through the sound barrier. Fragments of conversation with Loomis drifted back into his mind.

. . . O'Meara . . . surfaced two days later . . . he had gone underground to another base . . . a couple of months . . . he'd handed Lou Carson his identification log book . . .

Tweed began to feel drowsy. He closed his eyes and fell asleep. It was the steep angle of descent which woke him. They were landing at London Airport. It had all been a dream. He had never been away at all. When he arrived at Park Crescent McNeil's expression prepared him for the shock.

Sunday May 31

Clint Loomis parked his car in a different place when he returned from Dulles alone. He knew every inch of the shoreline on both banks and this time he chose an abandoned shed at the end of a dirt track to house the vehicle. Then he started the long walk back to where the outboard was concealed.

It was another brilliant sunny day and the heat beat down on the back of his neck as he dragged the dinghy to the water's edge, got inside and fired the motor. In the distance the cruiser *Oasis* was gleaming, the sun reflecting off the highly-polished brass. For a moment he was reminded of Tweed when he heard the sound of a helicopter and saw the machine disappearing in the direction of Chesapeake Bay. Then he concentrated on navigating his small craft.

Waldo was waiting for him, barking his head off at the top of the ladder. As he was tying up the dinghy Loomis vaguely noticed a second power cruiser rather like his own heading on a course towards him from Chesapeake Bay. He went through the same security precaution — tipping Waldo overboard and waiting while the dog swam round the boat before hauling him aboard.

The odd thing was Waldo only displayed signs of agitation when he was back on deck. He was shaking himself dry — and Loomis grinned as he recalled how Tweed had taken the brunt of the water the previous day — when the dog stopped, still dripping. His body tensed, his ears lay flat, his teeth were bared and he stood rigid while he emitted a slow, drawn-out snarl.

'What's the matter, boy? Tweed got you nervy . . .'

Loomis followed the direction of Waldo's stare and his expression changed. Waldo was gazing at the oncoming cruiser which, unless it changed course, would pass close by them on its way upriver. Loomis could see no sign of anyone on board, which was odd. You would expect someone on deck on such a glorious day. He ran down into the cabin.

In a locked cupboard the ex-CIA man kept a small armoury. Opening it, he looked at the machine-pistol, the double-barrelled shotgun, the three hand-guns. He chose the shotgun.

It was like a ghost ship, the oncoming cruiser, Loomis thought as he came up on deck. Tinted glass in the wheelhouse windows which masked the presence of men who *must* be inside. Damnit, one man must be at the wheel. Chugging slowly and ominously, a cloth over the side concealing the name painted on its bow, it closed with *Oasis*.

Waldo was a coiled spring, hairs bristling, the softness of the growl from deep in his throat infinitely more menacing than his normal barking. Loomis glanced round to see if help was near at hand. Only a vast expanse of empty water greeted him.

He crouched low, his shotgun out of sight. If this was trouble one blast through the wheelhouse window was liable to take out anyone inside. The helmsman certainly – which meant the vessel would no longer stay on its remorseless course.

It was due to pass within yards on the port side, the side where Loomis waited. The hell of it was he couldn't initiate any action in case they were peaceful sailors going about their lawful occasions as the Brits would phrase it. The thought made him wish he had Tweed on board. He had a feeling Tweed would not just have sat and waited. But what the hell else could he do?

Stand up and address them through his loud-hailer? And present someone with a perfect target. Already he was working on the premise that the approaching cruiser was hostile – without one shred of evidence. Yes! Waldo was evidence – his reaction to the vessel was unusually violent ...

They set about the task in a way Loomis had not foreseen. They were almost alongside *Oasis* when a flutter of dark, pineapple-shaped missiles sailed across the water separating the two vessels and landed in various places. On deck. On the foredeck. At the foot of the companionway. *Grenades!* Jesus Christ ...!

They had slightly different time fuses. One landed underneath Waldo and detonated on impact. The dog disintegrated into a flying mass of bloody meat and bone, smearing the woodwork. Loomis went crazy. He stood up.

'*Bastards!*'

His shotgun was levelled point-blank at the tinted glass of the other vessel but before he could pull the trigger a grenade which had landed just behind him exploded. All feeling suddenly left his legs and he found himself floating backwards, falling down the companionway. He landed at the bottom just as one of the grenades which had ended up in the cabin also detonated. It sliced away half his head.

A boathook grappled *Oasis*'s side when ten separate explosions had been counted. The man holding it wore a frogman's suit. The engine of the killer cruiser had been stopped and another man, also wearing a frogman's suit, leapt nimbly abroad holding a sub-machine gun.

He took only two minutes to search *Oasis*, to note that Loomis was dead, that no one else was hiding aboard. Then with the same agile movements he returned to his own cruiser, the engine started up and the vessel set on a new course which took it far away from *Oasis* as swiftly as possible.

In the burning-glass blue of the sky the pilot of a helicopter turned his machine and headed it away from Washington. Over his radio he spoke one word repeatedly.

Extinction . . . extinction. . . extinction . . .

Sunday May 31

The headquarters of *Bundesnachrichtendienst* – the BND, the German Federal Intelligence Service located at Pullach – is six miles south of München. Erich Stoller's nerve centre was surrounded by a wall of trees and an inner wall comprising an electrified fence. Stoller, with his dry humour, referred to it as 'my own Berlin Wall'. He had just made this remark over coffee to Martel.

Tweed, due to catch the 13.05 flight back to London, was still fast asleep aboard the *Oasis* owing to the difference in the time zones. They sat in Stoller's office inside a single-storey concrete blockhouse of a building. Through the armour plate-glass window a stretch of bare earth showed where armed guards patrolled. Beyond was the electrified fence and beyond that dense pine trees. It was another hot morning and the temperature was rising rapidly.

'I spent four years in Wiesbaden with the Kriminalpolizei,' the German told Martel. 'Then I transferred to the BND.'

'And after that?'

Martel watched Stoller's dark eyes as he drank some more of the strong coffee, his manner relaxed, his voice expressing friendly interest.

'A year here and then two inside the Zone ...' Stoller's tone became sombre at the recollection of his time in East Germany. 'You know what it's like – going underground. It felt like ten years. Every hour of your waking day on the alert, every waking minute expecting a hand to drop on your shoulder. And you don't sleep too well,' he concluded with a wry smile. 'I thought you knew about that period ...'

'Tweed doesn't tell me everything,' Martel lied easily. 'How long have you been back in civilisation?'

'Four years – if you can call Bavaria civilisation just at the moment. The riots are getting worse. The neo-Nazis march, the left-wing people counter-march, the two lots meet – and *Boom!*'

'The state government elections in a few days should solve all that,' Martel suggested.

'If Langer's moderates win. The trouble is Dietrich's party and the frequent discovery of Delta arms dumps may drive people into Tofler's left-wing bear-hug. Then he'll set up Bavaria as some kind of so-called Free State – detached from the Federal Republic ...'

'You don't really believe that, Erich ...'

'I do believe you've just been subjecting me to some kind of personal interrogation and I'm wondering why.'

Martel swore inwardly. He'd had to take the risk Stoller would catch on. Maybe he'd been stupid to try the experiment – facing a fellow-professional. He set out to repair the damage.

'Why so edgy? If we're to work together I like to know about a man. Maybe I can provide you with my career sheet ...'

'Sorry!' Stoller raised a hand and smiled his slow, deliberate smile. The German did everything deliberately. He even sipped his coffee as though testing for a suspect ingredient.

'I am edgy,' he went on. 'You would be if you faced a crucial election – just when the Summit Express is crossing your territory with the West's top leaders aboard. My responsibility is the sector from Strasbourg through to Salzburg ...'

'And the German Chancellor?'

'Kurt Langer boards the train at München Hauptbahnhof – but I still have the other three to guard through the night from Strasbourg.'

'You sound as though you expect trouble,' Martel suggested.

'I do.' Stoller stood up behind his desk. 'Shall we collect your friend, Claire Hofer, and drive to München?'

'Can I make one phone call to London before I leave?'

'I'll go and entertain Miss Hofer. No, no! You may prefer to talk in private.' Standing up, Martel reflected, the German was an imposing figure; not the sort of man you would expect to survive behind the Iron Curtain for two years.

'I will be in the canteen where we left her while we talked,'

Stoller informed him. 'Just ask the operator for your number, press the red button and you're on scrambler . . .'

While he waited for the Park Crescent number Martel studied a wall-map of Bavaria. It showed where caches of Delta arms and uniforms had been found. Flags indicated the discovery dates.

He found it strange that the rate of success was accelerating. No wonder the polls were showing increasing support for Tofler's party as Election Day approached. Each discovery increased the voters' fear of a Delta win. The phone rang and he heard McNeil at the other end of the line. He asked her to supply 'photos of the four principals . . .'

'Tweed is out of London,' she told him quickly. 'He asked me to give you a message, Keith. Tomorrow, Monday, catch the first available flight to Heathrow where you will be met. You can give me the flight number? Good. And the ETA? Bring a passport picture of Miss Hofer. As soon as the meeting is over you fly back to Bavaria. Time is running out . . .'

'Don't I know it,' Martel replied.

It was a hot Sunday morning in Paris.

Howard had stayed in the city at the urging of Alain Flandres for a further discussion with O'Meara about security precautions aboard the Summit Express. The train was due to leave the Gare de l'Est late Tuesday evening, June 2 – only three days' hence.

Despite Howard's protestations Flandres had insisted he would personally drive his British opposite number to Charles de Gaulle Airport to catch his London flight. Howard had a shock when he stepped out of the lift with his bag into the reception hall of the Hôtel de France et Choiseul ready for his departure.

'Tim is flying to London with you,' the Frenchman announced.

'Decided I'd call at the Embassy there and check out certain unfinished business, then fly back here for *Der Tag*,' O'Meara explained. 'It will give us a chance to get better acquainted . . .'

Howard said nothing as he contemplated the two men, contrasting their styles. They were opposites – the slim, elegantly dressed Alain, every hair in place, his movements nimble and precise, and the large American in his check sports jacket who exuded aggressive self-confidence.

'I have to pay my bill,' Howard said and walked to the counter. His eyes scanned the guests seated in the lounge area. A slim, fair-haired girl, fashionably dressed and with her superb legs crossed, sat reading a copy of *Vogue*. A blue Vuiton suitcase stood by her chair and she glanced up briefly as Howard passed her.

It took only a few moments to settle the bill, he lifted his case, went back to the entrance and Flandres led the way to where a blue Citroen was parked. He opened the rear door and Howard was forced to join O'Meara in the back. As the car left the kerb the fair-haired girl with the Vuiton case emerged and climbed inside a waiting cab.

During the journey the Englishman encouraged O'Meara to talk and maintained an almost uninterrupted silence. Without appearing to do so he was watching Alain behind the wheel who frequently glanced in his rear-view mirror. Howard gained the impression they were being followed.

He was on the verge of asking the Frenchman if he had spotted a tail when something made him keep quiet. At de Gaulle Alain accompanied them to the barrier and bade them an effusive farewell.

'... until we meet again here in Paris aboard the Summit Express,' he murmured.

He watched as the two men stood on the escalator carrying them up inside a transparent tube elevated at a steep angle. A fair-haired girl passed him carrying a Vuiton case followed by a small, stocky man wearing a trilby. The tails were in position. Renée Duval would report on all Howard's movements and contacts. Georges Lepas would perform the same operation on O'Meara. Alain Flandres was a professional, his favourite maxim *trust no one – particularly those close to you.*

Because something was wrong ...

*

Münich Hauptbahnhof. The location Charles Warner had haunted on his visits to the Bavarian state capital. Martel and Claire had asked Stoller to drop them at the Four Seasons Hotel in the centre of the city. As soon as the German had departed Martel picked up both bags and shook his head at the hotel porter.

'We're not staying here ...'

They walked a short distance before Martel hailed a cab and gave an address close to the Hauptbahnhof. After he had paid the fare they separated, each carrying their own bag. When they entered the vast station there was nothing to indicate they knew each other. Claire followed Martel at a distance, thankful for the pistol concealed in her handbag.

Both got rid of their cases in self-locking storage compartments and Martel began his search. Why had Warner found this place – and its alter ego in Zürich – important enough to record in his notebook? Knowing it would help identify him to any watcher, he strolled into the Sunday turmoil with his cigarette-holder at a jaunty angle. Behind him Claire checked for shadows. They were now in the middle of the spider's web.

Erwin Vinz felt desperate – which he knew was bad because a mood could cause him to make a mistake. After two fiascos in Lindau – Gross's unsuccessful attempt to kill Martel in the fog followed by the elimination of the wind-surfer execution squad – Reinhard Dietrich had flown into a fury in his Münich penthouse apartment.

'You had Martel! You had him in the palm of your hand in Lindau. What happens? Gross is killed by Martel while you stand by! Are you degenerating into some kind of amateur? If so, there is always a remedy ...'

'I do have a plan ...' Vinz began.

'Wonderful! Just as you had a plan at Lindau! I hope you also realise I hold you partly responsible for my nephew, Werner's demise?' He paused, choking on his emotion. The news had come over the phone from Erich Stoller of all people, the

Intelligence creep Dietrich loathed. Vinz made a great effort.

'I am sure that Martel will surface in München. He is likely to come in by train. He uses trains a lot. He travelled to St. Gallen from Zürich by train. He left St. Gallen aboard the München express last Thursday ...'

'And you lost him,' Dietrich broke in sarcastically.

'I have crammed München Hauptbahnhof with our soldiers,' Vinz persisted. 'They have his description. The station is so overcrowded an accident can occur and no one will notice. A man falls off a platform under a train ...'

'Dangerous,' Dietrich said thoughtfully as he lit a cigar, 'to draw attention to the Hauptbahnhof ...'

'Only if the Englishman realises its significance – only if he survives to pass on the information ...'

'Kill him!' Dietrich crashed his fist on the desk, his face red with fury. *'Kill him for Werner! Now – get out ...'*

The Hauptbahnhof was an inferno: the noise, the chaos incredible. Martel was caught up in the mob of passengers hurrying for trains, getting out of the city for a Sunday break. Expresses arriving, departing ...

Saarbruecken, Bremen, Frankfurt, Zuerich, Dortmund, Wuerzburg ... The destination boards carried the names of cities all over Europe. Under the tall roof in the cavern below were platforms 11 to 26. A sign pointed to an adjoining *second* station – the Starnberger. There was even a third station for platforms 1 to 10.

Wartesaal, a huge waiting room. Rows of telephone booths. A cafeteria. *Kino* – a cinema open from 0900 to 2100 hours, entrance six deutschemarks, for which sum you could sit there all day and in the evening. A score of different exits – including one to the complex U-Bahn system.

Martel was like a sponge, soaking up data, smoking his cigarette, strolling among the hustling, shoving crowds. At the back of his mind an idea was forming. Warner had noted down this rendezvous of strangers as important. Was the reason staring him in the face?

168

The noise was appalling, trapped by the overhang of the roof, the noise of voices, trampling feet, Tannoys booming. An assault on the nerves. The heat, again trapped inside the cavern by the roof, was exhausting – the clammy humidity, the sweat of God knew how many hurrying passengers.

Patiently, her handbag under her left arm, her right hand close to the flap and the pistol inside, Claire Hofer appeared to drift into the whirlpool as she doggedly followed the Englishman. Then she saw him. *Erwin Vinz ...*

She was sure the killer would not recognise her. When he came into the reception hall of the Bayerischer Hof late in the evening he had not even glanced at her. But she had been trained never to make easy assumptions. From her handbag she took a pair of tinted glasses and slipped them on. She had to warn Martel.

Keith Martel's attention was absorbed by something else. He had the uncanny feeling that he was surrounded by hostile forces, that amid the surging crowd was a more compact, organised detachment of men. Then he saw a man wearing a Delta symbol in his lapel, a man waiting by the barrier where the München Express from Zürich was gliding to a halt.

More people poured off the platform into the station. Martel pretended to study a timetable board while he watched the man. One of the disembarking passengers showed his ticket but retained it – so it was a *return*. It happend in seconds – showing the ticket, the shaking of hands with the waiting Delta man and then they walked into the cafeteria. The new arrival also wore a silver triangle in his lapel.

'Erwin Vinz is here. Wearing the same clothes as in Lindau. He is standing by a loaded trolley behind you – he's seen you ...'

Claire Hofer gently rubbed the side of her face to conceal the movement of her lips as she stood alongside Martel, also appearing to consult the timetable.

'Watch *yourself*,' he warned. 'I think the place is crawling with Delta types. Two have just gone into the cafeteria ...'

He left her and she remained for a few moments studying the

times and scribbling them in her pocket notebook. When she turned round Martel was disappearing inside the cafeteria. Erwin Vinz had spoken to a man she had only a brief glimpse of: she had an impression of tanned skin, large sun-goggles and the man vanished towards the exit.

Inside the cafeteria Martel ordered a cup of coffee, paid for it and selected a table close to one of the doors to the concourse. He sat in a chair with his back to the wall. The two Delta men were absorbed in conversation. The recent arrival from the express handed to his companion a thick envelope which disappeared inside the companion's breast pocket.

A glance, the briefest lifting of eyes in Martel's direction by the man who had waited at the barrier, warned the Englishman he had walked into a trap.

They crowded round the nearest exit, blocking his escape route – five well-built men wearing Tyrolean hats and carrying beer steins. One of them sat down at his table as Martel grasped the pepper pot. The man put his stein on the table, reached inside his pocket and produced a notebook which he laid on the table. He had not looked once in Martel's direction.

He put his hand in his pocket again and it reappeared holding a felt-tipped pen. He held it below the level of the table, pressed a button and the needle shot out into the action position. Martel ripped off the top of the pepper pot and tossed the contents into his eyes. He screamed – and his scream coincided with a louder sound. The explosion of shots fired from a pistol.

Martel jumped up and pushed over the table, tipping the killer opposite and his chair sprawling to the floor. The men round the door were stumbling against each other and their faces registered stark fear. They were desperate to get away from the door they had been blocking a moment earlier.

'This way out!'

Martel had a brief vision of Claire standing in the doorway, the pistol she had fired three times gripped in both hands and aimed at the Delta men. Her earlier shots had gone over their heads. Martel ran forward, using the stiffened side of his hand to chop down a man who made an attempt to stop him.

Then he was outside. Claire had rammed the pistol inside her handbag and he gripped her by the arm, hustling her across the concourse. Behind them they left a scene of confusion and shouted curses as frightened customers panicked and struggled to leave the place.

'*U-Bahn!*'

Martel shouted the words close to Claire's ear as he continued moving her fast among the crowds, elbowing people out of his way, forcing a swift passage towards the main exit and the escalator to the U-Bahn system.

'Tickets . . .' Claire reminded him.

'I bought a couple earlier when I was prowling round – to give us a line of retreat . . .'

Before entering the U-Bahn it is necessary to buy a ticket which you insert into an automatic punching machine and then descend the escalator. Still moving rapidly, still gripping her arm, he headed for the U-Bahn entrance, weaving in and out among the passengers.

He was careful now not to force his way through, to merge into the background. They had a short head-start; the U-Bahn must swallow them up before the Delta men inside the Hauptbahnhof arrived. They reached the machines, punched their tickets, went below and arrived on a platform as a train was pulling in.

As it moved out Martel was certain no one had followed them on to the train. He looked at Claire sitting beside him. She removed her dark glasses. Her forehead was glistening with beads of sweat – but other people in the coach sat in shirt-sleeves and mopped their own foreheads. She looked back at him uncertainly.

'We go straight to the Clausen,' he told her quietly. 'It's a small hotel in a side street. We can go back for our bags later – much later.'

'Was it all worth it?' she asked.

'You tell me. I know now why the Hauptbahnhofs are important.'

*

The Sunday Concorde flight from Washington departed 1305 hours local time and arrived at Heathrow at 2155 hours local time. The cab deposited Tweed at Park Crescent – where McNeil, forewarned by his call from Dulles – was waiting for him in his office. The clock on the wall registered thirty minutes before midnight.

'The news has just come over the telex.'

McNeil made no attempt to soften the shock she knew Tweed would receive. The one thing her chief detested was any kind of fuss.

'What news?' he enquired.

'Your old friend, Clint Loomis, has been murdered ...'

She handed the telex to Tweed and sat down, her notebook at the ready. She doodled while she waited, carefully not looking at Tweed who sank into his swivel chair and eased his buttocks into the old cushion. He read the signal three times.

Ex-CIA agent Clint Loomis killed by unknown assassins this day ... aboard power cruiser Oasis ... attorney fishing witnessed second cruiser sail alongside ... grenade attack killed Loomis and the guard dog ... FBI investigating with full cooperation CIA ...

'That damned helicopter,' Tweed muttered. 'He wouldn't take any notice ...'

'I beg your pardon?' McNeil queried.

'Sorry, just thinking aloud.' His voice became crisper, he sat up erect in his chair as he pushed the telex strip back across his desk. 'Put that in the shredder. No one else is to see it. Any word from Martel?'

'He phoned me from Bavaria. He's coming in early tomorrow and I have booked the necessary hotel accommodation at Heathrow. He has given me the flight details so you can meet him there.'

Tweed swivelled in his chair and gazed at the blinds which were closed over the windows. They were as blank as his thoughts. He was very worried.

'Things are coming to a head,' McNeil suggested.

'And only two days to solve the insoluble. The Summit Express leaves the Gare de l'Est in exactly forty-eight hours' time.' He swivelled back to face her. 'You've been going through all the dossiers. No hope, I suppose ...'

'There is something,' McNeil replied.

The call from Washington came through just before midnight and Manfred was asleep in his Münich apartment. He switched on the bedside light, slipped on his gloves and picked up the receiver. The identification procedure was concluded and the American-sounding voice gave its message briefly.

'Loomis' contract has been terminated. We decided not to renew it ...'

'Thank you ...'

Manfred replaced the receiver, got out of bed and began padding round the room. All was going well. Nothing could now stop Crocodile. The big killing would be carried out on schedule.

CHAPTER 21

Monday June 1

'We have the rest of today and part of Tuesday before the Summit Express leaves Paris for Vienna tomorrow night,' Tweed said.

'And in those few hours,' Martel commented, 'we have to identify the target out of the four western leaders. And we have to track down the security chief who is the rotten apple – again from four potential candidates ...'

At the London Airport Hotel McNeil had reserved three bedrooms – all in different names. The accommodation would only be used for the short time while Tweed conferred with Martel, but this would not seem strange: it was common practice among international business executives.

They were esconced in the middle room. Earlier Tweed had checked the rooms on either side to make sure they were empty. Martel was inserting a cigarette in his holder after his comment. He had arrived a short time ago on a flight from München. Once they had talked he would fly straight back to Germany.

'Any ideas?' Martel asked. 'Does the Loomis murder tell us anything?'

'It is pretty certain that after my signal was read out in Paris to the security conference by the British Ambassador one of the four security chiefs present reacted. He had me followed to London Airport when I boarded Concorde. There just wasn't sufficient time to kill Loomis *before* I talked to him ...'

'What about Alain Flandres? His earlier history is pretty thin in the files. Then there's O'Meara – that absence from his West Berlin base for two months Loomis told you about. It could have been spent in East Berlin.'

'That is my reading of the situation ...'

'Except that I have another candidate – Erich Stoller of BND. He spent two *years* under cover in what he called "The Zone".'

'I didn't know that,' replied Tweed. Intrigued, he leaned forward over the coffee table. 'You dug up this fact?'

'No, he volunteered it, implied you knew about it. He also knew I was interrogating him, but on the surface it hasn't affected his cooperation ...'

'I didn't know, but Erich is clever,' Tweed leaned against the back of his chair and stared at the ceiling. 'He may be pre-empting the possibility we'd find out in his dossier. So we have two possibles – O'Meara and Stoller. And after we've finished here I'm flying to Paris to meet Alain. I want his version of his past.'

'And Howard?'

'The least likely.' Tweed took off his glasses and rubbed his eyes. Martel noticed traces of fatigue. 'I don't like him,' he continued, 'but that's irrelevant. We're looking for a traitor who has practised his trade of treason for years ...'

'So you're ignoring Howard?'

Without replying Tweed burrowed inside a brief-case he had

propped against the side of his chair. Extracting the photocopy of a file he handed it to Martel. On the front was the security classification, file reference number and three words. *Frederick Anthony Howard.*

Martel began skip-reading as Tweed explained. 'We have McNeil to thank for that. How she got the original out of Central Registry and made that photocopy I'll never know. I think she has a duplicate key to the dossier cabinet ...'

'Christ!' Martel looked up, stupefied at the thought of the risk McNeil was running. 'She's never told you that?'

'No,' Tweed said quietly. 'That is her way and I don't ask her questions. Have you come to it yet?'

'Come to what?'

'Page 12. Several years ago Howard spent a tour of duty with the Paris Embassy as Intelligence Officer. While he was there he took a spell of leave – six weeks. In *Vienna.*'

'Normal leave?'

'No, sick leave. He was on the edge of a nervous breakdown – "mental exhaustion" is the phrase used by the quack. The medical report is there. He was away January to February. Think of the Austrian climate. Damned funny place to go for sick leave ...'

'If he knows Vienna that will help him protect the PM.'

'That's another odd note,' Tweed commented. 'He's never made a single mention of the fact as far as I know.'

Martel handed back the photocopy and sat puffing his cigarette. Tweed produced an envelope with four glossy prints. 'You wanted photographs of Flandres, O'Meara, Howard and Stoller ...' Martel put the envelope in his pocket, stubbed out his cigarette and spoke with great vigour.

'Time is so short we have to put maximum pressure on all four security chiefs – in the hope that the unknown assassin makes a wrong move. We stir up the cauldron ...'

'How?'

'By telling each of them on the quiet the part we left out. I can deal with Stoller – you'll have to pass the word on to Howard, Alain and O'Meara ...'

'What word?'

'That the same unimpeachable source which told us one of the Western leaders is marked for assassination aboard the express also told you that the killer is among the four security chiefs.'

From an inside pocket Tweed extracted a card protected by a plastic folder and gave it to his companion. Martel studied the card, which carried his photograph, as Tweed explained while he wandered restlessly round the room. So far he had not reacted to the audacious suggestion Martel had put forward.

'Keith, we shan't meet again before the Summit Express leaves the Gare de l'Est tomorrow night. That card enables you to board the train at any point en route. No one can stop you – not even Howard ...'

Permission to board ... every facility to be given to the bearer, Keith Martel ... specific permission to carry any weapon ...

Across his photograph was inscribed the neat and very legible signature of the Prime Minister. She had counter-signed the reference to weapons. Martel stared at Tweed.

'In God's name, how did you get this?'

'I approached her directly through the Minister. I spent half an hour with her. I told her one of the four security chiefs may be an assassin ...'

'She must have loved that ...'

'Took it very calmly,' Tweed replied. 'She even said she would feel perfectly safe in *our* hands. She went through your dossier while I was there. Incidentally, you brought a good passport picture of Claire Hofer with you? Good. Do you trust her?'

'With my life – I *have* done already. *Twice* ...'

'Give me her photo.'

Tweed sat down at the table, produced a second card, a duplicate of Martel's but without the photo or signatures. Taking a tube of adhesive from his pocket, Tweed carefully affixed Claire's photo in position. He then extracted a pen Martel had not seen before and proceeded with great care and skill to forge the PM's signature twice. He looked at Martel over his glasses.

'I have her permission – and she loaned me her pen to do the job. Here is Miss Hofer's card. One thing I must remember to do above all else.'

'What's that?'

'Return the PM her pen. She'll give me hell if I forget. One thing more is exercising my mind – before we go. *Manfred* ...'

'What his next move will be, you mean?'

'I know,' Tweed replied. 'I have duelled with him long-distance before and I should know by now how his mind works. Sit in his chair for a moment. He has been informed that we know one of the four western leaders is marked down for assassination. When we reveal to the security chiefs that one of them is the assassin he will react – he may already have put into action the next phase of his strategy ...'

'Which is?'

'*Smokescreens*. To conceal the identity of the killer he will try to divert our suspicions to the wrong man. He will aim for the maximum confusion in our minds – simply put, so we don't know where the hell we are. And we have no time at all left to locate the guilty man.'

'You agree my idea, then,' Martel said and stood up, checking his watch.

'Yes. We tell the security chiefs one of them is a phoney. And then watch all hell break loose ...'

Reinhard Dietrich was in a state of controlled fury as he drove the Mercedes 450 SEL from his apartment to the underground garage which Manfred had designated as the meeting place. On the phone it had almost been in the nature of a summons for Dietrich to come immediately – alone and with just sufficient time to get there.

Inside the deserted underground garage Manfred sat behind the wheel of his BMW hired under a fictitious name with false papers. He had deliberately arrived early and positioned himself so his car would face Dietrich's on arrival.

He heard Dietrich coming, driving on the brake.

The garage was dimly lit and Manfred timed it perfectly. As the millionaire appeared driving towards him he turned on his light full power. The unexpected glare blinded the industrialist who threw up a hand to shield his eyes and cursed as he reduced speed and pulled up alongside the BMW. Manfred promptly turned off his lights, which further confused Dietrich's vision.

He saw a vague image of a man wearing a dark beret, the face turned towards him concealed behind large sun-goggles. Switching off his motor he lowered the window. Manfred was already talking as the window purred open.

'If you lose the election you go ahead with the *putsch* as planned. Your men in full uniform. You march on München – make it as much a replica of Hitler's 1923 march on München as you can.'

'Hitler didn't succeed,' Dietrich pointed out. 'He ended up in Landsberg Prison . . .'

'Where is the new weapons dump?' Manfred interjected. 'I see . . .' He paused. 'We are so close to zero hour you should use armed guards to protect the place this time. That is all . . .'

'*Wait!*'

Manfred had not even heard the plea. He was driving out of the garage, his red tail-lights disappearing round a corner. Dietrich swore again, took out a cigar and lit it. The arrangement was he should wait two minutes before he also left.

Arriving back at München Airport, Martel took a cab to the corner of a side street in the city. Waiting until the cab had gone, he walked the last four hundred yards to the Hotel Clausen where the Swiss girl was staying. He was relieved to find Claire safe in her room.

'I've been busy while you were away,' she announced. 'I spent a lot of time at the Hauptbahnhof . . .'

'That was foolhardy – you could have been spotted . . .'

'When will you learn I'm not stupid?' she flared up. 'I change my clothes before each visit. A trouser suit in the morning, a skirt and blouse with dark glasses after lunch ...'

'Sorry.' Martel dropped his brief-case on the bed and stretched his arms. 'I'm tensed up. The Summit Express leaves Paris tomorrow night and we're no nearer knowing who the target is, let alone the assassin ...'

'The dossiers that woman in London is checking? She has found nothing?'

'It could be Flandres, Howard, O'Meara – even Erich Stoller. Any one of them. But she's persisting. The Hauptbahnhof ...'

'You never told me what *you* had noticed after we ran for it,' she reminded him.

'Your impressions first.'

He slipped off his shoes, lay on the bed and propped his back on the bedboard. While she talked he smoked and watched her, thinking how fresh and appetising she looked. He felt a limp, sweaty, mess: the humidity in München was growing worse.

'The Hauptbahnhof here,' she began, 'and probably in Zürich – for the same reasons – is the *mobile* headquarters of Delta. Which explains why Stoller has never managed to locate their main base. The *schloss* Dietrich has in the country is a blind ...'

'Go on.'

'It makes an ideal headquarters because of all the facilities. It is always crowded. So a meeting between two men – or several – is unlikely to be noticed. Couriers come in on trains, deliver their messages – and depart on other trains. They never actually go into München! How am I doing?'

'Promising. Do go on.'

'You observed one of those meetings – the man off the Zürich Express. Plenty of meeting-places – far less risky than any so-called safe houses which might be located and watched. The cafeteria, the cinema, and so on. They even have fool-proof communications which can be used with the certainty no call will ever be intercepted. The payphones.'

'I think you've got it,' Martel agreed. 'But suppose they are spotted?'

'Look at the number of exits available. They can even rush

on to a train just leaving. Remember how we escaped – by diving down into the U-Bahn ...'

'That's what I think Warner worked out – all you've been saying. And it explains his reference to the Hauptbahnhofs in his little notebook.'

'I did observe one thing which worried me,' Claire went on. 'I saw men coming in on different trains, tough-looking customers who all made for the self-locking luggage containers. They had *keys to the lockers* and collected large, floppy bags – the kind you use to conceal automatic weapons. Then they walked out into the city ...'

Martel whipped his legs off the bed and frowned in concentration. 'You mean Dietrich is sending in an élite force – probably placing them in hotels close to strategic targets like the TV station, the central telephone exchange – all the key centres of control?'

'That was my guess ...'

'We should contact Stoller,' Martel was pacing the room. 'The trouble is we don't know whether the assassin we're trying to pinpoint is Stoller. If he is, he'll thank us – and do nothing.'

'Can't we do one damned thing?' Claire protested.

'We can try ...'

'Alain,' Tweed said quietly, 'we know one of the four passengers aboard the Summit Express leaving for Vienna tomorrow night is the target for an assassin ...'

'We must certainly assume that, my friend,' Flandres replied.

They were eating dinner in a small restaurant at the end of a court off rue St. Honoré. *Le patron* had escorted them to a table in a secluded corner where they were able to converse without being overheard. It was an exclusive place and the food was excellent. Alain was in the most exuberant of moods.

'What I am going to tell you is completely confidential – just between the two of us – and because we have known each other all these years. How long is it?' Tweed ruminated.

'Since 1953 when I left the Army – I was Military Intelligence, you recall? I then joined the Direction de la Surveillance du

Territoire. An orphan, I have spent all my adult life engaged in the traffic of secrets. A strange pastime.' Flandres sipped at his wine glass. 'I do not like your Frederick Anthony Howard,' he said suddenly. 'He is not sympathetic – like a man who fears to say much in case he reveals more than he wishes to ...'

'I find that impression interesting, Alain.' Tweed spoke in all sincerity: he greatly respected the Frenchman's acumen. 'And you chose Military Intelligence when you joined the Army?'

Flandres laughed, a vibrant laugh. 'My God, no! My whole life has been a series of absurd accidents. Military Intelligence chose me! Can you imagine it? Two weeks after I put on uniform I am commissioned overnight – and all because of two accidents! My predecessor got drunk, fell out of a window and broke his neck! And my second language was German – because I had been born in Alsace. So I am attached to General Dumas' staff as Intelligence officer since at that moment he was advancing through Bavaria. Absurd!'

'And later you were demobilised ...'

'That is so. I return to Paris. My only trump card is a commendation from Gen. Dumas. I show this to the DST and to my utter astonishment they take me on. Even the commendation is an accident. Dumas mixed up the documents! He intended it for a quite different officer! It is a mad world. Now, what were you going to tell me? Something amusing, I hope?'

'Anything but amusing, I fear ...'

Tweed looked round the small restaurant, shook his head as *le patron* caught his eye and moved towards them. He was not happy about what he had to say – and he was enjoying a pleasant evening with his old friend.

'This is a message from a dead man – I prefer not to identify him. I believe he told the truth but I cannot prove it. He reported that the assassin who will kill one of the western leaders aboard the Summit Express is – one of the four security chiefs charged with their protection.'

'That is a really terrifying prospect,' Flandres replied slowly.

He sipped more wine, his dark eyes pensive. 'Is there any clue as to which of the four is the guilty man?'

'None whatsoever ...'

'It could even be me? That is what you are thinking?'

'I have an open mind on the subject – some people might say my mind is blank ...'

'That is something I cannot believe. You will have ideas. You will have investigated. How long have you known this?'

Flandres was in one of his rare solemn moods. But his surface temperament had always been mercurial. Only those who knew him well realised he was possibly the most astute security chief in the West.

'For the last few days,' Tweed replied. 'I have told no one else – not even Howard. Officially I'm not concerned with this Summit Conference ...'

'And unofficially?'

'I root around,' Tweed replied vaguely.

'In Europe? In America?'

'In my mind. I do have a prime suspect. There was, shall we say, an incident? It could point in one direction only. It needs further checking. As regards the Summit Express, let no one board that train without impeccable credentials,' Tweed warned.

'I shall lose a little sleep,' Flandres assured him. 'I am not entirely happy that the train leaves the Gare de l'Est at 11.35 at night and that it will still be dark when it crosses the frontier into Germany.'

'I understand it is the normal train with a section of coaches sealed off from the rest of the express for our illustrious passengers? Plus their own restaurant ...'

'That is so. Which means there are six stops before the express reaches München. There Chancellor Langer boards the train ...'

Flandres threw up both hands in a gesture of frustration. 'All because my own President will not get into a plane – so the others agree, seeing it as a chance to confer during the journey so they present a united front to the Soviet leadership in Vienna.'

'Well, you can't alter that, so let's talk about something more congenial ...'

For the rest of the meal Flandres was his normal ebullient self, a tribute to his exceptional self-control. But Tweed thought he could see in the Frenchman's eyes an unspoken question. Who was the Englishman's prime suspect?

The caller gave the code-name Franz to the operator at Stoller's Pullach headquarters and said he would ring off in twenty seconds if he was not put through without delay. It was late on Monday evening but the BND chief was waiting hopefully in his office.

'Erich Stoller here . . .'

'Franz speaking again. I have more information for you – the location of the largest arms dump yet. This time it will be protected by Delta men . . .'

'Let me get a notepad, I'll only be a moment . . .'

'*Stop!* I know that trick! Make your notes afterwards. Wait until the dump has been built up – organise your raid for tomorrow, the day before the election. The location of the dump is . . .'

Having provided Stoller with the information Reinhard Dietrich had given him earlier in the underground garage, Manfred replaced the receiver.

CHAPTER 22

Tuesday June 2

FREISTAAT BAYERN! TOFLER! TOFLER!! TOFLER!!!
FREE STATE OF BAVARIA! TOFLER . . .

The banners and posters had appeared overnight and were everywhere. Small planes flew over the cities cascading thousands of leaflets bearing the same message. Two days before the election Bavaria seethed in a turmoil.

There were marches by Delta men wearing peaked caps, brown shirts and trousers tucked into jackboots. They sported armbands carrying the Delta symbol.

There were counter-marches by Tofler's supporters waving banners and dressed in civilian clothes – each cavalcade preceded by small groups of teen-age girls carrying flowers – which made it tricky for the police to intervene for fear of hurting the girls.

Münich was like a cauldron with motorists shrieking their horns as planes above fluttered leaflets like confetti. Standing by a window in the office reserved for him at police headquarters Erich Stoller's expression was grim as he spoke to Martel who stood beside him.

'It's getting out of control. And the news tomorrow that we've seized the biggest Delta arms dump yet isn't going to help ...'

'Your informant again?' enquired Claire who stood behind the two men. 'There has to be an informant for you to have traced so many weapon caches recently ...'

'Yes, Franz phoned me again ...'

'*Franz?*'

'The code-name for my informant.' Stoller made a gesture of impotence. 'I really have no idea who he is – but every time we react to his brief messages we find a fresh dump ...'

'The timing is interesting,' Martel commented. 'This business of the arms dumps has been rising to a crescendo – and the climax, oddly enough – will coincide with the Summit Express crossing the Bavarian sector. There is, incidentally, an item of news I should pass on to you. Just before Werner Hagen caused his own death at the water-mill he made an alarming statement.'

'What was that?' Stoller asked quietly as he went to the table and poured more coffee.

'He alleged – and both Claire and I believed him – that ...' He swung round and stared at the German as he completed his sentence. '... the assassin who will kill one of the western leaders aboard the train is one of the four security chiefs assigned to protect those leaders ...'

*

A hush descended on the large room. Claire remained quite still, sensing the rise in tension. Stoller paused in the act of pouring coffee. Four sparrows settled on the window-ledge outside, which struck Claire as very strange. *Four*. There were four security men involved.

'Did – you – say – Hagen?' asked Stoller, spacing his words.

'Yes.'

'He said that just before he died?'

'Yes.'

'Which means you withheld this information for three days?'

'Yes.'

The two men faced each other like fierce dogs squaring up for battle. Stoller had gone very pale, his long arms close to his body. Martel watched the German as he lit a fresh cigarette. He asked the question casually.

'What was it like – your two years under cover in what you still call The Zone? That length of time must be something of a record – to survive undetected . . .'

'And what does that mean?' Stoller asked very quietly.

'Simply that my main job is to identify the rotten apple in the barrel – O'Meara, Flandres, Howard – or yourself. And the train is leaving Paris tonight. You're going to find the atmosphere aboard rather electric. Think of it, Erich, all four of you looking over your shoulders . . .'

'Why take Hagen's word?'

'Because my job is to tell when a man is lying – and I believe Hagen was telling the truth.'

'Would you think me rude if I asked you to leave? And at least you won't be on board the train . . .'

'Why the hell did you do that to Stoller? God knows he's helped us,' Claire raged.

They had returned to the Hotel Clausen and Martel was sitting on her bed while she stormed round the room. The Swiss girl was in a furious temper. She sat down in front of the dressing-table and began brushing her hair vigorously.

'We're letting them all know at the last moment. It's the plan

Tweed and I cooked up when I met him at London Airport. It will throw the killer off balance, may cause him to make a slip ...'

'They'll *all* know? Is that a good idea?'

'They'll be watching each other.'

'As you said, the atmosphere will be diabolical. One thing's for sure – you've made an enemy of Stoller ...'

'Only if he's guilty ...'

She swung round on her stool and glared. 'For God's sake remember what you said to him. We can't go near him again.'

'You think we're marooned?'

'Aren't we?' she challenged.

They were waiting for Tweed in his office after his return flight from Paris. Seated behind her desk, McNeil half-closed her eyes to warn her boss. Big Trouble.

'This is Tim O'Meara,' Howard began very stiffly, introducing the large American who remained by the window to avoid shaking hands with Tweed. 'Someone took this photograph while you were on board Clint Loomis' power cruiser on the Potomac ...'

Tweed took the glossy print and examined it carefully. It was a blow-up which had been produced with great skill, doubtless in the CIA laboratories at Langley. The print provided a clear reproduction of Tweed who was squinting as though gazing into the sun.

'Well?' Howard demanded.

'How did you come by this photo? It is important that I know.'

Previously Tweed had given O'Meara one brief glance on entering his office. The question was now addressed to him. Howard went purple at Tweed's reaction.

'By God, you're going to regret this ...'

'No,' Tweed corrected him briskly, '*you* are going to regret this if my question is not answered. I happened to notice when the photo was being taken.' He looked direct at O'Meara again. 'I need to know how you obtained this picture ...'

'Delivered by messenger to Langley,' O'Meara said

brusquely. 'I gather the messenger was held at the gate – normal procedure. He said he had been called by phone, told to go to the reception desk of a Washington hotel where an envelope would be waiting with my name on it. Another envelope contained the delivery fee and a fat tip.'

'You believe this?'

'We checked out his story, for Christ's sake,' the American snapped. 'Who took the picture we haven't a snowflake in hell's idea. It was obviously taken with . . .'

'A telephoto lens – then your technicians produced this remarkable blow-up. There was a message with the print and negative?'

'Yes,' said O'Meara, unconsciously confirming Tweed's query as to whether both print and negative had been delivered. 'It said that I might like to know an Englishman called Tweed had been aboard the *Oasis* before the unfortunate aftermath. All this stuff was flown to me top priority by Langley.'

'Manfred,' Tweed murmured.

'What was that?' Howard pounced.

'*Manfred!* He arranged it – the taking of the picture after he had had Loomis and myself followed from Dulles. He's playing his usual tactic – sowing confusion prior to launching Crocodile . . .'

Tweed then proceeded to play his own diversionary tactic before Howard could interrogate him about the Washington trip. Unlocking a desk drawer he lifted out three articles and placed them neatly on his desk top. A .38 Smith & Wesson Special. A black beret. A pair of large tinted sun-goggles. He added to the collection a dark blue windcheater.

'The interesting question,' Tweed remarked, 'is who was in London last Friday morning when Manfred-Carlos was in Piccadilly?'

'We were in Paris for the security meeting. I caught the noon plane,' said O'Meara.

'I was on the 10 a.m. flight . . .'

Like the American, Howard answered quickly, then stopped in mid-sentence. In a matter of seconds Tweed had reversed the roles, had become the inquisitor instead of the accused. He followed up his advantage before Howard could explode.

'That doesn't exonerate either of you. The wearer of these garments, the owner of the gun was seen by a policeman in Piccadilly at nine o'clock in the morning. As you know, shortly afterwards this little collection was found on a chair in the man's shop, Austin Reed. My question really is *who* did this mysterious man who vanished so quickly come to London to meet . . .'

He broke off as the door opened and Howard's deputy, Mason, came into the room. He was closing the door when Tweed spoke abruptly.

'Not now, Mason. And next time, knock first. It is customary.'

'But I was invited to attend . . .'

'You are now invited to leave immediately.'

Mason stared at Howard who looked away towards the window. He wet his lips as though about to say more when he caught Tweed's gaze. It was bleak and intimidating and Mason suddenly realised no one was coming to his aid. With a mumbled apology he left the room.

'Did you invite him?' Tweed asked Howard sharply.

'Not really . . .' Howard seemed as relieved as anyone to see the back of Mason at this juncture. 'He is, of course, my deputy . . .'

'Who has yet to work his passage,' Tweed replied caustically. 'Returning to the subject of this strange incident in Piccadilly, Special Branch — at my request — handed these items to their Forensic boffins for urgent analysis. No manufacturer's labels, of course. The beret is from Guyana, the windcheater and goggles from Venezuela next door. Origin of the gun untraceable. Does their report suggest anything?'

'South America,' O'Meara said grimly. 'Carlos again?'

'Except that it is rather obvious,' Tweed pointed out. 'And we are getting too many obvious signals. I'm looking for something not obvious . . .'

'What the devil do you mean?' demanded Howard who had

recovered his normal balance. 'And what has this to do with our over-riding concern – the Summit Express?'

'It's a question of timing.' Tweed was still addressing O'Meara. 'You should read a little more history. In the early part of 1919, when Germany was falling apart, a Soviet republic was established in Bavaria – so there is a precedent for Operation Crocodile. Luckily the so-called people's government was destroyed by the remnants of the German Army and the Freikorps. Look at the map ...'

Tweed opened *The Times* atlas and showed them Lake Konstanz and how its shape was like that of a crocodile with its jaws agape.

'That is the significance of Crocodile – it denotes the locale of the conspiracy. Bavaria is their immediate target. The plan is to set up a neutral government under this creature, Tofler – who has Communist links. Bavaria has a narrow section of the Konstanz shore – and reports had reached me that a secret factory in Czechoslovakia is building motor torpedo boats ...

'But Czechoslovakia has no coastline,' the American protested.

'So when Tofler takes over, the torpedo-boats are sent by road aboard giant trailers and launched into Lake Konstanz. Only a few would be needed to dominate the Rhine delta – even to help a campaign later to seize the Vorarlberg province from Austria ...'

'I find this sinister,' O'Meara muttered.

'A typically audacious Manfred plan,' Tweed assured him. 'To detach Bavaria from the rest of the Federal Republic – and then one-third of the land mass of Western Germany is severed from the main bulwark against Soviet Russia. The stakes in Crocodile are enormous ...'

'You could be dramatising the situation,' O'Meara suggested.

'No, he isn't,' Howard agreed, to Tweed's surprise. 'If by some twist of political events Bavaria were detached from the Federal Republic the Soviets have conquered western Europe. It is a scenario we have feared for years – not that I dreamt

Bavaria would be the key the Kremlin would turn to unlock Western Europe ...'

'This crap about a Soviet Republic in 1919 ...' O'Meara broke in aggressively.

'Is history,' Howard confirmed. 'It existed for a short time. Now I want to know the source of your information,' he told Tweed firmly.

'Werner Hagen, the recently deceased nephew of Reinhard Dietrich. What neither of you know,' he continued poker-faced, 'is that he also revealed that the assassin is one of the four security chiefs attached to the train ...'

Howard recovered from the shock first. His expression froze and he walked round the side of the desk to stare down at Tweed. His tone was clipped.

'For this I will have you thrown out of the Service.'

'If I'm wrong, you might manage it,' Tweed agreed. 'But if I am right you will have questions to answer at the highest level ...'

'The guy's crazy!' O'Meara burst out. 'First he gets involved in the Clint Loomis killing. Now he comes across with this lunatic accusation ...'

'Alain Flandres is taking it very seriously,' Tweed observed. 'I met him in Paris only yesterday ...'

'You did what!'

Howard was almost apoplectic. He thrust both hands inside his jacket pockets to regain control. Tweed gazed back at Howard over the rims of his glasses as his chief spoke with great deliberation.

'You have no authority to involve yourself in any way in the security of the Summit Express. You have grossly exceeded your brief and will be held answerable for this dereliction of duty ...'

'Washington will hear of this, buddy,' snapped O'Meara. 'They will be interested to hear a senior British agent has made this accusation about their security chief ...'

'I said *one* of the four security chiefs,' Tweed reminded him.

'There are precedents. Remember Chancellor Willy Brandt's closest aide, Guenter Guillaume, turned out to be a Soviet plant – which destroyed Brandt. Now I believe they have planted someone else.' He looked at Howard. 'The assassin could have been recruited many years ago. I rather think he was. You had better be extremely careful from the moment you board that train tonight ...'

CHAPTER 23

Tuesday June 2

Name: Alain Dominique Flandres. Nationality: French. Date of birth: January 18 1928. Place of birth: Strasbourg.

Tweed, alone again in his office with McNeil, studied the file she had handed him. Alain's personal description followed – his height, weight, colour of eyes, colour of hair. It matched the file's subject. He settled himself more comfortably in his chair to peruse the life history.

Career record: Escaped to England, April 1944. Commissioned as lieutenant in Free French Forces. Appointed to Military Intelligence due to fluency in German. At war's end transferred to staff of Gen. Dumas for French occupation of Vorarlberg and the Tyrol. Demobilised and returned to France, May 1953. Immediately joined Direction de la Surveillance du Territoire. Transferred to Secret Service in charge of special unit guarding President, July 1980.

Tweed finished reading the file and drank more tea while he ran over the details again. 'What about his marital status?' he asked.

McNeil replied from memory. 'He married Lucille Durand, daughter of a textile manufacturer from Lille in . .'

'That's enough,' Tweed interjected. 'What about the dirt?' he enquired with an expression of distaste. 'The yellow sheet — an appropriate colour for the things we record about people's lives. But sometimes that's where the clue lies ...'

'Seven different mistresses so far ...' McNeil was consulting a yellow flimsy. 'You want the erotic details?'

'No. Were all his women French?'

'The names look French to me. Who next?'

'O'Meara,' Tweed hunched forward in the chair, his eyes screwed up in concentration. 'This file will be meagre, I presume?'

'Here it is.' She handed him a slim dossier. 'And, as you say, meagre ...'

Name: Timothy Patrick O'Meara. Nationality: American. Date of birth: August 3 1930. Place of birth: New York City.

Career record: Served with Cryptoanalysis Section, CIA, Langley, 1960-1965. Assigned other duties, 1965–1972. Served with West Berlin station under Controller, Clint Loomis, 1972–1974. A two-man unit; other member (junior) Lou Carson. While in Berlin had affair with 18-year old German girl, Klara Beck. On return to US promoted to Assistant Director of Operations, Langley. Transferred to Secret Service on ...

Tweed stopped reading . 'He's married?' he enquired.

'Yes.' McNeil produced another yellow flimsy. 'He did rather well. Nancy Margaret Chase, educated Vassar and all that implies. Daughter of a powerful Philadelphia banker. What they call "the quiet money".'

'His first and only wife?'

'Yes. The yellow sheet hints his father-in-law's connections with the White House helped his rapid rise. O'Meara carries lots of clout. His next move may be to stand for the Senate ...'

'The yellow sheet says that?'

'No, McNeil says that. And you still haven't explained why you lit fires under Howard and O'Meara this morning ...'

'Just trying to arrange the key pieces on the board prior to the opening moves in the game. Again, I'm fighting Manfred long-distance – and already the bastard is breathing down my neck.'

'And your rogue piece – Martel? I wonder what he's up to?'

'I'm going to pay a call on Reinhard Dietrich at his *schloss*,' Martel informed Stoller, who greeted him with apologies on his return to police headquarters in München.

'You are completely mad,' the German protested.

'There's something very peculiar going on,' Martel continued. 'I suspect that – unknown to Dietrich – Erwin Vinz is operating a secret cell inside Delta, a cell controlled directly by the East Germans, which means ultimately by the Soviets. Dietrich is being manipulated, conned – and I think I can raise doubts in his mind. That could upset the whole Crocodile apple cart at the last moment – and with the Summit Express leaving Paris tonight *this* is the last moment . . .'

The tall German wandered over to the window with an expressionless face. 'What makes you come up with this bizarre theory – what is it based on?'

'Four attempts on my life so far, for God's sake. In Zürich, two in St. Gallen and one off Lindau. In every damned instance the killers wore Delta symbols – the worst type of publicity for Dietrich's movement. They even *left* a badge under Warner's dead body – because that didn't get there by accident.'

'How are you going to handle it?' Stoller enquired.

'I have phoned Dietrich who apparently had just returned to the *schloss*. I'm going as a foreign correspondent. Dietrich wallows in publicity . . .'

'And what paper are your pretending to represent?'

'*The Times* of London. I always carry credentials confirming my status as a reporter. I have one for *Die Welt* . . .'

'In your own name?'

'No, as Philip Johnson – who exists . . .'

He broke off as the phone rang. Stoller answered it, listened for a moment, spoke a few words and handed the receiver to the Englishman. 'It's for you – from London . . .'

At the other end of the line Tweed chose his words carefully. It was quite possible the call was being secretly recorded for Stoller to play back to himself later.

'Keith, a courier – carrying diplomatic immunity – is bringing you certain records for you to peruse in the hope that something will point the finger. The courier is my assistant. She will be arriving aboard an evening flight at München Airport. Have someone meet her. The flight details are . . .'

'Thank you,' Martel said. 'And goodbye . . .'

'I still think you are mad,' Stoller repeated as Martel replaced the receiver. 'You could get yourself killed visiting Dietrich at that *schloss*.'

The Englishman glanced at Claire who had remained silent during their conversation. 'At least you can't say I don't inform you of my movements on your patch, Erich. I'm driving down to Dietrich's place at once.'

'Don't delay . . .' Stoller paused. 'Late tonight I have to fly to Bonn . . .'

'I didn't understand what went on in Stoller's office,' Claire said later when they were leaving the outskirts of München with Martel behind the wheel of his hired Audi. 'I had a feeling that signals were being exchanged . . .'

'He was just showing he was sorry for his earlier outburst. And Tweed is sending in a courier with the dossiers on the evening flight to München. We're clutching at every last straw we can lay our hands on.'

'Why tell Stoller about your suspicions about Vinz and his secret cell? If it is Stoller who is guilty . . .'

'Then his reaction – or lack of it – will tell me something. Incidentally, Reinhard was most cordial when Philip Johnson of *The Times* phoned. He's looking forward to seeing me.'

'That's what worries me,' Claire replied.

'You say this British reporter who calls himself Philip Johnson has an appointment at the *schloss*? At what time? Dietrich, why did you agree to see this man?'

In the Münich apartment Manfred's gloved hand held the receiver tightly as he waited for the reply. It was pure chance that he had called the *schloss*, that the millionaire had then volunteered this information.

'Because I am convinced he is Martel, the man responsible for the murder of my nephew ...'

'*Why?*'

'Because I checked immediately with *The Times* in London.' A note of exasperation had crept into Dietrich's voice. Manfred questioned every decision he took. 'They confirmed they have no correspondent of that name based in Bavaria ...'

'No correspondent of that name on their staff?'

'I didn't say that!' Dietrich rapped back. 'They do have a man with that name on their staff, he is a foreign correspondent – but at the moment he is in Paris. This man who called himself Johnson is driving here this afternoon by the direct route from Münich in a blue Audi. Any more data you require?'

'Be very careful what you say ...'

Once beyond the outskirts of Münich Manfred drove his BMW like a maniac. The sniperscope rifle was concealed inside a zipped-up golf-bag on the seat beside him. His features were concealed behind an outsize pair of dark-tinted glasses. His hair was hidden by a soft hat pulled well down over his forehead.

He braked about half a mile from the main entrance to the Dietrich estate. His phenomenal memory had not let him down. Yes, the gate in the wall was there. And beyond it stood a ramshackle farm-cart abandoned long ago and which he remembered from his secret meeting with Erwin Vinz by the roadside.

The geography, also, was right for his purpose. Beyond the gate a field rose up steeply to a ridge surmounted by an outcrop of rock. An excellent firing-point. Getting out of the BMW, he opened the gate, lifted the shafts of the cart and heaved to get it moving.

Manfred possessed extraordinary physical strength. He had once broken the neck of a man weighing twenty stone. He hauled the cart into the road where he positioned it carefully. He could have blocked the road completely – but this would have been bad psychology.

If you are quick-witted, confronted by a barrier you turn your car swiftly on the grass verge and drive like hell back the way you have come. So he used the cart to block the road partially – to force an oncoming vehicle to *slow to a crawl* and negotiate the obstacle.

It also provided against the contingency that the wrong car could arrive first and the occupants might get out and shift the cart. As the cart was positioned they would simply drive slowly round it. He next hid the BMW inside the field behind a clump of trees, not forgetting to close the gate. His target would notice little details like that.

Five minutes later, confident from what Dietrich had told him on the phone that he had arrived first, Manfred settled himself in place behind the rocky outcrop and peered through the gun's 'scope. In the crosshairs the road came up so he felt he could reach out to touch it. Then he heard the sound of an approaching car. Martel's blue Audi came into sight.

'I still don't like this idea of visiting Dietrich,' Claire said as she sat beside Martel in the Audi. 'But, oh, this must be one of the most beautiful places in the world.'

According to the map Martel had studied earlier they were within two miles of the main entrance to the *schloss*. All around them the sweeping uplands of Bavaria were green in the blazing sun. At the summit of limestone ridges which reared up like precipices clumps of fir trees huddled. They had not passed another vehicle for some time.

'*You* are not going to visit Dietrich,' Martel told her. 'Before we get there I'm leaving you with the car while I walk the rest of the way. If I haven't reappeared in one hour you drive like hell to Münich and report to Stoller ...'

'I'm not frightened. I'm coming with you ...'

'Which means if I run into trouble there's no one available to fetch help ...'

'*Damn you, Keith Martel!* That's blackmail . . .'

'That's right. Now what, I wonder, is this?'

'It's a farm-cart someone has left in the road. You can drive round it along the verge.'

Martel was driving at fifty miles an hour when he first spotted the obstacle. He began to reduce speed, agreeing with Claire that to get past the obstruction he would have to edge his way round it along the grass verge. He looked in his rear-view mirror, expecting to see one or more cars coming up behind him. The mirror showed an endless stretch of deserted road.

He looked to his right and saw a vast field running away to the foot of an upland. He looked to his left and saw ahead, close to the farm-cart, a closed gate. Beyond the gate the land rose steeply, ending in a rocky escarpment which loomed over the road. He scanned the escarpment, reducing his speed further so that he would be moving at less than ten miles an hour as he nosed his way round the ancient cart.

The escarpment was deserted. Claire followed his gaze, shading her eyes against the glare of the sun. The escarpment had a serrated edge like a huge knife with large notches. In one of the notches she saw movement. She pressed her back hard against the seat as she shouted.

'*There's someone up there . . .!*'

In the crosshairs of Manfred's 'scope the windscreen of the blue Audi was huge. The sun was in an ideal position – shining from behind his shoulder. He took the first pressure on the trigger. The Englishman's features were clear – even the cigarette-holder at a jaunty angle. The girl beside him wore dark glasses, making identification impossible. It didn't matter. The car was crawling . . .

'*Hold on tight!*'

Martel yelled the warning as he did the opposite to what instinct dictated – to reverse and turn on the verge. He rammed his foot through the floor. The Audi surged forward. The farm-cart rushed towards them. Claire blenched. The accident would be appalling. There was a sound of shattering glass.

Martel heard the whine of the high-powered bullet wing past

the back of his neck. He kept his foot down, skidded as he swerved round the cart, regained control, drove off the verge and down the clear stretch beyond the cart.

Missed! On the ridge Manfred was stupefied. It was unprecedented. Following his normal cautious policy – which had enabled him to survive so long – he left the area immediately and drove back to München.

CHAPTER 24

Tuesday June 2

Name: Frederick Anthony Howard. Nationality: British. Date of birth: October 12 1933. Place of birth: Chelsea, London.

Career record: Joined Foreign Office, June 1958 ... Appointed to Intelligence Section, May 1962 ... Transferred to Paris Embassy, May 1974 as Intelligence Officer ... Owing to pressure of work took six weeks' special leave, January 1978 ... Appointed head of SIS, May 1980.

Studying the dossiers once again with McNeil in his Maida Vale flat, Tweed skip-read Howard's details. In any case he knew them from memory. He handed the dossier back.

'Anything?' she asked.

'I don't know. I'm intrigued by that special sick leave he took while in Paris and which he spent in Vienna. Intrigued because he has never mentioned the fact ...'

'You'd have expected him to?'

'I'm not sure.' Tweed took off his glasses and chewed on the end of one of the frame supports. 'Despite his apparent extrovert personality if you listen to him carefully he is highly vocal but says little.'

'A natural diplomat?'

'Now you're being cynical,' Tweed admonished. 'But the Vienna incident reminds me of someone ...'

'Who?'

'Kim Philby.' Tweed replaced his glasses. 'It was in Vienna that Philby was first contaminated by the plague – by a woman. So that leaves only Erich Stoller, thank God – I'm beginning to see double. Drag out his file and we'll see what we have there ...'

At the entrance to Reinhard Dietrich's *schloss* the noise was ear-splitting, the source of the noise terrifying. A pack of German shepherd dogs snarled and leapt towards Martel, restrained only by the leashes held by the guards. The Englishman immediately recognised Erwin Vinz. The German walked forward and stopped close to the visitor.

'Yes?' he enquired, his slate-grey eyes studying Martel.

'Philip Johnson of *The Times*. Mr Dietrich expects me ...'

'Why do you arrive on foot?' Vinz demanded.

'Because my bloody car broke down a couple of miles back. You think I'd walk all the way from Münich? And I'm late for my interview – so could we stop wasting time?'

'Credentials?'

Vinz extended a hand and took the press card Martel handed him. Somewhere high in the warmth of the azure sky there was the distant murmur of a helicopter. It reminded Martel of the humming of a bee. Vinz returned the card.

'We will drive to the *schloss* ...'

He led the way to the large wrought-iron gates which were opened and then closed behind them with the dogs and their handlers on the inside. The guards were dressed in civilian clothes and wore Delta symbols in their lapels.

Vinz climbed in behind the wheel of a Land-Rover-type vehicle and gestured for Martel to occupy the front passenger seat. When they were moving Martel glanced back and saw the rear seats were occupied by two burly guards.

He lit a cigarette and made a display of checking his watch. As he did so he looked surreptitiously into the blue vault of the sky over Bavaria. The tiny shape of a helicopter was receding into a speck.

It was a good five minutes' drive through parkland dotted with a variety of trees before they turned a corner in the curving drive and the *schloss* appeared. It was not reassuring – a grey-stone walled edifice like a small fortress complete with moat, drawbridge and raised portcullis gate in the arched entrance.

Vinz slowed down as they bumped over the wooden drawbridge, crossing the wide moat of green water. They passed under the archway and the main building came into view, enclosing a cobbled courtyard. At the top of a flight of steps a man and a woman waited to greet their visitor.

Reinhard Dietrich wore his favourite country garb, riding clothes and breeches tucked into gleaming boots. In his right hand he held a cigar. His ice-cold eyes stared at Martel as he dismounted from the vehicle, but it was the woman who gave the Englishman a shock.

Dark-haired and sleek, she was dressed in a trouser suit with her jacket open exposing her full figure. There was a half-smile on the finely chiselled face, a smile with a hint of triumph. Klara Beck was obviously pleased to see their guest.

They led him inside the open doors of the *schloss* into a vast hall with a highly polished floor scattered with priceless Persian rugs. Vinz and his two henchmen had produced Luger pistols and escorted him across the hall into a large library overlooking the moat.

Martel was faintly amused at this display of weaponry – somehow it symbolised the poor imitation of Hitler's bodyguard Dietrich was aping – and the reaction helped to quell the cold fear growing at the pit of his stomach. He had not anticipated Klara Beck.

'Stay with us, Vinz – just to ensure our guest preserves his manners.' Dietrich gestured with the cigar he had lit. 'The other two can go dig the garden . . .'

Wary of Vinz's Luger, Martel took out his pack slowly,

inserted a cigarette in his holder and lit it. He sat down in a leather, button-backed chair in front of a huge Empire desk. An ash-tray of Steuben crystal was filled with cigar butts.

'You may sit down, Martel,' Dietrich said sarcastically. 'We can dispense with the charade of Philip Johnson, I suggest ...'

'We all seem to be making ourselves at home ...'

Martel gestured to Klara Beck who had perched herself on the arm of his chair. She crossed her legs and even the trousers could not disguise their excellent shape. Taking off her jacket, she revealed more of her superb breasts. Dietrich glared at her, went behind his desk and sank heavily into his chair, his voice harsh when he addressed his visitor.

'What suicidal motive drove you to come here? And don't tell me that if you're not away from the *schloss* in half an hour Stoller and his minions will rush to the rescue. I read the papers. The BND commissar is flying to Bonn – doubtless to escape the humiliation of witnessing my victory at the polls ...'

'Your *defeat* ...'

Martel was watching Beck as he spoke and caught the flicker of surprise in her dark eyes. *Surprise* – not alarm or disbelief. Dietrich exploded.

'You bloody amateur! What do you know of politics in Germany? I hope you don't imagine you will leave this place alive? Where is the witness to prove you were ever inside the grounds, let alone the *schloss?* Why the hell did you come here ...'

'To tell you that you are being conned, Dietrich,' Martel replied harshly. He ground out his half-smoked cigarette in the ash-tray and lit another. 'You have been manipulated. Right from the start you've been a pawn in a game you were never equipped to play ...'

The atmosphere in the library had changed. Martel could sense the change and, resting against the back of his chair, he was watching everyone in the room under the guise of an attitude of nonchalance. He could *feel* Beck's nervous reaction, the tensing of her muscles which subtly shifted the chair leather.

Vinz reacted differently. He tried to freeze his emotions but he shifted nervously from one foot to the other. Dietrich, who was no fool, noticed the movement. He frowned but concentrated his ire on Martel.

'Bloody hell! What are you talking about ...'

'I'm talking about your betrayal,' Martel continued in the same even tone. 'Betrayal by someone you trusted. Why does Stoller keep locating the Delta arms dumps so easily and swiftly? He has an informant – that is the only answer ...'

Vinz took a step forward and waved the Luger. 'You are asking for a mouthful of broken teeth ...'

He got no further. Dietrich stood up and moved round his desk with surprising agility. With the back of his hand he struck Vinz across the face. The German stood very still as Dietrich stormed.

'Shut your trap! Who do you think is in charge here? Get out of this room and go fishing!'

Martel waited until Vinz had left and then went on speaking. 'Ask yourself the question, Dietrich. Is there one other person only who knows the location of the dumps? If so, that has to be Stoller's informant. Maybe a series of anonymous phone calls? If you are wondering why, every newspaper headline reporting discovery of another dump swings the polls a few points more against you. I say you are being manipulated by a mastermind ...'

There was a flurry of activity. The door into the library burst open and one of the guards rushed in. Dietrich glared at the intruder.

'What is it, Karl?'

'The gate. They have just phoned through. A convoy of cars is approaching the entrance – they think it is the police ...'

Dietrich stood considering the news for a few seconds, staring at Martel. Then he barked out an order and two more men appeared from the hall through the open door.

'Put him in the cellar – he can shout his head off down there and no one will hear him. Search him first ...'

He moved across to a bookcase and removed a volume.

Behind it was a button which he pressed. A section slid back with a purr of hydraulics, an addition to the *schloss* no doubt built by his Stuttgart technicians. Martel carefully did not look at Beck as he extracted the smoked cigarette from his holder and stubbed out the butt in the messy ash-tray.

'On your feet!'

Karl had spoken and his Luger was aimed point-blank. Beyond the dark well exposed by the secret door Martel could see a staircase curving down out of sight. He followed one of the guards across the shag carpet as Karl gestured with his gun, walking slowly. The muzzle was rammed into his back. As he stepped through the opening he heard Klara Beck speak urgently.

'Empty that ash-tray – it contains his cigarette stubs ...'

Trust lovely Klara not to overlook any little detail, the bitch. A smell of damp, of mustiness rose to meet him as he descended the spiral with the guard in front and Karl behind. Dietrich called out a final threat.

'Later you will talk – or we open the moat sluices and you drown slowly in that pit ...'

At the bottom of the steps a doorway led into a stone-walled cellar. Karl thrust a hand against the small of his back and shoved him forward. He lost his balance, sprawled full-length on the floor. When he stood up he was alone and the door was closed and locked.

The BND motorcade, comprising three six-seater black Mercedes crammed with armed men in civilian clothes, pulled up in a semi-circle round the entrance gates. The chief guard inside panicked and gave an order.

'Release the dogs!'

The gates were opened and the pack of unleashed dogs rushed out, jaws agape, snarling as they leapt at the cars. Beside the driver in the lead car sat Erich Stoller. He gave the command at once.

'Shoot those beasts ...'

A window was lowered, a machine-pistol appeared and a

fusillade rattled. The vicious animals stopped, some in mid-leap as the hail of bullets swept over them. Within seconds every dog lay inert in the roadway. Stoller stepped out followed by two men.

'Cut the communications in the gatehouse,' he ordered.

The two men ran forward and inside the building as one of the guards held the phone to his ear calling the *schloss*. One man grabbed him. The second ripped the instrument from the wall. Shaken, the guard still protested.

'That's illegal ...'

'You're under arrest. Charge – obstructing the authorities in the performance of their duty ...'

Outside another guard was shouting at Stoller. 'You will pay for this – killing the dogs ...'

'I noticed one of them was foaming at the mouth,' Stoller told him. 'I suspect rabies. Tests will be carried out.' He returned to his car and spoke to the driver. 'Burn rubber to reach the *schloss* ...'

The motorcade swept up the curving drive, spinning round corners. One minute after leaving the entrance Stoller saw ahead the walls of the *schloss*.

'Keep up the speed – they may try to lower the portcullis ...'

He was right – as they approached the drawbridge the hydraulically operated portcullis began to move down. All three cars swept through the archway and the gate closed behind them. At the top of a flight of steps stood Reinhard Dietrich, hands on his hips. Stoller, followed by his men, jumped out and ran up the flight.

'You cannot enter,' Dietrich told him. 'And when I am elected you will be booted out of Bavaria ...'

'This warrant ...' Stoller waved the document under Dietrich's nose '... signed by the Minister-President, allows me to do what I like – tear down the place stone by stone should it be necessary. Are you going to invite us in or attempt obstruction?'

Dietrich turned away and walked back into the hall followed by Stoller. Inside the industrialist began moving towards a room on the left. Stoller noticed a door to the right which was half-open. He made for it and entered a large library. An attractive dark-haired woman holding a glass sat on a sofa and looked at him over the rim as she drank.

'Your name?' Stoller demanded.

'This is outrageous!' Dietrich had hurried after Stoller and was standing behind a huge desk. 'I shall complain to the Minister-President ...'

'There is the phone.' Stoller turned to the woman again and his manner became polite. 'We have full powers of search. Could you please give me your name ...'

'Don't answer,' Dietrich told her, reaching for a cigar.

'Klara Beck,' the woman replied and smiled. 'I am Mr Dietrich's secretary and personal assistant. Is there any other way in which I can help you?'

'You can let me know the present whereabouts of an Englishman who called here within the past hour. His name is Philip Johnson ...'

Klara Beck. One of the names Stoller had checked out when Martel had reported the conversation he had eavesdropped on in the phone booth at Lindau Hauptbahnhof. The Stuttgart number had been traced to a penthouse apartment owned by Dietrich GmbH. There was also an interesting file on Beck which went back to her early days in Berlin.

'I have been working in my office upstairs and just came down to the library before you arrived,' Beck replied. 'I have never heard of anyone by that name ...'

'You live here at the *schloss*?'

'What bloody impertinence ...!' Dietrich exploded from behind his desk.

Stoller ignored the industrialist, concentrating his whole attention on examining the room and questioning Beck. His men were at this moment searching the rest of the *schloss*. Dietrich knew this, yet he had left Erwin Vinz to keep an eye on them. He seemed most reluctant to leave the library, which convinced Stoller he was in the right room.

'I have an apartment in Stuttgart,' Beck replied as she took out a pack of cigarettes and inserted one between her lips. Stoller leant close to her with his lighter and ignited the cigarette. As he did so she watched him with her large eyes and there was a hint of invitation. A dangerous woman.

'It is a company apartment,' she went on. 'One of the advantages of working for the owner.' Her eyes again met Stoller's directly. 'And I'm very good at all aspects of my job.'

'I'm sure you are.'

Stoller bowed courteously, then resumed his slow stroll round the room. The ash-tray on the desk had recently been hastily cleaned. There were smear-marks of ash round its interior. He looked up as one of his men entered the room followed by a colleague.

'Anything so far, Peter?' Stoller enquired.

The man shook his head and Stoller told both of them to wait with him in the library. He noticed Dietrich was beginning to enjoy his cigar, to relax in his chair.

'Who has told you this fantastic story about this mythical person being anywhere near my home?'

'The aerial camera – plus the co-pilot's field-glasses. The film taken will, when developed, provide the evidence. We used special film which shows the exact date and time pictures are taken – one of the products of your company, I believe?'

'Camera? Pilot? Have you gone mad?'

'A helicopter tracked Johnson up to the *schloss* – with a cine-camera recording the incident as I have just explained. What cigarettes do you smoke, Mr Dietrich? The brand, I mean.'

'I only smoke cigars – Havanas.' Dietrich was mystified by the turn events were taking and shifted restlessly in his chair.

'And Miss Beck smokes *Blend* – as I noticed when she took out her pack ...'

Stoller was walking along the line of bookcases. He stopped and stooped to pick up a cigarette stub half-hidden in the shag carpet at the foot of a bookcase. He showed everyone the stub which he had spotted a few minutes earlier.

'Interesting. Dietrich – on his own admission – smokes cigars.

Miss Beck smokes *Blend*. This stub is *Silk Cut* — a British cigarette. It was lying at the base of this bookcase. I find it hard to surmise how it comes to be there — unless it was dropped when someone walked through a solid wall. Or is the wall so solid ...' He began taking out volumes from the shelves and dropping them on the floor. To speed up the process he swept whole sections of the calf-bound volumes on to the carpet as he nodded to his two men. They produced Walther automatics and held them ready for use. Enraged, Dietrich strode round his desk.

'Those volumes are priceless ...'

'Then show me where the catch is which releases the concealed door.'

'You are mad ...!'

Dietrich stopped speaking as another half-dozen books went on the floor and Stoller gazed at a red button set in a plastic frame which had just been exposed. He pressed the button and a section of bookcase slid back revealing the spiral staircase beyond.

'Peter,' he ordered, 'go and see what is down there. Should you meet any resistance use your gun.' He glanced round the room. I doubt if I have to remind anyone terrorist kidnapping is punishable by long terms of imprisonment ...'

'I was upstairs helping Klara,' Dietrich began.

'Was he, Miss Beck?' Stoller enquired. 'Be careful how you reply since criminal proceedings may be involved.'

'I'm confused ...' Beck started choking on her cigarette but was saved from saying more by the appearance of Martel brushing dirt from his sleeve. There was dried blood on his knuckles where his hands had hit the cellar flagstones. Peter came into the room behind him and spoke to Stoller.

'He was imprisoned in a cellar like a pig-pen but they left the key on the outside of the door — it saved shooting off the lock.'

'Well, Dietrich?' Stoller asked.

'He is an imposter ... I was sure he was an assassin sent to kill me ... After he made an appointment I phoned *The Times* in London ... They told me Johnson is in Paris ... I have many enemies ...'

The Delta leader was talking like a machine-gun, gesturing to indicate his alarm, the words tumbling out as he struggled forcefully to make his story sound plausible enough to make Stoller doubt the wisdom of preferring charges. It was Martel who guided Stoller to a decision.

'I suggest we get to hell out of this den of nauseating clowns. The atmosphere here smells even fouler than it did in that filthy cellar ...'

'The three BND cars reached the exit, turned past the heap of dog corpses lying in the road and headed back towards München.

'In a minute,' Stoller said to Martel, 'we come to where I left Claire Hofer parked in your Audi – where you left her. She recognised me and blasted hell out of her horn to stop us. Then she blasted more hell out of me to hurry to the *schloss*. That girl likes you,' Stoller commented with a sideways glance.

'I'll bear it in mind – and thanks for keeping tabs on me with the chopper – and for battering your way into the fortress ...'

'Why did you visit Dietrich?' the German asked.

'To set the enemy at each other's throats. To convince him he is being betrayed, which I believe is the truth. It may throw a last-minute spanner in the works of Operation Crocodile. And God knows we're close to the last minute ...'

Claire made her remark as Martel drove them in the Audi back to München. Stoller's motorcade had long since vanished as he hurried to reach the airport to catch his flight to Bonn.

'I assume we cancel out Erich Stoller now as a possible assassin?'

'Why?'

'For God's sake because he rescued you from the clutches of that swine, Dietrich ...'

'And what will be the prime objective of the security chief who is the secret assassin?' Martel enquired.

'I don't follow you,' she said with a note of irritation.

'To act in a way that will convince Tweed and me that he is not the man we're looking for.'

'You can't mean Erich Stoller is still on the list.'

'Yes. He is no more cleared than the others. Let's hope those records we're collecting from Münich Airport do tell us who we're looking for.'

CHAPTER 25

Tuesday June 2: 1400–2200 hours

Name: Erich Heinz Stoller. Nationality: German. Date of birth: June 17 1950. Place of birth: Haar, Münich.

Career record: Served with Kriminalpolizei, Wiesbaden, 1970–1974 ... Transferred to BND, 1974 ... served as undercover agent inside East Germany, 1975-1977 ... Appointed chief, BND, 1978 ...

Tweed again skip-read the file McNeil had handed him. Examining dossiers produced this reaction: the more you tackled the faster you absorbed them. Tweed pushed the file back across the desk to McNeil. He rubbed his eyes and yawned before asking the question.

'What do you think of Stoller? You never met him – which can be an advantage. His personality doesn't intrude, you concentrate on the facts.'

'He's by far the youngest of the four – in his early thirties. Isn't that unusual – to become chief of the BND at his age?'

'Chancellor Langer personally promoted him over the heads

of God knows how many more senior candidates. He has a reputation for being brilliant ...'

'I detect a "but" in your inflection,' McNeil observed.

'Well, he did spend two years behind the Iron Curtain ...'

'But you said he was brilliant ...'

'So we start going round in circles again.' Tweed frowned and leaned forward to tap the neat pile of folders McNeil had arranged. 'I'm convinced that in one of those folders is the answer – a fact pointing straight at the guilty man. It's at the back of my mind but I'm damned if I can bring it to the surface.'

'Maybe Martel will spot it when he reads the copies I'm taking with me to München this evening ...'

'It worries me, McNeil,' Tweed said quietly, 'you're breaking all the regulations by taking even copies of those dossiers out of the country ...'

'I'll be covered by my diplomatic immunity pass. Martel will meet me as soon as I get off the plane. Nothing can happen while I'm in the first-class section of the plane. I'm quite looking forward to the trip ...'

'I'm having you escorted to München with an armed guard,' Tweed decided. He reached for the phone, dialled a number, gave brief instructions and listened. 'He'll be here in half an hour,' he told McNeil as he replaced the phone. 'It will be Mason – he says he's the only one available.'

'At least he will be company on the flight.'

Tweed looked at her and marvelled. Some of these middle-aged English women were extraordinary. They undertook the most dangerous missions as though they were taking a trip to Penzance. He watched as she packed the copy files in a special security briefcase. Her own small bag had been packed hours ago.

'You're not to chain that thing to your wrist,' he told her.

'Why not? I'm doing this job.' She spoke sharply as she locked the case, extended the chain from the handle and clamped the cuff of steel round her wrist, snapping shut the automatic lock. Both knew why he had said that.

Tweed would sooner lose the case rather than subject McNeil

to a frightful ordeal – and instances had been known where attackers used the simple method of obtaining such a case. They chopped the hand off at the wrist.

1800 hours, the American Embassy, Grosvenor Square. In a second-floor office Tim O'Meara stood holding his executive case while his deputy, James Landis, listened on the phone, said yes and no, and then replaced the receiver.

'Well?' O'Meara demanded impatiently.

'Air Force One is on schedule over the Atlantic. It will touch down at Orly in good time for the President to be driven direct to the Gare de l'Est and the Summit Express ...'

'Then let's get to hell out of here so we're at Orly ourselves in good time ...'

'A curious report came in about a half-hour back, sir – concerning the investigation into the murder of Clint Loomis on the Potomac. Apparently a nosey international operator in Washington listened in on a call which came through from ...'

'I said *come on!*' O'Meara blazed, cutting off his deputy in mid-sentence.

1800 hours, Elysée Palace, Paris. In the courtyard outside the main entrance and behind the grille gates leading to the street Alain Flandres watched the anti-bomb squad going over a gleaming black Citroen. In a few hours this car would transport the French President to the Gare de l'Est.

As always, Flandres could not keep still – nor trust anyone except himself. As two men directed a mirror at the end of a long handle underneath the car he stood to one side and watched the mirror image.

'Hold it there a moment!'

He stared at the reflection and then called out to a leather-clad man nearby. 'Get underneath this car and check every square centimetre. The mirror could miss something ...'

He ran up the steps inside the Elysée and went to the operations room where an armed guard opened the door. Two men were hunched over powerful transceivers while the third, a cryptographer, checked decoded signals. He looked up as Flandres came into the room and tried to hand his chief a sheaf of messages.

'Just tell me what they say, my friend! Why should I ruin my eyes when you are paid to ruin your own?'

There were grins at the sally and the tense atmosphere lightened with Flandres' arrival. It was part of his technique to defuse any heightening of tension. Calm men took calm decisions.

'The American President lands at Orly at 2300 hours ...'

'Which leaves exactly one half-hour to drive him from airport to train. We had better close off the route – they will drive like hell. It is the Americans' idea of security. A demonstration by Mr Tim O'Meara of his efficiency! Long live the Yanks!'

'The British Prime Minister will land in her special flight at Charles De Gaulle at 2200 hours ...'

'Characteristic of the lady – to allow sufficient time but not so much that she wastes any. A model passenger!'

'The German Chancellor is scheduled to board the express at Münich Hauptbahnhof at 0933 tomorrow morning ...'

'That I know – it has long been planned ...'

'But there is an odd signal from Bonn I do not understand,' the cryptographer told him. 'We are particularly requested to stand by in the communications room aboard the Summit Express for an urgent message from Bonn during the night.'

'That is all?'

'Yes.'

Flandres left the room, walking slowly along the corridor. The Bonn signal was a new, last-minute development which he could not understand – and because he did not comprehend its significance it worried him.

1800 hours, The Chancellery, Bonn. Erich Stoller left the study of Chancellor Langer in the modern building on the southern outskirts of the small town which overlooks the Rhine. The tall, thin German wore an expression of satisfaction: his dash by private jet from Münich had been worthwhile.

During the flight Stoller had wondered whether he could manage it: Langer was notoriously unpredictable, a highly intelligent leader with a will of his own. And it had taken only ten minutes' conversation to persuade the Chancellor.

Stoller had sent off the coded signal – prepared in advance – while he was still in Langer's study, the signal to control H.Q. at the Elysée in Paris. Alan Flandres would by now, he hoped, have received this first signal. It was the second signal, timed to be sent later when the train was on its way, that was vital.

'I have pulled it off,' Stoller said to himself. 'The plan is working ...'

1800 hours, Heathrow Airport. Flight LH 037 took off for München on schedule, climbing steeply into the clear blue evening sky, leaving behind a vapour trail which dispersed very slowly. Two passengers had come aboard and settled themselves in the first-class section at the last moment. Special arrangements had been made in advance to receive the couple.

Neither McNeil, carrying her brief-case locked to her wrist with a metal hand-cuff and chain, nor her companion, Mason – who carried a Smith & Wesson .38 in a shoulder holster – passed through normal channels. Once identified, they were hustled to an office with a sign outside. *Positively No Admittance.*

They remained inside the locked office until a phone call to the uniformed police officer sharing the room informed them all other passengers were aboard. They ran down the covered way leading into the aircraft where stewardesses waited to escort them to reserved seats.

'Isn't it nice to be VIP's?' McNeil whispered as she sipped her champagne and the plane continued its non-stop ascent.

'All in a day's work,' Mason replied, his expression blank.

1930 hours, Heathrow Airport. Flight BE 026 departed for Paris on schedule. Tweed – who was deliberately travelling economy class – had a difficult job timing his boarding of the flight. As he knew from McNeil's private intelligence service, Howard was travelling on the same flight, but first-class.

Tweed, therefore, entered the final departure lounge just as the last-but-one passenger disappeared down the ramp. The steward on duty beckoned frantically.

'The flight is just departing!'

'So I'm just in time,' Tweed responded as he rushed down the ramp. Damnit, he had paid for his ticket.

As the stewardess ushered him aboard he glanced into the first-class section on his left. The back of Howard's head was just visible. Fortunately when disembarkation took place the custom was to let off first-class passengers ahead of the plebs. Tweed chose a seat he hated, a seat at the rear of the plane. He detested flying.

He sank into his seat and after take-off forced himself to gaze out of the porthole window. In the evening sunlight the full glory of Windsor Castle revolved below. For Queen and Country. A bit old-fashioned these days, but Tweed never bothered about what impression he might create on the rest of the world.

Flight LH 037 had crossed the German border when Mason excused himself to McNeil. 'I want to send a message to Martel confirming we are aboard this flight – the pilot can radio it for me ...'

'But he's expecting us,' McNeil reminded him.

'Expecting is not the same thing as *knowing* we caught the plane. With what you're carrying we can't take any chances ...'

He made his way towards the pilot's cabin and was stopped by a stewardess. He took out his identity card and gave it to her. 'Show this to the pilot. I have to send an urgent radio signal. The pilot knows we are aboard ...'

After a short delay he was shown into the cabin and the door was locked behind him. Mason introduced himself and then turned to the wireless operator. The pilot nodded that it was all right and the agent asked for a pad to write the message. It was addressed to a Münich telephone number.

'The signature is a code-name,' he explained as the operator read the wording. Mason nodded his thanks to the pilot and left the cabin as the operator began transmitting.

Telephone number München . . . McNeil and I aboard Flight LH 037 from London. ETA . . . Please arrange reception committee. Gustav.

In the München apartment a gloved hand picked up the phone as soon as it began to ring. The operator checked that she had the correct number and then began to transmit the message.

' "McNeil and I aboard Flight LH 037 . . ." '

'Thank you,' said Manfred, 'I have that correctly. Goodbye.'

The gloved hand broke the connection, lifted the receiver again and dialled a München number. It was answered by Erwin Vinz whose voice changed when he realised the identity of the caller.

'You will take a team of men to the airport . . .'

Manfred's instructions were precise, although masked in everyday conversation. When the call was completed he checked his watch. It was convenient that the airport was close to the city – Vinz's execution squad would be in position by the time Flight 037 had touched down.

And Mason, who was still over twenty thousand feet up, would have been appalled had he known the instructions.

'Kill them both – the man as well as the woman . . .'

Martel stood by a bookstall inside the exit area at München Airport, apparently studying a paperback. He also appeared to be on his own, which was not the case. At the other side of the large hall Claire, wearing dark glasses, stood with a small suitcase at her feet like a passenger.

The arrival of Flight LH 037 from London had been announced over the Tannoy. Passengers who had disembarked were hurrying across the hall for cabs and the airport bus. Martel scanned the small crowd and saw McNeil, carrying a brief-case in one hand, a suitcase in the other. He also saw Mason alongside her.

'Tell you what,' Mason was saying to her, 'I'll just dash over to that kiosk and get a pack of cigarettes – you go and grab a cab and then we shan't have to wait . . .'

'But we're being met . . .' McNeil shrugged. Mason was gone.

Martel saw the separation and frowned. He dropped the paperback, picked it up and quickly returned it to the revolving rack. Claire was waiting for the signal and now she recognised McNeil from the description Martel had given her.

She also knew something was wrong. The dropping of the paperback had warned her. Had Martel simply returned the book to its rack it would have been no more than a recognition signal. Inside her handbag she gripped the 9-mm pistol. McNeil, an erect, slim woman, headed for the exit.

A man dressed in the uniform of a Lufthansa pilot standing near the exit produced a Luger equipped with a silencer from a briefcase. Erwin Vinz, carrying a light raincoat folded loosely over his arm, walked into the hall, dropped the raincoat and aimed the machine-pistol the garment had concealed.

'*McNeil, drop flat!*' Martel yelled.

It was remarkable: Claire was amazed. The middle-aged Englishwoman fell forward, dropped her suitcase, used her hands to cushion the shock of the fall and lay quite still, hugging the floor.

Martel pointed the Colt .45 snatched from his shoulder holster and aimed at the most dangerous target – Vinz and his machine-pistol. He fired rapidly. Three heavy slugs hammered with tremendous power into Vinz's chest, hurling him backwards. His shirt crimsoned as he crashed to the floor, still clutching the weapon. He had not fired a single shot.

The Lufthansa 'pilot' aimed his Luger point-blank at his agreed target – Mason, who stood near a cigarette machine. Two bullets struck Mason who fell forward against the machine, clawing at it as he sagged to the ground. Claire aimed, steadying her pistol over her left arm. It was remarkable shooting – clear across the hall. Two bullets hit the killer and he toppled forward.

'*McNeil, stay flat!*' Martel yelled again.

Three men apparently waiting for passengers had produced hand-guns.

Martel had just shot Vinz . . . Claire was firing at the 'pilot' . . .

The three new Delta professionals were aiming their weapons at the still-prostrate form of McNeil ... There was panic spreading among the other passengers ... A woman screamed and went on screaming and screaming ...

A steady drum-fire of fresh shooting filled the hall and Martel watched in amazement as all three Delta assassins fell to the floor. Men in civilian clothes appeared from different parts of the hall armed with Walther automatics. One of them came up to Martel, an identity card held up in his left hand.

'BND, Mr Martel. Josef Gubitz at your service. The others you see are my men.'

'How the hell did you know ...'

'The plane's pilot transmitted the message the Englishman on the passenger list named Mason had sent, transmitted it to Stoller as instructed.'

'Who instructed him?'

'A man called Tweed in London. Any signals sent by Mason from the aircraft to be immediately transmitted to us. Stoller reacted from Bonn by sending us here. It was kind of complicated ...' The German, a small, well-dressed man, looked over his shoulder at the carnage in the hall. '... but it worked.'

'Thank God for that – and thank you.'

Claire was helping McNeil to her feet who was looking down at her grazed knees as Martel joined them. She looked at Martel. 'You know something? My nylons are ruined. Do you think I could indent for a new pair?'

Martel, Claire and McNeil were sitting in the Englishman's room at the Hotel Clausen. The two women drank tea as Martel checked the four photocopy dossiers McNeil had brought him. McNeil sat in an armchair next to Claire and placed her cup on the table. The Swiss girl was marvelling at her placidity.

'That tea you poured me was just right,' McNeil announced. 'It was nice and strong – just a dash of milk and no sugar. You can't beat a cup of tea after a bit of a dust-up.' She paused. 'Mason tried to get me killed, didn't he?'

'Yes,' said Martel. 'And they wiped him out because by now he had served his treacherous purpose. I'm certain he bugged Tweed's office. I'm equally sure he dressed up in the wind-cheater, beret and sun-goggles, made sure he was spotted by a policeman in Piccadilly and then took off his things – probably in a lavatory – and left them with the gun on a chair in Austin Reed's ...'

'Why?' Claire asked.

'To confuse us. Manfred was never within hundreds of miles of London. And it must have been Mason who followed Tweed to London Airport before he boarded Concorde – then repor-ted it back to Manfred. It's odd Howard ever took on a man like that ...'

McNeil was watching Martel who had closed the last file. 'Do they tell you anything?' she asked. 'Tweed gave the impression he couldn't find anything but I believe it's there ...'

Martel took a sheet of the hotel notepaper, scribbled some-thing on it and showed it to McNeil. She read what was on it, tore the sheet into small pieces, got up and walked across to the toilet. They heard her flush the loo and she came out and sat down again.

'Well?' Martel enquired.

'I thought so, too,' McNeil replied. 'You can't trust Tweed, of course – he keeps so much to himself. The trouble will be proving it ...'

'So we leave you here until it's all over with Stoller's armed guard on the door. Claire has some distance to travel – and I'm heading for a different destination. What scares me is we have so little time ...'

CHAPTER 26

Tuesday June 2:
2030–2335 hours

Charles de Gaulle Airport, 2030 hours. Flight BE 026 landed on schedule. Howard was among the first passengers to disembark. His special pass took him straight through Customs and Immigration and Alain Flandres was waiting for him with a large Citroen.

'This is what I call service,' Howard remarked as they settled back in the rear and the chauffeur-driven car glided away.

'We pride ourselves on our organisation,' Flandres replied with a cynical smile. 'Since the change of government we have little else to pride ourselves on.'

'As bad as that?' Howard glanced sharply at his companion who, as always, was the soul of relaxation. 'Is everything proceeding according to plan?'

'There is something I do not understand – and in the situation we are faced with incomprehensible things disturb me. I have had a signal from Bonn warning us to expect an urgent communication from Germany during the night. Stoller is not at Pullach . . .'

'Well, that's his problem . . .' Howard dismissed the whole thing with a curt wave of his hand.

'It might be our problem as well,' Flandres responded.

Under Flandres' instructions French security forces at both Orly and Charles de Gaulle were checking all arrivals for known faces. But they missed one person who came in on Flight LH 323 from Münich via Frankfurt. The aircraft landed at Charles de Gaulle at 2215 hours and the passenger, who had travelled first class, passed through the security checks unchallenged.

Elegantly clad in a black Givenchy dress and wearing a string of pearls, she also wore a hat with a veil. Porters carried her Gucci luggage to a waiting chauffeur-driven limousine. She raised her veil briefly for Passport Control.

'I wonder how many ingots of gold she is sitting on in the Bahnhofstrasse,' the Passport official murmured to a colleague after he had returned Irma Romer her Swiss passport and she moved away.

'I wouldn't mind having her sitting on me,' his colleague replied. 'She *is* a beauty . . .'

Settling herself in the spacious rear of the car the woman with the veil spoke to the chauffeur as the car was driven away from the airport.

'Emil, we have one hour before the train leaves – so you must drive slowly, kill some time. I must board the Summit Express five minutes before it departs.'

'My instructions were clear, Madame,' Emil replied. 'There will be no problem.'

'There *must* be no problem.'

Having issued this injunction, Klara Beck crossed her long legs and relaxed. It had been a rush to drive from the Bavarian *schloss* to catch the plane at München but she was sure she had successfully eluded the man who had tried to follow her. That would be Stoller's doing, of course.

'Stick Stoller,' she thought inelegantly and checked the time by her diamond-studded watch.

Gare de l'Est, 2300 hours. The twelve-coach express stood in the station. At the front the giant locomotive which would haul its precious cargo gleamed under the lights. It had been polished and polished again like a jewel. The chief engine-driver, Jacques Foriot, was the most experienced driver in the whole of France. He stood checking his array of dials and controls and then peered out of his cab.

The first six coaches immediately behind the engine were reserved for the train's illustrious passengers. The Prime Minister of Great Britain, typically, had arrived first. She had gone to bed without delay in Voiture One, the coach attached to the locomotive.

Voiture Two would be occupied by the French President who was at this moment climbing aboard after his swift ride from the Elysée. Alain Flandres stood on the platform, his eyes everywhere as the short, stocky President mounted the steps and disappeared inside. Flandres let out an audible sigh of relief.

'One more worry off my mind,' he remarked to his deputy, Pierre Buzier, a giant of a man with a bushy moustache who towered over his chief. 'And now one more worry on my mind,' Flandres continued with a shrug of his shoulders.

'But he is safe now,' Buzier reassured him. 'It was the drive from the Elysée that bothered us ...'

'And you imagine that the next seven hundred-mile ride across Europe does not worry me, my friend?' He squeezed Buzier's huge arm and smiled cynically. 'It will be a long night — followed by a long day ...'

The makeup of the express had been the subject of considerable study and much discussion by the security staff at the Elysée to ensure maximum safety. Voiture Three was reserved for the American President who was expected to arrive from Orly at the last moment. And Voiture Four would be the preserve of Chancellor Langer when he boarded the train at München at 9.33 a.m. on the following morning.

Behind these four coaches was attached the communications coach which carried some of the most sophisticated equipment available. One section was devoted entirely to a link between the train and the White House in Washington. The president would be accompanied, as he was everywhere, by an official carrying the black box — the sinister device for signalling a nuclear alert in varying stages of urgency.

Flandres and his technicians had devoted a great deal of energy to equipping this coach, cooperating with the Americans who had installed their own devices.

As though to counter the austere purpose of this coach, the one behind was taken up by the restaurant car for the exclusive use of the western leaders. It was expected that during daylight hours they would confer at length while they hammered out a united policy before facing the Soviet leader in Vienna.

'I want more men on this barrier,' Flandres ordered as he passed through the second barrier temporarily erected on the platform, a barrier sealing off the VIP section at the front from the rest of the express.

'Surely we have enough men already,' Buzier protested.

'For practical purposes, yes,' Flandres agreed. 'For public relations' purposes, no. The Americans are great believers in numbers. Bring ten more men from outside the station. That should impress them, should it not, Pierre?' Again he smiled cynically.

'If you say so ...'

'I know O'Meara. If I am not mistaken I can hear the approach of the great man ...'

'The American President?'

'No – O'Meara! Accompanied by the President!'

Beyond the second barrier was the rest of the train, the public section which comprised another six coaches. Two for first-class passengers (one a sleeping-car), three for second-class and, at the rear of the express, the public restaurant.

As he passed them alone – Buzier had hurried ahead to gather up ten more men – Flandres glanced at each window. Most of the blinds in the sleeping-car were closed but the station pulsated with a sense of expectancy. As he continued towards the main ticket barrier the little Frenchman scanned the other windows and eager faces stared back. He stopped to request that a window be closed. Until the train was moving the order was all windows must remain shut.

In the corridors on the other side of the express armed men of the French security services stood at intervals. At the main barrier he saw Howard waiting and pursed his lips. Having seen his own charge safely aboard, the Englishman was going to be present when the President of the United States arrived.

The distant sirens shrieking like banshees came closer. He

must feel at home, Flandres reflected. He himself had been kept awake when he visited America by the hellish wail of patrol cars dashing through the night.

'He's only just on time,' Howard commented as Flandres reached the barrier. 'Why is it that Americans have to arrive at the very last minute?'

'Because they see no point in waiting. What they accomplish with the time saved is another matter . . .'

As the Frenchman had anticipated, O'Meara made a great performance of the arrival. When the motorcade swept into the station the American security chief leapt from the leading vehicle almost before it had stopped. Several men, their coats open at the front, followed him as he glared up the platform. The President rather spoilt the effect.

'I want men facing every window before the President moves up the platform,' O'Meara demanded.

'If they're going to take a pot-shot at me, Tim, they're going to,' said the President who stepped out from his car looking as cool and unaffected as a clerk walking home from work. 'And your remark is hardly a great compliment to M. Flandres . . .' He extended a hand. 'It is Alain Flandres, isn't it?'

'A pleasure to see you again, Mr President . . .'

They shook hands while O'Meara moved restlessly and gestured for the American Secret Service men to form a circle round Flandres and the President. 'Washington, two years ago – am I right?' the President said.

'You have a remarkable memory . . .'

There was tension as the procession of men made their way along the platform, so many alert to danger which might come from any quarter – and the potential target was the most powerful leader in the western world. Flandres was disturbed and felt he must speak.

'I don't like being hemmed in like this . . .'

The President, smiling and amenable, stopped. 'Tim, I think we must allow Alain to command the security operation. This, after all, is his territory.'

'More space, please!' Flandres spoke curtly to O'Meara. 'We

223

must have a clear field of fire in an emergency . . .'

At the foot of the steps leading up into his coach the President lingered to speak again to the Frenchman. 'I just want you to know that I feel perfectly safe in your capable hands. And now, if you'll excuse me, I like an early night's sleep . . .'

Three minutes from departure time two unexpected events occurred. A chauffeur-driven limousine drove into the station and an elegant woman alighted and presented her ticket while the chauffeur brought her bags. The ticket collector noted that she had a sleeping compartment reserved. At the same time the Passport controller – brought to check the identity of all ordinary passengers – noted she was Swiss.

'You had better hurry, Madame,' the collector advised. 'The train departs in three minutes.'

Further down the platform at the second barrier Howard watched the elegant woman walking gracefully towards him while her chauffeur carried her luggage. She disappeared inside the sleeping-car and Howard turned to his deputy, Peter Haines, a short, wiry man.

'I wouldn't mind joining that one in her bunk,' he observed and climbed aboard the train.

The ticket collector was closing the barrier when a cab drew up.

A compact figure wearing glasses and a rumpled hat who had paid the fare earlier got out. He ran towards the barrier, carrying a small case.

He had his ticket ready and a plastic card which he presented to the Passport official. The latter glanced in surprise at the card which bore a photograph of its owner and then turned to hold up his hand to the guard indicating that the train must wait.

The late arrival moved rapidly down the platform to the second barrier opposite which Howard was standing in the open doorway to get a last-minute breath of fresh air. As he saw the passenger his face went rigid and he stepped down on to the platform.

'Tweed! I don't know what the hell you are doing here but I'm forbidding you to board this train ...'

'I don't think you have the power.' Tweed showed his card with green and red stripes running across it diagonally. 'And you are holding up the train ...'

'Say, what the devil goes on here?'

O'Meara had appeared behind Howard. Now Flandres stepped down from the other end of the coach and ran along the platform to join them. O'Meara peered over Howard's shoulder.

'Jesus Christ! She signed the pass herself!'

'This is outrageous!' Howard exploded. 'I was not informed ...'

'You were not informed for security reasons,' Tweed replied. 'If you are worried, why not wake up the lady and check? But I doubt whether she will appreciate the interruption ...'

'Get aboard, my friend.' Alain Flandres had grasped Tweed's arm and was ushering him up the steps. 'You are most welcome.'

Tweed waited in the corridor as Flandres waved his hand towards the guard, climbed the steps and closed the door.

'Alain, there is one I would like checked as a matter of top priority. At the barrier the Passport controller told me the lady who came on board at the last moment is travelling on a Swiss passport, that her name is Irma Romer. Can you use the communications set-up to radio her details to Ferdy Arnold in Berne? Ask him to confirm whether their people have issued Irma Romer with a passport – that she does in fact exist ...'

'Why bother about her?' Howard demanded.

'Because her car was parked in a side street for some time before it drove into the station. I arrived earlier myself, you see ...'

The train was moving now, the huge wheels of the locomotive revolving faster as the Summit Express emerged from under the canopy of the Gare de l'Est and headed east on its historic journey for its final destination, Vienna. Seven hundred miles away.

CHAPTER 27

Wednesday June 3: 0100—0810 hours

'Has anything unusual happened yet, Haines?' Tweed asked.

'Unusual?' Howard's deputy enquired cautiously. At one o'clock in the morning he had a haggard look.

'Unexpected, then.'

They were sitting at one end of the communications coach where two bunks had been installed for security chiefs off duty. Haines glanced towards the far end of the coach where the three security chiefs were gathered round the teleprinter.

The express was ninety minutes away from Paris, moving at over eighty miles an hour as it thundered through the dark. The coach swayed round a curve. No one felt like sleep.

'I'd sooner you addressed that question to Howard,' said Haines.

'I'm addressing it to you.' Tweed reached towards his pocket as he continued. 'Perhaps you are unaware of my authority?'

'There was something, sir,' Haines began hastily. 'While he was at the Elysée Flandres had a message from Bonn warning us to await an urgent signal aboard the express. Stoller has disappeared ...'

'Disappeared?'

'Yes. We don't know where to communicate with him. The secrecy of the whole business is worrying Flandres ...' He looked again at the far end of the coach. 'I think something is coming through on the teleprinter.'

226

It was Howard, beginning to look strangely dishevelled, who came with the telex strip which he waved at Tweed with an expression of satisfaction.

'Signal from Ferdy Arnold in reply to your query. The Swiss can be damned quick. Irma Romer was issued with a passport four years ago. Widow of an industrial magnate — engineering. She's travelling outside the country somewhere in Europe. So can we now forget about your paranoid aberrations?'

'Can I see the telex, please?'

'I've just read the damned thing out to you!' Howard threw the strip into Tweed's lap. 'Admit it,' he snapped, 'it's a wild goose chase.' He turned and stepped on the right foot of O'Meara who had come up behind him. 'Do you have to follow me everywhere?' Howard demanded.

'People apologise when they bump into me,' O'Meara rasped.

Tweed watched the two men over his spectacles. Already they were getting on each other's nerves — because under the surface there was a terrible suspicion that one of the security chiefs was the enemy. And with the windows closed tightly for the sake of the communication experts the atmosphere was growing torrid. Something had gone wrong with the air-conditioning.

Flandres, who had witnessed what was happening, came rapidly to their end of the coach. 'Gentlemen, we have the most nerve-wracking assignment any of us has probably faced — let us face it calmly and help each other ...'

'What I'd like to know,' O'Meara demanded, 'is who is in charge of British security — Tweed or Howard ...'

'I would say Alain is in supreme control for the moment,' Tweed said quickly. 'We are passing across French territory ..'

'Still nobody answers my Goddamn question,' O'Meara persisted.

Tweed read through the Berne signal and looked at Howard. 'You left out a bit, didn't you? Arnold ends his message with the words *further details to follow as soon as available.*'

'What further details do we need?' asked Howard wearily.

'Her full description,' Tweed replied.

Nobody slept inside the communications coach as the express sped on through the night. The atmosphere grew worse as the air became more clammy and oppressive. Conditions were not improved by the cigar O'Meara smoked as he lay half-sprawled in the lower bunk.

Tweed moved away and sat in a swivel chair screwed to the floor, his head slumped forward, apparently asleep. But he was aware of everything going on as the thump-thump of the train's wheels continued its hypnotic rhythm. The factor he found most disturbing was Stoller's disappearance.

They had arranged a duty roster for one security chief to patrol the corridors of the four coaches where the VIP's were presumably asleep. This was at Flandres' suggestion despite the armed guards from each contingent occupying the corridors of their respective coaches. At the moment Flandres himself was on duty.

The Bonn signal arrived at the ungodly hour of 0431 – after the express had left Strasbourg and ten minutes before they were due at Kehl on the German border. Tweed sat up in his chair because he saw the cypher clerk decoding the signal which had arrived. He held out his hand as the clerk walked towards O'Meara who appeared to be asleep.

'I'll take it . . .'

'What the hell is it now?' O'Meara suddenly demanded.

The American – who had obviously not been asleep – was stripped to his shirt-sleeves, exposing the holstered gun strapped under his left arm. He leaned over Tweed's shoulder and the Englishman caught a whiff of stale sweat from his armpits. Howard, who had just entered the coach, joined them as all three men perused the signal.

'Christ Almighty, what is going on?' O'Meara growled and lit a fresh cigar. Howard's reaction was a tightening of the muscles of his jaw, Tweed noted.

Urgent change of schedule. Chancellor Langer will board Summit Express at Kehl, not München. Repeat Kehl not München. Stoller.

'It's a nightmare,' Howard said. 'What does it mean?'

There were pouches under his eyes betraying his fatigue. The underlying strain of mutual suspicion and mistrust was beginning to take its toll on the three security chiefs. Flandres had now joined them and was mopping moisture off his forehead with a silk handkerchief. The atmosphere was becoming claustrophobic. Each man was conscious of being cooped up inside a confined space he could not escape. Only Tweed seemed relaxed as they re-examined the signal.

'He has given us less than ten minutes' warning. It's just not good enough. What *does* it mean?' Howard repeated.

'It appears to mean,' Tweed suggested, that Stoller is using his considerable ingenuity to protect his leader. That is,' he added, 'assuming Chancellor Langer is the assassin's target . . .'

He was watching the three men as he spoke, searching for a clue in his blunt reference to the assassin. The American chewed at his cigar and spilt ash down his front.

'You're not making sense,' he complained irritably.

'The timetable of the western leaders for their journey to Vienna has been widely publicised,' Tweed explained patiently. 'Including the fact that Langer was scheduled to board the train at München when he had made his brief speech outstide the Hauptbahnof. By coming aboard much earlier this unexpected change may throw the unknown assassin off balance.' He stared round the trio hovering over him. 'It *has* already thrown you off balance . . .'

'You're assuming Langer is the target,' Howard pointed out.

'True,' Tweed agreed. 'The target may already be on board. I am not sure . . .'

'Just as you're not sure of any of us,' Flandres said amiably.

'True again. And the train is slowing down – we are at Kehl. So the fourth suspect, Stoller, should join the happy band . . .'

There was a further surprise when the express drew into Kehl and Flandres opened the door of Voiture Four to find

Chancellor Kurt Langer staring up at him, his lean face wearing an expression of amusement. Like the French security chief, the German spoke fluent English and, wearing his well-cut business suit, could have passed for an Englishman.

'Alain Flandres, how pleasant to see you again. I trust my early arrival did not get you out of bed?'

'None of us have had much sleep . . .'

Flandres ushered the Chancellor quickly aboard into the corridor and away from the open doorway. He peered briefly out into the early morning. The gloomy platform, glowing with sepulchral lamps, was lined with BND men facing *away* from the express. Flandres frowned and turned to speak to the Chancellor.

'Where is Erich Stoller, Chancellor? Surely he is accompanying you?'

'I have no idea where he is,' Langer answered affably. 'He is as elusive as a lark. The train can leave when you are ready – I go this way? Thank you . . .'

Flandres signalled to the guard and closed the door. The train began to move again, picking up speed, the coaches swaying slightly as they started to cross Germany, heading for Bavaria. Flandres wasted no time making sure Langer was comfortable: the Chancellor was notorious for his dislike of fuss. He hurried back into the foetid atmosphere of the communications coach where the others sat waiting for him.

'Stoller did not come aboard,' he announced. 'And Langer tells me he has no idea as to his present whereabouts . . .'

'That's crazy,' O'Meara protested.

'It could also be very serious,' said Tweed.

His remark did nothing to lighten the highly nervous mood which had now spread to the communications technicians. Howard left the coach to take up his duty roster, glaring at Tweed as he passed him hunched in his swivel chair.

The early hours when morale is at its lowest crawled and no one spoke unless it was absolutely unavoidable. Friendly cooperation had long since given way to raw-edged nerves and outbursts of irritation over trivia. Only Tweed remained detached and watchful – like a man awaiting an event he has foreseen and which is inevitable.

When they had at last settled down into some kind of neutral silence the second signal came in from Berne.

Subject: Irma Romer. Height: 5ft. 4 ins. Weight 120 lbs. Colour of eyes: brown. Age: 64. Married to industrialist, Axel Romer, 34 years. Destination: Lisbon. Arnold, Berne.

The second signal promised from Berne reached the communications car of the Summit Express as it was pulling into Ulm Hauptbahnhof at 0805 hours. Tweed automatically converted the details from the metric system as he read the message and passed it to Howard.

'The elegantly-dressed woman who came aboard at the last moment at Paris,' he commented. 'The one you said was of no significance. The description doesn't tally in one single detail . . .'

'We had better go to the sleeper coach at once,' Flandres said. 'With armed guards,' he added. He looked at Tweed. 'Coming?'

The two men passed through the restaurant coach where breakfast was being laid for the four western leaders to the end door which was kept permanently locked, sealing off the coaches occupied by the public. A guard unlocked the door and Flandres, followed by Tweed, hurried along the corridor of the sleeping car.

'Come with us,' Flandres ordered two of the guards standing in the corridor. 'Have your weapons ready. Good, there is the attendant . . .'

The uniformed attendant in charge of the sleeper was making the morning coffee and looked up in some trepidation as Flandres began questioning him. He then explained that the passenger, Irma Romer, had left the express at Stuttgart after complaining that she felt unwell.

Stuttgart . . . The timetable details flashed into Tweed's mind. *Arrive 0651; Depart 0703.* A twelve-minute stop, the longest of the whole trip except for Münich. Flandres looked at Tweed and made a gesture along the corridor.

'So, once again you are right, my friend. We should examine her compartment?'

'Yes,' said Tweed.

The attendant opened the door which he had locked after the passenger had left. Tweed stepped inside followed by Flandres. The Englishman raised the wash-basin lid.

'The soap is untouched. She hardly used the place ...'

'The bed has not been slept in,' Flandres pointed out. 'So she sat up all night ...'

'Waiting until she reached Stuttgart,' Tweed said thoughtfully. 'I don't like this, Alain, I don't like it at all. Why should she book a sleeper, spend the night in it from Paris to Stuttgart and then get off? This business of feeling ill is nonsense.'

'Well, she is off the train – and we are moving again, thank God. I hate these stops. Let us go back and check with Howard and our American colleague ...'

It was only a two-minute stop at Ulm. An essential element in the overall security was that at each stop one of the security chiefs climbed down on to the platform to check who was leaving or boarding the public section of the train. As they made their way back through the restaurant car Tweed asked his question.

'Who was watching the platform at Stuttgart?'

'O'Meara volunteered for the job ...'

'And he wouldn't recognise Irma Romer,' Tweed remarked. 'He has never seen her.'

'And there was a fair amount of activity at Stuttgart. It will remain a mystery ...'

In the first-class day coach a woman passenger sat reading a copy of American *Vogue*. Her hair had a tinted rinse and she wore horn-rimmed glasses which were also tinted. She was dressed in an American trouser suit and perched on the luggage rack above her was a case with a bright tartan cover.

She was travelling on an American passport in the name of Pamela Davis and her occupation was given as journalist.

Taking out a pack of *Lucky Strike* she lit a fresh cigarette. By her side the ash-tray was crammed with half-smoked butts – but on top in view were fully-smoked stubs.

After complaining to the sleeping-car attendant of feeling ill, Reinhard Dietrich's mistress, Klara Beck, had got off the express at Stuttgart carrying her large Gucci suitcase. It was, she knew, a twelve-minute stop. She made her way to the ladies' room.

She had changed into the trouser suit behind a locked toilet door. She had used a hand-mirror to adjust carefully the rinsed wig which concealed her dark hair. Inside the large Gucci suitcase were some expensive clothes but it was mainly occupied by a smaller, tartan-covered case.

She had used a steel nail-file to force the locks on the Gucci. When it was found it would be assumed it had been stolen, certain contents taken and then abandoned in the toilet. There was no way the suitcase could be linked with its owner.

She had put on the tinted glasses, filled her new handbag with the contents of the one she had carried earlier, and substituted the Pamela Davis American passport for the Irma Romer Swiss passport. In her handbag was a fresh ticket purchased in advance from Stuttgart to Vienna. The transformation was now complete.

Klara Beck had overlooked nothing. Her actions had neutralised any check which she felt pretty sure would be made on the occupants of the sleeping-car. She was now ready for the final stage of the operation.

Normally Tweed would have been standing on the platform at Ulm during the two-minute stop – and Tweed was the man capable of recognising Claire Hofer. Martel had not only given him a verbal description of the Swiss girl during their meeting at Heathrow; he had backed this up with the passport photo attached to the special card. Instead it was Howard who checked passenger movement.

Claire was waiting on the platform when the Summit Express came in. She carried a small suitcase and her handbag. And she wore a pair of glasses with plain lenses which gave her a studious air. When the train stopped she approached the entrance to the first-class coach and showed her ticket to the waiting official.

'And your passport, Madame – or some other form of identity,' another uniformed official requested.

Claire produced her Swiss passport and this immediately satisfied the German. She climbed aboard and began moving along the corridor glancing into each compartment. The first one with only a single passenger was occupied by a tall man wearing lederhosen – the leather garb seen so often in Bavaria. His hat was tipped over his eyes and he appeared to be asleep.

She went inside, closed the door and heaved her case up on to the rack. The fact that it was a smoker had influenced her choice. And she wanted a quiet compartment so she could think. Inside the next compartment – only a few feet further along the corridor – sat another lone passenger, a woman carrying a passport in the name of Pamela Davis.

'What a pleasant surprise, Miss Hofer . . .'

She nearly jumped out of her skin. Her hand slid to the flap of her handbag which contained the 9-mm pistol. The tall man tipped back his hat as he spoke softly.

'No need for protection. I'm quite harmless,' he continued.

Stupefied, she stared as Erich Stoller stared back at her. The express began moving east again. It was exactly 8.07 a.m.

CHAPTER 28

Wednesday June 3: 0800–0845 hours

'The Blumenstrasse cemetery. I haven't much time . . .' Martel told the Bregenz cab-driver.

'Where you're going they have all the time in the world . . .'

The cab-driver's response was typically Austrian, taking life as it came – and went. But Martel's urgency communicated itself to him and he drove away from the solid wall of buildings along the lakeside at speed.

The Englishman made an effort to contain his impatience. Away to the north the Summit Express was speeding across Germany and, if on schedule, was approaching Ulm. At the eastern end of Lake Konstanz a grey drizzle blotted out the mountains. Through the open window moisture drifted in and settled on his face.

Arriving at the entrance to the cemetery, he paid the fare, added a generous tip and told the driver to wait. Then he plunged into the sea of headstones, his eyes scanning the maze. It was such a long shot – a remark made to him by a gravedigger when he had last been in Bregenz.

But it was the right day. He checked his watch. It was also the right time. 8 a.m.

'She comes every week without fail,' the gravedigger had told him. 'Always on the Wednesday and always at eight in the morning when no one else is about . . .'

Martel buttoned up the collar of his raincoat against the rain. The only sound was the low whine of a wind. Clouds like grey smoke were so low you felt you could reach up and touch them.

As the mist parted occasionally there were brief glimpses of the forest on the precipitous Pfänder mountain. Then he saw behind a headstone the crouched form of the gravedigger. He was levering his spade, adding to a mound of freshly dug earth.

'Back again, sir.'

The old man had straightened up and turned. His moustache dripped moisture and his cap was soggy. He regarded Martel's expression of surprise with amusement.

'You didn't startle me. Saw you coming soon as you entered the Friedhof. Thank you kindly, sir . . .'

He pocketed the sheaf of Austrian banknotes Martel had earlier counted from his wallet, then leaned on his shovel. Martel had one hand clenched behind his back, the nails digging into his palm to conceal his frustration. It was no good asking direct questions immediately: that was not the way of the Vorarlberg.

'You work in all weathers?' Martel enquired.

'They don't wait for you on this job...' The gravedigger then surprised him. 'Looking for that woman who comes here each week? She's just coming through the main gate. Don't turn round – the slightest change of atmosphere disturbs her ...'

Martel waited and then glanced over his shoulder. Beyond the pallisade of large headstones a woman wearing a red head-scarf was walking briskly. She wore a fur coat and carried a spray of flowers as she headed in a diagonal direction away from them.

'She's not short of a schilling,' the gravedigger whispered to Martel. 'Saw her in town once – my wife said that fur is sable.'

'Whereabouts in Bregenz?'

'Coming out of a house in Gallus-strasse. Now's your chance.'

The woman was crouched with her back to them laying the flowers on a grave. Stooping low, Martel ran among the maze of headstones which reminded him of huge chess-pieces.

His rubber-soled shoes made no sound as he came up behind her and stopped. It was the same grave. *In Gottes Frieden. Alois Stohr. 1930–1953.* The woman stood up, turned and saw him.

'Dear God!'

Panic! A slim, shapely hand clutched at her mouth as she stifled a scream. Large luminous eyes stared at Martel in sheer fright. A reaction which was hardly justified. Startled – yes, Martel would have expected that. But her reaction was too extreme – like that of someone whose dreadful secret had been discovered. He spoke in German.

'I have to ask you certain questions ...'

'Questions?'

'Police.' He produced the special pass which gave him access to the Summit Express and showed her only a glimpse. Documents were designed to delude the innocent. 'Security from Vienna ...'

'Vienna!'

'I need information on Alois Stohr – as he is called on the headstone ...'

Afterwards he could never have explained why instinctively he chose this approach – only another trained interrogator would have understood. 'Seventh sense,' Tweed would have commented tersely.

'Why do you say that?' There was a quaver in the woman's voice. She would be in her late forties, Martel estimated. Still a very handsome woman. She must have been a beauty at eighteen, say. In 1953 when Alois Stohr was buried. 'I come here to put flowers on the grave of an old friend,' she went on.

'A friend who died nearly thirty years ago? You come here each week after all this time? To recall the memory of a *friend*? The man who died in 1953 when the Vorarlberg was under occupation ...' The words poured out of Martel in a torrent as he aimed blind, hoping to strike a sensitive spot. He went on, saying the first thing which came into his head. '... occupation by French troops – that is, French officers and Moroccan other ranks ...'

He stopped.

He *had* struck home – he could tell by the brief flicker of alarm in her eyes which vanished as swiftly as it appeared. Martel felt he had a lousy job to carry out but there was no other way.

'You know then?' she asked quietly.

'I am here,' he replied simply. One wrong word would lose her.

'I keep a taxi waiting ...' She stooped and gathered up the loose cellophane wrappings in which she had brought the flowers. The cellophane was printed with the name of a florist and was moist with the mist. 'You want to come back with me?' she continued quietly, her voice soft and weary. 'Here ...' she gestured at their surroundings. '... is hardly the place.'

'Of course ...'

Her taxi was waiting behind his own at the gate, the drivers

237

chatting together. Martel paid off his own driver and climbed into the back beside the woman who gave an address in Gallus-strasse.

The bookseller Martel had talked to on his previous visit had informed him it was one of the wealthier residential districts. As they drove away Martel recalled a remark the gravedigger had made about the woman. *Not short of a schilling*. It was all beginning to make hideous sense.

The four-storey villa in Gallus-strasse had cream-washed walls, brown shutters and was a square, solid edifice. Eight steps led up to the front door. Alongside the door were eight names, each with its own bell-push. There was a speakphone grille. One of the names, Martel noticed as she unlocked the door, was Christine Brack.

She had an expensively furnished apartment on the second floor. When she offered to make coffee he refused – he was desperately short of time. She removed the head-scarf, the sable coat, and underneath she was wearing a dark dress with a mandarin collar. As he had expected, she had an excellent figure.

Sitting down on a chair close to his own and facing him, she used both hands to shake loose long black hair. She was a very attractive woman.

'I suppose I have been waiting for you to arrive all my life – ever since it started ...'

'May I smoke?' Martel asked.

'Please do. You can give me one ...'

Was it a reaction to the state of extreme tension affecting him? He felt a wild desire to pick her up and carry her to the bed he could see through a half-open door. She followed his glance and crossed her shapely legs.

'Will the money stop now?' she asked. 'Not that I really care. It has felt like blood money all these years. And going to the Post Office to collect the envelope seemed undignified. Does that make sense, Mr ...?'

'Stolz, Ernst Stolz ...'

238

'You know, of course, I still retain my maiden name, Brack?'

'Yes, and I understand the blood money feeling,' Martel probed cautiously. 'Although I think you are wrong ...'

'We were deeply in love, Mr Stolz. When the accident happened we had just got married ...'

'It was an accident?'

He was – to use another of Tweed's phrases – creeping over thin ice. She looked startled.

'But of course. My husband was driving the American jeep alone on a dangerous road in the Bregenzerwald and it was winter. He skidded over a precipice ...'

'Who confirmed it was an accident?'

Perplexity mingled with suspicion in her expression as Martel struggled to draw her into the web of revelation. 'The two security men who brought me the news,' she replied.

'They wore civilian clothes? Had you ever seen them before? Do you speak French?'

'In the name of God what are you suggesting?' she demanded.

'It would help if you answered the questions ...'

'Yes! They wore civilian clothes. No! I had never seen them before. And no! I do not speak French ...'

'So, from the way they spoke, you would not be certain whether these two men were really French – because naturally you conversed in German?'

'That is correct. They explained to me how important it was for my husband's death to remain a secret – he was part of a long-term anti-Soviet operation. They said I owed it to his memory that his work should continue – probably for many years. They told me that his real rank was much higher than the one he had borne – that of lieutenant – and that each month I would therefore receive via the post a generous sum of money as a pension. From the amount I get he must have been a colonel at least ...'

'What about the burial? Who identified the body?'

'I did, of course! In a private mortuary in the mountains. He had broken his neck but there were few other injuries.'

'And who was buried in the grave? Alois Stohr?'

'My husband, of course ...' Christine Brack was shaking. 'He was buried under a different name because the long-term anti-Soviet operation depended on pretending he was still alive. They told me he would have wanted me to agree to the deception ...'

They had committed two murders, Martel reflected. The man whose neck had been broken – and some poor devil of an Austrian whose body had probably been weighted and dumped in the nearby lake. It had been vital to kill and remove the unknown Stohr because of the death certificate regulations and so on – when all they had needed was his name.

Christine Brack, too, would have been killed except for one snag. A third murder might have loaded the dice against the conspirators. Instead they had told her black lies and provided money. He was now at the crux of the whole business. As he reached into his coat pocket for the envelope he realised his palm was moist.

'I want you to look at these photographs and tell me if you recognise anyone. Prepare yourself for a shock. These photos were taken recently.'

Martel waited, concealing a sensation of turmoil. Everything depended on what Christine Brack said during the next minute. She spread out the glossy prints on her lap and then uttered a little exclamation. Her expression was frozen as she held out one photograph.

'That is my husband, Mr Stolz. Older yes, but that is him. I have been dwelling under some terrible illusion for thirty years. What does it mean ...'

'You are quite sure?'

'I am certain. Incidentally, I will now tell you another man came to see me recently but I told him very little.' Martel realised she was referring to Charles Warner as she returned the photographs to him.

'That is *not* your husband,' Martel said gently. 'It simply looks very like him. And you have been living under no illusion – your husband did die thirty years ago.' He stood up. 'You may well be under observation and in grave danger now I have called. Can you pack a bag in five minutes and come with me to a place of safety for a few days?'

Shock made her amenable and she agreed to his suggestion. Also she was a woman able to pack in five minutes.

Martel hurried her down Gallus-strasse to the lake front where he found a cab and told the driver to take them to a nearby airstrip. The pilot who had flown him from Münich was waiting with his plane.

'I have to be in Münich so I reach the Hauptbahnhof by 9.30 at the latest. And first I have to drop this lady at a hotel ...'

'We're going to have to move,' the pilot warned.

'Then *move!*'

As they settled into the plane Martel prayed to God that he would not be too late. It had certainly been *German* 'security' men who had fooled Christine Brack all those years ago. And he now knew for certain the identity of the assassin.

CHAPTER 29

Wednesday June 3. München

The arrival of Erich Stoller in the communications coach after the express had left Ulm caused a sensation. Howard was furious and did not resort to diplomatic language.

'Where the hell have you been? You realise the three of us – O'Meara, Flandres and myself – had to assume the responsibility for the safety of your own Chancellor ...'

'Who is where at this moment?' Stoller broke in.

'Still locked in Compartment 12. The others are impatient for their breakfast but felt they had to wait until he emerged ...'

'Follow me,' the German suggested. 'And surely you mean

the *four* of you?' He glanced at Tweed who remained oddly silent. 'So, had someone hurled a bomb through the window of Compartment 12, you feel it would have been due to my negligence?'

'That's how I see it,' O'Meara replied.

They were following the German who led the way from the communications coach to Voiture Four. He stopped outside Compartment 16 and raised his hand to rap on the door.

'Wrong damned compartment,' Howard snapped.

Stoller rapped on the door with an irregular tattoo and it opened from the inside. Framed in the doorway stood Chancellor Kurt Langer, fully dressed and smoking one of his inevitable cigarettes. He wore a fresh business suit and an enquiring look.

'Time for breakfast, gentlemen? The others must be ready for a good German meal. May I rouse them myself so I can officially welcome them on German soil?'

O'Meara, Howard and Flandres – who had come hurrying up behind Tweed – were stunned into respectful and bewildered silence. They stood aside as Langer, chatting amiably, returned with his fellow-leaders and escorted them to the restaurant car. When they were alone Howard exploded.

'Stoller, you owe us an explanation ...'

'He owes us nothing,' Tweed intervened. 'We are now in Germany and he can take whatever action he likes. But he may wish to tell us the latest score. Something in the public section of the train worries you, Erich?'

'It was all arranged with the Chancellor in advance when I flew to Bonn,' Stoller told them as they returned to the communications car. 'I boarded the express secretly at Kehl as a passenger while the Chancellor distracted your attention ...'

'But why?' Howard demanded.

'Because,' Tweed again intervened, 'he sensed there is danger in the public section. I suspect he checked every passenger while pretending to be one of them ...'

'Correct,' Stoller agreed.

'And,' Tweed continued, 'I imagine you checked the sleeper?'

'Again, correct.' The BND chief permitted himself a wintry smile. 'For the sleeping-car I donned a uniform and examined credentials soon after the train left Stuttgart at 7.03 when they would have had a good night's rest. I found something curious – a woman left the train at Stuttgart, said she was feeling unwell. I'm unhappy about her . . .'

'All of us are,' Tweed replied and explained the mysterious disappearance of Irma Romer who had proved to be an imposter.

A subtle change had come over the relationship between the security chiefs since Stoller's arrival. Before his appearance the personality of Alain Flandres had dominated the group. Now, without seeming to, Tweed had assumed authority.

'I'm going along to the breakfast car to make sure all is well while they breakfast,' Howard suggested. 'Want to join me, Tim?'

Tweed said he would stay with Erich. Stoller waited until they were alone and guided Tweed to the end of the communications coach out of earshot of the technicians. He sat on one of the bunks and lit a cheroot. Tweed thought he looked badly in need of sleep. The German kept his voice low.

'Claire Hofer, Martel's Swiss assistant, came aboard at Ulm – she's by herself in the first-class coach. It worried me . . .'

'I'll go and see her in a minute,' Tweed replied.

'You know where Martel is? He's gone missing.'

'No idea. I think you have something on your mind . . .'

'I know who is the target for the assassin – it's staring us in the face,' Stoller asserted.

'I agree. But you tell me – and why you think so.'

'My own Chancellor. The state election in Bavaria is knife-edged – with Tofler, the Kremlin's creature, using the neo-Nazis to frighten the electorate into voting for him. So, what would be the effect of the assassination of Langer today?'

'Panic. A potential landslide for Tofler, leading ultimately to Bavaria becoming a Soviet republic – as it briefly was in 1919.'

'So we agree,' said Stoller. 'And you know where I'm convinced the assassination attempt will take place?'

'Go on ...' Tweed was watching Stoller through half-closed eyes.

'München. He insists on making a brief speech outside the Hauptbahnhof during the stop there and I can't dissuade him. Have you made any progress in locating the assassin?' he asked casually.

'No,' lied Tweed. 'But I'm going along to have a quiet word in her compartment with Claire Hofer. Did you bring any of those new alarm devices your boffins invented.'

'Half-a-dozen were put aboard. I'll get you one ...'

Stoller walked to the far end of the coach and returned with a square rectangular plastic box he carried by a handle. 'This is The Wailer. It's designed to look like a powerful torch – but if you press this button a siren starts up. All hell breaks loose.'

Tweed picked up the 'torch' and made his way along the speeding express through the restaurant. The four western leaders were eating breakfast and the American President, as relaxed as ever, had just cracked a joke which was making his companions laugh. As Tweed passed their table the PM looked up and smiled at him.

Tweed walked on, showing the guards his pass, and moved into the first-class coach. He heard the door being locked behind him and nodded at the two guards outside. Walking slowly along the corridor, he glanced into each compartment.

The one before Claire's was occupied by a single woman wearing what the Americans called a pant suit. He noticed she had a tartan-covered suitcase on the rack and she was smoking as she stared out of the window. He wasted no words as he sat down beside Claire Hofer and showed the pass with his photograph.

'Miss Hofer, my name is Tweed. Keith Martel will have told you about me. Where is he?'

She examined the pass carefully before returning it. 'He flew to Bregenz in Austria late yesterday evening. He ordered me to board this train at Ulm.'

'Bregenz? Then I was right. But we need *proof*. Where will he board the express?'

'At München – he was flying back this morning. I just hope that he makes it . . .'

'He has to make it. The target is Langer. The attempt will be made at München. There is a thirteen-minute stop. Langer insists on making a speech outside the Hauptbahnhof – in front of a vast crowd. The assassin has to be identified and exposed before Langer mounts that podium . . .'

'Which means Martel must be on the platform and ready to board the express instantly . . .'

'I don't like the split-second timing,' Tweed confessed. 'And now I must go . . .' He tapped the plastic box, explaining how the device worked. 'Don't forget The Wailer. You see anything wrong, you press the button . . .'

Alone again in the compartment, Claire was beset with anxiety. What could she possibly hope to see that was wrong?

'For Christ's sake, move faster! I've paid you enough,' Martel rapped at the cab-driver. 'Use the side-streets . . .'

'The traffic – the one-way system . . .'

The driver lifted both hands briefly off the wheel to indicate his own frustration. München was jammed with cars. People on foot were streaming towards the Hauptbahnhof to hear Langer's speech. And Christine Brack was now safely ensconced in the Hotel Clausen.

They passed the river Isar where it debouched into an intricate system of sluices. Martel remembered the rendezvous a man called Stahl never kept at the Embroidery Museum in St. Gallen. Stoller had later told him of the body found trapped in one of the sluices, a body whose only identification had been a wrist-watch engraved with the word *Stahl*. Then the memory was gone.

Martel contemplated getting out and running the rest of the way. Then he saw they were passing the Four Seasons Hotel. Too far yet. He would never make swift progress through this mob of Langer supporters.

He checked his watch again in an obvious gesture which the driver saw in his rear-view mirror. It was 9.23 a.m. The Summit Express was due to arrive at the station in exactly ten minutes' time. The turmoil following the Chancellor's assassination would be appalling. It could easily sway the election into Tofler's hands.

Like Tweed, Martel had worked out that the target was the German leader. And now he knew the identity of the assassin – but only he could confront the killer and prove his identity. He stared in the rear-view mirror and met the driver's eyes.

'Here I can try a side-street,' the man said. 'It could save a few minutes ...'

A few minutes. They could make all the difference to the future of western Europe – of the whole of the West.

Manfred's nylon-clad hand lifted the receiver the moment the instrument began ringing. He was aware he was gripping the receiver tightly. His packed case stood by the apartment door.

'Ewald Portz speaking,' a voice said. 'I am in position ...'

'Watch your timing – it must be perfect ...'

'We have gone over it a score of times,' Portz snapped.

'Then just remember – this is not a rehearsal ...'

In a phone booth at Münich Hauptbahnhof Portz, a short, stocky man in his thirties, glared at the phone he was still holding. The line had gone dead. The bastard had rung off.

Inside the apartment Manfred picked up his case and kept on his gloves while he opened the outer door, closed and locked it. Only then did he remove the gloves and stuff them in his pocket. The main thing was that Portz – the *decoy* – was ready and in position. Armed with a pistol loaded with blanks he had to aim and fire at the Chancellor at the same moment as the real assassin. Then he would run like hell in the confusion, making himself prominent as he disappeared inside the U-Bahn.

This tactic should divert attention from the real assassin who, once he had done the job, would make his way to the adjoining Starnberger Hof, the station for trains to the mountains. Then he would travel only a few stops before he left the train, was met by a waiting car and driven to a nearby airstrip.

Getting behind the wheel of his car parked at the kerb, Manfred adjusted his spectacles and drove off to the underground garage for his final meeting with Reinhard Dietrich.

It was hopeless. The traffic was getting worse the nearer they came to the Hauptbahnhof. Martel rapped on the window, gesturing to the driver to stop. He had the money for the fare – in addition to the earlier tip – ready in his hand as he leapt out.

'You will catch your train?' the driver enquired.

'This is the one train in the world I *have* to catch . . .'

Martel disappeared and the driver shook his head. What a statement. The English, they were all mad. Perhaps that was why they had won the war?

Martel barged his way through the crowd, elbowing aside men who shouted after him as he plunged on through the milling mob. He could *see* the Hauptbahnhof now. It was 9.31 a.m. Only two more minutes before the Summit Express arrived – before the Chancellor, noted for his briskness, left the train and made his way to the specially-constructed podium Martel could see. He forced a path round the edge of the jostling mass.

Reaching the road in front of the Hauptbahnhof he encountered a fresh problem but he was ready for it. In his left hand he held the special pass which allowed him to board the express. The new problem was police guards who held back the crowd. He shouted at the top of his voice.

'*Polizei!* Make way! *Polizei* . . .!'

'Stop . . .!'

A uniformed policeman drew his Walther from his holster as Martel dashed past him and across the open space. He zigzagged, risking a bullet in the back. The voice called out with greater urgency.

'Halt or I fire . . .!'

Only at this critical juncture did he have some luck. He recognised a man in civilian clothes as one of Stoller's aides –

and the aide recognised Martel. He raised a bullhorn and bellowed the order to the policeman.

'Hold your fire! Let this man through . . .!'

Martel dashed past him and the station entrance was ahead with more sightseers behind a cordon of police waiting for a glimpse of the Chancellor. Beyond he saw the locomotive of the express just stopping. He ran on . . .

As the express slowed to a halt Klara Beck was walking through the corridor towards the exit, carrying her tartan-covered suitcase. She did not even glance into Claire Hofer's compartment. Something about the way she moved made Claire study the woman.

Lindau! Claire had seen Beck arrive in the reception hall of the Bayerischer Hof. From the elevated terrace above the harbour she had observed Beck walking rapidly towards the Hauptbahnhof. Klara Beck!

Claire stood up, grabbed The Wailer and left the compartment, following the woman in the trouser suit. When she reached the exit the door was open and Beck stepped down on to the platform.

Half-way along the coach Beck paused, stood the case on the platform, twisted the handle through a one hundred and eighty degree arc and walked on, leaving the case. Alain Flandres had descended from the restaurant car and glanced quickly round as though looking for something suspicious. Then he walked swiftly through the ticket barrier to the side of the station. Chancellor Langer had left the train and waved a hand, acknowledging the crescendo of cheering.

Claire dropped The Wailer on the platform and pressed the button. She nearly jumped out of her shoes as a hellish wailing sound like a police siren blasted out, its high pitch penetrating the cheers. Langer paused uncertainly. Stoller appeared beside him, a gun in his hand, followed by O'Meara. Beck glanced back and recognised Claire.

There was a searing flash of light as the magnesium flares packed inside the paper-thin walls of the tartan-covered case

248

exploded. It was the five-second moment of distraction the assassin was waiting for. Ewald Portz raised his pistol and began firing the blank shots. Martel appeared behind him, the Colt .45 in his hand. He gripped the butt with both hands and elevated the muzzle.

At the side of the station Alain Flandres aimed his Luger equipped with a silencer point-blank at Langer. Martel swivelled his weapon and snapped off three rapid shots. The bullets missed the Frenchman but ricochetted all round him. He ran for the entrance to the Starnberger Hof station and disappeared.

Klara Beck was on the verge of pulling the trigger of her pistol pointed at Claire when Stoller fired once. Beck stooped forward, the pistol falling from her hand, and sagged to the ground.

O'Meara had produced his .38 Smith & Wesson and took deliberate aim at Portz. After firing his blanks the German was fleeing towards the U-Bahn. The American's bullets slammed into his back and he sprawled on the concrete, leaving behind a smear of red as he lay inert.

As Alain Flandres ran on to the platform a train was just leaving the Starnberger Hof. The timing had been vital. He grabbed a door-handle and heaved it open. A train guard shouted at him as Martel came round the corner. Flandres had heaved himself up on to the step and was about to hurl himself inside the compartment. Martel fired twice and both bullets rammed into the target's back.

The train was gathering speed as he hovered, half-inside the compartment and half on the step. He stayed poised like a figure frozen in a tableau. Then his body jack-knifed, toppled backwards into space and hit the platform like a sack of cement. He was dead when Martel reached him.

Wednesday June 3

'The Soviets – using East Germans as proxies – replaced a young French lieutenant in the Army of Occupation in Bregenz with their own man thirty years ago,' Martel said and accepted a cigarette from the German Chancellor who sat opposite him in the restaurant car of the Summit Express.

The train had left München and was heading east for Salzburg and Vienna. Martel was not in the least embarrassed by his audience which included his own Prime Minister, the American and French Presidents, together with Tweed, Stoller, O'Meara and Howard. He just felt unutterably weary.

'How did they manage that deception?' Langer asked.

'By a process of elimination, I assume. Everyone has a double. I happen to know you have your own for security reasons – and never use him. They had a man – my guess would be an Armenian – and he looked very much like the real Alain Flandres. They undoubtedly scoured the French forces in the Vorarlberg, the Tyrol and Vienna searching for their double. Poor Alain was made to order.'

'In what way?' Langer pressed. 'And drink some more cognac ...'

'The real Flandres was an orphan. No one back in France knew him well. He was being demobilised and planned to join the Direction de la Surveillance du Territoire – an outfit where everyone would be a stranger. Damn it, Chancellor – if you don't mind my recalling the episode – Chancellor Willy Brandt was compelled to resign when his chief aide, Guenter Guillaume, turned out to be a KGB agent. An even more difficult plant than Alain Flandres.'

'You're right,' Langer agreed. 'And I am most grateful that you saved my life. But how did you detect Flandres?'

'It's a tragic story. We had a previous agent, Charles Warner, who was murdered. In his notebook was an intriguing reference to Bregenz. I showed Warner's photo round the town and that led me to a cemetery — to a grave still visited by the woman who married the real Flandres just before he was murdered ...'

'She knew about the impersonation?' Langer queried.

'The East Germans fooled her, kidded her up with a story so her dead husband was buried under another name. They had to do that if the fake Alain Flandres was going back to France to infiltrate the security services ...'

'We were not very clever,' interjected the French President.

'Every security outfit has been penetrated at some time — even the KGB overlooked Col. Oleg Penkovsky. We worked on a process of elimination ...'

'What exactly do you mean by that?' Howard demanded.

'Let Mr Martel continue,' the PM reprimanded Howard sharply.

'It looked like O'Meara at one time,' Martel said, staring at the American. 'When Tweed visited Clint Loomis to check up your background Loomis ended up dead ...'

'Hell, I'm not taking that ...'

'You are taking that — and whatever else comes,' the President of the U.S. told him mildly.

'As I was saying, Loomis ended up dead. But that was to point us in the wrong direction — Manfred's doing, we suspected. Plus a missing two months when you were in West Berlin and absent from your base.' Martel tactfully omitted to mention that O'Meara had spent time with the now-deceased Klara Beck.

'You, sir,' Martel switched his gaze to Howard, 'posed a problem. While attached to the Paris Embassy you spent six weeks' leave in Vienna. You've made no mention of this fact since this operation started — even though Vienna is our destination.'

'Purely personal reasons,' Howard responded stiffly and lapsed into silence.

'Then there was Erich Stoller.' Martel glanced at Tweed. 'You might like to go on ...'

251

'Erich was the obvious suspect,' Tweed began briskly. 'He had spent two years underground inside East Germany. Plenty of time for him to be trained by the state security people in Leipzig or East Berlin. *Too* obvious. Had he gone over to the other side, after a year or so they'd have faked an imminent exposure which made him dash back across the border. That would have built up a nice credit balance of trust. The fact he was there two years proved he was just damned good at his job.'

'So we came to Alain Flandres,' Martel explained. 'Likeable, lively Alain who seemed above suspicion. Until it occurred to us that his early background was the vaguest of all four security chiefs. And now, if you don't mind, I'd like to snatch a little sleep. I'm getting off at Salzburg . . .'

'I shall also get off there,' said Tweed.

'Well,' Howard broke in boisterously. 'I think you can safely leave security for the rest of the journey in our hands . . .'

'Now that *they* have located the assassin,' the PM interjected cuttingly.

Manfred received his first warning when he drove into the underground garage to keep his rendezvous with Reinhard Dietrich. To his surprise he saw Dietrich's Mercedes had already arrived — although it was strictly understood that Manfred would be there first.

He checked his watch. No, he was not late — Dietrich was early. In the deserted cavern Manfred swung his car in a semi-circle and backed rapidly to position his vehicle alongside the six-seater Mercedes. He used one hand on the wheel while the other opened the automatic window and then grasped from the seat beside him a Luger with the silencer screwed on the barrel. When he switched off his motor he realised Dietrich had kept his own engine ticking over.

'You are early,' he called out. 'Another mistake — I trust you do appreciate the whole manoeuvre has failed?'

'Entirely due to you,' the millionaire replied.

Dietrich was sitting in the automatic car with the gear in drive, the hand-brake off — and only his pressure on the foot-brake preventing the car moving forward. The front passenger window was open, his right hand gripped a Walther pistol, his left hand a metallic sphere, and the passenger door was not closed.

'Your meaning?' Manfred asked quietly. 'Because Langer was not assassinated his party will win?'

'That, of course. But it is not pleasant to grasp that I have been tricked from the beginning. You supplied the arms to Delta, I told you every time the location of the dumps. You, alone – and myself – had this information. Stoller must have been delighted as you relayed the locations to him. You are a bloody Bolshevik ...'

Both men reacted at almost the same moment. Manfred raised the Luger and fired twice. *Phut-phut*. Dietrich had used his right foot to kick the door open wide as he leant forward and aimed the Walther. He was too late.

Manfred's bullets thumped into his chest and he slumped sideways over the passenger seat. His hand holding the large sphere lost its grip and, unseen by Manfred, the 'rolling' bomb thumped on to the concrete floor and disappeared beneath Manfred's car.

The new device designed by Dietrich's boffins in the secret research section of his Stuttgart factory was like a massive grenade. The button Dietrich had been holding depressed was released, the device activated and timed to detonate in five seconds. Dietrich's foot slipped from the foot-brake and the Mercedes glided forward.

Manfred turned on the ignition at the very moment the rolling bomb exploded with tremendous power. Compressed between concrete floor and chassis, the blast soared upwards and *elevated* the car. The sound was deafening, the ruination total. Afterwards they were never able to find enough of Manfred to make any kind of identification possible. He was literally blown to pieces.

The three of them – Martel, Tweed and Claire Hofer – stood on the platform at Salzburg Hauptbahnhof watching the end of the rear coach grow smaller as the Summit Express headed on the last lap for Vienna.

'I'm flying back home,' Tweed announced. 'I shan't expect you for three weeks, Keith.' He glanced at Claire. 'I expect I can keep Howard at bay until you return ...'

They watched the compact figure of Tweed striding briskly away, his shoulders erect, looking from side to side, still observing all that was going on around him. Martel turned to Claire who spoke first.

'He'd make a marvellous chief of your SIS. He's so amazingly cool under pressure. When he came to give me The Wailer just before the train reached München the tension must have been terrific. You would have thought he was on holiday.'

'Talking about holidays, you're going back to Berne to report?'

'Yes ...'

'On the other hand there's no rush, surely? I'm going to pick up Christine Brack from the Hotel Clausen to take her back to Bregenz. I want her to know the man who impersonated her husband is dead – psychologically it may close a long, painful chapter in her life. Bregenz is on the way back to St. Gallen. Didn't you find the Metropol a comfortable hotel?'

'I think I'm going to find it even more comfortable this time,' she replied, linking her arm inside his.